FAMILY
OF
KILLERS
Memoirs of an Assassin

STEPHEN W. BRIGGS

Black Rose Writing | Texas

ISBN: 978-1-68433-857-3
PUBLISHED BY BLACK ROSE WRITING
www.blackrosewriting.com

Printed in the United States of America
Suggested Retail Price (SRP) $20.95

Family of Killers is printed in Bookman Old Style

*As a planet-friendly publisher, Black Rose Writing does its best to eliminate
unnecessary waste to reduce paper usage and energy costs, while never
compromising the reading experience. As a result, the final word count vs. page count
may not meet common expectations.

To my wife and children,
Carolyn, Carson, and Jacob.

In memory of my Dad,
whose stories always entertained me.

FAMILY
OF
KILLERS
Memoirs of an Assassin

PART ONE
The Early Years

CHAPTER ONE

Portadown, Northern Ireland, 1977

An abrupt shake to his right shoulder and the panicked whisper of his mom's voice woke David.

"David wake up, David, wake up, get out of bed and get dressed!"

David, a seven-year-old, brown haired-boy with lots of freckles on his face, was in a deep sleep. His mom, Elizabeth, continued to shake him with more urgency.

David was deep in a dream of driving a Formula 1 car, a car that now headed towards a wall of bright lights as he slowly woke from his slumber.

"David, open your eyes. Luv, wake up—get out of bed and get dressed, we have to leave, now!" his mother said as she shook him more vigorously.

David wanted to get back into his race car dream. He rolled over in his bed, turned his back to his mom and pulled his favorite Rupert the Bear bed sheet over his head.

"Mommy, it is still dark outside. You said I could sleep past eight today because there was no school and we have vacation," David said.

"David get up, get dressed and get downstairs. We have to leave the house right away, I will not tell you again," his dad said, bent over David.

David rolled back over to face his father. Finally, he opened his eyes. Lights danced on his bedroom walls. Confused and groggy, he looked around at his room and out to the hallway.

"What's wrong Daddy, why are the lights off and other people here? I thought Mommy said I could lie in today," David said.

He saw shadows of people, in the hallway with flashlights, as they rushed past his bedroom door. He could hear footsteps of people moving on the main floor.

"I will fetch Amy," Elizabeth whispered to James. "You get your son up and ready to go."

"What time is it?" David asked his dad.

"It's very late, and we have to go on a wee trip."

"Then why are all these people in the house, what is wrong Daddy?"

"Everyone here is helping us pack the car so we can leave quickly."

"James, where do you keep your kit?" asked Scott, David's uncle, and James' brother. "We should take that with us now, you might need it later."

Scott went silent when he saw Elizabeth exit Amy's bedroom with his niece in her arms. Amy, David's younger sister by five years, grasped her mom's neck tightly as she looked around the upstairs hallway confused. She was still in her pajamas and her long ginger hair looked like a bird attempted to build a nest with it. Like her mother and brother, she was also ripped out of her deep sleep and brought into this panicked surge of people.

James attempted to get David out of bed. He held a flashlight just over David's head. It highlighted the poster of Rupert The Bear that hung over David's headboard. Rupert looked back at them, from an imaginary forest.

"Son, get out of bed and get dressed now!" James said.

"Why are all these people here and why are the lights...?" David said.

"David, not one more sound, aye?" James interrupted. "Get out of your bed and move now, before I redden your backside, I do not want to tell you again."

"James, I am going to take Amy downstairs to gather a few more items and wait by the door for you two," Elizabeth said. "David, hurry up and get dressed, stay with your daddy, don't leave him."

David nodded in acknowledgement. Elizabeth grasped Amy around the legs and chest, like a running back, not wanting to fumble the ball.

James grabbed David roughly by the shoulders and pulled him out of his bed. David saw more flashes of light pierce his room; his teddy on the dresser, given to him by his nannie at his birth, his Matchbox cars lined up in a race car grid on the play bench his dad and grandfather built for him for his third birthday. The light moved again, it highlighted his stuffed animals, their eyes reflected strange colors and shapes on the walls. They were all given names and personalities by David as he organized them on the floor.

Scott stuck his head into the room again, "James, we don't have much time, five minutes at the most."

"Aye, Scott, I am working on this wee one," replied James. "If he doesn't get his feet moving, we will be leaving him here."

Everyone came to a stop as a gun released a bullet in the distance. The screams of a neighbor from a couple of houses away confirmed the urgency for the family's evacuation. The rush outside of David's room sped up to a new level of frenzy as a neighbor continued to scream in fear or pain.

David understood of why his family was up and out of bed in the dark and why there was a panicked feel throughout the house.

Those who grew up in Northern Ireland in the 1970s knew what a gun sounded like, hell most people knew the difference between PC4 and dynamite when it exploded. As a child you were taught when you heard a gunshot or explosion, you ran the other way! There was no duck and cover or hide under a desk, not in this part of the world. When you heard a loud noise like that you ran, you ran fast, and you ran away from the sound. As a seven-year-old, David knew those lessons better than his ABC's or sums.

"Where did that gunshot come from?" David said.

"Stop asking questions, son," his dad said, as he grew impatient with David. "We have to leave here for a wee bit on a special trip, I need you to get dressed. RIGHT NOW!"

James grabbed David's clothes from on top of the dresser drawers.

'Mom would leave my clothes there for the next day every night, maybe for this very reason,' David thought.

"Is this because of the meeting in the shop?" David said.

His father pulled his pajama top over his head, in silence.

"Daddy, I didn't tell Mommy about the meeting tonight, I promise, if that is why we have to leave, I didn't tell anyone. Did something happen with Granda?" said David.

"Look son, I said no more questions. You need to move very quickly. You can ask all the questions you want later. I know you didn't tell mom. Just help me get you dressed and downstairs."

David suddenly had the urge people get when they wake up and become vertical, like a tap, ready to be turned on.

"I have to go pee right now, Daddy," he said as he jumped off the bed.

His father handed him a flashlight, "Here use this but don't shine it around any windows, keep it pointed down and hurry back."

David rushed out of his bedroom. He saw his mother at the top of the stairs with tears on her cheeks. She had handed Amy off to his Uncle Scott. David wanted to run over to say 'hi', but his bladder had other ideas.

"Daddy said stay focused," he whispered to himself.

"David, where are you going?" his mom asked through her tears as a man pushed by her to get downstairs.

"Pee Mommy, I have to go real bad."

David ran into the bathroom; he narrowly missed a large man by the window with a gun at his side. The man, Brian, turned and acknowledged David but did not leave his position beside the bathroom window. David's bladder screamed at him as he stood by the toilet. He was usually too shy to urinate in public, but there was no time to have Brian leave.

"Who are you? Why are you in the bathroom hiding?" David said as he shone the flashlight in the face of Brian. "Oh, you were at the shop tonight, I remember—Brian," David said, pleased with himself that he remembered the man's name.

David ran back down the hallway towards his room where his father and mother waited for him. Elizabeth had returned with shoes and a coat for David to wear, if he ever got dressed.

He entered his room and heard his mother angrily whisper, "This is your fault James, you were in too deep, you are a husband and a father, not a militant or a gun runner. You promised me you had left that part of your life behind. Now look at us. Our neighbors are being shot, tortured, or killed, and we are packing up to run from our home. We are leaving our lives behind to go where—where? I know you said this could happen but..." she stopped when she saw David's silhouette in the door frame.

"Elizabeth just finish packing any wee items for the kids, we will be back in our home shortly, just a few days away till things sort themselves out. We were going on vacation anyway, so..." James said.

"This talk isn't over James, not even close," Elizabeth snapped back.

Calmly she turned to David and said, "David, your trainers and coat are on your bed, make sure you put them on before you leave your room and hurry up, luv."

"Daddy, why is Mom saying those things, are we moving? What about all my toys? She didn't pack them."

"What did I say about questions David, not until later. We will be back, we don't run son, now be a good wee soldier and put your clothes and trainers on, and get downstairs," James left David's room as he reminded him, "Hurry, we have to go right now, and we won't wait for you."

David smiled at his dad and saluted him in acknowledgement through the dark. He jumped on the bed and put on the rest of his clothes and his shoes. A man, David did not recognize, entered his room, and saw David struggle with his shoes.

He bent down to help David and said, "Time to get going Davy."

David hated being called that name.

"My name is David," he told the stranger angrily. "David."

"Aye, David," said the man. He shrugged at David and headed downstairs to where the others were gathered.

David, finally dressed, quickly jumped off his bed and ran over to his dresser and toy bench. He used his flashlight to see all his toys. He grabbed as many of his favorite cars he could and stuffed them in his coat pockets. Then he grabbed his teddy. He wasn't going anywhere without Teddy. David looked around to see what else he could grab quickly. He felt he would never be back to this room, not in the way it was now and not while the family was together.

Scott did one last sweep of the upstairs to ensure they took all the bags. He passed David's room and saw David beside his bed, crying.

Scott knelt in front of his nephew and spoke in a comforting tone, "David, you are all right, things will be fine, but please get downstairs."

"I know Uncle Scott, but I want all my toys to come too," David said between sobs.

"You will be back to see all your toys, if not, I promise, your aunt and I will make sure you get them all. Right?"

"Aye," David said.

"You need to remember one thing for me, you have to help your dad take care of your mom and sister. You are Amy's big brother and your parent's big helper. Family is all we have; family is all that matters. Remember, family first. I love you kid, and I will always be here for you, always!" Scott said.

He pulled David towards him for a hug. David stopped sobbing and smiled at his uncle as he embraced him.

"Stiff upper lip," David whispered in his best fake English accent. A statement his grandfather would say to David, to lift his spirits. David and Scott both laughed at the comment and the attempted accent. He grabbed Scott's hand, and they carefully made their way downstairs.

"Hurry up," Elizabeth said angrily to Scott and David as they came to the front hallway.

Brian, the man David encountered in the bathroom, was the last man down the stairs.

"We are all here. Are we ready to run to the vehicles?" Brian said. He carefully surveyed the street from the front bay window.

"We will all ..." A sound of an explosion nearby cut off James' words. The house shook and the glass in the front door rattled in its holdings. A bright flash temporarily lit the front hall, as bright as a rare sunny day in Northern Ireland.

A car was just blown up. The explosion was close enough to shake the windows and David felt it vibrate through his body.

The car bomb was likely targeted for another family like David's. The number one rule in Northern Ireland was before you started a vehicle, check under it for any extra parts. That explosion was either; someone got in their car and did not do a thorough inspection of the undercarriage or a terrorist had just blown himself up while he armed the bomb under a car.

James held Amy and spoke again. "The four of us," he pointed to Elizabeth, Amy and David, "will drive with Scott and Edward in the Austin, you two will take the van. Let's try to stay together, if we can, you know the meeting place."

Edward, Elizabeth's brother, looked at Scott, "I will drive, you ride shotgun."

"Aye, if only we had a wee shotgun," Scott said, with a smile.

"I will drive the van," Brian told Bill, the man who called David, 'Davy,' in his bedroom. Bill smiled at David.

David did not smile back at Bill. He hated Bill even more when he messed up David's hair and said, "Ready to head out, Luv?"

Brian and Bill grabbed the remaining bags from the front stoop and ran up the walk to the van. They loaded them into a brown Morris Half-ton van at the end of the front lane, parked by the fenced front garden.

Brian pulled out a couple MAC-10 rifles from the back of the van and tossed one to Bill. He headed to the driver's side to start the van. Bill surveyed up and down the street, the road was clear. Bill whistled to notify James and his family to head out.

The family left the house. David still felt he would never be back, never see the toys he left behind, never see his friends on the street. He believed this might be the end of his life living in Northern Ireland.

Amy, in Elizabeth's arms, had begun to cry. Elizabeth covered her face with a blanket to muffle the sound.

Scott took the lead and waved at the family to follow him closely. David's left arm was pulled hard when James clinched him tightly by the wrist and followed Scott. David scrambled to catch his footing as his father pulled him along the stone path. Edward closed the front door and followed behind the family as they moved past the small patch of grass to the front gate, just past the rock garden James had worked hard on the previous summer, with some help from David. James pushed David's head down to get him lower to the ground. The family briskly moved towards the Austin.

"David, move quicker," his father said.

Edward pushed David from behind. They left the front walk and headed across the short laneway as someone fired a gun.

'Was that gunshot aimed at his family? Did someone just get shot around me?' David wondered, as he struggled to keep his footing.

David did not have time to ask his dad, they were now in a full sprint to the car. James dragged him behind and pushed Elizabeth in front. His father's tight grip released as he threw him into the backseat of the Austin. His father, mother and sister piled into the car behind him. David crawled across the blue cloth seat. He frantically tried to make room for his family. His father grabbed the back of his head and pushed him lower towards the floorboards of the old car.

"Keep your heads down. Everyone stay low," James said.

Brian and Bill, in the van, pulled away with no lights turned on outside the vehicle. Edward prepared to do the same in his vehicle with David's family stacked on top of each other in the back seat.

CHAPTER TWO

James and Elizabeth adjusted their positions in the car to make room for the kids, crowded around them. Elizabeth held Amy, she twisted, and now had Amy secured on her lap. Scott sat in the passenger seat with a MAC-10 rifle on his lap. He opened the glove box and handed James a loaded Browning pistol, a family favorite.

David had seen lots of guns in his young life and had been in cars before where his uncles handed out loaded weapons.

Edward pushed in the clutch and jammed the gearstick into first gear. He mashed the gas petal and released the clutch, the Austin pulled out of the laneway, spinning the tires.

"Hold tight," Scott said.

Both vehicles left the housing estate and were on the Armagh Road. They headed east as the police and fire brigade approached them from town. When they passed each other on the road, Edward checked the car's rear-view mirror to see if any police cars turned around. None of the emergency vehicles followed them. Edward sped up to catch up with the van. With no cars behind them, Edward took the most direct route to the meeting location. He split off from the van's planned route.

The car took the Armagh Road to Jervis Street then a quick right onto West Street, towards St. Marks Church, the core of downtown Portadown. If they were followed, this was where

Edward would see the vehicles. At this time of night no one would be driving through town except police who patrolled the downtown core, and they were all by James' housing estate.

David smiled a little, he loved the way his uncle drove. His uncle was a very good driver and would do all kinds of stunts with David when they drove around town or the countryside together, but David was never allowed to tell his mother. For the first time since David woke up, he felt somewhat normal.

David turned to his dad and looked at the gun. David swayed with the turns in the car, he couldn't help but wonder if he would see his dad shoot at someone tonight.

Panic and fear ran through David's mind, *'If Dad is shooting at someone, then they would shoot at us. I don't want to die. Why are we running from our house, anyway? Granda always said we stood our ground and fought; we don't run from anything.'*

"Dad, will you have to use the gun tonight, to shoot someone?" David asked.

The tires screamed, as they looked for grip around a corner.

"No, no he won't, luv. It is only with your dad, so it doesn't rattle in the glove box. Everything will be fine," his mom replied. "Your father would not use a gun to shoot a soul. Would you, James?"

Edward looked in the rear-view mirror and smiled at James.

David knew every word his mom just spoke was a lie, he had seen his Dad and Uncle Scott point a gun and threaten a man before.

James looked over to her and saw a look of anger flash at him repeatedly as the streetlights temporarily illuminated the car, the familiar look he would get when he rolled into bed late at night or when he would leave for 'a short business trip.'

Amy fussed in her mother's arms. Elizabeth pulled out a soother from her coat pocket and placed it in Amy's mouth. Elizabeth tried to comfort Amy.

She spoke out to anyone that would listen in the car, "Where do we go now? What are we to do, run for the rest of our lives? James this is your father's doing. When he left the army, he couldn't just live a normal life, get a regular job, and raise a God-fearing family. No, no, he had to involve you, your brother, my brother and how many other innocent souls in his new life of government worker and superhero for the British. How..."

"Elizabeth, catch yourself on, this is not the time or the place for your moaning," Edward interrupted.

"We will get you out of the country, sort this all out, and have you home by Christmas. You were heading to Blackpool for vacation, anyway. Just look at it as an extended vacation," Scott said, as he tried to break the extra tension in the car.

They crossed over the Bann River, where a large massacre of protestant settlers happened in 1641. Protestants and Catholics fought over what David's family was still fighting over 300 years later.

The bumps as they drove over the bridge loosened the soother from Amy's mouth, and she cried wanting it back.

"Don't worry, dad always had plans for a quick evacuation of one of our families. We will be fine," James said over Amy's cries.

"Do you have to drive like this Edward, no one is chasing us and now Amy is crying again—and we will not be fine," Elizabeth said. "If it was going to be fine, we wouldn't be running from all that trouble back at the house. We wouldn't be pulling our kids out of bed at two in the morning or running away with Scott and Edward and the others in the van with guns loaded."

"Elizabeth, be quiet. No one needs this lecture now, there will be time for it later," James said to Elizabeth over the noise of tires looking for grip and Amy's screams.

James put his arm around David and pulled him close and whispered, "Don't listen to your mom. It's going to be okay. You will be on a new adventure that one day you will tell your kids and even your wee grandkids!"

David looked up to his dad and smiled, "Okay Dad, but mom seems pretty mad."

David felt drained from the late night and early rise. His mind spun as he went through many emotional stages in his head. Fear and confusion were turned to anger and frustration. He looked out the window as the streetlights flashed before his eyes.

•   •   •

Earlier in the evening was strange for David, even before the evacuation from his house. Usually, his dad brought him home, but tonight Uncle Scott took him home shortly after some men stopped by the shop, people David had never seen before. James shuffled David into the office so the adults could talk on the shop floor. David watched as they talked and waited for someone to wave him back out.

As the meeting dragged on, Kenton became agitated with James. Once that happened, Scott brought David home while James stayed at the meeting.

David had only left the shop without his dad twice before. Both times his mom was furious with James when he finally did get home. This time Elizabeth brought Scott into the front hallway to talk. She told David to take off his raincoat and head to his bedroom, get changed and climb into bed.

Elizabeth yelled at Scott about things David did not understand at his young age. One of the few words he understood was divorce, he heard it a lot from a friend at school who now only lived with his mom in council housing. David lay in bed and listened to his mom tell Scott how 'the bunch of them were going to Hell,' another word he knew about from Sunday School. He did not think his family was that bad to go to such an evil place, but maybe mom knew better. When Scott finally left, his ears were ringing, and she had beaten his spirit down. Elizabeth headed up to David's bedroom to check on him.

"Mom, why are we all going to Hell, my Sunday School teacher told me, if I say my prayers and was a good boy God will take me to heaven when I am old," David said.

"No, you are not going to Hell. Hell is for bad people, you are a good wee boy, so you don't need to worry," she said with a quiet voice he rarely heard when his dad was around.

"What about Dad and Granda and the others, I stay with them in the shop, and you said they were going to hell. Should I stop going to the shop? Is the devil really there, like you told Uncle Scott downstairs? I have never seen him, at least I don't think I have," said David.

"No, no luv, don't worry. Did you say your prayers before you got into bed?"

"Yes, mommy and I asked God to make the Devil leave the shop so I can be safe there."

"Okay, that is good, God will listen to you because you have a good soul."

David got his kiss on the cheek, the one he received every night, and rolled over to fall asleep.

• • •

David was snapped back to reality when his head bounced off the window. Edward took a corner too quick, and the back end of the car got away from him. When he made the steering correction, the car swerved before it snapped back in line.

David really wanted to go home and get back into bed. He was angry at his dad for the meeting last night and all the people that chased him from his house. He did not know where his family is going but somehow, he knew wherever they ended up his Granda Kenton, would be there to protect him.

The vehicle continued through the old narrow streets of Portadown. David looked out the window, he knew where he was now, and he thought he knew where they were headed.

"Dad," he whispered into James' ear. "Are we going to Granda's shop?"

"Yes," his father said. "We will be safe there."

• • •

"Your dad's shop? You three are a bunch of eejits. This is the master plan you came up with, the bleeding shop? How can this be better than our house? Will someone tell me what is really going on here? What happened tonight that has caused this? Catch yourselves on, how is this a plan for our safety?" Elizabeth said.

"Elizabeth," Edward said, "you need to stop this negativity now. We know what we are doing, we have planned this for a while. Dad would not be happy with you right now if he was alive."

"Aye, and why isn't he alive, maybe the stress of me marrying into this family broke his heart. Then you joined this boys' club after he passed. He must be rolling in his grave," Elizabeth said with venom in each word.

"Kenton has been good to us and mom, Elizabeth," Edward said. He looked for second gear with the shifter for a hard right turn at an intersection and continued to speak. "We are all family; you knew before you married James what your life could involve."

James put his hand on Elizabeth's hand to settle her down. Elizabeth knew this wasn't the time or place for the fight she wanted, especially with David in the car. She went quiet and looked out her window as she rocked Amy in her arms.

The car turned down another street, and finally David could see the familiar street he had been on many times. The facade of the shop gave the sense of security he wanted, even with his mom yelling and fighting with his father and uncles. As they approached the side of the building, the bay door to the shop opened. The van had taken a different route to the shop and pulled on the street just in front of the car.

"Well, I guess this proves both routes are the same time after all," said Scott, as he tried to break the tension.

David smiled; his grandfather had a large shop where David spent a lot of time.

CHAPTER THREE

The vehicles pulled into the shop, as the bay door moved on its tracks. For the first time since he was shook awake by his mother, David could see properly with decent lights.

David looked out the car window and saw the inside of a very familiar workshop. The vehicles moved to a corner of the shop. They originally built the stone building in the late 1800s as a warehouse for textiles, Portadown's primary industry. With a bit of financing from a military contact, Kenton purchased the property in 1964 and converted it into a large workshop. The shop was used to repair equipment, machine new parts for factories in the area, and make automatic sub-machine guns. The business sold the weapons built in-house and many other kinds of weapons to paramilitary groups in Northern Ireland, Ireland, Europe, and the Middle East. With Kenton's business partner in Canada, they had strong ties with both the Canadian and American governments. Several underground groups, like bike gangs and the Italian Mob, frequently used the family's services.

• • •

David surveyed the shop; he noticed the big presses in the back corner. He was not old enough to work on them just yet, his grandfather would remind him. The lathes, drill presses and milling machines were closer to the parked vehicles. Behind them were multiple work benches with large metal toolboxes partnered to each bench. Kenton's office had windows looking out to the shop and work bench area. It was located near the front right of the shop. Beside Kenton's office was a large sliding door with a man door built into it, another area of the shop they forbid David to enter. The wall at the front, divided the shop from the reception area and had one-way bullet-proof glass. Those in the shop could see out to reception, but no one could see back into the shop. The waiting area beyond the glass had some chairs and a counter where customers picked up or dropped off their smaller parts. On the shop side of the glass wall beside Kenton's office, was a corner of the shop where a small kitchen and table existed for break time or lunches.

•   •   •

David was happy to be somewhere very familiar and very safe, even if his mom did not think it was. He spent many evenings and weekends at this shop with his dad, uncles, and grandfather. David saw this place as his second home. Even at his young age his grandfather would say, 'you're never too young to learn.' They taught David how to use basic hand and power tools. He would assist on the bigger machines like the lathe and mill.

There were other skills he had learnt; how to lie to protect those in the shop and how to keep secrets from his mom. When he was younger, she would ask what he did at the shop or where he went with his dad, uncles, and grandfather. The older he got, the more they reminded him to not tell Mom any stories about being out with 'the boys.' If he told her, he would not get to continue in the adventures they all had together. Sometimes James, Scott or Kenton would take him out on drives where they would meet people to drop off 'parts' or collect money. Some jobs would bore David, he sat quietly with his Uncle Edward, in front of someone's house noting who went in and who came out. A few times, but don't tell Mommy, they brought him on trips where he would see one of them exchange many weapons for money or information, usually down an old country road. They would leave him in a vehicle while his 'family' would walk into a building with masks on. Then after a few minutes they would run out. On those nights they would usually meet a military man after they finished the job and then go out and eat a lot of food to celebrate.

Other days they would drink orange pop and eat crisps in the shop, and on special days his nannie would bring sandwiches for dinner.

He knew this visit, after his quick awakening, would not be the same. David knew there would be no fun tonight.

This shop also had its dark side. He would hear the stories sometimes when they thought he was napping. He would hear stories about the hijacking and blown-up buildings, vehicles, or people. How they moved weapons, disposed of bodies, took special trips to do terrible things across the pond, or built bombs and of course the money made by all those jobs. He wondered if any of those things were the reason they were here in the middle of the night tonight.

•   •   •

David saw his grandfather. He was bent over a work bench in conversation with a couple of people. When David saw his Aunt Sarah, Scott's wife, he started to worry. 'Why would she be here tonight,' he thought? The other man, at the work bench, was an employee of his grandfather's. The man had an Avenger SMG, sub-machine gun, slung over his shoulder. That gun was the moneymaker of the shop. David's granda looked up from the bench, smiled and waved to David.

Tom, the man standing with Kenton as David arrived, headed to the roll-up door where his cousin Ken was. The pair headed outside to watch for any unusual activity.

The shop, on the corner of a dead-end street, made it easy to control the traffic in and out of the back area. The front of the shop opened to a main road, it made for a good secondary exit if needed. Tom and Ken worked for Kenton for years but were never let into the inner circle of the crew. Kenton always believed he needed to keep the inner circle very small, he would only allow close family into it.

"We are here, we can stay the night and move tomorrow," Scott said more to Elizabeth than the other passengers.

"This is your wee plan? Hide in your da's shop for the night? This is the plan you have always said would keep us safe if anyone came looking for you? Why would we come here? We should be on the road out of town away from here. If we are in so much danger, why are we coming here? Isn't this the first place someone would think to look for you?" Elizabeth said.

"Elizabeth, this is only a stop to load up supplies and organize ourselves before we move on. This shop is the safest place we can be right now, and you know it! Stop with the questions and help with the children," James replied.

Edward looked at Scott and nodded to get out of the car. Edward knew his sister all too well, and he did not want to be part of this family fight when it happened.

"All out," Edward announced to everyone.

Scott and Edward got out of the car as James reached over and opened the door for David.

"Okay son, climb out and wait for me by the boot," James said.

David exited the car. His dad took Amy from Elizabeth and climbed out behind him. The van doors opened beside the parked car, Bill and Brian got out of the van with their guns. They walked to the car to meet the others.

Elizabeth did not leave the car. She sat in the back seat on her own. She tried to collect her thoughts and understand what just happened to her family and her home. She knew one day James' past would catch up to him. But why now? They had planned to buy a new house and settle into life with young kids. Why now and why us?

She thought back to how James urgently woke her from a deep sleep. She woke up angry with James for having Scott bring David home and was ready to have the fight again about him being a better father. When he informed her there was a threat to him and the family, all the anger left her like air from a burst balloon. He explained she needed to get up, keep the lights off and help get the children dressed, and ready, to head to the car. James, Scott, Edward, and a couple mates were there to help get the family out of the house safely. Elizabeth, did not have time to understand the whole story and only heard 'family in danger.' The good part, if there was a good part, was she had packed for a vacation that evening, so the suitcases and travel bags were partially packed.

She knew the events that had happened since she woke up, and were still happening, would change her life forever. Selfishly she wished it had been Scott's family or even Edward, not her family. She had already sacrificed so much since she started dating James, now this.

Here they were hidden with their children in her father-in-law's shop. Amy won't remember this, but what impression will this have with David? The last thing she wanted was David to grow up in the family business. She did not want that worry, as a mother. She knew they would groom her wee boy to do whatever it was they did internationally to make extra money and support the troubles at home.

When she had time alone with David, she would ask him what he did at the shop with his dad and the family. David would respond as she believed he was taught. "*Worked on my go-cart and watched everyone work on the machines and tools, that was all Mommy,*" he would say.

She knew they taught him to lie to protect the others. A seven-year-old lying to his mother to protect 'the men'. What would God think of that, or worse, what would God think of a mother who would allow it.

Torn by the upbringing of David she knew she still had Amy, Amy was her girl, they would not take her to the shop or out on their adventures. Amy would stay home and not know what her family did, for as long as Elizabeth had any say in her upbringing. Amy would have a normal life as a good Christian girl and marry a good Christian man one day. One that did not have family ties to the UDA, British Intelligence, or any other militant group.

'Here I sit, in the back of a getaway car, torn from everything I know, all for my evil father-in-law and his activity with the British government, and his partner in Canada,' she thought.

She knew she would have to do as she was told, because in this family there was no such thing as separation or divorce. No, you just ended up another statistic in 'the troubles.'

She would not put it past Kenton to have this look like a rescue and escape just to increase his territory in the America's with John, Kenton's partner.

She gathered herself, and wiped the tears that flowed down her cheeks and chin. Elizabeth knew she needed to get out of the car. She checked her emotions, took one last deep breath, and smoothed her skirt, a nervous habit she had.

She confidently said to herself, "you need to have a talk with James before this goes too much further. You need to find out where your family's future is going."

Her tears flowed again as she slowly exited the car. She walked around the car to James and the others. She took Amy, who had also begun to cry again. James smiled at Elizabeth as he reached out to her and pulled her in for a hug. David saw the three of them as they embraced each other. He ran over and wrapped his arms around his father's and mothers' legs. The four held each other for a moment as a unified family.

•　　•　　•

Elizabeth broke away from the hug, "These kids need to get some sleep. Where can they lay down?"

"David knows where he sleeps when he is here. There should also be a cot setup for Amy in the office," James said.

"James, we need to talk about all this," Elizabeth said.

"Go put the kids down first," James responded.

"No, we should have had this talk a couple years ago, and I just ignored the signs, I want to talk now. You at least owe me that," Elizabeth said.

"Later, I have other things to deal with right now," James replied, annoyed with her persistence and lack of support in front of the others.

"Elizabeth, you will get a chance to talk to him later. Let's worry about getting the kids back to sleep," Edward intervened.

"Aye, you are right, for now," she said.

Elizabeth walked off to where the others gathered. She gave James the same look of anger and rage, which had become too familiar. Their conversation was not over. She knew she would not win and whatever was planned she would not have a say in, but she needed to say how she felt.

"David, come with me," she said.

Scott looked at James and nodded, "Good luck with that chat, mate."

"I heard you, Scott," Elizabeth said, through her anger and tears.

Once Elizabeth could not hear the group speak, James said, "I don't know how close that was, but we are here now. There was a lot more action than I was expecting and thought we had planned."

"I know we staged some of it, but the explosion and the gun fire as we ran to the car was not part of our plan. Now that we are safe here, I can confirm we did not do all of that. I believe they were a lot closer to getting you and the family James, than we first believed," Scott said.

"I will do some digging once you are out of the country, James. See what information I can gather about who was on your street when we were leaving," said Edward.

The group of men hugged each other like a team celebrating a World Cup win. They laughed for no reason except that they made it to the shop in one piece.

"At least we weren't followed," said Bill. "Not with these two Jackie Stewarts driving, no one could keep up to that bit of speed."

"Well, when I realized there was more action happening than we had planned, I figured we needed to move quickly," said Edward.

Bill and Brian went to the van and unloaded the luggage. James, Scott, and Edward followed Elizabeth to see Kenton and Sarah. Three short knocks and two louder knocks sounded from a window on the far side of the shop. Everyone froze. James ran to his family and moved them behind a lathe. He had them crouch down behind it. Kenton turned off the lights to the shop and the snap of bolts on guns echoed through the shop.

A two-way radio crackled to life with Ken's voice, "We have a car slowly driving on Goban Street. Not sure what the intention is, but we are setting up a trap to have it stopped. The target has now turned onto our street."

James pushed his family even lower to the ground. David could hear and see others move around the shop with low light flashlights, they took up tactical positions around the perimeter of the shop.

After a couple more minutes the radio came to life again, "Target has been intercepted and removed. All clear. There is no other activity to be seen. The target is being brought to the shop door. Over"

"10-4. Over," Kenton replied to the radio.

"Shh, stay quiet and still for just another minute," James told his family.

David heard the bay door open and saw a car pull in. The headlights were off, and the motor was not running. Once the door was closed, they turned the lights to the shop on and David could see the new car in the shop. A beat-up silver Ford Falcon was parked just inside the bay door. Ken sat in the driver's seat.

"All sorted out, I am just going to put this in the holding area for tonight," said Tom.

He walked over to the wall and opened the two sliding white doors. Scott and Edward ran over to help push the car into the area and closed the doors behind them. Bill left his position and went into the room with the car.

This was the area of the shop David was not allowed to visit, "Ever," his grandfather would say, "and no peaking when the door is open, you have to be much older to work in that part of the shop."

David knew bad things happened in that part of the shop; he heard screams one time. He had peeked another time when the doors were wide open. There wasn't much in that area of the shop. There were tools on the wall, lots of hammers, screwdrivers and cutting shears. A couple stools and a metal chair with belts attached to it, was pushed up against the wall. The chair did not look very comfortable to David. There was enough room for a car, but not much more. The doors were always closed and usually locked.

David heard bangs coming from the boot of the car as the men pushed the car into the forbidden room. *'That is where they had stashed the bodies of the men that were originally driving the car,'* David thought. *'They were not going to enjoy their visit in that area.'*

James let Elizabeth and the kids out of their hiding spot. David scanned the shop looking for his grandfather. He did not see his grandfather at first, but his Aunt Sarah was there looking at him, he ran to her, jumped into her arms, and gave her a big hug as he cried.

"James, where are the people that were in the car," Elizabeth asked as they followed David.

"Luv, do you really want to know? Or, do you already know and just want to hear me say it? And please don't ask what will happen to them. You already know that too," said James.

The group in the shop gathered. Kenton, the troublemaker, Elizabeth would call him when James couldn't hear her talking, Sarah and Scott, Edward, Elizabeth's younger brother who she believed they tricked into this little club of Kenton's, Bill and Brian, employees of Kenton's.

The adrenaline had left David and he felt very tired. It was half-past three in the morning and David was woken around two o'clock. David saw his grandfather. He ran over to him and jumped so hard into his arms; Kenton had to step back to keep his balance. They hugged tightly and David gave him a big kiss on the cheek.

"Granda, what is going on tonight?" David inquired as he tried not to show he had been crying.

His grandfather smiled and said, "Not now David. You look like you need a wee sleep and I think your mother wants you to go with her to the office. Your couch is waiting for you."

"David come with me," Elizabeth called to him. "You need to get some sleep."

David wanted to stay with his dad and grandfather, but the urge to sleep was greater.

"David, your blanket is in the cupboard as usual," Kenton said as he pushed him towards Elizabeth.

The rest of the crew from the vehicles all stood around the table. They shook hands and hugged. It had been a stressful couple of hours, but things had worked out.

"Phase one has been successful," Kenton stated as he shook James' hand. "We can bunker down here tonight and get you moved to safety tomorrow. I am so glad my contact from the Falls Road passed that information to us, or else the four of you would be dead by now."

"Yes, I know Dad. That was too close for all of us. Elizabeth is not happy at all about any of this, you should be ready for her, she won't leave here before you get a mouth full from her," James warned.

"I know, I am fully expecting the tongue lashing of my life, worse than any commander I ever had in the military."

"Dad we are turning her world upside down and uprooted her and our children, she has every right to snap."

Elizabeth, who was over with Sarah, walked over to James just as he finished his quiet conversation with Kenton.

"I am putting the kids to their makeshift beds, if you can break away from your boys' club, come see them before they fall asleep," Elizabeth said to James.

David loved the old couch; it was where he would nap after he worked hard in the shop. He enjoyed it when he could come to a meeting or hangout with his family at the shop. Here he was an employee, his grandfather would give him small jobs to do like organize screws or clean the floor but to David he was part of the team! When he was there late in the evening or on the weekend, he would sneak away to the office for a nap. He would lie on the right side of the couch; it was less worn and would give him a good view of the shop as he dozed off. Many people, cars, guns, and other stranger items would pass through his field of vision as he fell asleep. His father and grandfather constantly reminded him, 'whatever you see or hear in the shop you can't tell anyone, it is all to stay here, you can't even tell your mom or your teddy bears. If you do, someone could get hurt and you won't be allowed back.' David, even at his young age, knew how to keep secrets, especially from his mother.

David went to the cupboard and grabbed his blanket, the red one with the tartan pattern on it, and climbed up on the couch. Aunt Sarah came to help with the blanket as his mother placed Amy in the cot.

"Aunt Sarah, I have a couple questions," he said once he was wrapped up in his blanket.

"Okay, but you need to sleep so only a couple of questions, David," she replied.

David revisited all the questions he had asked since he woke up earlier, "What is happening? Are we going to die? Will I see you or Nannie again? Will I get to go home to my toys and...?"

"Shhh, not now, we can talk tomorrow, now you need to sleep, you have a busy couple days ahead of you. Your mom and dad are going to need you to be at your best, you can only be your best when you get all your sleep," she said. "Close your eyes and know we all love you here David, now try to go back to sleep. Maybe tomorrow, if there is time, your dad and granda will talk to you about your questions."

Sarah hummed a song to him, Abide with Me, to calm him. He lost the fight with sleep. She kissed him on the forehead and left the office.

James noticed the kids were almost asleep as he came into the office. Elizabeth looked over her shoulder at him and stared at him with eyes of rage.

"Don't you dare wake either of my children," she whispered.

James shook his head and walked over to David.

He leaned over David and whispered, "Love you son, this will all make sense one day." He leaned in and kissed David on the forehead. "Sleep well luv, tomorrow a new life begins for all of us."

He pulled the blanket up a bit higher to David's chin and walked away. James saw Elizabeth leave the office. He walked over to Amy; her thumb was in her mouth.

James bent over her and whispered, "Hopefully this will all be a dream to you when you are older, I never meant for you to see any of this. Love you, Princess Amy."

He leaned in to give her a kiss while she fussed, James gently swept her hair from her forehead, kissed his hand, and tapped her on the nose.

"Sleep my luv," he whispered.

• • •

James finally had a quiet moment, he became overwhelmed by the situation and cried. He couldn't let Elizabeth, or the others see him in this moment of weakness. She already questioned the madness in her life and the life of her children. He had to be decisive and strong for the family, for his father. James quietly sat on the office floor with his back against the old maple desk and his knees pulled into his chest. The tears had stopped, and the urgency of the moment had returned to him. He wiped his eyes and took a deep breath. One last moment of peace. He knew that when he walked out the door, the peace would turn to chaos. He still had to finalize the plans with his dad and deal with an assault of questions from Elizabeth. *'I might have been better off if the IRA had captured me, then have to face Elizabeth tonight,'* he thought to himself.

Elizabeth noticed James had not come out of the office. She stood by the office door to see if the children were okay. James rose to his feet and into Elizabeth's sight. He smiled at her angry face.

Before he could close the door to the office Elizabeth spoke, "Before you go back to your little gang of misfits we need to talk."

"Quiet, they are sound asleep," James said, as he raised his finger to his lips.

"Yes, I know James, I was there with them taking care of them while you were over celebrating your great escape. Where can we talk without being interrupted?" she said.

"Luv, it can wait..." he began.

"No, it will not wait any longer," she said. "We need to talk about us and the kids and what you think we are doing."

"Aye, come over here."

They walked by the table where Sarah sat waiting for the kettle to boil. She looked at Elizabeth then at James as he passed, she gave him a half smile, half, I feel so bad for you look. The same look you would give an innocent man going to the gallows.

He led her to the front area of the reception room. They would be alone, and the walls were soundproof, which could be good or bad for James.

"Over here Elizabeth, we can sit here and talk for a minute."

"This will take more than a minute James, our future deserves more than a minute," she said.

•　　•　　•

"So how do we start this conversation, luv?" James asked as he put his hand on her knee.

Elizabeth moved her leg quickly away from him. "Don't touch me," she said. She tried to control her voice and emotions. "Don't you even think of trying to comfort me right now James Grant, I am so worried—angry—furious—scared, I just want to hit you, hit them," she said.

She pointed through the glass to where she believed her brother and father-in-law stood. "Why have you let this happen? What will happen to us, to the kids..." her emotions now won, and she cried.

"Luv, calm down," James said. "I can answer all this for you but just not right now, I promise tomorrow we will have lots of time to have this talk, tomorrow I promise I will tell you everything. For now, I need you to be strong and to listen, with no interruptions please. We will leave here tomorrow and go to Canada," James said.

"Canada? I don't think we will be moving halfway around the world. No, NO, NO! This was all a setup to get us to move to Canada to help John's side of the business? There is no way I am leaving Northern Ireland. What about my side of the family? I can't leave my mom alone. We can hide here for a few days while this blows over, then go to Blackpool like we planned. Canada? I don't think so," she responded through her tears.

"Elizabeth listen, we will be going to Canada to live, you will like it there, away from all this trouble, we will have a house there, all our stuff will be sent to us in time," James said in a calm voice.

"We don't have the money to move to Canada, what about the kids how do we explain this to them?" she asked.

"We don't, not right now. One day David will know all this, but we can't tell it to Amy she doesn't need to know any of this. Elizabeth, please just listen, I will tell you everything tomorrow, I promise," James said.

"Know what, James?? This was the plan all along, you and your father planned this. James, I can't believe you would do this—Canada to John? This is so obvious now! How much more is there to tell me? I thought I knew everything! I thought you always said, 'no secrets between us.' But there is, oh aye, there certainly is," her voice rose with each word. "You have never told me the truth, have you?"

She swung her hand at him to slap him, but he stopped her. "Listen Elizabeth we need to leave here. We need to protect ourselves and our children. This life we know here can't happen anymore; we need to leave. We will have plenty of time tomorrow and I will explain it to you then. But now I need to get back with the crew and review our exit from here, you need to sit down and shut up, help make some meals and take care of the kids. Just stay out of the way."

She saw something in James' eyes and face she had never seen before, fear. He was truly worried for his kids, wife, and self.

"Okay, okay, I think I am beginning to understand we need to go, and this situation is well above my understanding, for now. But I want to know everything and no more secrets between us. If—IF we move to Canada, it will only be the four of us. So, you need to be completely honest, aye?" she said.

"Aye, we will be on a boat to England tomorrow or tonight, I have lost track of time. I will explain it all to you, I love you and never want you this mad at me again," he said.

She nodded at him. "Maybe this is a good thing, getting away from all this. Maybe a new, honest, no secrets start is what our marriage needs. Just the four of us with no more lies, no more secrets and our kids raised without the troubles dragging them to your father's level of society."

James did not respond to her comments. "Please help Sarah as I meet with Dad to keep the plans rolling. I promise, you will know everything tomorrow, no more secrets, after tomorrow it will be the four of us on our own."

"Okay until tomorrow when we talk, I will trust you and follow your instructions."

Elizabeth pulled herself out of the chair, still angry, still confused, but she now understood her children needed her to follow whatever instructions James asked of her, for now.

As she walked by him, he grabbed her arm and spun her around to face him. "Elizabeth, I love you, always have, always will," he said.

She gave him a small smile, "Okay, love you too." she responded without emotion. "Can I see my mother before we leave?"

"Yes, I will ask Edward to pick her up after breakfast, until then please let me work on getting us out safely," James pleaded.

"Aye, I will."

Once she left, James took a big breath. "Okay, now to try to keep my word."

•   •   •

Elizabeth sensed there was more at play with this escape. Something seemed fabricated, something seemed orchestrated. All her fears and worries ran through her mind again. She needed to have a say in this relocation of her family. She also knew she could be in a shallow grave by teatime tomorrow if she asked the wrong question or poked around into business that wasn't hers to see. She would have her day, but today she would play the role of the scared, angry, but faithful wife. She would play her part for now, but she expected to get her answers tomorrow.

She would not speak up and embarrass James any further. His men respected him and admired him; she knew that. A man who did not have his lady under control, that was a sign of weakness to this group, and she did not want to know the repercussions of showing disloyalty towards James or the family.

Right now, what she needed and wanted was some quiet time in the office with her kids, alone.

CHAPTER FOUR

James reviewed the exit strategy with Kenton, Scott, Edward, and Brian. Elizabeth sat with her children. Sarah made tea. She poured out a second cup and headed to the office to sit with Elizabeth.

Kenton and James broke away from the group to talk by the presses.

"Before we continue with this plan, will she be okay?" Kenton asked as he nodded in the office's direction. "We can't risk her spoiling the plans we have finalized with John. A lot of talk and work has gone into this. I know she doesn't believe it, but I love her like my own and I want her to be happy."

"Aye, Dad, she will be fine. She just needs to wrap her head around what is happening to her and her family. I haven't been able to explain the whole situation to her yet. She knew something like this could, and probably would, happen. And here we are running from the boogeyman. She had no warning. Maybe I should have prepared her more. She did really think I was out of the front-line activities. If she knew what we were planning and doing, she would have taken David and Amy and ran far away," James said.

"Does she suspect you know anything about this being planned?" Kenton asked.

"No, I played it well. I hate the fact that I had to lie about this to get her to move, but we both know my family will have a better life in Canada and I can work with John to grow our network. The guns and equipment we can move through the Americas will pay for any of her concerns over and over," James replied. "I will have to tell her one day, maybe tonight on the boat. The thing is, yes, it was partially staged, but once I explain I was identified on a job she might see it our way. She may never forgive me for the way we did it, but here we are with no choices left but this way. We have talked in the past about getting away from the troubles and having the kids raised in a peaceful country. But I believe she would have wanted more input on the timing and the location. She is a strong woman, stubborn in her ways, but hopefully she will understand."

"Okay son, it is still the right thing to do for us and your family. You know there is a large price on your head, and I don't want to see it cashed in. Even with it being a wee bit staged tonight, someone was poking around outside the shop and Scott said there was a lot more activity at the house than he had planned. The last thing I ever want to do is have to explain to your kids, my grandkids, why you were not around, so you do need to leave the country."

"Yes, I know Dad and I am glad we didn't hesitate to do this tonight. I don't think they will follow us to Canada."

"Alright son, we have a busy day ahead before we move out this evening. This has been a very successful night from a tactical, and a father's view."

The two men hugged and walked to the waiting group to review the next stage of the extraction for the family.

"Brian, dismiss the others for now. Thanks for your help tonight mate, tell them they won't need to come back to the shop for three days. I will need you back tomorrow to take care of the car and its contents in the back room. I will let Gary know we will have a delivery for him with some cargo in the boot. Give him a hand if he asks."

"Yes, Kenton, consider the job completed," said Brian.

Brian rounded up the others and headed to the back of the shop.

"Okay, let's review the checklist," said Kenton. "Scott, you have secured a boat to get them to England?"

"Aye, it is in Bangor Harbor, our regular fishing crew. Captain Peter cancelled some scheduled trips to help. We don't have to worry about him asking any wee questions when we arrive. I gave him a general rundown of the situation," said Scott. "The crew will get them out of the harbor and over to England."

"Is the transportation to the airport in London confirmed," Kenton said as he continued down his list.

"Aye, Leslie will have a car waiting for us at the marina in Blackpool, full of gas and reliable. He will leave it at the dock tomorrow, about an hour before we arrive. The keys will be under the passenger seat and the plates are legal. Once my family is at the airport, we will park the car in the usual parking area, to be disposed of later," said James.

"Alright, those are the easy parts," said Kenton. "I have secured airline tickets; they are in the travel bag in the office. The bag also has new ID's if we choose to go that route, five-thousand Canadian dollars and cheques for a bank account John set up for this purpose. I don't think you will need the fake IDs for this trip. If you decide not to use them, leave them in the car's boot and they can be disposed of properly."

"Aye John," said James. "What about him? Will he be at Toronto when we arrive? Or will there be transport for us?"

"Yes, it has all been arranged. John will be at the airport to pick you up and get you to Guelph. He will have a place for you to stay for a couple weeks while he finalizes your immigration paperwork over there."

"Aye, it is just a lot different for me flying over there to work than bringing my family permanently," said James.

"Okay, so we wait out the day and leave around half-past six tonight," said Kenton.

"I know I have said it before, but I feel bad uprooting my family like this. I know this had to happen now because we—I—blundered the last job. But why are we getting into bigger, more hazardous jobs for the government? When we kept it small, with the guns and bombs, we were all making money and could feel relatively safe in our houses. Now these bigger, higher risk jobs are breaking apart the family and putting us all at risk," said James. He flailed his arms and tried to look angry.

James would not question his father's decisions, it was just the way he was raised, but he knew Elizabeth would look through the window of the office and if he did not show he was fighting for his family to stay here, she would question his commitment to them.

Kenton expected the dramatics, as they had discussed it last evening, and played along. He added some extra physical theatrics to his response, "I know son and I am sorry, but this is the path we need to go. One day we will look back on this and be glad we took the higher risk, higher paying jobs. It won't benefit us, but it will benefit David and Amy, and when Scott and Edward have wee children, they will see the fruits of our work too. I will talk to Elizabeth if you want. I can explain it all to her, all the parts you have hidden from her to protect her and your mother-in-law."

"No, we will talk on the boat, I will have lots of time then to chat about tonight. Hopefully she doesn't throw me over the side," said James with a smile.

•   •   •

"We should get some breakfast started before I open the shop for the day," said Kenton.

The sun peeked into the high windows, by the roof of the shop, and into the office windows where Elizabeth, Sarah and the kids slept.

"It has been one hell of a night, one we won't forget for a long time," said Scott as they headed into the small makeshift kitchen.

"One day very soon, I want to open the wall up and put in a small apartment, so you have somewhere to stay when you come back to work with us, James," said Kenton.

"Aye, it wouldn't be a bad idea Dad. Maybe we should make a room for David as well. Just don't tell Elizabeth," James said as he walked over to the office door.

He looked into the office, the sun shone on Elizabeth's and Sarah's faces. Elizabeth woke up from what looked like a very uncomfortable sleeping position.

James opened the door and whispered, "Morning you two, Dad is starting breakfast."

Elizabeth turned and glared at him. She walked over to Amy and checked on her and then to David. Both kids were sound asleep. Elizabeth followed Sarah out the door.

"How's about Ye," said Sarah to James as she walked by.

"Alright?" he replied.

Elizabeth walked out without greeting her husband. James grabbed her from behind and pulled her to him. "Morning Luv, how did you sleep in there? It's a bright sunny morning, do you want to go out for a quick walk while Dad makes some breakfast?"

"Get your filthy hands off me, you think I am just going to wake up this morning, after sleeping on an old office chair, and forget what happened last night? Well, you have a lifetime of misery heading your way if you think that! What are we doing? What brilliant plan do you have for us now after your night of scheming," she whispered angrily, like a snake rattling its tail before it strikes.

"We will discuss it later," James said as he let go of her waist.

"It's always 'later' or 'I have to meet my father', when will there be time for me and your kids?" she asked, her voice raised for the others to hear.

"Soon, I promise. Soon it will just be the four of us, together."

The aroma of bacon and eggs in the pan filled the air.

"Morning," Elizabeth said to the group with a very insincere smile on her face.

"Alright Luv," asked Kenton.

Elizabeth did not reply she just gave him a look, *'if only looks could kill'* she thought, *'that one would have stopped, if not exploded his heart.'*

• • •

The aroma of bacon made its way through the open door and into the office. David lay awake with his thoughts, *'was last night all a dream? Was I just waking from that strange dream after napping in my granda's office like I had done so many times before? No, it was all real. There was no dream, not this time.'*

He got off the sofa and walked over to Amy to see if she was awake. She was still asleep, so he left the office quietly. He looked around the shop and walked over to his father. David rubbed the sleep out of his eyes when he approached James.

"Hi Daddy, can we go home now," David said.

"No son, if you remember last night, we talked about going on an adventure together. Today that adventure begins. Tomorrow you will get to fly in a big jet airplane," said James.

Elizabeth heard Amy crying. She headed into the office.

David turned from his dad and said loudly, "Mommy, I get to fly on a plane tomorrow. A plane, Mommy! I can't wait."

"Aye son, a large plane to another part of the world away from our family and all your friends," she replied, as she gave James and Kenton looks that shook their very souls.

"Elizabeth luv, don't be like that, it is a special day for him," noted Kenton.

"Aye, a special day indeed," said Elizabeth.

• • •

With breakfast ready Kenton said grace, "Dear Heavenly Father, thank you for the food we have to eat this morning and the health and safety of this family. Be with those who will travel and those who stay here. Thank you for the lessons of forgiveness you teach in your gospels and as the days go on let us all remember those lessons. In your name we pray, Amen."

The group repeated "Amen" together.

They each took a plate of food and a cup of coffee or tea. James made a plate for David and Elizabeth prepared one for Amy. The group sat around a couple of work benches, quiet as they ate, each in their own thoughts of what they were assigned to do or what would happen to them over the next few days.

"Edward, can you leave after you eat, pick up our Doris and bring her back here for a visit. She can spend the day with the wee ones as we repack the cars and prepare to depart. Drop Scott and Sarah over to Gary's dealership to pick up the spare cars I ordered for us to use tonight to move everyone to Bangor Harbor," Kenton said.

"Aye, I will drop them off, then do the usual loops to ensure I am not followed. I hope they don't have eyes on mom's place," Edward replied.

David sat with his father; he was so excited about this new adventure he couldn't contain himself. "Dad, how big will the plane be? Where will it land? Can I see the driver?" he said.

"David, eat your breakfast and stop asking questions," his mother said.

Amy chewed on a piece of bacon and laughed at David.

•   •   •

Kenton knew Doris showing up would be a distraction for Elizabeth and the kids while the rest of the crew prepared for the family's departure.

The others left to run their errands while David worked with his grandfather on a milling machine. He sat on a high stool with big, oversized safety glasses while his grandfather removed a 1000th of an inch from a block of aluminum.

"Granda when we go away, will I see you again?" David said.

"Of course, you will. Once you are a little older you can come visit in the summer when the weather is nice. I would love to take you to places for visits," his granda said.

David sat for a minute and thought about what his granda just said.

"Can we go to the old castle we pass on the road to Bangor?"

"Aye, and there are even bigger ones to see if we head west."

David smiled at the thought of bigger castles and getting to visit them with his grandfather.

• • •

Edward entered the shop with his mother behind him.

"Nannie!" David yelled.

Doris, David's grandmother, smiled at the loud, loving welcome from her only grandson.

Edward had updated her on the events from the previous night and the plans going forward. David couldn't see it, but her eyes were puffy, and her cheeks were red, her heart was broken from the news. Doris, like the others, knew a day like this would come. Edward drove around town a couple times to calm her down before they arrived at the shop.

David jumped off the stool and ran towards her. Edward crouched down and opened his arms, as if he thought David was running to him. He knew better. David ran by him without even acknowledging him, everyone gave out a loud laugh. David jumped up into his nannie's arms and gave her a big hug. Once he climbed down from his hug, they walked over to Elizabeth and Sarah hand in hand.

"Nannie, we are going away tonight, and I get to go on a big airplane. Will you be coming too?" David asked.

"No, son, I won't, but I will come visit you at your new home in a wee while. I will visit a lot and you can come visit me too," she replied.

"What, you won't be coming with me? I thought everyone was coming," said David. The joy in his face had quickly changed to disappointment.

"David, can you come over here please for a minute," said his dad.

David let go of his nannie's hand and ran over to his dad. Doris picked up Amy and gave her a hug.

"David let's go into the office for a minute," James said.

"But Dad, I want to see Nannie."

"It will only be a minute."

"Right, did I say something wrong Daddy," David said.

The two of them walked into the office together and David jumped up on the desk chair while James sat on the couch.

"David, it will only be mom, Amy, you and me going on this trip, no one else," explained James.

"What?" said David. "I thought we all were going. I don't want to leave everyone here." Tears welled up in David's eyes. "I thought we were all leaving together to start a new life. It's just us? Will I ever get to see them again? Daddy, why is this happening?"

James looked down at the floor in shame. He tried not to look at David. The emotion in David's voice and the tears in his eyes caused James to choke up.

'Now wasn't the time for emotions to take over,' James thought.

"Daddy, are you okay?"

James coughed to clear his throat, "Yes son I am and we all will be for a long time. Go out and see Nannie I am sure she wants to be with you for the day before we head out on our big trip."

David did not have to hear that twice; he was off the chair and out the office door like a rabbit being chased by a fox.

As James rose from the couch Kenton poked his head into the office, "Alright?" he asked.

"Aye, I am fine. Just some moments of doubt," James said.

"I understand, be strong son, for all of us," Kenton said.

"Aye, I always have Dad," James said, as he struggled to make a smile.

• • •

Doris played with the kids and Elizabeth sorted through the suitcases. She wasn't sure they had packed the proper clothes for James, herself, and the kids. There were some items she really wanted to go home and get, but Kenton refused to let her leave the shop.

Kenton wasn't sure what was going through her mind and to let her out of the shop was not part of the plan. He needed to make her feel this was where she could remain safe until they moved out tonight.

"Elizabeth, whatever you are missing, we will ship to you over the next few months. And if it is something you need right now, there is enough cash traveling with you to buy it in Canada," Kenton said.

"I know it is just some sentimental items my dad gave me before he passed," she said.

"Your mom and brother will make sure you get them all, you have my word," he said.

"I know Kenton, it is just I wasn't prepared for this at all. This is just a lot to take in right now, I am sure we will be happy in Canada once we get settled. My mom, will she be able to visit or are we going to be in hiding over there?" she asked.

"No," he replied. "You won't be in hiding. Once you settle in, I will personally pay to have your mother flown over to visit. She can stay as long as she wishes. We will all be over to visit, and you will be back here too. Think of this as a way to get the kids away from the troubles."

"Aye. So, you won't expect James to return to do your dirty work for you?"

"I didn't say that, now did I," he said.

"No, no, you didn't. But he will not be taking David for any of this. The sea will separate my son from here, and I plan on raising him my way. You can have James back for your 'jobs', but you will not be getting any of my children."

The look of confidence and denial on his face made her blood boil.

"We will see," he said. He smiled at her with his smile that either had a person raging or a women's knees turning to water.

Elizabeth walked away and sat on a chair in the reception area by herself.

The arrogant sound of his voice had annoyed her for as long as she has known him. It had a high pitched nasally sound that always seemed to have a condescending tone to it. She believed Kenton felt she was not good enough for James and she had to prove her worth to Kenton every time they were together.

Sarah saw Doris with the kids but did not see Elizabeth. She checked the office, then the front reception. Elizabeth sat on one of the reception chairs with tears dripping off her chin. Sarah sat down and put her arm around her, nothing needed to be said at that moment. Sarah felt bad for her, trapped in her marriage, and now being forced to move halfway around the world. She knew Elizabeth was too stubborn to accept the family for what they were.

●　　●　　●

Elizabeth sat at the front of the shop alone as the roll-up door at the back of the shop opened and two used cars drove in, a black Ford Escort and a gold Austin Maxi. Once again Gary had pulled through for Kenton, he sent two cars that were average family cars. These cars would not stand out at a checkpoint or parked downtown. That he sent an Austin Maxi was a bit of a joke between the two men.

The first time Gary sent an Austin was for a job in Cookstown before James and Scott were old enough to be involved. The job was to take out two British IRA informants and set explosives in a barn where the IRA had a weapon depot. The only problem with this job was when the Austin did not make it back to the shop. After the four-man crew had successfully completed the job and were almost back to Portadown and the shop, the Austin's engine had its own explosion. A piston failed and came out the side of the engine block. Luckily Kenton and his crew had enough explosives with them to destroy the car and create a four-foot crater under the car. With the car destroyed, the crew had to hike back fifteen miles to the shop.

Ever since then Gary has kept one Austin for the crew. They painted it multiple times. The motor was rebuilt and improved from the 1500cc sewing machine motor to an impressive motor that could outrun most cars in the country. The car had customized hiding spots, located in the car so weapons or explosives, would not be detected at checkpoints. This was the crew's car. Everyone had used it for jobs, and this was the car Scott learnt how to drive a standard transmission. Gary would pull this car out for special occasions. The Austin had to be used for this trip; it was part of the family and should take James' family on their next adventure.

Scott and Sarah got out of the cars.

Scott said with a big smile, "Look what Gary gave us."

James, Edward, and Kenton walked over to the cars.

"Hazel, our good luck charm," said James.

•   •   •

Gary Rose, one of Kenton's business contacts in Banbridge, owned car dealerships of new and used cars.

When Kenton was posted in Northern Ireland with the SAS, he purchased his first car from Gary's dealership. With that transaction they developed a friendship. Kenton, always looked for an opportunity to make money. He approached Gary 'with a deal you can't refuse.' Gary accepted the deal. They built a professional relationship, and he became the unofficial car dealership of the British Military in Northern Ireland.

As they deployed British military personnel and Special Forces to Northern Ireland, Kenton recommended Gary's dealership as the place to purchase a new or used car at an affordable price. Gary, always loyal to Ulster and the British gave soldiers and their families special prices. He also rented cars to those who were not staying long term on the Island.

The military, government and new soldiers purchased and rented cars from Gary, Kenton's SAS crews used the dealership for other matters. As Gary's business grew, so did his partnership with Kenton. Gary separated his new car business from the used cars and set up multiple dealerships for the sale of vehicles. The used car dealership had a large service area for customers vehicles and a couple of private car bays for any cars Kenton needed tuned or worked on. As the business grew, Kenton and Gary, laundered money through the car lots, lots of money. The discounts Gary gave on the personal sale of vehicles to military staff were always accounted for and paid in full when Kenton needed a favor of a spare or 'clean' car.

Gary would never reveal how his dealership grew to one of the biggest in Armagh County, but certain groups investigated his loyalty to the Queen or to the Republic.

Gary proved his loyalty to Kenton in 1973, when one of his new car dealerships burnt to the ground, all the cars were destroyed on the lot. Republican sympathizers took three salesmen and Gary hostage. They believed he was too closely involved with the British military and should rethink his business plan. Gary never broke, during his interrogation. Kenton, James, and a few of their crew were able to locate Gary and his salesmen. Kenton and his crew broke in and killed the kidnappers, all but one. The only injury suffered to the captives was to Benny, Gary's sales manager, who they shot in the ankle while he was interrogated. After he recovered Benny walked with a noticeable limp.

Kenton's crew brought their hostage back to the shop and after a few days of torture and questions, the crew were able to take down eight IRA hideouts in the Belfast area. They released the whistleblower back into his own area of town for his own people to deal with. He was found dead two days later in an alley with all his fingers and toes removed, his eyeballs packed in the front pocket of his dress pants and an inverted cross carved into his forehead.

Gary had two special services he offered his special clients, first; untraceable disposal of vehicles that were no longer needed after covert operations. Gary, or another trusted employee, would strip the cars down. Then they shipped the parts around Europe or melted them down at the local foundry. The second service offered was the ability to clean a car of all identifying marks. If they needed a vehicle as a transport car for a bomb or other unusual activity, there would be no fingerprints, distinguishing features, or VIN identification on the car. The license plates were always legitimate and matched the car they were hung on. This would ensure no issues at any military or police checkpoints. The plates were never used twice, just like the paint color on the car. Most times they returned the cars to Gary's lot undamaged. Back at the dealership they would clean, paint, and prepare the car for the next request.

There was always at least a two-day delay before they received a car, five days if there was a request to have it 'cleaned.' Those cars rarely came back to the lot. Gary had an agreement with his customers. If they knew the vehicle would not be returned, Gary would purchase, or take a car from his lot. An old basic car that no one would notice in a crowd. It would receive a 'sanitization' and a tune-up to ensure it was reliable. As Kenton would tell people, there is nothing worse than having a car break down on the side of the road with fifty pounds of C-4 and TNT on the way to a job. You need a reliable vehicle.

• • •

"Okay, let's get the cars loaded up with luggage and food for the trip," Kenton said.

The crew loaded the luggage and weapons into the cars as they reminisced about the adventures they had in the Austin, or as they called it, Hazel.

The remainder of the day went slowly for everyone as the kids played with Doris and they finalized plans. Kenton had a few scheduled customers pass through the shop doors, but business was quiet.

The group were having tea and cookies when the front door opened. In walked a man none of them had ever met before. Kenton cautiously walked to the front counter from the shop.

"We are closed, I was just heading to the front door to lock up," Kenton said.

James and Scott jumped up and headed to the office to grab a couple guns. Edward headed to the back door.

"Won't take but a minute of your time. I was looking for a James Grant, I was told he worked here," the stranger said.

Kenton noticed the man was overdressed for the weather outside. Kenton watched the customer's hands and body language. He had been in these situations enough times that he would know the stranger's next move before the stranger did. Kenton moved along the service counter to the cash till where a pistol was taped to the underside of the cabinet.

"No. He doesn't work here; I have heard his name about town. Maybe in a pub one night. He is bit of a problem for some I hear," said Kenton. "Is there something I can help you with. I own the business.

"Oh, and your name is?"

"John Phillips. I own this shop and would like to close it up for the day if you have no business for me."

"Aye, I have none, mate. I was told I could find James here, but I must of wrote the wrong address on my notepaper. I owe him some money."

Edward had left the building through the back door. There was no one in the back area, so he proceeded to walk the perimeter of the building. The car the man had driven up in was empty and there were no other cars on the street.

Edward entered the front door like the other man did. He walked up to the counter and stood behind the man in conversation with Kenton.

"Well, if you see him, I would really like to pay him what I owe him," said the stranger.

"Aye, I will tell him, if I see him, or hear his name at the pub," Kenton said casually.

The man turned to leave, he bumped into Edward. It startled him to see another person in the front area that he did not hear come in. "Beg your pardon, sir, I didn't hear you come in," said the stranger.

"No problem mate, I was hoping to pick up my parts before they closed. Luckily you being here has kept the shop open a wee bit longer than usual," said Edward.

Edward stepped around the stranger and asked, "Are my parts done yet? I was in the area and thought I would pick them up."

The stranger turned to say something, then decided not to and left the shop. Edward followed him out. Kenton locked the front door. The stranger got back in his car, waved to Edward, and drove down the street. Edward returned the wave, then turned to watch the car leave.

Edward entered the back door and grabbed a piece of paper and pencil from a bench. He wrote down the plate number. "Have Matthew run this plate, Kenton," Edward said as he handed Kenton the piece of paper.

"Aye I will have Matthew check it out."

"That was strange, do you know the man, James?" asked Edward.

"No never seen him before."

"It was strange, the big over coat he was wearing," said Kenton.

"When he bumped against me, I could feel a gun in a holster on the right side of his chest," Edward said.

"I wonder why he came here, I would have thought they would be watching the house," Kenton said. "If we didn't have your move happening in a few hours, I believe I would have him in the shop answering a lot of questions or squealing in pain."

"Aye, let's not let our guard down tonight, obviously the price on your head is public knowledge," said Scott.

"Aye," said James, hoping Elizabeth did not hear the comment.

•   •   •

Elizabeth and Sarah prepared a steak and kidney pie and a chicken pie with chips for supper. The crew gathered around the work bench and ate together. Elizabeth's mood had improved, at least with most of the people at the table, James and Kenton were not as fortunate.

The group had one last cup of tea together while David had an orange pop and Amy some milk. There was an air of heaviness over them all. No one wanted the family broken up. Not like this, but most understood why it had to happen. They knew they would not be together much longer, and the plans to move James' family out of the country needed to be reviewed one last time. The time to leave was close and everything and everyone needed to be ready to go.

They checked the cars for all the luggage. James, Elizabeth, and the wee ones said goodbye to Doris. There were a lot of tears, a lot of *"I don't want to leave Nannie, I want to go home,"* from David and Amy. That only made the wedge with Elizabeth and James' marriage that much wider. Elizabeth had lost her father, and now she was losing her mother.

CHAPTER FIVE

While David and his family said goodbye to Doris, Kenton went to his office and called John. This move was one of the most important things they had ever done together.

"Hello old friend," said Kenton when the man on the other end of the line answered.

"Hello partner, everything still on schedule with James and his family?"

"Aye, still a go."

"We have been through a lot together, but this is the biggest, hardest job we have done, at least emotionally. I have been thinking about you guys ever since you called the other day. I can only imagine the emotions going on in the shop right now," said John.

"Aye, even for a hardened, crazy old man like myself, I am having problems keeping my emotions under control. Thank you for doing this John, you know how I am about family. You know you are a big part of this family. Take care of my son and his family."

"I will, everything is ready to go on my end," said John.

"Thank you. We will leave here shortly. I will call you once the boat leaves the dock with hopefully all its cargo."

They loaded David, his family, and their belongings into the Austin. Scott, Edward, and Sarah loaded themselves into the Ford. David always liked to drive with his grandfather. Kenton taught defensive and tactical driving when he was in the SAS. This meant, when he drove with David, they would take corners sideways and run roundabouts like a race car driver would take a turn. With this drive none of that would happen for David, his grandfather would drive defensively, so no attention would be brought to the family running from home.

There wasn't much conversation as the vehicles left Portadown. The kids had fallen asleep, and Elizabeth sat in the back of the car while James and Kenton discussed the plans and other family matters quietly up front. The cars drove nose to tail all the way through Belfast and to the turn at Helen's Bay. Outside of Helen's Bay, Scott pulled over, Kenton pulled behind him, he was worried they had a mechanical issue with the car. Scott walked back to Kenton's window and informed him that radio chatter had reported a British military check point two miles ahead. They knew, if it was a real checkpoint and not an ambush, it would have helicopter support looking for cars that turned around. Kenton decided they would have to go through the checkpoint.

Kenton mumbled as they walked to Scott's car, "They didn't tell me about this check point. I hope it is a checkpoint, we have no way to confirm it now. We can't be sure it is a British checkpoint, so be ready for anything. Do you have a map in the glove box?"

Scott opened the glove box and pulled out a map. He opened it on the bonnet of the car. James and Edward stood with flashlights pointed on the map. Kenton quickly reviewed the map, he looked for any choke points or high hills in the location of the checkpoint. He decided they would proceed spacing the cars at one quarter mile apart. They all headed back to their vehicles as Kenton reminded everyone to be ready for a possible ambush.

Kenton's car approached the checkpoint first. The guards instructed him to pull up into the bright, temporary lights the Army had set up on the roadway. Two heavily armed British Soldiers approached the car, one went to the driver's door and one to the front of the car. Scott pulled up to the checkpoint as the two soldiers reached Kenton's car. David knew, more soldiers would be in the ditch behind the car, just in case someone tried to attack the soldier at the driver's window. Then there would be another crew about a half mile up the road for those foolish enough not to stop at the checkpoint. The British army did not hide this information as they wanted anyone who lived in Northern Ireland to be aware they would not survive running through a checkpoint.

The soldier asked the usual questions of Kenton. 'Where are you going, who was in the car and can you show ID.'

Kenton flashed his old military ID to the soldier. The soldier spoke to him for a couple minutes as another soldier used a large mirror to check the undercarriage of the car. The soldier finally stepped back and saluted Kenton. Waving to the guard house, they raised the control arm and admitted both cars through the checkpoint together.

• • •

The group arrived at the dock in Bangor ahead of schedule. David could see the old familiar fishing boat they would be taking. He had been on this boat with his father and grandfather many times to either fish or to feed the fish. Sometimes James and Kenton would meet with other people in the cabin while David fished with the crew. They always reminded him not to tell his mother, or he would not get to come back.

The boat was a seventy-five-foot-long fishing boat. It slept at least ten people; the fishing deck was behind the wheelhouse, as were the sleeping quarters. The boat had new paint since David was last on it. The blue and red, was gone and it was now forest green above the waterline and white below. The crew scurried around the deck with last minute preparations for their departure. The captain in the wheelhouse checked the weather and water conditions. Seeing the cars pull up the crew came to the car to get the luggage and the passengers. David knew the crew from all the previous times on the boat. The Captain was the man who showed him how to put a worm on his fishing hook properly. The last fishing trip was the first time David had caught the biggest fish over everyone else. It made for a delicious dinner that night.

•   •   •

Scott and Edward helped the crew load the boat while James and Kenton walked over to the side of the dock by themselves. Elizabeth sat in the car while Amy slept on her lap. David noticed his dad and granda, at the edge of the dock, he got out of the car. Elizabeth grabbed his arm and pulled him back into the car. David tried to shake her grip, but she tightened her grasp.

David turned to her, he tried to free himself from her grip.

"Let me go mom, please. I want to be with Dad and Granda."

Elizabeth struggled to keep him with her, but she finally let him go, not just physically but emotionally too. She knew the life she had tried to protect him from, the life she did not want for him, but they had already ingrained it in him. Her seven-year-old son had already picked his destiny, or rather, had it picked for him. The only hope she had now was a move halfway around the world would separate him from this life, this continuous turmoil he was forced to grow up in. Her fear was, David, like his father and grandfather, would continue in the family business. She tried to stop David, but today she could not fight any longer. After the last twenty-four hours, she had no fight left in her. Her son would become what his father and grandfather made their income as, what took them away from their family and put their loved ones in a constant state of worry and fear. She added this to her mental list of things to discuss with James when he finally gave her the time to talk. She subconsciously handed her only son, David, over to the family business. The illusion of losing David was too much for her to handle and she cried.

David ran over to his father and grandfather. James welcomed him with a hug and kiss on the head. James looked towards Elizabeth as he held David's hand. He couldn't see Elizabeth in the back of the Austin. If only the three of them knew the anger, betrayal, disappointment, and abandonment she felt in that moment.

•   •   •

The boat pushed off and set sail for Blackpool. The hugs, kisses and blessing of a safe trip were completed. The crew reviewed the trip details, as everyone's tears dried. Elizabeth and Amy were already in the boat's sleeping quarters. David held James' hand as they waved to the family they were leaving behind. David was torn between leaving everyone he knew and the adventure of a new place to live and the flight he would take to get there.

The boat moved out of the harbor and Kenton headed to a pay phone by the dock's bar. He made a call to John informing him they were on the boat, all four of them thankfully. John and Kenton's question if Elizabeth would not leave was no longer a concern.

John had about seventy-four hours before they arrived, plenty of time to finalize food, cash, and clothing for the family. He knew what to expect of the family and what they would have with them.

The crew had prepared a couple of rooms for the family to sleep. The small bunk room, they set up for David and Amy, was not much bigger than the bunk beds in the room. Elizabeth had put Amy down for the night in the lower bunk when David and James came down to the crew's quarters.

"David, you need to get into bed and have a wee sleep, you didn't get a full night last night, and you have had a very busy day," said his mother.

She showed David the room he would sleep in, so small, she had to step out for David to get into the room. When David saw he would get to sleep on the top bunk, he climbed the ladder right away with a big happy smile.

"Aye Mom, I could use a wee sleep and I get to have the top bunk; I always get this top bunk when we go fishing," said David.

"Aye luv, top bunk. Get to sleep, love you."

"When he gets to sleep, we need to have that talk, James," Elizabeth reminded James.

James knew there was no escaping the talk now unless he jumped ship.

David's head did not even hit the pillow before he was asleep. James and Elizabeth checked on Amy, kissed both kids and left the room.

"Now for some time together, to sort this out James, and I only want the truth to the questions I ask. If this marriage is going to last this trip to England, I need answers and only the truthful ones, no wee fibs, no yarns with these answers either, only truth. Our Edward would tell me everything if I asked, I am sure." Elizabeth said.

"Aye, let's head to the kitchen area we can have a spot of tea and chat," James replied.

Elizabeth made two cups of tea while James went up to the captain and told him he didn't want any crew to interrupt them down below until they pulled into the Isle of Man to refuel.

Elizabeth was at the table with the teas made when James returned.

"Okay, Luv, what questions do you have for me?"

"I am ragin' right now; I really don't know where to start with you. You told me you had stepped away from this mess you and your father were in, so let's start there," she said.

"Right, no, I have not stepped out, I am more involved than ever, as you can tell. You know there is no getting out of anything with this family. So, to answer your question, I have been lying to you. The meetings I told you I had for church or working evenings in the shop were mostly lies. Some were planning, some were actions, but I am still involved heavily with all the parts of the business. I know I told you I was only dealing with managing the shop and the legitimate side of the business but no, I have been on major newsworthy jobs with Dad, Scott and yes—Edward too."

"So why the lies James, WHY?"

"You know what you married into, so don't ask why. I didn't even think you were believing me anyway when I said I was out in meetings. Maybe it was a way to protect you and the kids from the dangers of what I was doing. The less you know about the family the better."

"And what about David, would you have him at the shop and other places while doing this work?"

"Yes, Elizabeth, he helped in certain situations, but we kept him away from a lot of it. He is a wee boy wanting to be with his father. We would put him in the office when we would have meetings, and I never took him anywhere that he would be in real danger. But we took him out to jobs when we were all going together. That being said, he knows about the guns and I am sure he has figured out a lot more of what was going on. We always told him if he told you anything besides working on his go-cart or watching us build a die or plate for a customer he couldn't come back. I might not be the best dad, but we all liked having him at the shop. It kept us all together. It reminded us we were in this as a family, not just business partners."

"James, how could you? Did he ever see, you know, a body or anything like that come into the shop?"

"Umm, I would say no, but he is a smart boy, and he would watch out the office windows when we were busy with things like that. We reminded him never to go in the back room and if we were interrogating someone Edward would take David out for a treat, just in case things got loud."

"You mean, someone screaming, begging for their life."

"Aye."

"The big question, how did we get here? I want it all, not the short quick version. Why did I pack up my kids and get on this bloody boat? Truth, James!"

"Okay, John, you met him a few times when he was here to visit and at our wedding. We all run the businesses together. He will meet us in Toronto, he will set us up in Canada. John needs help over there. I am going to help and continue to build our business over there. So that is part of why we are here on this boat."

"What? We are putting our future in a couple of international criminals, and you might be one now too? James, how could you let your father talk you into this."

"He didn't Elizabeth, this had to happen, and it had to happen immediately. Yes, Dad, John and I had plans to move me—us, to Canada, but you were to be part of the decision and without full support from you it would not have happened. But the other night I was on a job and that was when all this changed. It changed all our plans and our family's future."

"Why, what happened, James? Why did all the plans change? We could disappear on our own, just the four of us. Abandon our families and start a new life."

"You know there is no way that would ever work. It's absurd to even suggest."

"I know," she said. She knew it wasn't just her marriage that were 'till death us do part.'

"Okay, this is the part I don't know if I want the truth to, but I need to know, and you must be honest James. We can't start this trip with lies, tell me the truth about the other night, what really happened to you or the guys before you came home and woke me. Why did we have to leave like that, it all seemed 'put on' to me James. It felt like you planned it. Yes, we heard gun shots but nothing in our direction and the shooter wasn't even close. I know that much! No one chased us, and I don't believe the car you guys pushed into the other room had anyone in it, I think it was a prop. The whole night felt staged, James. If you have a price on your head I need to know, I need to know if this bounty will carry over to Canada and haunt us the rest of our lives. Was all this done for extra money, I cannot understand or accept that. But you have to tell me the truth and all the truth."

"Aye, I will tell you, but don't interrupt me while I talk. Right?"

James got up and grabbed the tea pot and topped up both their teacups.

"This is a full teacup story. Let me tell you the whole tale without interruption. I can start at the beginning, way back. My story of being in the Orangemen or at church was just a cover for the truth. Again, I didn't even think you believed me half the time. I have done a lot of things in the name of the Protestant church and this family of killers I was born into. I have terrorized Catholics in Northern and Southern Ireland and even done some things to the Prods just to set up some IRA people. I have done work around the world. Mostly North and South America, but there has been some work in the Middle East and Asia. John would bring me to Canada for work to assassinate people or help with shipments of goods. I know where we are going to live in Canada and you will love it, I promise. The trips where I told you I was going on were not actual work, church or Orangeman related they were to ensure our products were being sold properly. I would help move our competition, mostly the soviets, out of our areas or do work for others who needed people out of their way."

"How could you," she said with shock and disappointment in her voice.

"It is part of the business and the skills I was taught, luv. Again, I don't think you actually want all the details?"

She shook her head.

"You knew when we were dating and getting married what my family did. Yes, we have expanded the scope of our work to become a large player in the underground world of arms trading. We each have our own specialty skills that people, and governments use around the world. So that catches us up to present day. The night in question I was out on a job with Dad, Scott, Edward, Brian, and Bill. The request was to hit two targets in Belfast, both in the Falls Road area. The one job was to remove David Smith. You have seen him on the news, a Northern Ireland Member of Parliament. He would pass critical information to his IRA contacts. He was to be at the Falls Road area, and we were to remove him from a house and interrogate him for information. We were to give the information to our British contact and dispose of Mr. Smith's body quickly, in a non-recoverable manner. Meaning we would chop it up and spread it through farms so there would be nothing to identify. Everyone would consider him a missing person. Dad, Brian, and Edward were assigned the removal, questioning and handling of David Smith. Scott, Bill, and I were to blow up a pub where a large depot of explosives was being kept. I was to locate Nigel, the bomb maker. Nigel is one of their top bomb and explosives builder. He does mostly IRA stuff but has freelanced for many other groups around the world. Scott had tracked him all day, and I was to meet Scott for the kill. My expertise.

"What? You do the kills? James, you—how do you— expertise?" Elizabeth was so shocked she couldn't form a sentence to respond.

"Let me finish. Scott tracked him to a pub that night. Nigel used the back storage area of the pub to build his bombs. I met

Scott, and we waited for him to leave the pub. I always use a knife, like Dad taught. A simple cut of the throat to avoid the noise of gunfire.

"You kill people? You never told me that, and up close with a knife. Then come home, kiss me and hold our kids with the same hands."

"Again Luv, I thought we agreed no interruptions."

Elizabeth pretended to zip up her lips with her right hand.

"So, Dad's job went fine and after twelve hours of chatting we had all the information they asked us to gather from Mr. Smith. The crew then disposed of the body."

"That was on the news yesterday, he was missing, I remember."

"Scott and I were not so lucky. Bill was in a car waiting to get into the back of the pub after Nigel left to blow up the depot of explosives and probably half the street with it. We had time between Nigel leaving the pub and the pub closing, so Scott came to help me. We saw Nigel head down the street, so we hid behind some shrubs. That way it would be easy to pull him behind a hedge and do the job quietly and out of sight. We pulled down our masks and as he walked by the opening in the hedge, we jumped him. I pulled him back behind the hedge just as a few people came out of a house across the street. They must have seen us because they came running to help him. I was able to get my knife on him but as I pulled his head back to expose his neck, a boot connected with my arm."

James pulled up his sleeve to show her the boot size bruise, it covered most of his biceps.

"That moved my arm causing me to stab Nigel in his ribs, I punctured his lung. The hooligan who kicked me fell over, and I was able to slice an artery on his leg. I believe he passed on the scene. Another person reached for my head and pulled off my mask. Scott swung and connected with his jaw, knocking him out cold. As more people came to the rescue of those guys, I stabbed one in the stomach and another in the thigh as I was trying to stand up. Scott kicked some lad so hard he broke the hooligans shin bone. The noise of the bone breaking was louder than the commotion going on around us. At this point others saw what was going on behind the hedge and ran away, but they all saw my face, including Nigel. Some were calling out for help. Lights came on in bedrooms up and down the street. I should have taken another moment to cut Nigel's neck as we originally planned, but Scott was already pushing through those around us to get a path out of the area. I didn't want to be left behind the hedge alone. People were coming outside to see what all the commotion was about. We ran back towards the car where Bill was waiting for us to finish the job in the pub. There were two-gun shots in our direction, but we made it to the car. Bill knew something was wrong when he saw us running and me without my mask. Dad has a contact at the hospital where they took Nigel. He told Dad, Nigel was rushed to hospital, and the Doctors kept him alive. Dad knew if Nigel gained consciousness, he could identify me as the one who made an attempt on his life. We got back to the shop and Dad had our Doctor check my arm and Scott's hand. I came home that night knowing we could be in danger. The next day I went to work as usual and picked up David after school to come to the shop, like you knew I would. At this point none of us knew anyone had identified me or that Nigel was conscious. If we did, I would never have had David at the shop, and we would immediately had you and the kids locked in the shop. We were all working on some jobs for Dad. David was biking around the shop pretending he was in a race when one of Dad's contacts, Greg, called and said he would be at the shop with information for the family. When he arrived, I brought David to Dad's office so he wouldn't hear the details. Greg told us how Nigel survived the attack and had identified me. Dad's contact told us Nigel was being heavily protected, and he had spoken to many IRA leaders about who I was and what had happened. When the police showed up to investigate, they told them Nigel did not want to press charges. We discussed killing Nigel in the hospital with the help of Dad's contact, but with the new information we knew the risk was too high. He had already identified me to the IRA and many others. The next day there was a wee bounty put on my head. That was when Dad decided we needed to get out of the country."

"How much was the bounty?"

"Eighty-thousand pounds, why does that matter?"

"I might cash it myself. Me and the kids could do well with the money."

"Elizabeth, really?"

"No, but...it is a good load of money," she said. Inside she was still mad but happy her man was alive and with her and the kids.

"Greg then left and promised he would continue to update us if he heard of any plans. We decided it was time to move me, well us, to Canada. We had plans ready for an incident like this one. It was to get any of us out of the country safely and to safety in Canada with John. Dad's main concern was he didn't want the kids growing up without a father—me! Dad stayed at the shop calling people, waking people, whatever it took to get this boat, flights and of course let John know we were coming. I came home, and we got the family to safety. Now here we are on a boat to a new beginning in Canada. I did not plan for this to happen and we cannot go back home as a family. And that is what got us here. I honestly did not think you would agree to any of this, so that is why we added some drama when we were leaving the house. The only thing was the gunfire and explosion was more than we expected and was not part of our plans. So, I believe we might not be alive if we had stayed in the house for the night. I am sorry we had to do it that way, but none of us, including Edward, thought you would leave any other way. We discussed just waking you and telling you the situation, but honestly, would you have left? Would we be here right now?"

She shook her head, "Aye, you are right I would have fought you on this. What about the car at the shop?"

"The car outside, was real. There really is someone, or was someone, in the trunk. The person and the car will be dealt with, never to be seen again. Just like the guy at the end of the day, word spread quickly of my bounty. If you want, you can have the boat turn around and head back to port. The kids will come with me and I will leave you with your mom to make your own new life without me, my family, or the kids. This was the first job where I was identified. All the jobs around the world and this is what got me. I am sorry."

"Okay, first I am not going anywhere without the kids or you. We will endure this together; I wouldn't want to let you off that easy from this mess we are in. When we get to Canada will we become normal people leading dull boring lives, the life I want for us and our kids?"

"No, we won't, I will travel back and forth helping Dad when he needs it. There is more to us moving to Canada. But maybe we can discuss that later?"

"No, it all comes out now."

"How much have I told you about John?"

"Start from the beginning, please."

"I know I haven't told you much about John over the years and probably should have. It was part of the business I didn't think you would ever have to see or involve yourself with. John owns a plumbing shop and wholesaler. It is set up just like Dad is here, as a front for all kinds of other businesses. I will work there with him as a partner. John and the family own many businesses and have our hands in many things, none you need or would want to know about. The same set up as we have here. I have done a lot of work for John and before we met, I even lived with him when I had to hide one time before. He has a great son the same age as David. They can play together at the shop after school, just like here. I will continue to be doing all kinds of jobs with John and Dad so that won't change. The nice thing, Canada is so open it would be a lot harder to find me if something went wrong on a job. Wait till you see the open space and the countryside, the kids will have so many opportunities that are just not available here. We will still have our income supplemented, very well supplemented. Your mom and all our family can visit as often as they would like. Dad will arrange the travel plans so we know no one follows them. When we get established, we can make your mom a granny flat, so she has her own place when she visits. I think that covers all the big issues on why we are here. I really could use some sleep and you look like you need some too."

"I still have a lot more questions for you, I feel like I don't know you at all, but those questions can wait. You answered the main concerns I had, and I am exhausted too. You kill people and are good at it? Don't answer, please. One more question, with all this traveling did you ever cheat on me? Do you have a family—?"

"No, never. Never would, never could, Luv. I don't need other women complicating my life, it is complicated enough. It was always business only. It might be hard to believe, but I love you and the kids too much for that."

"Okay, because if you did, I would turn the boat around and take my chances back home."

"Do we have somewhere to sleep?"

"Yes, the captain's quarters, of course, nothing but the best for you," he said.

She followed James to the captain's room.

"James, I didn't realize the stress you were under. Living two lives. I feel you have so much more to tell me, but not tonight. I need time to think about all that you just told me. But I will have many more questions for you. I love you and I want to support you. Just promise me you will come home after each job; I don't want to be a widower and the kids need their daddy."

"I love you and will always try to be back home after each job."

The two lay on the bed and before they slept, they made love with a passion they hadn't experienced since before the kids were born.

CHAPTER SIX

David, slept on the boat with his family as it traveled to the Isle of Man where it was refueled. The crew brought food on board for the hungry family to eat when they woke. David and his family slept through the stop and the boat was back at sea before they began to wake. David, lying on his top bunk bed, knew his dad, uncles and grandfather were doing bad things but he never thought he would have to leave his home, his toys, and his friends because of it.

The family woke and sat together with the crew for breakfast.

David sat beside his mother and asked her, "Where are we going?"

His mother replied, "We are heading to Ontario in Canada."

"Canada? What's that," David said.

"Our new home, I guess," his mother replied.

David sat quietly. He ate the ham sandwich he was given and thought about going home to his family, his friends, and his house.

The boat sailed to Blackpool through some choppy water. Amy became sick after breakfast as the boat rocked against the waves. Amy's sea sickness made Elizabeth sick too. She couldn't wait for this leg of the trip to be over.

Finally, off the boat and with the car loaded, the crew wished James and his family safe travels. James loaded the kids into a car while Elizabeth had one more load of vomit to discharge from her stomach.

The four of them sat together, in a car that would be demolished a few hours after they dropped it off at the airport parking lot, ready to start a new life.

James stopped in a village to get petrol. Elizabeth ran across the street to the market and picked up some food and drinks for their lunch. She walked back to the car with a paper bag full of food, drinks, and a newspaper hung under her arm.

They decided to have a picnic and get some fresh air in the countryside. Somewhere, James could see vehicles coming towards his family. He stopped at a small pasture with sheep, and they found an old blanket, for the family to sit on, in the car's boot. David ate his food beside Amy, as they both looked through the fence at the sheep. David pointed out to Amy, funny things the sheep did which gave his parents a chance to relax. James, on his back, looked up to the cloudy sky deep in his own thoughts. Elizabeth dug into the newspaper. She searched for any Northern Ireland news. On page six was an article about a house attacked in Portadown. The intruders killed the family but failed to burn the house down. Further down the article they revealed the address and family name. As Elizabeth processed the numbers and letters then sent them to her brain, a noise came out of her mouth from deep in her subconscious. The kids turned around for a second, then went back to naming the sheep.

James, concerned, sat up and looked at her, "Alright?"

Elizabeth did not respond.

"Hon, what's the matter?"

She pointed to the newspaper.

"Read the article," she said.

James scanned the article. When he got to the address, he put the paper down and hugged Elizabeth. The address was their neighbor's house, three houses to the right, good friends of the family. They had kids, almost the same age as David and Amy.

"They—those guys—whoever they were went to the wrong house. They went to the wrong house, James. The Wright's are dead. It was meant for us. James, they died because of you," she whispered as she pushed herself away from him. "The kids died because of you. How do you live with yourself? How many times has something like this happened and you come home, kissed me, and went to sleep? James, the entire family is dead. It could have been us."

She forgot any good feelings she had struggled to find earlier during their talk. She was angry, disappointed, and a little relieved.

Last week the families were outside, the kids played in the field together with other families. Now they were gone, and she couldn't even go back to pay respect to the family because her family was on the run.

"How can my life have turned out like this?" she said. "I should have listened to my friends and others and not have gotten involved with you, James. Clean up, I will wait in the car."

She walked back to the car. James sat holding the newspaper. He felt bad for his neighbor, but Elizabeth did not know the whole story about Mr. Wright, and she never would. James would carry this burden to his grave before he would tell her anything else. He gathered up the food and blanket while David brought his sister to the car. Elizabeth never spoke to anyone for the rest of the trip to the airport. She continued to read the newspaper, reading the article a couple more times, she hoped maybe she read the wrong address. She stared out the window and thought back to when James was courting her and what her friends would say about his family.

● ● ●

Kenton had someone else in mind for James to wed but that plan did not work out. When Mary, James' former girlfriend, found out what the family's business included she broke up with James. After the break-up she threatened to tell the police or army and even some members of the IRA what she had been told. At that point she had signed her own ticket off the planet.

Kenton personally ensured she would not talk to the police nor have the opportunity to talk to anyone about his family's business. James did not want to see her killed but did not want to marry her either. He stepped out of the way and let his father do what he thought was best for the safety of the family and the business.

Her parents reported her disappearance. Authorities recovered her body the day after she went missing. Her body was found floating up the Bann River, there was no sign of foul play, just a teenage girl who had disappeared two nights earlier while at a small field party with some mates. The official police report was, she had left the party and walked along the shore to take the short way home. She had slipped into the river and knocked her head on a rock, as there was a cut just in-front of her right temple. That was the official police report, but some people believed it was the report Kenton gave the police to release.

When Elizabeth and James began to date, rumors were still around about what had happened to Mary at the party and how her body had ended up in the river. Elizabeth had known James and his family since childhood. James and Elizabeth had attended the same school and church since they were young. The two families would visit and spend time together as James, Scott, Elizabeth, and Edward grew up. They attended Sunday school, youth group and choir together. After Mary died and James courted Elizabeth their relationship quickly flourished. Many people warned her about James, and his family's business. None of the chatter she heard had any evidence, but the rumors continued.

Elizabeth's father passed away from injuries incurred while being a spectator at the annual Isle of Man motorcycle races. Kenton stepped in to support her family. He paid for anything they needed while Doris adapted to the life of a widower. That was when Kenton took Edward under his wing and brought him into the family business. Edward worked with Scott and James on smaller jobs, not mentioning any of this activity to Elizabeth.

James always promised Edward, he would tell her everything before they committed their lives together in marriage.

The day James asked Elizabeth to marry him was memorable as he did it in a castle on the west coast of Ireland. Scott and Sarah had joined them for a weekend getaway, or so the ladies thought. Scott and James had alternative reasons for the trip, as per Kenton's instructions.

James proposed to Elizabeth on the Saturday afternoon at Parke's Castle. Of course, she said 'yes'. They all went out and celebrated together that evening. Once the party had ended and the ladies went to bed James and Scott headed out on the real reason for the trip.

In the wee hours of the night, they broke into three houses and killed four members of the UDF (Ulster Defense Force). Each one, killed by a knife, guns were too noisy and did not allow an assassin to be up close to confirm the kill. The bodies were not found until later in the morning. They killed the four men as an example to the many others who were becoming sloppy in their work to 'Keep Ulster British.' James and Scott got back to their hotel, cleaned up and just made it to bed before the women woke up, another sleepless night for Kenton's crew. The four of them had a great weekend together. Scott and Sarah took the car they all drove to the coast in while James had a Jaguar reserved for Elizabeth and him to drive home. James did all the speaking on the way home, he told Elizabeth what his family did for a legitimate living and some of the extra activities they did on the side. He explained Edward's involvement, and what she would be part of because of their marriage. They say love is blind and Elizabeth is proof of that. With all the information James gave her she still stood by him, unlike most people (Mary) who would have ran far, far away.

Before the wedding, Kenton took her on a road trip. On that trip with Elizabeth, he explained some of the things she could expect as James' wife, he also told the story of Mary to her and gently explained it would be a shame if something like that had to happen to her. That was when she knew she was in this marriage 'till death us do part'. Kenton had the same talk with Sarah before her wedding. Sarah and Elizabeth would talk between themselves about those trips they each had before their, big day. But neither one wanted out, they loved their husbands.

Kenton had set up Doris in a nice little home close to where James and Elizabeth lived. Elizabeth could walk to visit her mom daily. The money James made allowed Elizabeth to stay home and take care of the house and when the kids came along there was money for the best prams, cribs, and toys. Elizabeth never asked how they could afford any of the things she had, she just enjoyed them.

She lived a princess's life until the other night. They took away her whole fairy tale marriage and life, like a big slap of reality had hit her hard across the face. Now she was on the run with her children, brother and mother left behind. All for Kenton, 'the man behind the troubles,' as her friends would call him before she dated James.

"Luv, the airport is just a few miles away. Can you wake up and start getting yourself ready?" James said.

"Aye, I wasn't sleeping just had my eyes closed thinking of better times," she said.

• • •

A lot had happened to David in the last couple days. When David saw the British Airways 747, he was about to embark on, all that was behind him, for now. David sat in the departure lounge staring out the large glass windows. He looked at this giant monster plane and wondered how it would ever get into the air with all the people on it. He could see other planes take off and land through the window.

Once on board the plane and seated in the middle four seats with his family, the flight hostess spoke to David and his parents. She asked if David would like to become a Junior Jet Club Member.

"What does that mean," said his mother.

"He will get his British Airways wing pin, a logbook, and get to meet the captain in the cockpit once we are over the Atlantic," replied the flight attendant.

"Can I Mom, please?" asked David, loud enough the other passengers looked at them.

"Yes, we will enroll him," said his mother.

The stewardess left to attend to other passengers.

The plane took off and leveled out. After about twenty minutes the pilot announced they were 'flying over Ireland the Emerald Isle.' James thought, *'Yes, it is pretty from up here, not so pretty in certain areas when you are down on the ground.'*

The stewardess reappeared with a small envelope for David. She handed it to him and said in her Liverpool accent, "Open up the packet and look through it, have your mommy or daddy help fill out the information, I will speak to the Captain and see when you can visit the cockpit."

David took the package and smiled the biggest smile. He could only imagine what a cockpit for a plane like this would look like.

David opened the packet and found his travel log and a shiny metal pin with wings on the side. He immediately had his mom pin it to his blue woolen sweater.

The stewardess came through the cabin and handed out drinks to those passengers who requested them. David bounced in his seat while he waited for the stewardess to take him to the cockpit. Once she served the drinks the tall slender stewardess came to ask David if he was ready to go. David walked up the isle holding her hand and entered first class. David's jaw dropped when they passed through the curtain to the front of the plane. There was a set of spiral stairs and a lot less seats. She led him up the stairs as he passed people sleeping or eating. Finally, he got to the cockpit where the stewardess knocked on the cockpit door. When the door opened David saw right out the front windows of the plane, he couldn't believe all the buttons, dials, and switches. The captain welcomed him and signed

David's flight log. After he asked a few questions and sat in the co-pilots seat, David had to return to his seat. He excitedly told his parents and the people in the surrounding seats all about the adventure. Elizabeth repeatedly asked him to keep his voice down, but he was too overwhelmed with the whole trip. He told his story three times before he fell asleep.

• • •

The plane landed smoothly at Pearson International Airport, just west of Toronto. Like some of the other tired travelers, David's family disembarked from the plane in a new country, with a new start on life. The only thing James knew at this point was John, his business partner, would wait somewhere in the arrivals area of the airport.

James had collected the luggage from the luggage carousel, a unit David thought would be more entertaining as an amusement ride. The family went through customs with the routine questions; what is the reason for your visit, how long will you be staying, who do you know in Canada? James answered the questions as if his family was on a vacation. Finally, they went to the reception area of the airport. James instructed his family to wait with the luggage by the exit doors while he went to find John.

John was internationally known for his skill of transferring undocumented 'new Canadians' into the country. Back in the eighteenth-century northern people would rescue slaves through a system of tunnels into Canada. John had his own *underground railroad*. There was a difference between John and those heroes of the past. John brought wanted criminals and crime lords into Canada, not slaves looking for a better life. John had a secluded safe house located just outside the sleepy little town of Erin. He would hide his customers on the property until they completed all their new documentation.

A wanted mobster from New York resided in the house when Kenton called John to inform him James and his family needed out of Northern Ireland.

The night John received the call from Kenton, the safe house burnt down. The mobster, John was protecting, had too much alcohol, drugs and four clumsy hookers from Toronto in the house. John received a phone call from the exhausted group in the early hours of the morning. They had walked into Erin to call John from a pay phone. Once John heard what happened to the house, he rushed to Erin with a couple of employees to meet the group. Luckily, the fire happened at night, so no one saw the smoke or called the fire department. Once John rescued the group, he brought them back to the smoldering remains of his safe house. There John took the time to burn the mobster and one hooker alive before he carefully placed their remains back in the house as the other three watched. Once done with that chore, John and his helpers dragged the others into the bush at the back of the property. They tied them to trees, cut their throats, and left their bodies for wild animals to feast on. When he finally called the fire department, John made sure the proper inspector reviewed the damage and the charred bodies.

John had to scramble to find a place to relocate James' family. He was able to secure a long-term hotel room for James in downtown Guelph, above a strip joint. It was owned by an associate of John's. This would be a perfect spot for the family to ensure no one followed them to Canada. John had the room painted, new furniture brought in, and the rooms on either side of the family's room emptied to avoid any noises that could carry through the walls.

John and his wife shopped for the family, they filled the fridge and cupboards with food. Brenda, John's wife, purchased winter clothes for Elizabeth and the kids and a large selection of toys. John moved James' clothes from his room in the plumbing shop to the family's new accommodations.

John had purchased a house for James' family to move into. The house would be ready for occupancy two weeks after the family arrived in Canada. He purchased a blue Ford LTD station wagon as the family car. It wasn't flashy and it would not bring any attention to them either. John wanted everything to be perfect for James and his family when they arrived in Canada. Of all the people he had ever moved, this one was the most important.

• • •

John arrived at the airport early, he had a couple business transactions to make before his guests arrived. When John finally got to the arrival floor of the airport, he confirmed with the arrival board that the plane had landed.

John paced the arrivals floor of the airport. He looked for an exhausted family dragging suitcases. What he found was James, who looked like he just stepped off a private plane ready to party.

"James" he called out.

Before John had called out his name, James had picked him out of the crowd and was headed his way.

John stuck out his hand to shake James' hand but instead he was wrapped up in a large hug from James, "John how are you mate, it is so good to see you."

"James, you guys made it safely. It is good to see you here. Your dad will be pleased to hear your family arrived safely," said John.

"Aye he surely will and thank you for this John, I really mean it. If you had asked me a week ago what I would be doing today, this wasn't even a thought in my mind, but here we are!" said James. "Of all the trips I have made here, this is only the second time you came to the airport; first time was when I came here with Dad as a teen to work and now this time with my family. Just be ready for Elizabeth, she is still upset; you might replace Dad as her new villain."

"Yea your dad warned me. Where did you leave the rest of your family?"

"Just down the hall, I didn't want to make them haul all the luggage this way if you were down the other way."

John flagged a porter from the doorway, slipped fifty dollars into his hand and said, "Come with me, this family will need help with their luggage."

"Yes sir," said the porter. His smile got larger, and his bad day just got a little better as he looked at the money in his hand.

James walked back to his tired family by the set of exit doors.

"Let me introduce the family, you know Elizabeth, my wife." John stuck out his hand to shake hers. Instead, she stepped towards him, reached for a hug.

"Thank you, John, for your help in securing our passage to Canada and meeting us here," she said.

"Anything I can do for Kenton's family is a privilege," he said.

Elizabeth smiled as she stepped back.

"This is David, my oldest," said James.

David took his hand out of his pant pocket to have it shook.

"Well, look at that," said John as he took David's hand and gently shook it. "I have heard so much about you, it is a privilege to meet you. My son Phil is very excited about meeting you."

"And this is Amy, our little girl," said James as he pointed to the stroller Elizabeth had been pushing.

"Welcome to all of you. Welcome to Canada, a loving peaceful country and a great place to raise children," said John as the porter loaded the luggage onto the cart.

"You have a son?" asked Elizabeth.

Before John could answer, "I loaded the luggage, sir. Where did you park?" asked the porter.

"There isn't much here, where is all your stuff?" asked John.

"Back home where we should be," Elizabeth said.

"One more piece, sir," John said as he lifted David onto the luggage on the cart.

David smiled as he rode on the cart. The group approached the sliding glass doors to the outside.

They stepped through the door and out to the cold November weather in Canada. Neither Elizabeth nor the kids had felt cold air like that before. James reached to hold Elizabeth's hand on the stroller handle, she pulled it away from him. John crossed the roadway between the airport and the parkade as the family followed behind.

"Dad, the cars are on the wrong side of the road and it is so cold," said David.

John laughed and said, "You will find a lot of things different here in Canada, but you will get used to them."

The family arrived at John's black Lincoln Continental. The porter loaded the stroller and bags into the trunk while the family got comfortable in the vehicle.

"Alright, we have about an hour-long drive to Guelph from here so sit back and relax. We will be driving on a highway that is straight as an arrow, not like your roads back home. I have a hotel room in downtown Guelph prepared for you. I reserved three rooms so you would not have any people beside you. The plan is you stay there for a couple weeks," John said as he pulled out of the parkade. "It is above a strip joint and is very secure. Your house will be ready in about two weeks. I have a car for you and a job you can start when you are ready."

John did not know how much James had told Elizabeth about the move, so he wasn't sure how much information to reveal.

"So, you and Kenton are old buddies from the war? Now you are business partners. John, was this evacuation of the family planned," asked Elizabeth.

"Honey not now, we are all tired, there will be plenty of time for those questions to be answered. You said I satisfied you with the conversation we had on the boat. Can you just trust I am doing this for the betterment of the family?" said James.

"Oh, I know, I just want to know whose family," she replied with an edge to her voice.

"So, what do you think, David, have you ever seen a road like this before?" asked John.

David did not hear him or even know there was a conversation going on. David's brain could not keep up with what his eyes were showing him of this wide-open country. The highway was bigger than any road back home, and the car was the size of a bus, to David.

His mom elbowed him gently in the ribs. "David, you are being spoken to, don't be rude."

"What, huh? What was that, Mom?" David asked.

"John asked you a question, can you answer him please?"

"David," repeated John with a smile. "I think I already know the answer but, have you ever seen a road like this before? They call it highway 401."

"No, I haven't seen anything like this before. I don't know what to say about all this."

"If you look over your shoulder and look real hard, you can see the CN Tower. It is one of the tallest structures in the world, if you see it then you see downtown Toronto."

David, James, and Elizabeth all turned to look over their shoulder.

"There," said David.

CHAPTER SEVEN

Guelph, Ontario

The family settled into their new home and into a routine of Canadian living, a different pace from what they were used to back home. David was happy to have his own bedroom again after a couple of weeks stuffed in a hotel room with his family. His new bedroom was bigger than the one back home, and he received some of his toys from Northern Ireland like his uncle promised.

David made new friends at school and church. He had to explain, repeatedly, why he talked with a funny accent and where he originally came from. He routinely visited the shop in the evenings and spent time with his new friend Phil.

Elizabeth attended a Baptist church with the kids and sometimes James, when he wasn't busy with his business. After Christmas, of the year they arrived in Canada, Doris came for a visit and helped settle Elizabeth's homesickness.

James spent a lot of time at the plumbing wholesale shop. He traveled back to Northern Ireland or other places for The Family. Elizabeth's and James' marriage continued down a path of destruction. A path, he reminded her, that did not end in a lawyer's office, but with a mortician, one that James and John knew. Often James would leave on 'trips' for work. He told the kids they were camping, hunting, or fishing trips. David always wondered what these trips were about, and where he went.

Before James left on a trip, David's parents would have a few big fights a day or two before. Once James left for the trip, David's mom would cry for hours. Alone, his mom would dive into depression, David would take care of Amy.

She would always say to David and Amy, "if your father asks you to go on one of his trips do not go, I couldn't handle two of you leaving me together."

David figured out his dad traveled back to Northern Ireland due to the escalated fights in the house between his mom and dad, the arguing upset David, and as Amy got older it upset her too.

Elizabeth would argue with James, thinking the kids couldn't hear, about how he did the devils work back home or on a trip outside the country. She had re-found Jesus and was a lot more judgmental of James and his family's business. James would remind her he fought for the victory of the protestant church over the catholic church back home. Elizabeth saw it as greed for money and power and maybe she could believe that story back home but not here in Canada. She would fight with James about the businesses money and that she needed to buy nicer things for herself and the kids. James would never agree. His dad brought him up to live as a middle-class family in his home city. He taught him not to raise any attention to yourself, your family, or the businesses. She had the best of everything at their vacation homes and boats, but she wanted it every day for the sacrifice she made for his family. She could not accept the humble life she had to live in Guelph.

David spent more time after school and in the evenings with James at the plumbing shop. His friendship with Phil continued to grow as they worked hard together around the shop. They had many duties to do weekly for their dads. As they worked, they were taught about plumbing parts and how to pull materials for the plumbers vans. When they were not busy working, they would play in the basement or attend martial arts classes at the dojo.

Elizabeth did not approve of the time David spent with James. She would try to keep David and Phil involved in youth activities at the church, but it was always a struggle. There was no help from Brenda, John's wife. She had accepted her place in the family and enjoyed the many privileges that came with her marriage. James and John would try to get the wives together and hoped they would develop a friendship, but Elizabeth had built a wall with whoever associated with James and that part of his life. Brenda would reach out for supper dates, tried to spend time at the vacation homes with Elizabeth and even attended church with her, but there was always a barrier there she could not break down. Elizabeth did not like that James and his family had taken David, her only son.

For David's twelfth birthday James bought David a knife and the family a larger house, closer to John. Now David and Phil could attend school together. With all the time they were together, they became segregated from others their age. David chose to spend more time with his Dad, John, and Phil. When James traveled for work, John would pick David up and bring him to the shop to work with Phil. The boys started to sit in on some meetings with John and James. They would do small jobs for both businesses, they delivered parcels or watched someone's house, taking notes as they biked the assigned area. With all the time the boys spent together, they had issues at school and church socializing with other their age. Elizabeth believed they were being rushed to grow up and not allowed the chance to be boys and young teens.

The more James traveled back home, the further James and Elizabeth grew apart. Doris spent six months at a time in Canada with Elizabeth and Amy. James and David spent more time together. They attended sporting events, golfed, and worked on building the business.

Elizabeth became more involved with the church. She attended most Sundays, James periodically attended with her to keep a normal happy family image that she wanted others to believe was real. She became very friendly with other families in the church, and would have dinner parties or social visits with these people. She always invited James, which infuriated him as it took time away from his time with John and the work they were doing.

He would remind Elizabeth, "Having people visit the house could reveal what our family's history truly is. If there was a slip of the tongue and someone revealed any of it, do you want to move again, this time to Australia?"

$$\bullet \quad \bullet \quad \bullet$$

David stressed over the two lives he was leading, one as a normal Christian boy, where he attended school and church. The other, as a boy who delivered packages, sat in on meetings where people discussed illegal activities or spied on people's houses for John and his dad.

Again, like he did in Ireland, David had to keep quiet about the activities Phil and he did or things they heard and saw. Elizabeth would ask him what he did at the shop and he continued to lie to her.

Phil and David continued to grow together as best friends, becoming one team, each one knew what the other thought. Just before his thirteenth birthday David got to shoot his first gun, not at someone, but at a target in the barn by the safe house. A farm they all owned north of Orangeville. David had a talent with a gun, knife, or his bare hands. Phil struggled with swinging a knife or shooting a gun, but he picked up the business side quicker than David.

John and James saw the natural progression the two boys made and the skills they developed. James spent more time with David, he trained David the way Kenton had trained him.

• • •

"Dad, what happened to you that we had to move to Canada? Not that I am upset we live here, but I wish I was back home with the others and Granda. I assume a job went really bad and they must have identified you. Am I close?" said David as he swung his knife across the neck of the practice dummy.

"Alright, let's pack up. We can talk once we clean up and are ready to head home," said James. "I knew one day you would ask."

They cleaned up the practice dummies and locked up the farmhouse. They sat in the car and James told David the details of the job where they tore his mask off and revealed his identity.

Once James completed the story to the point, he woke David in his bed, he gave David a chance to ask questions.

"Is this guy that identified you still alive?"

"Yes, Nigel still builds all kinds of explosives around the world," said James.

"Why have we never tried to hunt him down and kill him?"

"He is very well protected. He lives in Southern France on an estate owned by a few middle eastern businessmen. We have attempted to get on the property, but it has too much protection. I believe, the last details we received, the estate was housing a few people and their families who were wanted for all kinds of crimes around the world. The Americans have the same protection for some of their allies on an island in the Pacific. Just like we have a few farms here for our customers."

"The Americans have an island to protect people?"

"Aye, I have been on it a few times to close up a few loose ends for them. People are not always moved there to have a long, happy life."

"So, this bomb maker, Nigel, will we ever get our hands on him Dad?"

"Aye, we track him and many of our informants know we want him alive. We almost had him when he was in Beirut. I missed him by four hours that day. I was doing a job in Turkey when I got the call from granda to get to Beirut. One day he will slip up or his bosses will finish with him. Then they will release him to the open market and hopefully we can get him before another agency does.

"Dad, I would love to meet him, have a chat, and practice my knife skills on his neck one day for how he broke up our family."

"Aye, we all would. Granda and I joke that the worst punishment we can imagine for him would be to tie him to a chair in a locked room with your mom. It would be a slow, painful end to his life."

David laughed, "Yea I would almost feel sorry for him."

"Let's grab some food and head to the shop," said James.

They left the property and headed back to Guelph. David sat quietly thinking of Nigel, wondering what he looked like and imagining what he would do to him if they ever met.

•   •   •

James mentioned to David and Elizabeth at David's thirteenth birthday party he would take David back to Northern Ireland on his next trip, David would get to visit with family and spend time with his granda. David was excited about this opportunity to head home with his dad. Elizabeth controlled her emotions at the party for David's sake. But after the party she yelled at James to the point she lost her voice. Elizabeth explained how she forbid a trip and that she was still David's mother and should have some say in his life.

James understood why she felt that way, but David had more questions and wanted to be involved in the business. James wanted David's first job to happen back home with his family and not in Canada. Elizabeth repeatedly reminded James she was against the thought of David heading back home for more than a normal family visit. All the times they had gone home for a vacation together was tense enough for Elizabeth but now to send her only son home with James on a trip to put her son in danger was out of the question.

James reminded her, "There would come a time when David would work with him. It could either be here or back home, but it would happen. If it was back home, he would have his family around him to protect him while here the jobs were more isolated to single man jobs."

James finally convinced her to let David travel with him after his fourteenth birthday. She knew she had no say on the matter and there was no way to win this fight. Just like other times, where she would disagree with James, she could only push so hard before he reminded her there were other options if she wanted to resist. They both agreed they would still leave Amy in the dark about the family's true history and business. She also knew if she wanted the lifestyle she was used to, the family needed David to make money.

· · ·

The spring David turned fourteen, John and James sent the boys on a small trip to Hamilton to see how they would handle themselves.

The boys left the shop, ready for a job like this, in a spare vehicle. David drove while Phil sat in the passenger seat, he needed to prepare himself for the job.

David drove on highway six to Hamilton, he pulled onto the shoulder of the highway when a yellow police car with flashing lights pulled in behind him.

"Play it cool Phil, I wasn't speeding, and I was driving carefully," said David.

"Yea I know, we got this," Phil replied.

The tall, muscular officer with a slight limp approached the driver's side window. David had already lowered the window and had his fake driver's license out of his wallet.

"Afternoon, son. License, registration and insurance please," asked the police officer.

Phil opened the glove box got out the insurance and registration, he hoped his dad had given them a legitimate car and not a borrowed one.

"Do you know why I pulled you over this afternoon," asked the officer in a monotone voice.

"No sir," said David calmly. He had been through enough check points with military soldiers carrying big guns back home to know how to answer any questions the officer might ask him.

"Well son, when you passed by my car you looked like a couple of kids driving a stolen car." He leaned on the door and looked at Phil. "Have you even started shaving, kid? Can I see your ID too, please?"

Phil fumbled for his wallet and passed his fake license to the officer.

"Sit tight, I will be right back," said the officer.

David watched in the mirror as the officer radioed in the plates and their IDs to his dispatch.

"Well, I guess we will find out how good our ID's and license plates are."

"Dad wouldn't send us out on a job with bad paperwork. We both know that," said Phil.

After what felt like an hour to the boys, the police officer returned. "Okay, so where are you heading today and why?"

"Well sir, my mom asked me to go to Hamilton to pick up a couple of items at our church headquarters for the Sunday School class she teaches. Then we thought we would grab supper and head back," said David.

"Okay, where is this place located," asked the Police Officer.

"410 Upper James, up the mountain," said David. "Look, we have a map here."

Phil pulled the map from the pocket in his door.

"Okay then, have a safe trip," said the officer as he returned their documents.

"Thank you, officer, you too," said David.

The officer walked back to his car as David pulled his car back onto the road.

"That was close," said Phil. "You handled that very cool even throwing out a fake address."

"Yes, you too, especially grabbing the map to confirm my story."

• • •

They arrived on the street where the guns were to be delivered, an old section of Hamilton where the very low-income community lived.

A loud motorcycle pulled up beside them. "What business do you have on this street?" asked the rider in black jeans and a leather vest. His chest hair billowed out above the buttons.

"We are here to see Arsenic, your VP. We have a delivery for him—and you I guess," said David.

The biker waved to follow him. He directed them into a yard behind a rundown semidetached house. David parked the car and got out.

"What is James doing sending two kids," the bald, overweight man in a tank top and leather vest said to the guy they followed into the yard.

"Excuse me," questioned Phil as he stood beside David in front of the car. "We are here with your delivery. If you don't want it from kids, we can turn around and leave now. I am sure James and John will still want their money, or some form of payment, so go get us Arsenic before we get back in the fucking car and leave."

David shocked at Phil's response went back to the driver's door and pulled out a pistol from under the seat and purposely let them see him put it in his waistband.

"Fuck you kid, don't talk to me like that," the man said as he approached the boys.

A large man with a mohawk and a long grey beard came out onto the back porch of the semi, his leather vest had VP sewn on his vest. "What the fuck, did John and James open a daycare? I am not sure if I should be upset or privileged to have a couple of kids deliver our package, I am Arsenic the one you wanted to talk to. Everyone just calm the fuck down. These are allies not enemies even if they still feed from their mommy's tits."

"Hey, we are here bringing you your shit, and this is the welcome we get. Fuck you. Let's go Phil, John can deal with these fuckin' idiots I am done with being disrespected," said David. He motioned to Phil to get back into the car.

"Whoa, whoa calm down you little shit, you must be either James's or John's kid. I am thinking James's boy. Cocky little bastard. Where is the package? I got shit to do," said Arsenic.

David opened the trunk and pulled out the seven duffle bags and the twelve cases of ammunition from the trunk. "Here you go, I guess you will want to check them. I personally know the man who built these weapons."

Arsenic stood in front of Phil and smelt like rotten meat, "It would be a shame if you were killed by a gun your granda built. We don't need a fucking history lesson, just the delivery."

Arsenic directed another member of the gang, with treasurer sewn on his worn-out leather vest, to check the inventory. The treasurer stunk, like he hadn't had a showered in months, but still not as bad as Arsenic. David had been with James on a couple of meetings with other bike gangs, for some reason they always stunk and tried to be repulsive to David. It never worked and did not work this time.

They thoroughly checked and counted the inventory.

The treasurer handed David an envelope. "Here kid, this is what you want. Tell your dad we will request more in two weeks. He can expect a call before the end of the week. We got some girls in the house who would love to pop your virgin bubbles if you have time."

David counted the money, shook the treasure's hand and said, "Thanks for the offer, but I don't think those are the type of women we need to be spending time with. If they smell as bad as you guys, I wouldn't be able to get hard."

Arsenic laughed at the comment, "Why don't you two come back when you have hair around your dick's."

"Whatever, we are out of here," David said as he entered the car where Phil already sat.

They pulled around the yard and headed back up the street, two bikers escorted them.

"Well, that went well, I think. But why do they always stink? What do they get from that?" Phil said.

.   .   .

Back on highway six, Phil said, "Well again, we handled that well, but I was scared out of my mind. I don't know why Dad deals with those dirtbags, we could have a better class of customer."

"Look in the envelope, they paid twenty-five thousand dollars for those guns, cash, that's why," David said.

"Yea I know, I guess I just need to get used to dealing with people like that, Dad has only brought me on the higher-class meetings like with government people, the military or bankers," said Phil.

"Yea, Dad had me on a couple trips with these guys, the one he had me stay in the car, I'm pretty sure someone died that day," David said.

"You know how we have been talking about having a meeting with them about our futures and other things? I think after this trip we are ready for the talk, don't you?" asked Phil.

David agreed, the time was right with the extra jobs they gave them lately, the extra responsibility around the shop and how they were put into more difficult situations. It was time to discuss and plan their future.

The boys drove home while the police officer and Arsenic gave their reports to James and John. They both explained how the boys had handled themselves during their encounters. John and James also were ready to discuss the future with their sons.

PART TWO
Time to Work

CHAPTER EIGHT

Guelph, Ontario, 1984

The meeting between the boys and their fathers was scheduled. Phil and David were nervous and could not concentrate in class that day. They both skipped out of school at lunch and took off on their bikes. They headed to Exhibition Park to review what they wanted to discuss in the meeting. They both agreed they would hold firm and stick up for each other.

John and James were happy the boys had taken the initiative to call a meeting with them, but also a little upset, as fathers, that their sons felt they needed to schedule a meeting.

"Instead of having the meeting in the office, let's do it in the back of the shop, that will throw them off a little. See how they handle it," said John.

"Agreed, I am not sure what this is about. I hope our wives haven't gotten into their heads," said James.

David and Phil pulled up to the front of the shop on their bikes and brought them to the counter.

"Hey Frank, do you know where my dad is?" said Phil.

Frank, the shop manager and John's bodyguard said, "They are both out back waiting for you two. I am not sure what you two did, but they seem upset."

David and Phil walked to the back of the shop. They both felt like they could throw up. John had set up four chairs and a card table to meet around.

"I thought we could do this in your office," said David once they completed the pleasantries.

"No, out back is better," said James. "Do you guys think you are ready for an office meeting?"

"Yes, we do," said Phil.

"We will decide that," John answered. "So, what did you two want to meet about? We are busy organizing a movement of more guns for you two to deliver this weekend."

David and Phil previously agreed, David would start, and Phil would take the second part of the meeting.

"Well Dads, and I mean that, you both treat Phil and I like sons and so do our moms, and we appreciate it."

John looked at James and smiled.

"Since we were wee boys' you guys have trained us," David said.

"And trained us hard," Phil interjected.

"You have used us on small jobs, surveillance and scouting out areas for any security issues." David said. "We have both done whatever you asked and kept good-ish grades. We have worked at the shop doing whatever you need as we learn about the plumbing business. We have seen and heard things that we have never told others about and never would."

"Well, you know the rules," said James.

"Yes, we are aware of them and abide by them," Phil said.

"So, what are you getting at here, we are busy and need you two to pull some fittings for the plumber's jobs tomorrow," John said.

"Well, we do a lot of work for you guys and, we—look at the delivery last week. Police, bikers, and we handled ourselves well, we think. We enjoy working for umm, with umm you, but we want to be, well we want to be paid, when working for you," Phil said. He wasn't sure if he would be laughed or yelled at for the comment.

"Paid?" John raised his voice as he responded.

"You had this meeting to ask for payments of service. Really? We give you a house, food, clothes, everything you need and now you want paid?" James said.

"Well, James, we have two ungrateful kids don't we," John said.

"No, no, no. Wait, that came out wrong," Phil said.

"No, you are right, you give us so much. It's not that we want paid, well we do, but that's not, we want more than that too." David said, his foot firmly placed in his mouth with his comments.

"What? You want the shirt off my back," James said as he unbuttoned his shirt.

"NO, no, listen," David responded. He regretted ever asking for the meeting.

"No, you guys are taking this all wrong," Phil said. "What we want is more of the action, more of the business, we see how you have been training us and we have been doing even more training on our own. We want to be with you in meetings and on real jobs. You guys won't be doing this forever and we want to learn the insides of the business, it's not too soon for us. We have more education in business than most people in college, we just want more, and getting paid would be nice."

"Dad, I want to go home with you and help with jobs there. I want to know more about what Granda, you and Uncle Scott do back home. That is why we called the meeting; we want more of the inside business. Obviously, you are training me for the 'get your hands dirty' side while Phil is learning the paper side. We are okay with that, but we need—want, more," David said.

"Okay this isn't what we were expecting at all from this meeting," said James. "Can you give John and I some time to talk?"

"Sure," said Phil.

At that point, he would have agreed to anything to get out of the meeting. The boys got up from the table and went to see Frank to get the paperwork to pull orders for the next day.

James and John discussed their meeting with the boys. John brought the boys down to his office to finish the meeting.

"Please come sit at the table with us," John said as he directed them to the large conference table.

David and Phil hesitantly walked to the table where they had seen the two men sit and work out business deals and other deals as they played in the corner as kids.

"So, you two wee lads want more actions from us, do you? You think this is something easy that a couple kids at fourteen can run? What exactly are you asking for in this deal?" asked James.

Phil spoke first, "Well, Dad—Dads," he smiled. "David and I have been talking together and we do a lot for you two, not in a bad way, you have both taught us so much. We try to learn as much as we can from you and what we see happening around us."

"Dad, there is a lot you and Granda do. I want to see and learn the stuff from over home as well," said David.

"So, what we want is more involvement in the business. We want to take on some extra responsibility, be with you guys on the more complicated jobs."

"Okay, you realize you will have to learn to bounce between two worlds, a normal mundane life and then a life in 'The Family'. The work isn't hard usually, living two lives is what will cause you issues. We have talked, and we are happy this is what you want, very happy actually," James said smiling.

"I agree, this is what we wanted to hear from you two, and especially coming to us together. We wanted you to come to us, we didn't want to force it on you. So yes, we will include you both in the business and we should have, in the past, paid you, so going forward we will set you up with money. I guess that means your first lesson will be on hiding and laundering your money," John said.

"David, I am scheduled to go home in two weeks to work with Scott and Dad, you will be coming with me. Telling Mom will be an issue, but she knows it is coming, maybe just not expecting it so soon. I was your age when Granda pulled me into his world, so now that you are asking, it makes sense. You have the skills, so it is now time to put them to use. But we need to discuss it with mom," said James. "That will be the hardest meeting you will ever have to attend. We are both very happy you two came to us. The fact you did it together shows the relationship is strong with the two of you, which is what you will need as you grow older. You will need each other, and you must always have each other's backs."

The four, new, business partners went out for supper to celebrate the steps the boys were taking in the business. James knew it would not be an issue with Phil and his mom, but his job just got a lot harder. He had a couple weeks to convince Elizabeth this step to manhood David just took, was David's idea, and it was time it happened.

• • •

A couple days before James and David were scheduled to leave for Northern Ireland, James spoke with David. They discussed the idea that this trip needed to look unplanned to Elizabeth. James thought it might make things a bit easier for her to accept. What was one more lie to add to the mountain both James and David had already built over the years? He explained to David that he had brought the idea up to her a few times since his thirteenth birthday. Each time she would get furious at the idea of him going home to work with Kenton. James needed him to be surprised, that he would be going but, in the end, would go with him. Throw in some 'I don't want to leave mom,' for good measure, James advised.

David's mom had been talking to him about being her innocent boy and how he could break the cycle of his dad's and grandfather's illegal activities and desires. David did not have the heart to tell her he did not want to break the cycle, he wanted to be fully engulfed in that cycle. He knew this was going to be a difficult day, but he felt he was ready for it.

The night before David's first trip back home, he overheard his parents conversation.

"This is why we are in Canada, you told me when we moved here none of your other life would follow David. You have lied again, and now you want to get David involved in your jobs over home? Does he not do enough for you and John here in Canada," she said.

David could not hear his father's response.

"I don't want him to see the other side of his father and grandfather. He sees you as a God-fearing man for the most part, not the animal you are around your father. I don't want him involved in any of your business transactions, especially the ones back home. Let him have a normal life and upbringing in Canada, without knowing the horrors his family are involved in back home and who knows where else."

David thought he knew all the horrors that involved his family, but now he second guessed this decision to go back to Northern Ireland. He questioned what he had asked for. Was there more to what he and Phil requested? They figured they knew everything their dads did. They sold guns, roughed up a few goons and hid people and money. Would he be asked to kill? Would that really be a part of what they expected of him? No, his dad would not ask him to do that. What his mom said tugged on his heart. Was she looking out for him and his safety? Were his dad's intentions the same? They would have to be. His dad would not endanger him. He knew his father was a killer, and he knew one day he might have to do the same thing. This is what Phil and he had asked for. They wanted in and he was about to find out what, all in, really meant. David panicked as he laid in his bed. He wondered if it was too late to get out of this.

Again, his father replied but he could not understand him except, "My father demands it of me."

"I don't care," his mother replied, "it's not fair to me or him."

"Well, he will be leaving with me, I am sorry, but I need to take him," James said.

•   •   •

The morning of David's first trip home to work, he woke with anxiety, a feeling that had become all too familiar to him.

The hour arrived for them to depart. John arrived to drive them to the airport. David had never seen his mother so upset. She yelled at James and at John through her tears. David again doubted the choices he had made with Phil over the last few weeks. He did not want to go; he wanted to stay here in Canada with his mom.

"I will never forgive you if something happens to him," she screamed from the porch. His mother gave him a big giant hug as her tears dropped into David's hair. She wasn't letting go, and this upset David even more. James pried him away from Elizabeth's grasp and walked him to the car.

"You better not come back without him," she continued to yell from the porch.

John opened the trunk and helped James put the suitcase in, David entered the back of the car. He wanted to cry, he wanted to tell his dad he was staying home. But he sat silent, alone, and ready to throw up.

"Bit of a rough departure?" John asked James.

"Yes, but it actually went better than I was expecting," he said.

"Really? I could hear her yelling at you as I entered the street," John said.

"You ready to go, David?" John asked, as he backed out of the driveway.

Panic flooded through David's body as the car drove away. The music from the car speakers seemed to fade further away from him. His vision became narrow, and spots filled his field of vision. His breath got shallow, as the car turned onto the highway.

David's breath came in short, shallow gasps, and his father turned to see his son black out in the back seat of the car.

"David," his father yelled. "Come back, take a deep breath. Focus on my face, do you see it? David, look here. David!"

James tapped David on the cheek a few times. "David it is okay; you are having a normal reaction to the situation you just went through. Focus David," he said.

He tapped David on the cheek a bit harder this time.

David pushed through the darkness and out of the panic attack. He breathed normally and color filled his cheeks.

"Dad, what happened to me?" David asked.

Before James could answer, David threw up on the back seat and floor. John cranked the wheel to the right; he crossed a couple lanes of traffic and stopped the car on the shoulder of the highway. David jumped out of the car and threw up in the ditch.

"Sorry John," James said. "We will need to stop at a petrol station."

"Yea, I guess so," John said.

David felt better after the second discharge of his breakfast. He got back in the car and apologized to his dad and John. After five miles they stopped at an Esso gas station.

"David sit here, we will be right back," James said as they got out of the car.

"Do you think he is cut out for this line of work?" John asked James.

"I hope so. He is our future and my retirement plan. We will know better once we are back in Canada."

The two men entered the store and went separate ways. John went to pick up some rags and car cleaner while James headed to get some Gatorade and gum for David. As they came back to the cash register James saw David at the side of the car, he threw up again.

John noticed David and said, "Hopefully he will make it out of Canada. Maybe Amy is the one you should be bringing."

They both laughed at the comment. But James was worried that David would not be able to handle stressful situations if he had a nervous stomach.

"Better get one of these too," said John. He grabbed a pine tree air freshener off the rack on the counter. "Maybe two."

They approached the car where David was leaned up against it. James asked, "David, are you okay."

"Yes Dad, there was just a little more left in my belly. I feel fine now!"

"Aye, here, slowly drink this," James said, as he handed him the Gatorade.

John and James worked to clean the vomit off the leather seats. "Here David hang this on the mirror," John said.

The men cleaned the back seat and David took the waste to the garbage bin.

"Alright, let's get going, we have a plane to catch," James said.

The car entered the highway and James instructed David, "Keep drinking the Gatorade. I have some Hubba Bubba gum for you when you finish."

"Thanks Dad, I am sorry John. I don't know what happened to me there," said David, embarrassed.

• • •

They drove east on highway 401 in silence. David looked out the window and wondered what adventure or trouble he would get into. He knew his father and grandfather did 'bad things' as his mother would say when his parents would fight. His mother was usually mad a few days before and after his father's trips, but nothing like what he had seen today. He had never seen his mother so mad or upset.

James did a mental check of things, passports, background stories for the airport and a prayer of safety for him and especially David. James knew if anything happened to David there would be no returning to Canada, Elizabeth would have him chased like a deer during hunting season.

"So, what is happening today, Dad, where are we actually going?" David said. "Will I see Nannie?"

"Yes, we will have time for short visit, not to worry," his father said. "We will talk about it once we get to the airport son, until then, just relax, you will be fine, there is lots to do once we get there."

John pulled up to the departure parking lot and found a spot to park. David opened the car door to get out. "Wait a second David, there are a few things we need to discuss," his dad said.

David closed the door and sat back down in his seat.

"Is this where I get told I am a kid, and you can't involve me in anything too risky?" he asked.

James got out and went to the back door of the car and climbed in beside David. James dug into a bag and pulled out a small book and some papers.

"Okay we have a few things to go over, don't interrupt and listen very carefully. I need you to listen, do you understand?" he asked.

"Yes, Dad, I do but..."

"No questions. Just listen to the end, then you can ask me questions. Okay?"

"Yes, okay."

"Okay David, we are now at the point of no return. You can either get out of the car with me or return home to mom."

"Dad, honestly, I don't know. My head says stay with mom, but my heart says go with you." David paused; James caught John's eye in the mirror. John smiled back at James.

"No, Dad, I am going with you. I love you Dad and I want to be working with you and Granda. Of course, I am going with you, this is what I want. I know it might not have started well for me but..."

"Okay, son, good. Again, we are not going back for a vacation, we are going back to work. Right? We don't want anyone checking flight manifests and noticing us returning using our names. That means we need to change our names for a little while. You can call me Dad, always, but I will have to call you William Thompson, okay? Here is your new citizenship card for Canada and your Canadian Passport. Do you understand, William?"

David chuckled a little at the new name and was about to answer, "Ye..."

"This is not a joke. This is what we need to do to get back home. If you think it's a joke or don't want to take it seriously you can go back to mom, do you understand? You have had fake identities before and had to use them with the police. But going through customs is a lot different. They train these people to look for any inconsistencies in your travel story, so you need to be a lot more aware of your words and actions, do you understand? This is the big league now. You can do this. It is what we trained you for," James said sternly.

"Yes Dad," David replied.

The tone of his father's voice sunk into David's heart. He knew somehow this was going to be very important. He would need to fool people with this new identity.

"David, take a minute to read the passport, your name and your hometown. What is your name," John said.

"William Thompson."

"Where are you from?"

"Owen Sound, Ontario," David answered, like a soldier at roll call.

"When we get home, you can use your given name. Just like here, David, when it is time to work, I need you to be focused and serious. The job we are doing back home requires total commitment from you. People could get hurt if you are not doing your part. Just like the jobs we send you on here. I am asking you one more time, do you want to come with me or head back with John? I will understand either way."

"Nope, I am heading home to work with you," said David.

"Good. Now keep practicing your new name," said James.

James reviewed the plane tickets and his passport, Gordon Thompson was his name for this trip, he hated the name Gordon, but he was stuck with it for a while now.

"Really John? Gordon? You know I hate using that name," said James.

"Oh, I know," John replied, he looked through the rear-view mirror with a giant grin.

"Okay, so the best way to not attract attention is just be yourself, act like you always do, act like you belong in the situation. Do you understand?" asked James.

"I think so, just walk and look around like a kid at the airport for the first time?"

"Yes, that is all you need to do, relax. Okay?"

"Yes, anything to get to see Granda and Nannie, Dad, and to do a job with the family. I am trying to learn my lessons here. I am sorry about throwing up, it was just, mom really upset me. I wasn't ready for all that emotion."

"It's okay, you are here now on your way to what you and Phil asked for. Take the emotion out, starting now, and focus. Okay, what is your name," his father fired at him.

"William Thompson."

"Where are you from?"

"Owen Sound."

His dad smiled and thought to himself, *'maybe David is born for this! Leaving the house was emotional for me too.'*

"Alright let's go son, we have a plane to catch."

They got out of the car, John had their bag out of the trunk and waiting for them. James hugged John as he whispered, "See you in a few days if all goes well."

"Yes, take care of David, I don't want to give Elizabeth any bad news, she will have me killed as the messenger."

James laughed, "No, I would not wish that on anyone."

James was proud, nervous, and concerned for this trip. He looked at David who had the biggest smile on his face, looking like a teenager with no worries on his mind.

James—Gordon checked in with the airline and dropped off the suitcase. They headed to the security check. James handed the passports and tickets to the customs officer.

"Just the two of you tonight?" the security guard asked.

"Yes, a special trip for a special boy," James said.

"Well, it all starts here, gate twelve is to the right, enjoy yourselves," said the guard.

"Thanks," said James.

"Thank you," David responded.

They walked to gate twelve and waited for the plane to board. "You did great back there," James told David.

Once settled into their seats on the plane, James said, "You need to sleep on the flight, I don't know how much sleep you will get once we land. When we are home in Portadown, or when you are on any job as you get older, sleep when you can because there is no guarantee you will get to sleep at night. Always remember that. Train your body to sleep when you can. Do you understand, William?"

"Yes, I think so, won't I get to sleep in a bed when we get there?"

"Hopefully you will at least a couple nights, but if you continue to travel with me and Granda a lot of your life will change. You will have to act one way with us and another around your friends, Mom and Amy in Canada. This is a test to see if you can do it. When we meet Granda, we will tell you what we are doing and rules you will have to live with for the rest of your life. I am very proud of you and Phil for approaching us and having the talk. John and I were going to have it with you two one day, but the fact that, well, it is good son, very good…"

David could hear the emotion in his dad's voice.

"Okay," David said nervously. He leaned in and hugged his dad. This trip scared him, but he was with his dad so everything would be okay. David put on his Walkman headphones and fell asleep to Van Halen's album, 1984.

David woke as the plane's wheels touched down on the tarmac of Heathrow Airport. At first, he thought his alarm was going off and he would be late for school. He then realized he was in an airplane, a 747 to be exact, headed on an adventure with his father.

"Are we in Ireland?"

"No," his father said. "One more plane ride."

CHAPTER NINE

Northern Ireland, 1984

Kenton and Scott picked David and James up at the Belfast airport. They got into the blue Ford Granada when David asked, "Can I sit up front with Granda?"

"Sure, you can, climb in," said Kenton.

David ran around to the passenger side and climbed into the vehicle beside Kenton.

"So, how was the trip from Canada," Scott asked.

"I don't remember much of it. I slept the whole flight," said David.

"Best to sleep when you can while traveling," his uncle said. "Sleep can be rare while on jobs so always take advantage of a nap when you get a minute. A two-minute nap can make all the difference with decision-making skills. Always remember that."

Kenton said, "So I hear you are looking to be involved more with us, David?"

"Yea, Phil and I think we are old enough to be part of the bigger jobs and see how you do things. I want to be able to work with all of you on the big stuff. Maybe even do some trips here on my own. Dad goes away all the time, maybe I can take some of those trips. Mom was panicking when we left and that freaked me out. But I am ready for whatever the plan is on this trip. I would like to see Nannie at some point, if I can."

"Yes, you can have time for a visit, but you need to remember this is not a family visit. We run these jobs as military operations. You have a lot to learn. Your dad has taught you a lot, but your real apprenticeship begins today. You need to listen, ask the right questions, and take care of yourself and your team. Your mom is one of the few people I truly fear on this planet and I do not want to tell her someone hurt you," Kenton said with a smile.

"Okay, so I know the shop is a front like John has with the plumbing business, so what is the plan for this trip? And what more is there for me to know?"

"We only have those discussions at the shop. We don't just throw out our missions while driving through a town. There is a place to chat and a place to discuss business, you need to remember that. You never know who is listening."

They drove through the streets of Belfast; they approached a British military check point.

Kenton looked at David, "Don't talk unless they speak to you. You remember that right?"

"Aye."

Kenton pulled the car in line to be searched. The military guards at the checkpoint asked the car ahead of them routine questions when suddenly they scrambled and threw down tire strips in front and behind the car. All six men at the checkpoint had their guns pointed at the driver and passenger. Kenton opened the glove box and pulled out a revolver and slid it into his coat pocket.

"What is happening?" David said.

"Looks like they didn't like the ID the one lad showed them," said Scott.

They removed the driver and passenger from the vehicle at gun point. They instructed them to lean up against the bonnet of the car and spread their hands and feet. The officer of the group gave instruction to two soldiers to open the boot. The taller and much younger soldier reached into the car and took out the keys. He walked to the back of the car and unlocked the boot. He jumped back in surprise as it sprung open. Inside, Kenton could see a body tied and gagged.

"Is that..." David began.

"Yes, it is, be quiet, David," said Kenton.

The soldiers called the officer as they reached in to help the man out. The man was tied at the wrists and ankles with rope, and his elbows and knees were taped with duct tape. An orange rag was taped over his mouth, and his eyes and ears were taped closed as well. He struggled with the soldiers as they removed him from the car. With his ears taped he had not heard all the commotion at the front of the car. The soldier who opened the boot placed the hostage on the ground. He removed the tape from his ears and eyes.

"Sir, it is okay. We are British soldiers, your captors are in our custody, sir calm down," the tall soldier instructed the man as he rolled him over to his back.

The captive's eyes adjusted to the daylight as the two soldiers helped him to his feet. He had a hard time standing, due to the small quarters he had just been in for an extended period. Aware of the traffic backing up, the soldier escorted him into the temporary hut they used during this checkpoint.

Kenton took in a deep breath, looked through the mirror to the two in the back of the car and whispered, "I know him, we have done work together. We will need to contact him tomorrow. I need to know how and why he ended up in the cars boot. Once again this proves there is no such thing as coincidence, everything happens for a reason."

"Okay, I will make a note of it, Dad. I will get the details from you once we get through this," said Scott.

"I don't want to use my ID, but I think these boys are now on high alert," said James. "If they ask, I will use the one John gave us for traveling. David, you will too, so remember your new name."

The car in front, a beat up 1960 blue four door Vauxhall Viva, was pushed to the side of the checkpoint.

"Those blokes will be stuck here for a while," said Scott.

"Aye, I wonder if someone tipped off the military for this one. This is a temporary check point, and it looks like they put it together in a hurry," said Kenton.

They raised the control arm and removed the tire strips. Two new soldiers waved Kenton's car through.

"Good morning, sir," said the one soldier with a thick Scottish accent, as the other stood to the side of the car with his HK MP5 automatic gun pointed at Kenton's head.

Living in Northern Ireland, you got used to checkpoints and soldiers with guns pointed your way.

"Is there an issue?" the soldier asked David.

Kenton elbowed David in the ribs, "Son he is speaking to you, it is not polite to stare!"

"What? What? Sorry." David looked past his grandfather to the soldier. David could sense the disappointment from his grandfather.

"No, sorry, I am just in shock about what I just saw. I have been living in Canada for over five years and have never seen something like that happen right in front of me. I've seen it on the news but not right there," he motioned to the space in front of the car. "I guess it will take me a bit to get used to home," David finished with a nervous chuckle.

"Aye kid, you get used to it, it's not going away anytime soon."

"No, I guess not."

"Can I see some ID please," the soldier asked.

Everyone had their ID out of their wallets and handed them off to the soldier. He looked in and checked everyone against their photo ID.

"Where are you heading today?"

"I just picked these two up at the airport and we are heading back to Portadown for a surprise family visit," Kenton said calmly.

"Okay, have a good day, and William," the solider said as he returned the IDs, "don't be the one in the trunk." He winked at

David then waved his arm to the second security gate. A soldier lifted the gate manually and the crew pulled through.

"Nice recovery, David," his grandfather said. "I thought we were going to be waved to the side for more questions."

"Alright, let's get going," said James.

They headed for the road to Portadown.

Kenton looked back at the two in the back seat, "Remember the job we did five years ago where we had to get information for the military on a house in Londonderry? We ended up cleaning the place out," Kenton stumbled on his words as he looked to David. "The guy in the boot was the one I had watching the house, for a week, to get me the information on the schedule their crew was keeping. Without him, we would have all walked into a poorly timed operation. Scott, have Brian chat with his family. He can meet them over the next few days and get the details. Make sure he brings a few quid to help them out."

"Aye Dad, he can pay them a visit tomorrow," said Scott.

"Alright David, we need to continue our conversation about the family business. You need to understand our history to see the future," said Kenton. "David, as you know, I was in the British army back in the '40s, '50s and '60s serving with one of the most elite teams in the world, the SAS. I have been all over the world with my teams. My last assignment was back here in Northern Ireland, where I grew up. I realized there was a need for a non-military contact and crew that could work outside the constraints of the government's red tape. I retired and worked the grey area of intelligence where I could help and do things I couldn't do while in the SAS."

"Okay Granda, what does that mean, like what John does in Canada?" David asked.

"Aye, I will get to John. I worked a network across Northern Ireland and across the British empire where I would finish things the military or government did not want to have their fingerprints on or legally couldn't be seen doing. I stayed here in Northern Ireland because this was where I could do the most for my old mates, still in the military. I brought your father and uncle up working with me and now you will be the third generation to do this work. We will train you and work with you, but you need to understand if you can't make it to the level, I need from you, I will not allow you to continue. Of course, you must never speak of the information you learn, just like when you lived here. Do you understand?"

"Aye, Granda," said David.

"Traffic is slow today, so I guess I have time to start from the beginning."

John and Kenton both grew up with similar childhoods but in different parts of the world. They lived on small farms in the nineteen thirties and forties, both had a list of chores to complete daily, and both were the oldest sibling of large families. They lived on farms outside of cities, one in Canada and one in Northern Ireland. Both families were poor and survived off what they grew and sold on their farms. John's dad would find occasional work in the wood mills and mines in Northern Ontario while Kenton's dad worked in the textile factories around Portadown.

As teenagers, John and Kenton would finish their farm chores then visit their schoolmates, they all talked about the war in Europe and how they could beat the age restrictions to get involved before they turned eighteen. The only thing they wanted to do, like most teens back in the early forties, was to fight the Nazis.

Before either boy turned eighteen, they were enlisted. They were on the same Army base in Southern England, with their regiments, as they prepared for the D-Day invasion. Both boys were in the first wave of platoons that hit Juno Beach on June 6th, 1944. They made it up the beach and to the safety of the surf wall. Unlike many of their mates who died on the beach, drowning in the water or bleeding from bullet wounds on the blood-soaked sand.

The first few months after the invasion, their Divisions continued east, they struggled daily to take back European cities from the 'Axis of Evil'. It wasn't until both armies worked together, Kenton in XII CTRE Field Company and John in the 3rd Canadian Division, that their paths and lives became tangled. Together their division and company marched through Europe, they were involved in battle after battle as they cleared towns of the enemy and repaired roads or bridges destroyed by the Nazi occupation.

A warm and muggy night in August 1944, when the united 'First Army' secured another city in Holland, was when John and Kenton's lives became entangled. They were assigned night watch together by their commanders, instructed to watch the southern quadrant of the city's outskirts with twenty other men—boys. John watched the main road that came into town from the south east. They positioned him behind a pile of sandbags to watch for any movement on the road. Kenton was on the other side of the road with the same assignment. In the early hours of the morning John crawled over to Kenton's larger pile of sandbags, and the two took watch together.

In the darkness, with the sound of bombs being dropped and guns being shot, the two strangers both talked about their lives back home. They joked about what they had seen and done while on their 'European vacation' and what they hoped their futures would bring if they made it home. With what they, and all the other soldiers, had seen in the last couple of months, no one expected to have much of a future. They looked out into the dark woods and the crater filled road, both hoped not to be shot. Kenton would tell John, 'We all need to find some reason to go home again.'

The two corps continued to move through Europe, they merged with other corps and platoons to strengthen numbers. Kenton and John spent the rest of the summer and all the winter trying to survive the war, and the weather. They grew a close friendship and a reputation as the corps' top killers. They were being noticed by the higher-ranking officers. Kenton had a total of 300 kills during the last year of the war. John and Kenton had become a team their superiors could count on. They were sent on scavenger missions and out to find dawdling Nazis'. They would command special security details in the towns and areas where their Corps would bed down. It had come easily to them and to a few other newly designed special teams. Neither man had a problem interrogating a Nazis through an interrupter. And after they collected the information and sent it back to headquarters, Kenton and John were the team being asked to 'finish the job, for King and Country.' Neither had an issue taking a life, sometimes it was quick and simple. Other times those SS men just needed to suffer for their sins.

Once the war ended John and Kenton signed up for an additional year of service and spent it living in Holland. They worked for their respective militaries, rebuilding and searching for treasures hidden by Nazis. They helped to rebuild war-torn cities and met many young ladies who survived the war. It was a good time to be alive for John and Kenton, heroes to the locals and work horses for the military.

Having been together through the tragedy and victory of war they had both come out the other side different men. Gone were the innocent young farm boys, replaced by hardened men who had killed and manipulated their way through a war. They had seen the worst of humankind and believed somewhere between the worst and the best lay an untapped world where they could make a lot of extra money for themselves.

Kenton found they could do some illicit work for family's torn apart by snitches who gave the Nazis too much information during the occupation. Those families paid Kenton handsomely for his work. Word spread that he would take a payment to hunt and kill those rats. Kenton hunted the Nazis who thought they could just drop their uniforms and hide in the larger cities. He accepted payment of money or sometimes a comfortable bed to sleep in with some nice company.

John found other ways to make extra money in Europe. There was a need for weapons, food and building materials in the cities destroyed by war. John found an abundance of those items, mostly at his military depots, when the money was right. John and Kenton could move those items to cities in the region without the need to go through the proper channels. John lost his taste to kill, but found he could organize and move people, weapons, and food efficiently. He organized and moved assets while Kenton disposed of people, quietly and quickly, qualities John just couldn't master.

John was almost killed on one job when he entered an abandoned house. A Nazi was hidden on the second floor and jumped him. Kenton saw John struggle and jumped on the assailant, he killed him while John escaped.

Throughout the year they perfected their specialized skills. Kenton destroyed while John rebuilt. They also shared a skill, the ability to make money. A lot of money.

In Liege, Belgium, Kenton, and John located six Nazi soldiers and two SS officers who had changed out of their uniforms the day the war ended and moved into a few abandoned houses, they helped to abandon, with the help of some Nazi sympathizers. Kenton's commanders would not have approved of what happened to those men and the people who helped hide them. Those living in that commune of the city were very thankful, once those people disappeared. The Colonel, John and Kenton directly reported to, had an idea these two were working an angle of the rebuilding efforts. He turned a blind eye to the inventory that disappeared or when they did not report for duty. He knew his percent of the profits would be tucked in the top drawer of his desk, weekly.

When they completed their one-year contract, neither one wanted to leave. They had a good business plan in place, but things were dying down as Belgium was becoming self-sufficient and most of the bad Nazis had been found.

The government asked John to come back to Canada and help start a new department in the Canadian Government, an intelligence department of the military, Communications Security Establishment, CSE for short.

Kenton applied to the still new SAS back in England. He joined the elite team and spent the next twenty years developing, training, and rising the ranks of the SAS. He traveled the world and was stationed back home to Northern Ireland.

While Kenton traveled the world with the British SAS, John worked hard in intelligence, he made contacts throughout North America and the world.

They would both take time to meet when they had furlough or vacation. They talked about what they had accomplished since the war. They wanted to work together; they knew they had something very special together. The way they operated for that year after the war could be duplicated in the private sector.

During the sixties both John and Kenton looked for career changes and into something freer, like they were the year after the war. Kenton was tired of being told when to wake, eat, shit, and shoot even though he was a senior officer, everyone had a boss.

Britain became involved with the troubles in Northern Ireland. Kenton saw an opportunity to do work for the British government, things they legally couldn't do. A senior member of parliament had unofficially asked Kenton if he would like to become a mercenary or as they were looking to call it a freelance combatant. They needed someone to run operations without the government's red tape and ethics. Kenton raised in Northern Ireland would be the perfect candidate.

John too saw changes in Canada, especially Southern Ontario. He had connected with some Italian families during his time in the CSE. There was an opportunity for him to leave his government job and freelance for others, maybe on the other side of the law. With the intelligence job, he had spent a lot of his time on the 'other side of the law.' He worked with members of society and governments that were not always boy scouts. He found there were opportunities to work that side for not only mobsters but governments around the world.

Kenton and John, with their families, took a vacation together in Berlin the summer after both had corresponded about getting out. While their wives shopped and visited historical sites, Kenton and John sat in pubs, parks, and hotel rooms. They discussed the future and how they could build an international business together. The opportunity Kenton had in Northern Ireland to work with the British was inconceivable. John had done his research too, and on his side of the Atlantic there were many opportunities. They spent two weeks in Berlin, they planned, created, and worked through issues until they felt they had a business plan they could both work under on either side of the Atlantic Ocean. Kenton would work on jobs for the British and sometimes Irish to keep the war ball rolling in Northern Ireland. He would work other parts of the world, doing hits, tactical attacks on buildings and gather information in ways militaries could not. He would manufacture and move guns around Europe and the world all from a machine shop he would set up in Portadown.

John would do the same, there was a plumbing wholesale and service business for sale in Guelph, he persuaded the seller to give him a good deal on the property and the businesses. Through the two businesses, John would launder money, he contracted hits for Kenton, and moved people and the weapons Kenton's shop built around the world. On a farm property, north of Guelph, they created a safe house, a new part of the business where they hid people from organizations or governments. John had the clients live on the farm while his team made them new IDs and lives. He would work with the Canadian, US or other governments and mobsters or others on the run. John staffed a couple forgers for any ID's or documents needed quickly.

With all this in place the seventies brought a prosperous decade for both men, the newly named war 'The Troubles' worked well for Kenton in Northern Ireland. The number of weapons built or passed through his shop was enormous, worth millions of dollars to Middle East countries, European Nations, South and Central America and to the IRA. Kenton worked many covert jobs for the British not only in Ireland but in other parts of the world. They both traveled back and forth to each other's shops or would meet at one of their many vacation homes. They discussed the future and how they could.

James traveled more for Kenton and John to allow them more time at their shops. John always showed James a good time in Canada and explained how he could really use him there. James did like the idea of the move to Canada, but he was still young and in love with a wonderful girl back home.

Kenton needed him at home as much as John needed him in Canada.

*   *   *

Kenton had raised Scott and James alone since his wife Karen, their mother, died in a car accident in Belfast in 1964. Kenton had a rule that he reminded the boys constantly, 'You don't kill out of anger, or for free. Don't allow emotions to be involved in a job because that is when mistakes happen.' The week after Karen died Kenton broke his own rule and found the man who was drunk the day he ran a red-light. He hit Karen's Ford, square in the driver's door. The impact broke her neck and killed her instantly. Kenton did not kill this man, no, that would be too quick in Kenton's mind, he killed the man's wife, his kid's, and parent's. He left Mr. Drunk to pick up the pieces and deal with the guilt, from all the deaths he caused. Kenton read in a newspaper a month later, the man had hung himself.

James and Scott were trained for the family business by Kenton. Who better than Kenton, he spent years in the SAS where he trained and developed members. He cross trained with Canadian, US, and Australian elite teams, where he made lifelong friendships. James and Scott specialized in different areas, James trained in all aspects of the business Kenton and John had built. Scott was skilled on building and using weapons and explosives.

John was not one for getting his hands dirty, that work was left to 'The Family' a nickname he gave the three of them that stuck, around the world. John took the money Kenton was making and cleaned it for him. There was a lot more variety of "investments" in Canada.

Together they bought a large property north of Orangeville and made it a safe house only for the two families. John was able to secure work from mobsters in Chicago, New York, and Italy. He had a large retirement community of mobsters and others who needed a safe place to hide in Oakville, Guelph, and Woodstock. He had a reputation as a relocation specialist.

John enjoyed bringing James to Canada to do jobs for him. James was precise and clean. Some of the mobsters or bikers John had hired for lower profile targets were sloppy, did not always confirm a kill, and were loose lipped when they drank. John already had to bring James over to deal with two loose lipped fools he had hired for jobs.

Kenton had his own problems in Northern Ireland. A shipment of weapons was hijacked from a couple of his vans while they were transported to a port where an oil tanker waited to leave for Iraq. He had to locate the weapons and the person who took them. That wasn't too hard. On the news, a couple of clowns in Enniskillen were filmed as they shot bullets into the air with the weapons they had just stolen. Kenton arranged for James and Scott to pay them a visit the next night. There were enough explosives planted in the building that the explosion was felt two miles away. The next day a top UDA official came by the shop and apologized to Kenton for stealing the weapons from an unmarked vehicle. Kenton killed him right in the front of his shop, apology accepted.

A major hiccup in their business came during Ronald Reagan's term as President when Lieutenant Colonel Ollie North slipped up. He was all over the news for the weapons he sold to

Iran and many other countries. Most of those weapons were either stored or transported from John or Kenton's shops. Kenton and John worked hard for a few months with their contacts in selective governments, they needed to ensure their names and shops were not identified on any paperwork from the investigation. During that time, they shut down and emptied the shops.

• • • •

"Yes, I am going to be James Bond!" David said with a laugh.

James swatted at David's head from the back seat of the car. "Smarten up, there is no joking about this."

"David," his grandfather responded. "I have never met a man like James Bond. There is no flashy high living, no supermodel girls waiting for you in your future. There is hard work, living a normal life, looking over your shoulder and a lot of money to hide properly. You will need to have two personalities, the one your dad and I will help you train and develop and the regular good citizen you will use most of the time, the two can't mix. You will set yourself up with John and have a successful career as a plumber and hide your money away for later. But don't be fooled, I have seen people pass away trying to walk this tightrope. We will teach you how to do it, but you can't get flashy about your hidden life or the money you have, at least not around your home."

"Okay, I see this with Dad and John. Mom and Brenda, always talk about living an average life when they have the money to live like queens. But it would raise too many questions. I know when they vacation, they do it with high class."

"Yes, that is right, there are ways to enjoy the money too. The thing is, it needs to be interwoven into our lives."

The history lesson he had just received shocked David. He had heard parts of it, but never the entire story from the beginning. He looked out the window of the car. The rolling green fields of Armagh farmlands passed through his field of vision. In his mind, he tried to understand everything he just heard. The killing, bombs, and terrorist actions. He knew something was going on from a young age, the secrets, the guns, the things he had seen in the shop when they thought he was napping. He was young, and those things seemed more like dreams, but the older he got they grew with him in his reality. How can he live with this truth? The way he was trained, the guns, the practice with knives suddenly sunk into his soul, '*I was being trained to kill and tactically work through the process of jobs where they end in blood. This is going to be hard living a normal life and doing those things.*'

"Can you pull over Granda please?" David asked.

"Yes, just let me find somewhere to stop. Are you okay?" Kenton asked as he found a laneway and pulled the car into it.

David opened the door and stepped out of the car; his mind was spinning.

"Not again," said James.

David had to decide, does he run away through the fields, or embrace the truths he was just told and find out what other secrets there are to learn. The last forty-eight hours were an emotional rollercoaster. He now thought differently about his dad, his family and future. Some of the things he thought about his grandfather and father were lies. They were hiding their true selves from him. Was his mother right, were the men in the car, evil?

James slowly got out of the car and walked towards David.

David turned to him, "Stay away from me, don't come any closer. I need to be alone for a minute."

"David, it's okay. Let's talk about this. John and I told you there was a lot more to this life than even we made it out to be.

I know it has been emotional for you, this last twenty-four hours. John is having the same conversation with Phil while we are here. Come, get back into the car, we are almost to the shop." James said. "Son, it is okay to be confused, I was too. So were your uncles. If you want to leave and not talk about this anymore, that is fine, we can drop you off to Aunt Sarah's and go about our business or you can come learn the rest of the family business with us. I don't know what you will go home to, but you are here now, so let's go. You tell us where you want to be dropped off."

"What about Amy and mom, do they know?" David asked.

"Ya, your mom knows. Why do you think she was losing her mind when we left together? Amy doesn't know and will never know, if possible. You cannot tell her anything about this. Your mom and I agreed not to involve her in this."

"Why does she not have to know, and I do? She gets to be a normal teen doing stupid things? How do I go back and hang out with friends from school or church?"

"Well, that is something you will have to sort out on your own. You have been told a few times you will need to live two different lives and now you know why. It was different for me because all my friends were growing up in this environment. I will tell you; Phil will understand and the two of you will have each other to lean on. Can we get back in the car and head home?"

"Yes, yes we can."

David and James walked back to the waiting car together. David was confused about what he had just heard. His life was messed up anyway, maybe he should just embrace the madness and take it for a ride. Who knows what he could learn from it?

"Dad, I will sit in the back the rest of the way; you can have the front."

"Okay. Are you okay?"

"Yes fine, just fine and a bit hungry," he said. James and David got into the car, James gave Kenton a smile and a wink. Kenton started the car, and the crew continued the trip back to the shop.

"Everything okay? Are you ready for this wee adventure?" Scott asked David.

"Yes, everything is fine, thank you," David said.

David turned and looked out the window, he enjoyed the view and now understood just how powerful his family was.

CHAPTER TEN

David walked into the shop, he felt like he had really grown up in the last fifty minutes. Sarah and Doris were there waiting for their arrival.

"Nannie, Aunt Sarah!" David yelled as he ran in their direction.

"David," his nannie said with excitement as he embraced her. "How are you, son? How was the plane ride?"

"It was good Nannie, I slept the whole way," David said.

"Hi Sarah, how are you," he asked as he kissed his aunt on the cheek.

"David, it is so good to see you here," she said.

The rest of the crew had made their way to David and the ladies.

"So, how was your trip here," Doris asked. She poured tea into mugs for everyone.

David looked at his grandfather and asked quietly, "Does she know?"

"Aye, she knows it all," Kenton responded.

"I don't agree with it all, but I know it all, Sarah does, too," said Doris.

The group drank tea and ate chocolates while David told them about life in Canada and his trip. He ended his story with the checkpoint, not speaking of the conversation he had just had about the family.

Kenton said, "David, let's go into the office and talk some more. Your dad needs to clean up from the trip and then Scott and he have some work to do for me. Okay?"

"Yes Granda, can I get some water as well, I am very dry!"

"Sure," Kenton said.

David headed to the office. The couch he lay on his last night living in Northern Ireland was gone and a new brown leather couch was in its place. The new couch was nice but did not look as comfortable to David as the old one he would bunker down on. His grandfather had updated the old office since he was last there. New pictures were on the wall, one caught David's eye it was of a crew jumping out of a helicopter onto a sandy beach. The new desk was bigger than the old one and had carved details of weapons on the desk legs. The desk had Kenton's black leather chair behind it and two chrome and cloth chairs in-front of it. These chairs did not look as comfortable as Kenton's. There was a board table in the office with nine chairs around it, maps and notes covered it.

David sat on the couch while Kenton got him some water.

"What do you think of the office now? A little different from your last visit?"

"Yes, I remember sleeping on the old couch. The one side was always better and more comfortable than the other."

Kenton placed the glass of water on the table beside the couch, "There you go son this will help."

"So, David, I guess you have a lot of questions and I should have a lot of answers. Do you want to start or shall I?" Kenton asked as he went back to the office door and closed it. "I can sit on the couch with you or behind my desk, where would you like me?"

"Behind the desk, is fine," said David. "Why don't you start, can I have a note pad to write questions down? That way I won't interrupt you."

"Yes, good thinking, excellent thought," said Kenton.

Kenton rummaged through the upper right drawer of his desk and pulled out a blank note pad. "Here use this one," he said as he handed David the pad and a pen.

"Okay so let me get into a bit more detail about our past. From then to where we are now. When I left the SAS and the military, I worked with some upper-level officers to obtain information they could not get legally. They would pass me cash to pay for vehicles and to pay off informants. You need to remember the British military has a long history of working outside the rules. You don't become an empire by playing nice. After doing a few fact-finding missions, they passed me onto other officers looking for a person who could move equipment and people without being noticed. With my background, I could complete those tasks, and they paid me well for this work. When I was in the SAS, most of my team's assignments were on the other side of the world. I don't have time to tell you all of them now, but we will sit down from time to time and discuss them, I used to use them as learning stories for your father and uncles and will pass them on to you as well. Maybe one day someone will write a book about them. So, I would travel the Middle East and the Far East mostly sneaking in and out of countries as needed. I also worked in Canada and in other ally countries. But once I retired, I wanted to be closer to home with my family."

David listened to his granda speak, he sipped his water and took notes to ask later. He looked out the window and saw his father and Scott approach the office. Dressed in black, they carried camera bags over their shoulders.

Scott knocked on the door and said, "Okay we are heading out."

"Aye, hopefully we can get what we need tonight and clean this one up tomorrow," said James.

"Aye should be simple enough," said Scott.

"No, never assume that, complacency is the work of the devil. Always be on guard, always be ready. Even a simple surveillance job can go sideways if you are spotted," said Kenton.

"Aye, right," said James.

"Godspeed you two, see you in a while," Kenton said.

The men shook hands, James leaned in through the door, "David, learn from these stories. Granda has enough of them to keep you here till you are twenty," he said with a smile. "Nannie and Sarah are still here too if you two get hungry."

"Okay Dad, be careful with whatever you are doing."

James smiled at David; it felt strange having David here. He had spoken to Kenton about this very moment last month when he was here. He asked how Kenton handled his emotions when he brought Scott and himself on their first job. 'Staying focused, if you know your job and are prepared you know your team will also be safe. Prepare for the worst, hope for the best and trust that your guardian angels are paying attention.' Kenton never sent anyone out for a mission before they reviewed every possible scenario. Kenton's success in the military and after was because of his attention to detail.

"We will get the information you need and be back before dawn," James said as he closed the office door. The two men left the shop on their mission.

"Anybody need anything?" she asked while the office door was open.

"Can I get more water Nannie please," David asked as he brought her his cup.

"Yes, of course, luv," she said.

When she returned, Kenton was back to his history lesson for David. Doris stepped inside the office and handed the cup back to David; she also had a cup of tea for Kenton. "I figure you will need this to keep yourself focused and your mouth from drying out."

"Thank you dear," said Kenton

Doris left the office and returned to Sarah; she had the BBC news on the TV.

"As I gained the trust of the officers, I had contact with MI6 and other agencies. That was when I recruited your father, uncles, and a few other friends. I used the money I was making to set up compounds offshore in case things went bad here at home. I began moving larger military equipment in and out of Northern Ireland for them. They asked if I would be interested in terminating a couple of fellas who were causing issues for the British forces in East Germany. I took some time to think about this, then decided I would do it. It was a big step to take as a civilian, but it worked out for me and us. Any questions so far?"

"Okay, we are assassins, enforcers, weapon builders and offer any service our clients ask of us?" David said.

"Well, sometimes it could be a simple kidnapping and beating as a warning, a killing or a kneecapping in front of the target's family."

"Is that what happened the night we left for Canada?"

"Yes and no. Your dad's life was in danger, there was and still is a bounty on his head. We orchestrated that night to convince your mother your family needed out of the country. It wasn't the best way to handle it looking back now, but I did it to keep our family safe."

"That night will be with me a long time," David said.

"So, as I worked with the military, I also made contacts around the world. The more I did the more business came my way all being controlled from this shop or John's. Our shops have helped many governments overthrow other governments in the Middle East, South America, and Africa. I organized and ran one of the first teams in the Falkland Islands dispute. Your dad told me about your meeting with Phil, John, and him. I am glad you approached him, and we did not force it on you. But living a double life, killing people you don't know, living on the fringe of society, it all takes a toll. Doing all this knowing you could become the hunted, that you can't tell anyone this side of your life, is this what you want? Because once you are in, you don't get out. 'He who fears death will never do anything great.' That is the mantra you need to uphold if you choose this path."

"Okay so how do I decide, Granda, you are asking a lot from me? I wasn't expecting this to be so big or complicated."

"No, I am not asking anything from you, God, the world, is asking. I am just the vessel here, right now. Many others in the past had to decide this too. We are the ones history will never know about. We are the few that help empires bring down others."

"Granda, I want to but how can I be sure? I don't know if I can kill someone or hurt them."

"If you have any doubt, then no, go home, finish school and be a plumber."

"I can try, I feel like I could do it, I could do it for you and Dad. I guess there is a difference between talking about it and doing it in the heat of the moment."

"You have to know you can do it for yourself. Self-control is what this job requires, planning, thinking on your feet, being ready for anything. It is never just about running into a building on fire. Planning, preparing, and looking at the situation from afar, not up close, is how we run our operations. Then you must put it all aside and return to your regular life until the next call comes. That is the sign of success in this line of work."

"Okay, I still want in, I want this Granda. I will need guidance from you and Dad, but what about training? What about everything?" David asked as he became overwhelmed again.

"David, it is already in you, you are the third generation of this, it will come without forcing it."

"Okay, so where are Dad and Scott now? And where is Uncle Edward?"

"They are out scouting the job you and your dad flew over for. We will move in on them tomorrow. We have found an IRA base, in a house where they are making explosives for Middle Eastern terrorists. My sources also believe this group were the ones that did the Brighton bombing last month. Our job is to know the targets, eliminate some of the targets and keep a couple for questioning. I have photos of the two we are to keep alive. If we get them, we are to bring them to a meeting place where one of my government contacts will retrieve them and hand them over to the Americans for questioning. As for Uncle Edward, he is working with an American right now moving weapons to a Central American country with a couple of John's contacts."

"Who is your contact?"

"A military man is all you need to know right now. Let's see how you make out tomorrow night before we divulge any more details."

"Okay," David said with a sigh. "This is a lot to take in."

"Oh, I know, I know."

"Go see your Nannie, she misses you terribly. I think you have had enough of a history lesson today. I have some work to do. Enjoy some of her baking and then get some sleep. We made a small apartment at the side of the shop for when your dad comes over. There is a room for you with a bed and clothes."

"Okay," David said.

David grabbed his glass of water and headed out to the shop. No one was out there so he walked around the shop. He looked at the machinery he used to work on as a little boy. His confidence in himself grew as the shock of all the information sank in. The small jobs, how his dad trained him as he grew up, the way he handled those filthy bikers, they were tests for him and Phil. They must have done okay, or he would not be here.

The way they taught him to sharpen and maintain his hunting knife, it was all for this, the job he was here for. David sat at his old work bench. He was ready for this. He had killed many animals to keep their freezers full. How would a human be any different? He would find out soon enough, he supposed.

The side door of the shop opened, and Doris walked in. She had an arm full of food with her. David jumped up and ran over to help her bring the items to the front counter.

"Nannie, what have you here?" he asked.

"Everything that hungry men need to focus on the task at hand," she replied.

"How are you feeling now, son? Did your talk go okay with Granda?"

"Yes, Nannie it was fine. It actually helps me understand my life in Canada better now too."

"Good to hear. So, you are becoming a member of the team?"

"Yes, I think so. I will know for sure before I go back to Canada."

"Your father will be happy to hear that, your wee mother will not be happy at all. Maybe I should plan a trip shortly to visit her."

"No, she will not. I was thinking the same thing. You seem to calm her down."

Kenton came out of the office and poked through the cardboard bakery boxes. "It's the box on the bottom," Doris said.

"How did you know what he was looking for?"

"Oh, I just know David," she laughed.

"Right, I guess so."

"Do you want some tea with your treats, David?"

"Yes, please Nannie."

"Okay, while she is making tea, grab your suitcase from the car and follow me David," Kenton said.

David ran over to the car and grabbed the suitcase from the trunk. He followed his grandfather to an area of the shop he did not remember. A door hidden by boxes opened to a small flat. Through the doorway, David stood in the living room that opened to a small kitchen and dining room. The area was fully furnished with new furniture. There was a hallway between the kitchen and dining area that led to a washroom and three bedrooms.

"Wow, I didn't know this was here," David said as he walked to the kitchen.

"This is our little secret place. We hide people we need to move or that need a few days out of the public eye in here, or nannie just uses it for us when we have late nights at work. The second door on the left is now your room while you are here, and no one will use it when you are away so you can leave clothes and other things in there. Here is the key to it."

David walked down the hallway to the assigned door. The door opened to a small room with a single bed and a wardrobe. "Unpack and then come get your tea."

"Okay. Cool."

David pulled his clothes out of the suitcase and hung them in the wardrobe where other items of clothing were already hung.

He knew the shop was about three quarters of the building, but he did not think they owned this part of the building. Once again, the reality David had once known was a far cry from the new reality he now knew. He left the flat and joined his grandparents for a snack.

"So how is school? Do you have a girlfriend yet?" Doris asked, getting the food out of the pastry boxes.

"School is fine, Nannie. No, no girlfriend yet. I don't know if that will happen anytime soon with all this changing in my life."

To David, those two questions felt like a life he was living light years away. The mind games he would have to conquer, between the two realities, from now on.

"Aren't there any nice ones at church you like?" Doris said.

"Not really Nannie, we are all just friends right now. Honestly, I don't know how I can go back to Canada and have a girlfriend with all the stuff granda just told me."

"It will be fine; you will learn to adapt. We all have. It isn't as hard as you think," she said. She handed him a sausage roll and turnover with custard.

David's mouth filled with flavors you just did not get in Canada as he ate the food. "This is what I miss most about here, the food is so much better," David said after a few bites of the sausage roll.

The shop door opened, and James and Scott walked in.

"Huh," Kenton said under his breath.

"That was a lot quicker than I was expecting. Did you guys get tagged by someone?"

"Aye, it went real well," James said. "David, can you come over you should hear this as part of the team."

James waited for David to run over to them, "They are all there and yes there is—was a group of them making bombs."

"What do you mean?" asked David.

"Well, we set up for a long night of surveillance. Scott took the first watch while I walked down the street to get a look at the back of the house. The two targets the client is asking for alive, left the building and headed for a house down the street, I guess that is their accommodations. About an hour later there was a massive explosion, it took the roof off the building where they were making bombs. There is no way anyone survived it. I guess they crossed the wrong wires," James said.

"This is a good lesson for you David. These guys were involved in small bombs for cars and for houses, no real production, just a couple bombs a month around here. One of their associates made a deal with some guys in the Middle East who needed bombs made on demand. They began building and shipping ten times the number of bombs they were making a year ago. Obviously, a mistake happened and now those guys will not be making anything ever again. Always stay within your means. There is good money in this business but when you get too big, you lose control of the situation and in this business losing control usually means a shallow grave somewhere. Never take on more work than you can do yourself, understand," explained Kenton.

"Yes, Granda," David said. "Can I ask a question?"

"Of course," said Kenton. "Let's go sit and have our tea, while we talk."

"These guys we want, are either of them the guy that identified Dad?"

"No, I know what you are thinking, David. But no, Nigel is much higher up the food chain. One day he will be around, I am sure of it. He only comes back for the higher priced targets.

The ones that must go right, either because of the large amount of money or the high-profile target. He associates with these guys, but he is not around."

"Tomorrow night will still be a go, it looks like it will only be an extraction now," said Scott. "The Americans will still get the two brains behind the operation."

"Aye, those two won't be leaving anytime soon, too many peelers around now. That should quiet down by afternoon tomorrow. To be safe, I will talk to Michael at the barracks and see if he can move his men tomorrow night so we can get in, take the targets alive. We won't be able to move in if the place is still crawling with SIU," said Kenton.

"Aye, the police shouldn't take too long on this investigation and the other two are shook up now, they won't know what to expect," said James.

"Aye, I will go back out in the morning and continue surveillance to ensure they don't run," said Scott.

The men raised their teacups and toasted the night. David, a step behind brought his up just in time.

James smiled at him, "Welcome to the family business, son,"

They all laughed.

● ● ●

"Dad, can I go to bed?"

"Yes. Did Granda show you your room," asked James.

"Yes."

"Alright I will come with you; I am beat too. The time change is a killer sometimes."

"Dad," James said, "I am hitting the bed. We can review the plans in the morning."

"Aye, no problem," said Kenton.

"I am heading home too," said Scott as he finished his tea. "I will head straight to the house in the morning."

"Aye, okay," said Kenton.

"We will head out too, unless Doris wants to sleep here tonight?"

"No, I would like my own bed tonight Kenton," she said. "You can drop me off round home then pick me up on your way back tomorrow morning so I can spend some more time with David."

"Then it is decided. I will be back in the morning to open the shop for business. You two sleep in as late as you want."

"Wake us no later than ten, we have a busy day ahead of us," James said.

"Dad, why didn't you tell me any of this before," David asked once they were alone.

"It wasn't my story to tell, Granda started this, Granda runs this operation over here. It was up to him to tell you. You saw what you needed to in Canada, but this side of the ocean is a lot more dangerous."

"Okay, well granda told me a lot but there is much more to tell, I think. But my brain is about to explode like that house did today if I hear more right now."

"Yes, there is son, for another day. I should call your mother; she will be getting ready for bed about now with the time change."

James picked up the phone and called a number, from that number it transferred to the house number in Guelph.

"Hello," a sleepy voice answered the phone.

"Hi honey, we are here safe and sound," said James with a cheerful voice.

"How is David, what does he know about the doings over there," Elizabeth asked.

"David is fine. Yes, he learned a lot more from my father."

"That eegit, he better not let my son get hurt," she yelled through the phone.

"No, no, everything is fine, don't worry."

"Well, I do worry, it is what mothers do. We worry about our children. Especially the ones halfway around the world playing war games with his grandfather."

"Okay, it's late here and we want to get to sleep. I will call you in the morning and you can talk to David then," replied James with a more solemn tone.

"Okay," she said as she calmed down. "Goodnight, stay safe and bring my boy home."

"Mom still mad, Dad?" David asked after his dad hung up the phone.

"A little," James said. "So, what room did Granda give you?"

"This one," David said, as he opened his door to the room.

"Oh nice," James said, but a sense of darkness was in his breath. Another story David will hear on this trip if there was time.

"Something wrong, Dad?"

"No, everything is fine, come see my room."

James traveled back and forth all the time and had a nice big room. They did not use his room for guests, so it was personalized. There were photos of his family on the wall, he already had a closet full of clothes and many other photos David did not recognize. One with his dad in military fatigues in a jungle. Another photo had him in front of the pyramids in Egypt. He had a photo on his dresser with David's mom, dad and granda with a couple kangaroos.

David looked at all the photos, "Dad, did you go to Africa to shoot a lion? Is that a photo of mom in Hawaii What are all these places you have been to? I didn't know you traveled to those places, Russia too?"

"Well, you have to use the money somehow. Traveling is the best way to do it. The others are work photos. You will have your collection one day too," James said. "David, it is too late to talk about it now, we both need to get some sleep. Let me just say we are a lot richer than you know. All part of the business. Now let me get you to bed."

"I am fine Dad; I am not five anymore."

"I know, but tomorrow I will treat you that way to keep you safe. Understand?"

"Yes Dad, but you need to watch for yourself too. Goodnight," David responded as he turned and headed out the door.

David left his father's room and went to his. *'How much richer,'* he thought, *and where did it come from? Granda said they got paid well for these jobs, how well?'*

David lay on the bed, Huey Lewis and the News played in his ears, and the crazy stories he heard played in his mind. He decided he needed to write these stories down. One day, maybe not until his father was dead, he would have one hell of a story to tell the world. As that thought played through his mind, David fell into a deep restful sleep.

CHAPTER ELEVEN

David woke to the smell of coffee and bacon. For a second, he thought it was a dream, or a nightmare, until he opened his eyes and looked around the room. He pulled himself out of bed and walked over to the window and opened the curtains. The light on his face was warm and bright, it reminded him of Canada and the other life he had there. He got dressed in his jeans and shirt and walked out to the living room.

"Morning, Son. How did you sleep?" James said.

"Hi, Dad. Fine, I guess. Breakfast smells good. What time is it?" David asked as he sat at the small dining table.

"Ten past ten. I was going to let you sleep to half past. I hope my noise in the kitchen didn't wake you up?" James said.

"No, I don't think it was you. I was having a dream, well what I thought was a dream, but it seems pretty real now."

"Yes, it is very real now. Like I said a few times on this trip, you can walk away from all this if you like, I know it would make your mother very happy. But when we leave for the job, you really will be locked in for life. There will be no more opportunities to get out after that."

"No Dad, I am in. I was thinking, all the stuff you taught me over the years, it was preparing me for this?"

"Yes, it was. I wanted you to be better prepared than Scott and I ever were. But don't think for a second your training is over. You have so much more to learn. How many eggs do you want?"

"Three eggs please, I get the feeling we sleep and eat when we have the chance and enjoy the quiet while it is available," said David.

"Yes, you are right about that. There is fresh coffee or tea, and cups are in the cupboard," his dad said, as he pointed the spatula at an upper cupboard.

David poured himself a cup of coffee and asked, "Is there bread?"

"Yes, in the right cupboard, I will have a couple slices too."

David opened the cupboard and took out the bread and the butter. He put four slices of bread in the toaster and searched for plates.

"Plates are one cupboard over," his dad said.

"Okay."

He opened the cupboard and saw plates and two pistols. He removed two plates from the cupboard and the two guns.

"Will we be needing these tonight?" he asked, as he put them on the countertop.

"Hopefully not, they stay here. We will have some guns with us if we need them. Eggs are ready, butter the toast and go out to the shop. We can eat in the office as we review the plans for tonight's job," James said.

"Okay. Dad, I am excited but nervous about tonight. Is that normal?" David said.

"Yes, if you don't have those types of feelings, then you are in trouble. A little bit of nervousness is a good thing."

James took the pan of eggs and bacon, and with his coffee, headed to Kenton's office.

David buttered the toast, picked up the plates, and his coffee, and followed James.

"Morning sunshine, sleep well?" Kenton said.

"Yes, I did," said David.

"Okay, come in, sit down and get some bacon before your dad eats it all. As you eat, I will review the plans for tonight's job," Kenton said.

James and David ate their breakfast while they reviewed the nights activities.

• • •

David followed James around the shop while they prepared for the evenings activities. His grandfather told him, the next job he will be responsible for certain aspects of the plans and preparation, but this time he was to listen, watch and learn. Scott spent the early morning at the house and reported only two men were in the house. Brian had taken over the watch to allow Scott to return to the shop.

Doris called the office to let Kenton know she could be picked up. When he stopped by earlier, she had slept in and still needed to 'put her face on.' Kenton asked David to take the van, fill it up with gas, then pick up Doris. A couple jobs David was happy to do. He had been stuck in the shop since they arrived yesterday and wanted outside for some fresh air.

This was the first time he drove on the left side of the road, not a big deal, except for when he turned right. He forgot to go over to the left side of the road. After a couple honks and a few rude gestures, from the natives, David got the hang of it. He fueled the van, picked up Doris and was back to the shop before an hour was up.

David watched Scott and his dad work, when things were quiet, he reviewed the hand signals his grandfather used in the morning meeting. David studied the map and the route. He reviewed the floor plans of the house and the pictures of the men they were to take, alive. David's father drilled into him from a young age the importance of attention to details, the small details, 'those details are what allow you to come home safe' he would say. The way the front garden was designed, the window on the second floor that opened to the roof, the way the stairs turn five steps before they end on the second floor. David wanted to show he was prepared and ready for this assignment. He reviewed his position in the house if the men were on the first floor and where he was to move to if the men or a man happened to be on the second floor. He mentally walked himself through the building and out to the van. David felt he was ready for this mission but knew it could all change when he met up with his dad and Scott later.

At 4 p.m., as planned, Kenton closed the shop, lowered the metal doors over the front windows and locked the front entrance. The four team members met back in the office. They reviewed the plans one last time. David answered the questions James and Kenton had for him, he responded completely and professionally to each question. When the meeting ended, James pulled David to the side of the office.

"Okay, Son, you did well today helping prepare for tonight. I am so proud of you right now. We all are. Stay with Granda and listen to him. Remember to keep your eyes and ears open and prepare for anything," James instructed. "We will all try to watch you, but we have our own assignments and our own asses to take care of."

"Yes, Dad, I will, I am still nervous, but I am sure that will pass," David said with confidence.

"Yes, it will Son, once the mission begins and you stop thinking and let your instincts take over it will pass in a hurry."

The two of them hugged and walked back to Scott and Kenton.

"You alright David?" asked Scott.

"I think—yes. Yes, I am," David replied confidently.

"You will be okay, Dad doesn't train fools," Scott said.

The four men joined hands and Kenton prayed for their safety and resourcefulness. Once the prayer ended, the crew hugged and went to their assigned jobs.

"Don't forget to empty the car out, Gary will pick it up once we leave and recycle it for us," said Kenton.

Scott and James left to watch the house. David and Kenton reviewed the plans one last time to ensure David had no more questions.

"So why are these guys wanted alive and not just killed on the spot? Who are they?" asked David.

"Their names are Martin and Allen," Kenton said. "Each job we do comes with a detailed package of the person, people or situation that needs our attention. Depending on who you are working for will reveal how detailed your information is. As you get used to your client's packages, you can scan it and pull out what you need for the job. We don't need a lot of details, but like I said, depending on who is preparing the package will determine how much info you get. The American government and agencies are usually the best for need-to-know info. Their reports are clean, concise and to the point. The Brits give too many details, and most other countries are somewhere in between. The Mob is the worst. With them, with any job, honestly, if you don't feel you have all the information, you do not do the job. Simple as that. Ask once, then walk away. If they want you bad enough, they will come back with the information you need and likely a little more money. Most times the backgrounds don't matter. We go in, take, or eliminate the target, and get out. Usually, it is that simple. But even with the information, always listen to your gut and do your own preliminary investigation. The details you pull from the report are important. You want to know if the targets have a stash of weapons or are trained in hand-to-hand combat. Notes like that are important but if you were to know this guy killed a family and their dog or was selling information, would that help you in your mission?" Kenton said.

David thought for a moment, "No, I guess it wouldn't, would it? Knowing their threat level would. I see what you are saying, we don't care why they need to be put away or delivered to whoever hired us, just that we are being paid for a job. We are expected to do it quietly, efficiently and completely."

"Aye, so we don't need to know that Martin might have four kids and a mortgage, we just need to know he carries a Glock on his left hip and has a boxing background. That takes any emotion out of the job and just keeps the facts at the front of your mind," explained Kenton.

"Okay, I see how that can help when facing a person, it takes the human part out of the equation, he is more like a hunted animal," David said.

"Alright we have some time before we go, I need to make some calls."

"Okay, I will go change, relax and listen to some music," David said.

He headed back to his room for the last hour. Once changed into the black clothes that were already in his wardrobe, he lay on his bed listening to the Van Halen album *1984*. The music helped with the nerves he had. It also pumped him up for the mission. He thought, *'would I have to kill someone tonight? What if I cause something to happen that effects the job or worse causes one of my family to be injured or killed?'*

He cleared his mind of those negative thoughts and thought of his role and how he was here to help them. His dad taught him a long time ago, 'You cannot worry about 'what if,' prepare for what is known, react to what your eyes see, and what your ears hear.'

• • •

The time arrived for Kenton and David to head out and meet with the other two. Kenton came and knocked on David's door, David had relaxed and drifted off to sleep. Kenton smiled and thought, *'anyone who could catch a nap just before a mission like this was born for this lifestyle.'*

David woke up and went to the bathroom to splash some water on his face.

"Are you ready for this," Kenton asked.

"Ready and willing," replied David

The two of them headed to the van.

• • •

The van sped past James' location and turned on the next street, where Scott watched the back of the house. Both men, saw the van and headed to the meeting point. The van turned down Connaught Park one last time and pulled in front of the house that had blown up the night before. Smoke rose from the ruins, the police had wrapped caution tape around light poles and the burnt-out hedges, but, as planned, there were no police in sight. Scott and James jumped into the back of the van and reported what they had observed while on watch.

"The two targets are in the house; Martin is upstairs in bedroom two and Allen is on the main floor, in the kitchen cooking. There has been no one in or out while we were watching," Scott reported.

"Okay, that makes it easier for us then. As discussed, you two take Allen in the kitchen, I will take Martin on the second floor. David, you will take watch in the front hallway, just like it was all planned, do not leave your post," instructed Kenton.

They put on their black overcoats and pulled down their balaclavas. David and Kenton left the van and walked to the front of the house.

Stealthy actions to remove the targets would be the plan. Kenton was never a fan of guns. He felt they were impersonal and noisy. On most of his missions' knives were the weapons of choice, quiet, up close, and personal. With a knife, you knew if the target was dead and not just wounded. With the police in the area, they would carry guns, but only use them if it was completely necessary. David checked his hip to confirm the knife his granda lent him hung on his right hip. The knife David wore had been custom made in Baghdad, by one of the world's top knife builders. Kenton purchased it when he was in the SAS on a special assignment.

James and Scott were at the back door. Kenton and David walked up the front path. James slowly opened the back door into the mud room. The two men waited in the back hallway for Kenton and David to enter the front door.

The house was quiet except for a rerun of 'On the Buses' on the TV in the living room. Allen moved from the kitchen to the living room and sat on a chair with a plate of mashed potatoes, baked beans, and smoked ham. James could see him through the doorway.

Kenton worked the lock at the front door as David kept an eye on the road for any movement. Finally, Kenton got the latch to release and slowly opened the wooden front door. Kenton knew the noise these old doors made as they opened. He only opened it enough for them to fit through. Through the narrow opening, David and Kenton stood in the front hallway. Kenton gave the hand signal to James to show they were in, all clear, and ready to move to the next step in the plan.

Kenton ascended the stairs with cat like quietness.

James slowly moved to the entrance of the living room; Scott waited at the back hallway door. David stood at his post by the front door, his heart raced as all his senses, even taste, were on extremely high sensitivity. David believed he could taste the beans and ham Allen shoveled into his mouth.

James moved in on his target. He stepped into the living room behind Allen who continued to ram food into his mouth, like he was in a race. Allen did not hear James as he moved closer to him. James swiftly stepped in front of the chair.

"What the Fu..." Allen said, as he recognized there was a stranger in his living room. James knocked the plate off his lap and pulled him to the ground. Allen chewed his last piece of ham as he fell. Allen fought back but was on his oversized belly faced down, winded, he choked on the ham. He had one of James' arms wrapped around his throat, preventing him from swallowing, while the other hand covered his mouth and nose. Allen kicked and yelled but was losing consciousness quickly. He thrust his body one last time to knock James off, but to no avail. James squeezed a little tighter, the flow of blood stopped to Allen's brain. Allen saw some bright lights and went unconscious.

James rolled off and took in a deep breath of his own. It was a stretch to get his arm around Allen's neck and the chokehold had caused him to spit up some baked bean juice which landed on James' hands and arm. James stuck a rag into Allen's mouth, hesitated, then pulled it out. With all the food that went in, James wanted to be sure there wasn't any left that Allen could choke on.

Once he had him gagged, he tied Allen's hands and forearms together behind his back. That would be all James could do right now until they walked him to the van. No one would volunteer to carry this oversized slob.

Kenton had made it to the top of the stairs when the first door on his right, the bathroom, opened. The man who stepped out was not Martin, the man they came to take. No one reported to Kenton this stranger was in the house. *'How did Scott and James miss this, they are very good at surveillance? This was one of their biggest fuck ups,'* Kenton thought as the man stepped towards him.

Kenton, in his early sixties, still had quick reflexes. He was able to sidestep the unexpected guest who lunged at him. Kenton pivoted and forcefully directed the stranger down the stairs. The unaccounted-for man fell forward and clumsily rolled down the stairs. He bounced and banged against the walls until he landed by David's feet.

David, shocked by the fact someone just threw a man down the stairs, noticed right away this man was not in the photos he had seen. He jumped back, in shock. This gave the man an opportunity to gather his thoughts and get to his feet.

Being outweighed by at least fifty pounds, David tackled the stranger onto his back. The man banged his head on the carpeted floor and let out a grunt. David followed the man to the floor, he landed on the confused stranger's chest. David smashed the stranger's nose with his forearm. David heard his opponent's nose break. The muscular man bucked his hips, David was thrown against the hallway wall. The man now straddled David's stomach and pulled a knife from his belt's sheath.

Scott saw the stranger on top of David and moved towards the fight on the floor.

David was on his back, he looked up at his assailant. The stranger paused with a look of confusion on his face and leaned in to get a closer look at David, as if confused by the age of the young eyes that looked back at him through the balaclava. The moment of hesitation was all David needed; David's arms were not pinned below his rival. He pulled his own knife out of its scabbard. As the man's head came closer, David reached up, grabbed a handful of hair and with his right hand injected the knife through the side of his combatant's neck. David pulled the knife towards himself; the motion sliced the neck wide open. He felt warm blood cover his eyes and nose as it immediately soaked through his balaclava. The body dropped onto David as he slid the knife out of the man's throat and drove it in a second time. This stab went in deep just below and to the back of the left ear. The man took a couple gasps of air and lay motionless on top of David, blood ran out of the two puncture wounds, David's coat and shirt were soaked. David pulled the knife out just as Scott arrived to help.

Scott, saw all the blood, pooling on the floor, and thought it was David's. He sprung at the stranger's body and drove it off David with such force the limp body, smashed into the wall on the other side of the hallway.

James heard the bang and came to the hallway.

David, wet with blood smiled at Scott who knelt in front of him. David pulled the balaclava off before Scott stopped him.

"Leave it on Junior unless you are hurt. What the fuck happened here?" Scott whispered.

"It's okay, this man fell down the stairs and attacked me," said David, still winded from the fight. "He isn't the one we want, so I had to kill him before he killed me."

"Where is the Boss," asked James.

"Still upstairs," said David.

"You need to keep your face covered, we are taking prisoners and you don't want them to be able to identify you. Remember, that is why we are in Canada!" said James.

• • •

Kenton heard the noise downstairs but continued with the mission. He had his job to do, and they had theirs. Kenton stood against the wall in the hallway and waited for any response to the noise from the lad he rolled down the stairs. There did not seem to be any. He did not see any movement from the shadows under bedroom two's door either. Kenton approached the door and slowly opened it. Martin read a magazine while he sat on a bed. He did not even notice the door open. By the time he noticed the door, Kenton was in the room. Kenton hit Martin in the chest with his shoulder, it knocked him back onto the bed. Martin had no time to respond. Kenton, in close on Martin, swung his elbow at Martin's jaw and connected perfectly. Kenton heard the jawbone break as Martin blacked out. He grabbed the body by the ankles and dragged it to the ground. He rolled Martin over, pulled out a handkerchief, and stuffed it in Martin's mouth. Kenton could feel the broken jaw move as he forced the handkerchief in. He tied the gag on Martin's face, then grabbed his arms and tied them behind his back. Martin still unconscious weighed more than Kenton expected as he rolled him on his back.

Kenton sat back and leaned against the bed. This guy was bigger than he expected and was glad he had the element of surprise. Kenton took a minute to catch his breath, he thought, '*I am not getting any younger.*' Always alert of his surroundings, Kenton knew the guys downstairs had handled the third man and must have things under control.

Martin came out of his forced nap. He woke to tied hands and the excruciating pain of his broken jaw, displaced due to the gag. He struggled as he realized his hands were tied. The look in his eyes was that of fear and pain.

"Okay are you ready to get up? We are going for a ride," said Kenton.

Martin's eyes opened wide, Kenton knew that look, the look a captive gave when they knew death was near but not without some form of pain to give up secrets that were held deep inside.

"If it means anything to you, I won't kill you if you behave," Kenton said.

Martin responded, but his broken jaw and stuffed mouth made it impossible for Kenton to understand him.

"Not sure what you are saying, and at this point I do not need to know," Kenton replied.

Kenton stood up and stepped over Martin's head, he bent down and grabbed his shoulder, "You can stand and cooperate, or I can knock you out again and drag you around like a lion does to its prey when returning from the hunt, either way will work for me," said Kenton.

The man motioned to stand up. Kenton helped him up and directed him to the door.

"Okay we are going downstairs to my team. I am not sure what we will see down there, but one wrong move and you go back to sleep. Understand?" said Kenton.

David heard the two men come down the stairs. He did not want to disappoint his grandfather, so he jumped up and went back to the door where Kenton instructed him to wait earlier.

Scott headed up the stairs to ensure Kenton was okay. He took two steps up and saw a man or a prisoner headed towards him. He smiled at Kenton, who was behind Martin.

"See, here is my team to help. Did everything go to plan down here," Kenton asked.

"Aye, as we planned, except for the intruder who came rolling down the stairs, Junior dealt with him," Scott said, careful not to use any real names and not call him dad.

"Junior dealt with him? Is Junior okay?" asked Kenton, as he exited the stairway.

"I am fine, sir," replied David, from his front door post.

James went back to the living room to collect Allen. He brought him to the kitchen. Scott stepped over the body in the hallway and headed to the kitchen.

David waited for Kenton to pass before he followed them.

Martin saw the body on the floor. He dropped to his knees beside the body and cried. Turning to Kenton he couldn't speak but his eyes were asking, 'Why, why did you kill him'.

David felt no sympathy for the man he killed. He did wonder if the men were brothers or best friends.

'Did he have to kill him,' David thought. A resounding 'YES' entered his head, 'the man was going to kill you,' the voice in his head yelled at him.

"Did you do this," Kenton sternly asked David.

"Yes sir," David said.

Kenton looked at David, "Okay, it wasn't part of the plan so you can explain it to me later."

"Up on your feet, before you join him," Kenton instructed Martin, as he pulled him up by his hair.

Martin, followed by Kenton, then David, stepped over the body and walked into the kitchen. The two prisoners looked at each other. The concern left Allen's face when he saw Martin. Allen knew the third man; Martin's brother was dead. He cried too. Scott, James, and Kenton looked at each other quizzically. They had never seen men cry like this, at least not men supposedly hardened by the troubles in Northern Ireland. But the loss of all their friends yesterday in the explosion and now this last one would overwhelm anyone.

"Is everyone alright?" asked Kenton.

"Aye, we are, just as we planned it," James said with a smile.

"Right," said Kenton, he pointed to Scott. "You and Junior bring the van up to the front door. Sorry lads, you will have to walk over your mate one more time to leave this place," Kenton said.

Scott and David headed out the back door while Kenton and James grabbed their men. There was a small struggle from Martin, but a tap on his jaw from Kenton put an end to that rebellion. The men walked toward their dead friend. The blood had pooled around the head and the knife holes faced up at the men as they stepped over him.

"Junior did this?" Kenton asked again as he pushed his man over the body.

"Aye, he did while the guy was on top of him from what I was told," said James, as he followed Kenton to the door with his prisoner.

"Dead on," said Kenton.

"Aye," James said with a smile on his face. "Not too bad at all."

•   •   •

The four men stood in silence in the front hallway, they waited for the van to pull up to the front walkway. Kenton saw the van crawl up the street without lights on. He pushed Martin out onto the front stoop and walked him up the front walkway to the road. James followed behind, he paused to close the front door. They led the men to the back of the van where David opened the doors from inside. Martin resisted getting into the van. David helped him up by grabbing a handful of hair and dragged him to his seat. James threw his man into the van, both Kenton and James climbed in the back door of the van and sat across from their prisoners.

Scott drove away as James tied up the men's legs and looked at Martin's broken jaw.

"How is your hand," said James to his dad.

"Too close, so I swung with my elbow," he lifted his arm up to show James. The skin was turning purple, black and red.

James laughed and said, "You are not a spring chicken anymore, you know."

Scott drove the van for an hour and a half, indirectly, to the agreed meeting point. A mile out from the location at the intersection of Knockbracken Road and Ballymaconaghy Road, Scott flashed the headlights. The flashes signaled to the scout crew the prisoners were in the van. A mile ahead, the recovery crew were told by radio the delivery was almost at the drop point. Scott pulled into a small laneway and killed the engine. There was a rap on the back door of the van.

"All clear," yelled Kenton from inside.

The back door opened to reveal six British soldiers, in black wool sweaters, balaclavas and camouflage pants. They had L1A1 rifles pointed into the van.

"Put those toys away," Kenton said. "They are packaged up and ready to travel."

"Good to see you again," stated a voice from behind the soldiers and their lights.

Kenton stepped out of the van with James. Scott and David met everyone at the back doors.

"Here they are, the one on the right has a shattered jaw, not sure he will say much for the next couple weeks," said James.

"Thank you," the voice in the background replied, "Well men don't just stand there get them out of the van and into our truck."

Two soldiers jumped into the van and grabbed the men by the ropes that tied their ankles and dragged them to the back door. Outside you could hear the thud of the prisoner's heads as they hit the metal floor. Outside the van they brought the prisoners to their feet and shuffled them away into the darkness.

A figure stepped out of the shadows of the trees and walked to the four men standing by the van.

"You gentlemen are early. I guess things went very well with this extraction," said the senior officer as he approached them. He was an old colleague of Kenton's who stayed in the army and worked with intelligence. As he got closer, David could see he had a canvas bag.

"David, you can finally take your blood-soaked mask off," said James. "There are rags in the van."

"Good. The balaclava was starting to dry to my face and my shirt is getting crusty."

David climbed in the van and found some rags, he wiped off some of the dried blood.

"Lads here's your payment for the delivery tonight, another successful job, for Her Majesty. Thank you for this, the information we can get from these two should help find some other men in the future and save a few lives. Then when the U.S. have their chat, well, they just are not as sophisticated about these chats as we are," said the officer as he handed Kenton the bag.

"One little problem, there was a third person in the house, we ended up terminating him. We can go clean that up and dispose of the body if needed," Kenton offered.

"No, no leave him. When the police find him, they might see it as a fight over who was responsible for the explosion and it could help with investigating these two disappearing," said the Officer. "I will let the police know, so they can send the right investigator."

"Aye, we will be off then," Kenton said.

"One last thing, who is this?" The officer asked, nodding towards David. "I know you three, but... No, no, no, this isn't wee David, is it? No, it can't be."

"Yes sir, I am David, have we met before?" David asked.

"Yes, when you were this high," he held his hand down around his knees, "you were four-ish. Well, you have grown into a fine young lad. The Army could use someone like you when you hit eighteen" he stated. "But the pay is shit and it won't be near as much fun as working with these lads."

"Always recruiting," laughed James. "The army can use him but not as an enlisted man. There is no freedom in a uniform. This is where you make the money."

They all laughed as the Officer shook David's hand.

"You have a good point. Well, I better let you men go. I will be in touch soon, Kenton. Another job for The Queen." he said and winked.

"Back of the van this time David, the old guys get the front," said James.

Kenton cranked up the radio, and the men headed back to the shop. One rule Kenton had, after a job, no one talked about the job on the way home. You listened to music and reflected on the job. The debrief would happen at the shop.

CHAPTER TWELVE

The crew returned to the shop early in the morning. The first thing Kenton did was put the kettle on for a cup of tea. David covered in dried blood from his first kill asked if he could have some time to shower. Kenton told him to make it quick so they could review the job. When the kettle boiled, Kenton brought a pot of tea into the office. James and Scott sat the conference table.

"Before David comes back from the shower, what the hell happened there tonight? How did you two not know there was a third guy in the house? Never mind, we will discuss that when David returns as a lesson for him. Who killed the third guy, was it our wee David," Kenton said.

"Dad, I didn't see anything; I was in the living room tying up Allen. I heard the commotion and by the time I got there it was too late to help David," said James.

"I was at the back door when I heard the guy thump and bang down the stairs. I could see parts of the fight as I ran to help David. The guy landed at David's feet. When I got there, David, the floor and the walls were covered with blood. I panicked, thinking it was David's blood. I dove at the body to knock him off David. As it rolled off, David sat up smiling, with his knife in his hand. I have never been so frightened. At that point James came around the corner. From what I saw, I was very impressed with how David handled the situation and took down the target. It will be interesting to see what he says about it," Scott said, while he poured himself a tea. "Honestly, I thought David was dead. It has been a long time since I have felt so many emotions in such little time."

"This was my fault, I sent him down the stairs without thinking of the consequences. Thankfully David was okay. He seemed to be okay about killing someone, let's just feel him out, see how he is about all this. James you will need to watch him when you get back to Canada as well. Sometimes, something this traumatic could take a few weeks or months to show any issues. We need to be careful about how we act when he comes back into the office. No celebrating or real concern until we see how he is doing," Kenton explained. He had dealt with many soldiers and their different emotions after their first kill.

"Aye, the emotional issues will be with Elizabeth, I think. We should maybe remind him, we only speak of these things around here," said James.

Kenton poured his tea. In his desk he had some whiskey, he used it to top up his tea. They sat silently, drank their spiked tea, and waited for David to come back from his shower.

• • •

David sat on his bed, he replayed the evening in his mind, *'I killed someone,'* he thought, *'I actually did it. What do they think of me out there? It came so naturally. Too naturally. Was that my training or am I crazy?'*

He took off his clothes and headed to the bathroom to shower. His mind raced with confusion and emotion. *'How do I go to school and act like I care about hair styles or what my next test mark will be? Life just got real.'*

"Oh, fuck me," he said out loud to no one. "MOM!"

He climbed into the hot shower and cried. *'What will mom think of me?'* he thought. *'What have I done? That man might have a family and I just killed him.'*

Once he cleaned up and calmed himself, he got out of the shower and headed back to his room and sat back on the bed. *'It did feel pretty good and if I didn't kill him, I would be lying on the floor, dead. I won the battle. That is the actual truth: either he goes home to his family and I am dead or...I won.'* he thought.

David headed back into the shop area. He was nervous, and worried about the debrief. He wasn't sure if he was in trouble for his actions or if he would be praised.

"There he is," said Kenton as David entered the office.

"Sit, sit here mate," said Scott. "We poured you a tea do you want anything else before we begin? Usually when we start the debrief, we don't stop until we complete the walkthrough of the job."

"I would love a bottle of Coke," said David.

The three sat around the table, they waited for David to take his seat. "Okay, I am ready, so how does this go?"

"We should start with you David, tell us how you feel the night went, your emotions and observations on the evening. This is where we review the operation and how we feel about it. We talk it out here so we can walk out the door and continue with society. It is an old military skill we used when doing special missions. There would be times guys would sit and have a wee cry or laugh through the whole debriefing. It is whatever you feel inside at the time, just don't keep it inside. There is no other place on this planet you can talk so freely," explained Kenton.

"Okay," said David. "So, I just talk about what I saw and felt?"

"Aye, just review the job. This will help identify any problems we can correct, and it helps us stay grounded," said James.

"This was one hell of a night. Wow. What I have seen and done in the last...," he looked at his watch surprised. "The last nine hours? Holy time flies. The mission began as we had planned, I was very nervous. I was feeling a lot of pressure on myself wanting to impress you guys and not just screw up or get one of you hurt. I wanted you guys to be proud of me when we finished." He paused, he looked for a response, and drank his pop.

"We entered the building as planned, and I focused on my location and everything going on around me. Oh, before we entered, I felt my hip to make sure I didn't forget the knife you gave me Granda. I probably should have done that before we got out of the van. I surveyed the hallway and for a couple seconds felt like I was blacking out. I pushed through the foggy feeling and felt a bit better. When you left to go upstairs, I felt alone, but I could just see Scott in the back hallway. Dad had moved to the living room to take care of Allen. I told myself the plan was working out well but to stay alert, 'always be ready for the unexpected' you would say, Dad. Then I heard the voices from upstairs and a loud bang as this big guy came rolling down the stairs. I thought it was you at first, then I realized it was not you or either of the men we were there to collect. At that point I was in a bit of shock and stepped back. The guy stood up slowly, and honestly it becomes a blur. I tackled him and he ended up on top of me. He stared into my eyes, maybe my age confused him, or he thought he recognized me, but something caused him to hesitate for a second. God or my guardian angel, I don't know. That gave me a chance to reach for my knife and slice at his throat. The blood spilled over my face, in my mouth and eyes. I then pulled out the knife and jammed it into his ear, or somewhere there, I couldn't see exactly as his blood was in my eyes. I could taste, smell and feel the warmth of his coppery blood over my face, running around my neck and soaking into my balaclava and the upper part of my shirt."

"That was when I arrived and pushed him off you, I saw the blood and panicked thinking it was yours, David. When I rolled him off, you looked calm and relaxed," said Scott, with a smile.

"My heart was racing, but I felt like, I don't know, I had total control of the situation like time slowed down for me. I knew he would kill me; I didn't hesitate, I just did what Dad had me do to the animals we hunted. I sat up as Dad came in the hallway, again with the look of fear in his eyes, worried about me covered in blood, I guess. I heard the gurgle from the guy's throat when Scott knocked him off, his dying breath, I guess. Then I heard you coming down the stairs Granda, so I got back to my post like you instructed as we entered the house. You too had a crazy look when you saw me covered in blood. I felt relief to see we were all okay and the mission was a success. I really thought I had messed up the whole operation. My only concern was that I killed him, and you would be mad, real mad. I knew he wasn't Martin or Allen, or else I wouldn't have cut his throat. I felt bad when Martin cried beside him. But even that emotion passed as I saw we were all okay."

"No, no, no. Whatever the mission is, you always take care of yourself first. If it is a recover and delivery and it turns bad, then you do what you need to do to get home. Plain and simple. The ultimate goal, is the team always comes home together, safe and with no injures," said Kenton.

"Okay, Granda, understood," David said.

"So, once we were in the van, how did you feel?" said James.

"Fine, I was okay at that point, I felt the mission was a success and I wanted a signal I had done the right thing. I hoped you guys understood I only killed him because I knew he wasn't one of the two we were looking for. I wanted to be reassured that I didn't fuck up the mission," David said. He still looked for acknowledgement for his actions.

"Okay, so we all agree, you did nothing wrong tonight. Aye, we are all pretty impressed with how you handled yourself and the situation. In fact, very impressed," said Kenton.

David could feel the tension in the room lift.

"So, we are telling you, what you did was fine tonight, no one is judging your decision. But we all need to know how you are doing. It was your first human kill. How are you? Are you alright inside? We need you to talk about your emotions and what is going on in your head," James said.

"Okay, I am confused, honestly. I sat on my bed and had a flood of questions and emotions." David paused and took a deep breath. "I cried in the shower, felt bad and good about it, if that makes sense," David said, embarrassed. "I feel like I should feel bad about killing him, but I don't. Dad, what is mom going to think of me now? Should I feel bad about it? How do I go back to school in a couple days and act like I did before we came here? This is where I am struggling Dad. What about mom? Mom won't love me anymore. She would tell me if I got involved in this stuff, she wouldn't love me anymore and I would not be her boy anymore. So do we have to tell her?"

"David, David, breath, son, breath. These are all normal emotions. Yes, I guess there should be some remorse for what you did, but no, you shouldn't feel any. We have all done it, it is hard to accept sometimes but you have to take the personal side away, it is just another animal, only we don't eat the meat," Kenton said, with a chuckle.

"This is your first of many kills," said James.

"You said, many kills, Dad. Does that mean you will have me back? I can become part of the team? I didn't screw up tonight in your eyes? To be honest, the job, as a whole, was amazing. There was a high I had that whole time that was," he sat back in his chair, "the craziest feeling I have ever felt. So please, if you will have me on this team, I am all in, whatever you need going forward. I want to travel as much as Dad does."

"Aye, you did your job. You did your job very well son, we wish it didn't have to happen like that, but we are very happy with the results. We will bring you back for more work," Kenton said. He stood up and walked to David and gave him a big hug. "The only thing I need from you is to talk to your dad when you get back to Canada about any questions, dreams, emotions that come from what you did tonight. We have a rule here and to stay sane you need to abide by it, it needs to be your creed. We don't kill because of emotion, we don't kill for fun, we don't kill for revenge, we kill for others who pay and pay well. No free rides. You need to kill for a purpose, I don't want to see you tagged as a serial killer in the news, no money, no blood, understand? It is like any other job. You don't work for free."

"Okay, cool Granda, I understand. So, one last question, what about my ma? Does she need to know?" asked David.

"What did I tell you before we left to come here David, we don't talk to anyone except us four about what happens here. Mom won't ask, and if she does, say you hung out here with Nannie and Aunt Sarah while I did some work with Uncle Scott. She won't ask for any details, trust me she doesn't want to know, even though, she knows," said James. He got up and hugged David. "This is where you need to learn about your two lives, this new one and the normal one, the one we live outside of the business. It won't be easy, but you will adapt."

"Okay, let's review the night," said Kenton.

The crew reviewed the job together as a team. They broke down each step to see where they could improve the plan or their personal skills. James took the blame for the third person in the house, even though no one pointed a finger. David received a lot of praise for his work with the third man.

There was only one thing left to discuss. Kenton spilled the money from the duffel bag.

"We received twenty-five-thousand pounds for this job. That's five each and a few quid to put into our pensions. Do we cut the wee one in, too?" asked Kenton.

"Well, he did muck about and watch the front door for us," said Scott. "I could give up a couple quid to him."

"Aye, I will too, at least his weekly allowance for the next couple weeks," James said. "After all, I had to get him an ID and ticket to come here, that wasn't cheap."

"Well, he made me some tea while you guys were out yesterday and it has been good to see him, so he can have a cut of mine too," Kenton said, as he smiled at David.

David was confused by the comments about the money. Would he really get paid for the job, he would do it for free just to spend time with his family.

"If I could get enough for a 99 poke before we go home, I would be happy."

They all laughed at David's comment, "Son, you will be able to buy the factory in a year if you keep up the work you did tonight," said Kenton.

"David that money on the table is yours, we already took our cut. We all get equal pay for our work," said Scott. "But you are buying supper tomorrow night before you head home. Take it, you deserve it for what you did, we are all very proud of you. Enjoy it, that is with expenses taken out too, there is good money in this line of work, David. Just don't get greedy."

"Or cocky," Kenton said.

The men sat at the table for a while longer and when the sun cracked over the roof of the factory across the street, they all headed to bed for a deserved rest. David was still pumped about being accepted into the family business; he could still see the face of the man he had killed, but that would pass as many faces would imprint on his memory in his future.

•   •   •

David and James arrived home a couple days later. David returned to school the next day. His note for the homeroom teacher explained his absents was due to an ear infection. Phil was still off school on a business trip of his own with John.

David sat in his classes and stared into space. He thought about how his friends and teachers did not have a clue about how the real world worked, especially his new world.

He sat with some acquaintances at lunch but couldn't care less about Jenn's new jeans or the bush party at the pits on the weekend. David was past that. He wanted to scream at the top of his lungs for everyone to hear, *'This shit doesn't matter! I killed someone halfway around the world the other day while you were teasing your hair and listening to Corey Hart. I FUCKING KILLED SOMEONE! And all you worry about is getting drunk on the weekend! I can't drink. I need to be ready for my granda's phone call saying come and work for me, while all of you wait for Duran Duran's next video to be released! FUCK ME WHAT HAVE I DONE!'*

But David just sat there quietly in the group as his mind turned like a giant Ferris Wheel, it stopped to release a new thought or image every few seconds.

'They don't know what the real world is about. If they did, they wouldn't be complaining about their curfew or their little brother using their toothbrush,' he thought.

•   •   •

At home, his mom was very distant with him. Amy thought David and James had been camping and did not see a difference, but Elizabeth knew, she knew what her boy had done. He would not go there for a visit. He worked for Satan himself, her father-in-law. She kept her distance from David. Her conversations were simple and short. He would try to talk to his mom, even attempted to get a hug, but she turned away from him.

The more David stepped back into his life in Canada, the more he felt out of place. The Friday night after arriving home his mom made him go to youth group at church. She told him he had to go to keep his Christian friends and get right with Jesus for any sins he might have committed back home.

He did not want to attend, especially without Phil. He even had his dad step in, but it did not work. He was going. He was stuck at youth group with all the holier than holy teens as they judged each other. David played it cool during the games part of the evening. The devotional that night was about, 'loving each other.' David couldn't control his emotions and had a panic attack during the video. He ran out of the room, he thought about the sins he had committed in the last week. No one took notice of his behavior. He splashed cold water over his face, controlled his breathing and heart rate and returned calmly to the group, to finish out the night.

James picked him and a couple friends up at the church, it was his turn to do the drop off of kids. Once he delivered all the kids home safely to their 'best Christian parents' David opened up to James.

"Dad, we can't go right home, we need to talk," said David. "I am freaking out, I just had a melt down at youth group, like huge. The devotional was about loving one another, even your enemies. Dad, am I broken, or have I sinned so bad God is making me go crazy?"

James laughed out loud. Then David broke down and cried. James pulled into a parking lot by the bowling alley.

"Whoa, whoa, David, sorry I didn't think it was this bad it has only been a few days," said James. "No, God is not punishing you, why did you say that? What is happening, what did we tell you back home? Don't hide your feelings, don't let them build up, talk to me."

"I know, but I thought I could handle it; I didn't want you to think I was a wuss. But I can't handle school, home, or church. My friends bother me with their petty worries, mom hates me, and I am constantly reminded at church that we are bad people. If they only knew we were fighting for their religion, in a way. I can't handle this, I felt comfortable back home, I never settled living here in Canada. Like mom, I always wanted to go back home and be with our family instead of isolated here. But now I am really homesick. These people don't understand me, and I don't understand them anymore. How do I forget I killed someone," said David. "This sliding between two worlds is a lot harder than you guys made it sound."

"I know David, the easiest thing to do is make peace with yourself, be happy in here," James said as he tapped David in the chest. "Whether it is you and your secrets, the girl in class who is anorexic, the boy at church who is gay. You all need to find your own peace inside. With that peace, the world doesn't matter. You can live each day to the fullest whether we are working with Granda or you are in the library trying to get a date with the cute girl from math class. If inside, you are at peace, nothing else matters. So, find that peace, David. For me it is playing soccer twice a week and gardening. For you it could be riding your bike, reading or tennis. My only rule is you will not, cannot, find peace in drinking or drugs. I will do you in myself if I see it. You need to be alert, at all times. Plus, with that stuff in your system you could talk too much or react the wrong way to someone and easily kill them or be killed. Do you understand? Never! We had to kill a cousin who worked with Granda years ago because he got drunk one night and started talking. Granda killed him right in the shop the next day. No questions, no excuses. He just came in for a meeting and was a missing person for three weeks."

"Okay. I was saving the money I made," said David. "Maybe I can do something with it."

"Son, you don't need to save it. Spend it, there will be plenty more, believe me. I keep some but most we splurge on holidays, as you know."

"What if I take some money and upgrade my bike, and pound out my feelings on the bike," said David. "There really isn't anything better than a few hours out in the country riding."

"That sounds like a plan to me son. You don't have to worry about impressing anyone, just be happy. Live for you."

"Okay, so what is up with mom, does she hate me now? Because that is the way it is coming across to me."

"No, she loves you. She has always had a hard time with all of this. She isn't happy in Canada but won't leave us or Amy. She will come around, just give her time. With her, just be her son, let her take care of you, that is all she really wants. Don't talk about back home, don't give her attitude, just be you, she will come around."

"And church?"

"Well, that one is tougher. Those people think their shit doesn't smell, especially that church. I think that is why your mom attends that one. She knows I can't stand the people. They all have their own secrets, but put on a big show at church. Just remember the God in the old testament is the same one in the new testament, so they teach. The one in the old testament would have the Israelites kill every living person and creature in a city. The new testament Jesus, even though they love to say he taught peace, said, 'I didn't come to this world to bring peace but with a sword.' So those at the church will always be judgmental and have their little groups, don't even think about it. Why do you think I don't attend? They look down on me because I don't attend a lot and I don't give much money. If you want to learn about money laundering and corrupt methods to run a business, study the churches business plans. They are not the oldest and richest business, in the world, by chance. I can talk to mom and get you out of some of the extra church activities."

"Okay Dad, I feel better now. It still won't be easy, but I will take that advice. I was still trying to do things to make everyone else happy. I just need to take care of myself or talk to you about any concerns. One more question, what about Phil? Will he be okay with me?"

"Phil will be fine; he is learning a lot on his trip too. Don't worry about that. You two will be even closer when he returns. Since we are here, do you want to go bowl a couple games? We can call mom and Amy to come join us, if they are still awake."

"Yea okay, that would be fun."

James dropped a quarter in the pay phone and thirty minutes later the family were together. They bowled a few games, as a family, happy together. David believed he knew how he could find the inner happiness his dad spoke of. It started with having his family, in Canada together, without the fights and hurt feelings.

David went and ordered a new racing bike from the new bike store downtown. He remembered as a kid how much fun it was to bike around the streets and now, he could replace his old Zellers Venture ten speed with a top-of-the-line Bianchi. The peace he needed to survive in his two worlds would be found pedaling on two wheels, no matter where he was in the world.

The next week Phil was back to school and the two boys used each other to buffer themselves from the other students and teachers.

Phil bought a bike too and they both toured the country roads around Guelph, free of the pressures of home, school, church, and the business they were to inherit.

CHAPTER THIRTEEN

Northern Ireland 1987

David frequently traveled home to work with Kenton and Scott without James. This allowed James to spend more time in Canada with John. James and John were busy, they had plenty of money to launder, mobsters to hide that were named in government investigations and the sale and shipment of weapons. The U.S.A used the group to move weapons and people to Afghanistan and African countries to fight the good fight against communism. David, and his multiple passports, became a world traveler with Kenton while he worked other jobs in North America with James.

David, Scott, and Kenton had just finished a job together, they took care of a few chatty members of the UDA. It excited Kenton how business was growing on both sides of the Atlantic Ocean. He spent more time with David, they trained together while Kenton told him stories of the past. David became the go-to guy on both sides of the Atlantic. Kenton wanted David to have his own handcrafted knife. A gift that would last a lifetime and be a memory of Kenton when he was gone. Each member of the team had a gift like this and like any good tradesman you needed your own tools to do the job properly. David had used one of Kenton's old knives, and that just wasn't the way this family did things. You had your own guns, knives, gloves, tools, and clothes. There was never a need to share anything. Kenton and James had taught David how to care for his weapons, how to sight his guns, sharpen a knife he had on loan from Kenton and the proper way to get blood out of black clothes.

"I am going to take you to Belfast to get you your own knife. We all have guns and other weapons to use in this line of work, but there is nothing more personal and reliable than your own knife, David. This is the proper way to dispose of a person."

"I have the knife you gave me from Baghdad," said David. "But I would like to start my own collection."

"Aye, a knife should be an extension of you. You know I don't like guns, even though we make so much money from building and selling them."

"I know. It is funny how everyone thinks guns are the best weapon. And they are in certain situations but not how we do jobs, Granda. The job we did a few weeks ago, causing all that chaos. How many rounds did we shoot into the crowd? We only had four deaths. I am currently at one-hundred-percent efficient with my knife. It isn't like the movies or is Rambo a better shot than us," David said.

"In the movies they always hit their targets and the bad guy goes down with one shot. That doesn't work in the real world. There are too many variables to consider and of course you give up your position and the element of surprise. You want to ensure the life leaves the body. You want to be up close to confirm you complete the job. Your clients will always want confirmation of the kill, you can't do that unless you are with the target. There is nothing worse than putting six or ten bullets in someone and not getting the job done. I have seen many targets survive being shot multiple times. Their lives might have changed but you can't collect the money if the target still has a beating heart. True professionals use a knife or their hands and don't rely on mechanical equipment to do the work for them. A knife is more efficient, especially in the hands of a professional killer," Kenton said.

The two men walked from the shop to Kenton's car.

"Right, like the jobs you and John get for me in North America," David said.

"Aye, like those. Do you want to drive? I could use a break," said Kenton.

"Sure."

"Head to downtown Belfast, we can stop to get food on the way if you want," said Kenton.

"No, I am okay, maybe after."

"As I was saying, over here, some of our work requires a gun. Hell, we would not be trafficking them for government agencies and others if they weren't a big part of the business. But the hit jobs with one or two targets those are the jobs you use your knife. One time, with the SAS I was in China. My mission was to sneak into an opera. The target was in a private balcony with three other people. I was able to get in, take out the target and get out before anyone noticed he was dead. His friends, they didn't notice till intermission, and by then I was long gone. That is the quality of work I expect from you, David. You need to be a silent killer, that is a skill lacking in the world today. Everyone wants to be Rambo and unload hundreds of rounds into a building and hope for the best. Not you. We trained you to get in, get out, and go before anyone even knows there was a hit on that person."

"Okay, will I ever be that good?"

"You have been doing this since you were a kid, so yes, you will surpass me and your dad in this profession if you keep honing your skills."

David smiled at that comment. His time with his grandfather was so important, a trip in a car was a history lesson and David couldn't get enough. Kenton would talk about jobs he did with the SAS or jobs he did with James, Scott, or John. Of course, there were lessons on ways David could improve himself. But David enjoyed the family history talks the most. It seemed there was never a repeated story. One day David would look back at these talks and wish he had written most of these stories down.

• • •

"How did Dad get involved in all this?" David asked.

"When I got out of the military and back into civilian life, your dad was twelve and Scott was nine. Your grandmother, God rest her soul, you never had the chance to meet her, was not well then. Part of the reason I left the SAS was to stay closer to home, to take care of her. She had issues with her kidneys that nowadays would be a visit to the Doctor and some pills would fix it. Back then it was potentially deadly. I had enough money to buy us a house and the shop in Portadown. I hadn't told your grandmother or the boys, but I had made some deals before I left to be considered, 'a civilian'. I brought an old friend from the military to help me with the work we would do here in Northern Ireland. John was doing the same thing over in Canada. Travel and communication were difficult back in the sixties, so most of our communication was through coded telegraphs. John grew his business while we set up shop here, preparing for, and helping, the troubles to ramp up. The British government had a plan that would not go over well with the nationalist. Our job was to help make things as uncomfortable for the nationalists as possible. Just like your dad did with you and Phil, I had the boys out doing errands for me, dropping deliveries off to people, watching others. The kind of jobs that would not raise suspicion with people. As your dad and uncle got older, they became more involved with the business. Your dad being the older one started earlier than Scott. When your dad was sixteen, your grandmother died. It was a very hard time for the three of us, very hard. I became more involved in the assignments from the government involving the troubles and some overseas work. John spent a lot of time here helping me deal with the loss and my own inner peace. A while after that happened your dad raged out on one job and turned what should have been a fact-gathering mission and taking some hostages into a blood bath. Your dad ended up killing twelve of them, made them kneel in front of him, then he just walked down the line shooting them all in the head, he only stopped to reload. This was a very low point for all of us. I shipped him to Canada for six months while things quieted down here. That was the first time he had a price on his head. Scott and I wanted to bring him home, but he didn't want to come home. Scott took the lead on a lot of jobs while your dad was in Canada. It actually worked out well because we were able to grow real strong bonds with John and the Canadian business. The two of them worked well together and grew the North American side of the business to a massive operation. When he came back, your dad was different, John had changed him, made him more of a businessman, took the anger and wild out of him. He had a lot more control over his emotions and would take the time to think through a problem instead of just reacting. I don't know how John did it because I couldn't as his father. Your dad began traveling more between the two countries. He always wanted to move back to Canada, even after you and Amy were born. He did many jobs with Scott and me. He is very calm in high-pressure situations, like you are. He can see how a job is going and can change the plan on the spot and make everyone aware of the change without giving up any positions or people. You are showing that skill too. Your dad is much happier now that he is back in Canada, your mom is not happy, but he is, and that is what is important to me. I have caused so much pain and death as has Scott and your dad. My main goal these days is to ensure you all are happy, and not just smile when told to be happy, but truly living your lives with smiles inside. I want you to do what you want, be happy with your choices and do the best you can at what you choose. If it is a plumber or killer or bus driver you choose, do it to the best of your skill level and whistle while you do it. Whatever you decide, just be happy inside, do it for you and no one else."

"Okay, Granda, right now I am doing that. Right here with you is what makes me very happy. Hearing stories like this always makes me happy. I do struggle a bit sliding between the two worlds. Lately I seem to be in this world a lot more."

"What about when you are on a job, are you happy then too?" Kenton asked.

"Yes, I would say so. I don't ask for a lot of information on my targets, I just need to know the basics like you told me. The more I know about their lives makes it harder to complete the job. But it has never stopped me."

"Good, and afterwards, do you do the meditation and relaxation like I taught you."

"Yes, it helps me get out of the—not depression—but negativity I feel after a job. I also try to debrief with Dad, John or Phil. Talking to those guys really helps. I think I will bring Phil with me to deal with the normal plans around the job, that way I can focus on the task at hand. I have talked to Dad about it, and he agrees to having a second set of eyes on the jobs. Dad has his guys that he trusts to gather information, my guy will be Phil."

"Good, good."

"So, what happened to your partner you started with?"

"Dead, died the hard way too, slowly. They tortured him for information. We were on a job in South Africa; it was to be a quick kill and deliver some guns. He went to meet with the crew buying our guns. It was an ambush, they had made a deal with the guy we were to kill, he was our competition on selling guns, a fucking Soviet. He set the whole thing up with the group that was to buy our weapons. He gave them a free shipment of weapons if they would get us to meet with them. I was checking out a lead on the Soviet while he went to the meeting. By the time I could get myself and some military buddies organized they had stripped his body of skin, teeth, and nails. We found birds pecking at it in an abandoned shanty where intelligence contact told us they had left him. Terrible thing to see. We went into the village and killed every family member associated with the men that took him. As they used to say, 'we went Biblical,' on them. Ended four entire family lines. They never caught the men, but they found three of the four dead a week after I was back in Northern Ireland."

"Wow, so that can happen."

"Yes, how would you react if you knew someone tortured me or your dad or anyone close to you?"

"Yea, I don't want to think of it, but I believe I would go beyond Biblical. Fucking Soviets. Dad and I took one out in Vietnam last month. I guess I am on their list now of people to meet. John has really tightened up my documents and travel plans to keep me safe. Speaking of John, he remarried to Brenda and they had Phil. You never remarried?"

"No, I had enough to do and inviting someone into my life would ask too much of them. The closest I get is with your nannie, she understands this life and will listen, but we would never get together, too many people would talk. Plus, your mom would probably come home and hunt me down herself."

Laughing, David said, "Yea and it wouldn't be quick for you, another possible 'going Biblical' situation. What about Edward, how did he get involved?"

"Well, he fell into it when your grandfather died, and your parents were dating. Your nannie wanted him to still have a father figure and your dad brought him into the shop. The next thing I know we are using him for smaller jobs. He never got into the inner circle, but he has skills, he never fully committed to the business, was never in with both feet. Now he is happy in Australia with your aunt and cousins, away from all this. I still send him and your Aunt May money. He still stays in touch with me."

"So, why did Dad start dating Mom? They never seem happy together and we hardly do anything as a family. Amy has no clue about any of this, she really thinks I am out camping or vacationing. Occasionally, she asks to come along with me and Dad. We actually have taken her camping couple times but mom never comes."

"Your dad and mom started dating after he broke up with a girl, I wanted him to date. They always seemed to be the odd couple. Your mom thought she could change him, get him to stop with what we do here. She didn't know how deep your dad was in. She found out that I didn't approve of her and then dug her nails into your dad deeper. I don't want to talk bad of your mom, but she is a problem. Your dad has handled her well, but one day if she spoke up, we would need to deal with her."

"Aye, I know, some days it wouldn't be too hard. She keeps her distance from me, says I am dad's kid and not to bother her. She does everything with Amy, which is fine, but if it wasn't for dad, I would be long gone from her."

"Aye, it is tough, your dad talks about it to me, a lot. Just know your father, me and your uncles, aunts and nannie love you a lot and we are all here to support you if you need it, anytime."

"I know Aunt Sarah is awesome, maybe because her mom was the same as mine, showing favorites and blaming us for everything wrong in her life."

"One last question. What happened to the man that identified Dad, the reason we had to all move to Canada? Where is he now? What does he do? I think I would like to meet him one day, ya know," David said.

"Aye, I put a large bounty on his head, but no one was able to collect. I believe he is still in France or somewhere around there. We still see his handy work on the island from time to time. But he has moved on to bigger and better paying jobs. One day he will miss something, if it is here in this country, we will bring him to the shop for safekeeping until your dad comes for a visit,"

"I want a piece of him too, I think we all should be here for that."

"Aye, with him identifying your dad, it was a bad thing, and that job went horribly wrong."

"Yea it took me away from you and the family, mom is always homesick, and I feel like I missed out on so much not growing up beside you."

"David son, don't think that at all. You have a better life in Canada. You can see and learn more things. John and your dad have been able to grow the business with you and Phil supporting them. It really was a better scenario for you and Amy. Turn right up ahead, we are almost there."

"Well, if I ever get the chance to meet him, I will do him in slowly," said David.

• • •

They headed towards the harbor to an acquaintance of Kenton's. The blacksmith shop had made knives since the 1600s. Their slogan was 'Cutting all kinds of meat for four-hundred years.' Rumor has it, this was the blacksmith shop that sold Jack the Ripper his knife. Kenton and David entered the shop front where a friendly new face Kenton had not seen before welcomed them.

"Welcome, how can I help you gents today," said the man behind the counter.

"I would like to speak to Charles, please," said Kenton.

"Charles is busy today, how can I help you, sir?"

"By getting Charles to come out front, he will want to see me," said Kenton with a raised voice.

"Unfortunately, I cannot do that, he instructed me to not interrupt him for any customers today."

"I will say this once more nicely, go fetch Charles for me and my grandson, tell him Kenton is here to see him. If then he still doesn't want to be disturbed, I will leave."

"Okay, but I already..." he said, as the back door to the shop opened.

"Kenton, why are you standing out here, come, come, this must be David," Charles said. He escorted them into the bowels of his shop.

Kenton and David smiled at the person as they walked by, "He told you," David said with a smirk on his face.

"Wow, you are a tall drink of water," Charles said to David. "Today we begin designing you a knife. You know I have supplied knives to your father and grandfather and their friends and probably some enemies too. I still remember Kenton bringing your dad here for the first time. Now a third generation, wow, what a family," said Charles.

Kenton laughed, "Yes, what a family, indeed."

They entered Charles's office and sat down at a drawing table. "Kenton told me you were overdue for your own wee knife, have you any ideas of what you want? Obviously, you want a slicing and stabbing one to start with, correct?"

"Yes, I really like the feel of my Dad's knife, it balances well in my hand, and the double edge makes for easy work. The one with the green handle," said David.

"Aye, right. You know I have one I was just playing around with. I balanced the blade and handle out to a good ratio and made the handle of ivory, a beautiful functional knife. You can see it and let me know what you think of it. Or I can make whatever you would like."

"I would love to see it," said David, with the excitement of a child on Christmas morning.

"Yes, I would too," replied Kenton, "I have nothing that nice in my collection. I am a little jealous."

The men laughed.

"Ken, bring the knife we just finished to my office please," said Charles on the phone. To David he said, "Kenton has told me a lot about you, so I made this thinking of your personality and what you would use it for. The metal is BG42 steel, it is strong and reliable, it stays sharp for multiple uses even against hard material, like bone. It needs some care, but I know your granda has already taught you how to maintain and care for knives. I made it into a six-inch blade with a thicker handle area, but it is all one piece of metal from blade tip to butt to improve the overall strength. I designed the butt of the knife with strength to allow you to use it as a dull force weapon. With the weight and a full swing, you could easily crack a skull. I shaped the quillons to slice in close combat, and if you use this knife right and take care of it, it will become an extension of your hand. I wrapped the handle in ivory for comfort and grip. It came from an elephant that was killed by poachers. I personally know the man that found the elephant and the poachers. His job is to hunt poachers in Africa. He found them celebrating the kill of that majestic beast. Let me just say they suffered a lot more than the elephant did as it died. The elephant and its ivory were taken to a tribe that lives close to the herd, where they blessed the elephant. It fed the tribe for a few weeks, as over there, nothing goes to waste. They blessed the ivory with a blessing of protection by the tribe's Shaman. Now this knife is yours with the protection and blessings attached to it. I made the leather scabbard from a piece of the elephant's skin, another connection to it."

"Wow," was all David could reply to the story he just heard.

There was a knock on the door and Ken, Charles's son, brought a box into the office.

"Gentlemen this is Ken, my son, and the one I will hand the business to when I decide I have had enough of this rat race."

"Hello," said Ken.

"Kenton, David, do you mind if Ken sits in on the rest of this meeting?"

"No, not at all," said Kenton.

Ken walked over to the side wall and grabbed a chair and sat beside David.

"Pleased to meet you," Ken said as he reached out his hand.

"Same," replied David.

"David why don't you open the box and look inside," Charles said.

David took the box from the middle of the table and slid it to himself. His hands were sweaty as he undid the leather straps that held the lid closed. He opened the box, he looked in at the knife. A piece of art that would be as comfortable in

David's hand as it would be hung in the Louvre Museum. David hesitated to reach in. The knife was too nice to touch. He looked up at the three men, they stared at him in anticipation of his reaction.

"Whoa," said David. "Very cool."

"Aye, come on luv, take it out, let me see this knife," said Kenton.

David reached into the box and wrapped his fingers around the handle of the knife. The knife felt like it melted to his hand. He had never felt anything so perfect. David raised it out of the box, he held it like it was part of his body, his first knife, blessed with protection, fitted to his hand. Simply perfect.

"Oh, come on Charles, you have never made something that nice for me," Kenton said, with a smile.

David held it in his right hand, then his left. He passed it between his hands, he changed the angles as he held it. He flipped the blade from a forward to a reverse grip and swung it through the air with ease.

"Do you want to take it for a spin, David?" said Charles.

"Sure, it feels good and balanced and fits well in my hand. What do you have in mind?" said David, still in awe of the knife.

Charles stood up from the table and grabbed a ring of keys. They walked to what David thought was the wall. Charles placed a key into a small opening in the wall, it revealed a hidden door. They entered the room followed by Ken and Kenton. David's jaw dropped. Inside the room was a bunch of punching dummies, bags full of hay and an assortment of medieval and samurai swords that hung on the walls.

"Here David, have a go at these guys, see how a stab feels with the knife or a slice across the throat," said Charles.

David stood behind one of the dummies. He grabbed the chin and lifted, just like his dad had shown him. In one motion David ran the knife across the dummy's throat, the knife cut deep enough to kill any live dummy he was paid to do work on.

"How was it," asked Kenton.

"That was effortless," said David. "Granda, compared to the knife I have been using it is like going from a Ford to a Ferrari.

He then pushed the dummies head forward and stuck the knife just below where the base of the skull angles up to the back of the brain. Again, just as they taught him. Charles looked at Kenton and winked. Kenton nodded back.

David removed the knife from the dummy's skull.

"Sold," he said with excitement. "I can't believe how none of the knives I have used before feel anything like this one. Wow."

"Well, I knew you were coming in, but I didn't think the sale would be so easy. Are you sure this is what you want? I will make whatever you ask," Charles inquired.

"No, this one calls out to me, this is my new partner, we will do a lot of work together," said David. "One day I want to go meet this tribe that blessed my new knife."

"I can arrange it David, just let me know when," said Charles. "Let me take it out back and touch up the blade, I will then give you a detailed lesson on the care of this knife. With this metal you will need to take care of it a little differently than other knives you have used."

"Thank you, Charles, Ken," said David. "Granda, thank you so much for this. I will cherish this knife forever."

He leaned into Kenton and gave him a big hug.

The four men reviewed the knife's needs, from when, or if the ivory got blood on it, to the care of the blade. After they reviewed how to keep the knife like new, they went out for supper so Ken and David could get to know each other better, the future to both elder men's businesses.

CHAPTER FOURTEEN

Washington D.C. 1989

Tom Elliott had worked on a case for the FBI for six years. He had lost his wife to divorce because he put this assignment ahead of her; she took the kids and the house; he did not put up a fight. His mother passed away two years into the assignment. He chose not to attend the funeral, fearful he could expose himself and his team's identity, he did not want anything to compromise the investigation. He finally had all the documentation compiled to go to the higher ups to reveal all his findings.

After a sleepless night, Tom arrived early for the meeting. A meeting of this importance would usually be held at FBI headquarters. To protect his identity, he requested the meeting be held off site in an office building owned by The Department of Agriculture. In the conference room he placed copies of the report and a glass of water at each seat around the large table. His hope was, with the documents and his presentation they would accept his request for, firm, fast action he needed to shut down this worldwide operation. This meeting would be the first time the entire operation and investigation would be revealed to anyone. Over the years he would compartmentalize his work, he never revealed all his findings, as his predecessor taught him.

"In government work, especially ours Tom, never have your team involved in all aspects of the investigation. That way no one person can ruin a large operation by getting drunk and talking. Always keep your team apart, don't let them know who the team is. You take the information from them and compile it. Only you should know the big picture. When you are done with them, have them reassigned away, far away, from your investigation and team. The best agents to work with are those close to getting out. They finish your job and retire somewhere on a lake," Sam said one warm evening in Nashville. That was only a few weeks before Tom was assigned to this investigation.

Tom stood at the front of the room, the light from the projector highlighted his salt and pepper hair and the wrinkles that had appeared over the last six years. Tom had never felt so much pressure to present a case as he did this one. The Director of the FBI and CIA, The Attorney General, two senators from oversight committees and Tom's boss from Operations entered the room and took their seats.

Tom welcomed everyone to the meeting. He started his presentation, he disclosed how in 1982, a twenty-year-old boy from France, escaped from a compound in Texas. That child revealed someone had kidnapped him, from a school yard, at the age of eight.

Tom methodically spoke on how this one boy was able to give details and identify people in the compound. From that information Tom was able to expand his investigation, he discovered he had uncovered an international kidnapping and pedophile ring.

The investigation showed the lowest level in the ring's organization was a group who identified children, by sex, age, client request, or a specific need to keep inventory numbers up. The victims ages were from two years old to eighteen years old. An 'agent' followed the chosen child until a schedule and routine was confirmed for the kidnapping. With the schedule approved, a 'removal crew' would come to the area and steal the child or preferably children from their families and get them to a safe house. Ten removal crews worked worldwide, each with their own assigned areas of the globe. The removal teams comprised of two people, would arrive on site, be briefed about the child and their schedule. The removal team would take the child within twenty-four hours of when they arrived on site. The child was placed in a safe house and the crew would fly out before the local police could organize a search. With some cases, they would have the child in a safe house and be on to the next job before the parents were aware the child had not made it to school, or home. If possible, the removal teams would try to take multiple kids in one visit to an area before they moved to a different country to continue their work. This routine would happen hundreds of times a year. Many third world countries did not even fully count the missing.

The safe houses were located outside of major cities as a holding spot for the children. Tom identified fourteen in North America, one in every European country, twelve in Asia, twenty-one on the African continent and nine in South America. He knew of more but did not have the resources to confirm them. He showed photos of some of the safe house's interiors. They were not great, but they were clean and well lit. Rooms were no bigger than a prison cell, but they had everything a child would want, except of course, their family. The idea was to preserve the kid's innocence and youthful wonder, not harden them or stress them out; part of the magic for the customers was the youthful innocence. The kids were fed, exercised, and washed daily. Of course, a blood sample was taken; only clean healthy children made it to the next stage of this trip.

Once the compound was ready for a delivery, it could be weeks to many months, the children were prepared to be shipped to their final destination.

The day before they moved the kids, they cut their hair, the child received a full body wash and were given traveling clothes.

The day they moved the detainees were transported by a private jet to their new, and usually final home, a large secure ranch that straddled the US-Mexican border. The compound was over 1000 acres of emptiness. For a property that size, it had better security than the White House, a private airfield and a large conference area attached to eighty-five cottages. Locals referred to it as 'the beef farm owned by some Arabs.'

Tom paused to take a drink, which gave his audience a moment to let the first half of his presentation settle in. He looked at the clock on the wall. He had talked for an hour. No wonder his throat had dried up. He looked around at his audience, they were all focused on his presentation, no one asked any questions. As the old saying goes, you could hear a pin drop in the room.

The second part of his presentation began as he warned everyone of graphic photos and details. He continued with details of the young prisoners, how they lived their shortened lives as sex slaves to the rich and powerful. His report had many details of the living arrangements and how the children were selected by the rich and powerful within the compound. Some children were reserved for a handful of customers, while others were shared freely with all the clientele. The victims were never reunited with their families.

Once the child's bodies and innocence were all used up, they were dealt with quickly. The compound had mass graves of unidentified bodies, far away from any house or barn. The last thing those innocent kids saw was vultures as they flew overhead. A few were not so lucky to have a quick death. Some customers purchased their favorite children and took them to a foreign land where they kept them as slaves. They would live out their lives as servants to kings, queens, or someone with money, power, and the ability to keep them quiet. Some would work for their owner, while others were kept only for pleasure.

Others, like the boy that started this whole investigation, were kept as staff to work on the compound, not for money but for the privilege of not being raped and beaten daily or weekly by customers.

After another short break, to let that all settle in, Tom started the last part of his presentation. He explained how his team received photos and information from the inside of the compound and some safe houses. Two contacts his team worked with became compromised and mysteriously never left the compound again. Those two people were able to report names of clients, get photos and reveal the horrors that happened in the compound. The list included government leaders of multiple countries, many CEO's, top level athletes, movie and TV stars and royalty. The list, Tom believed, was only the tip of the iceberg. His team discovered more names through flight manifests they recovered when they interrogated flight crew personnel. Unfortunately, that line of information dried up once three pilots and two other flight crew members mysteriously committed suicide in impossible ways. The strangest was one pilot, he smashed the back of his skull with a hammer, then stabbed himself in the back four times. A medical miracle, Tom noted! They were able to get one agent into the compound, two years ago, as flight attendant. She worked the flights from Asia when they brought and returned customers and children discretely to the compound. She gathered information from the pilots. Unfortunately, the plane she flew on had a mechanical failure while it landed in the compound. This failure and flight crew deaths was never properly investigated by the National Transportation Safety Board.

For Tom the presentation of the facts was the easy part and was now complete. He looked around the room, the faces showed shock, disgust, and confusion from his presentation. But still no one asked a question. Now he needed help from the top cops and attorneys in the country. He needed them for the arrests and shutdown of the compound and safe houses.

He began his requests with the need for specialized reconnaissance crews to get into the compound and get a closer look. There was one area at the back of the compound, it was legally part of Mexico, maybe they could find a way in there, he recommended. He was concerned when he asked for warrants as the one list had a Texas judge named on it. When the time came for the closure of the compound, he recommended they hit the safe houses around the world at the same time. Hopefully the teams could save and return some children, still in the safe houses, to their families. The hardest part of the operation would be rounding up the removal teams and the ones that identified the children.

There was one last issue, one piece of the puzzle he could never confirm; who owned the property? There was no name on any deed or piece of legal documentation.

Everyone sat in silence. Tom sat down at the table, exhausted. Finally, the silence from his audience was broken by a question.

"Tom, who else knows all these details and where are you storing all the documents from this investigation," asked the Senator from Georgia.

"Sir, I have all the information gathered in a rental office just outside D.C. and no one knows what you all now know. Like I said before, I kept everyone compartmentalized," said Tom.

The room went silent again.

"Tom, could you give us a few minutes to talk," asked his boss.

"Sure."

Tom left the room and headed outside for a smoke; he could use some fresh air. After his smoke he was brought back into the room. They told him they would take his information and review it with other leaders and countries. There was a lot of international logistics to work out. This was a large operation and would require a lot of planning before it could proceed. They took his office key to claim the rest of his paperwork.

They thanked Tom for all his work and personal sacrifice during this investigation. His boss noted that in six years Tom had not taken any vacation.

Tom was told, while they did their part to prepare documents for the arrests and raids on the compound, they wanted him to go on a vacation, to be somewhere safe. There was a vacation house just outside of Buffalo owned by the CIA.

He was to use it and if they needed him, they would call the house.

They thanked Tom again for the scarifies he had made for his country. He was told his travel details would be ready by the time he returned with some clothes for his holiday.

Three days later he rode his Harley, he was relaxed and worry free, just outside of Buffalo, New York.

• • •

Canada 1989

David had been busy with jobs for John and Kenton. He had done a lot of work with his dad to complete two to three big jobs a month during the last six months. He traveled back to Kenton and all around the world, all under different names. As he headed to the shop, he thought back to his last trip to Syria with his dad and a large shipment of guns. When they arrived, their clients asked if they had time to do three hits. All three hits James had David organize and run with a timeline of one week to complete them. They worked on them together, under David's leadership. On the flight home James told David, he was ready to do jobs alone. Those three hits were David's final test, and he passed with flying colors. James explained to David how he needed a break, and that David was years ahead of where he was at David's age.

• • •

David arrived at the office for a team meeting, his team's meeting. This would be his first job alone. He had met with Phil and the team who had tracked the target for the last week. John prepared David's documentation, IDs, and a blue Ford Taurus was delivered from the local car rental company. With the file on his target, David headed back to his house to pack for the job. David's team had done an exceptional job on the reconnaissance work for this one.

David pulled out a couple of bags from his closet and filled one with clothes. Every time a piece of clothing went into David's bag, he looked at the photos and reviewed the details of the target's face, the tattoo on his arm, the thick salt and pepper hair and the birthmark on his chin.

David finished packing the overnight bag and packed his biking bag. This was the bag that would hold the weapons and tools he needed to finish the job they hired him for. He packed some bike shorts and a jersey, a pair of coveralls, latex gloves, and a dust mask. He then opened his closet and took down a large, heavy wooden box which he kept locked. David lifted the vent cover and reached down. He felt the magnet and key that hung on the ductwork. He retrieved the key and opened the box. Inside was a collection of custom knives. Clean, sharp, and ready to use. David took out the knife, the one his grandfather purchased for him. He bounced the knife in his palm a couple times and placed it inside his bike bag, wrapped in its custom scabbard.

He took out a second knife as a backup, a boot knife they called it in the military. Your last means of defense if things went bad.

•   •   •

David loaded his car with the overnight bags and his bike. On the passenger seat was the file folder with the information to review one last time before he crossed the border. The drive to the border was on the QEW, Queen Elizabeth Way. A good name for the road that took him to a lot of his jobs. The road, named in recognition of the person who helped start this family business for his grandfather.

David was a little nervous, but confident in his skills. He pulled into a coffee shop and picked up a large double-double and a honey dipped donut. He sat in the car. He sipped his coffee and reviewed the details of the guy they hired him to kill.

'Tom Elliott, FBI, single, address of 3711 East River Road Grand Island New York. 'Kill quick and simple, no others if possible.' the report stated. There were more details about why the hit was out on him, what he did, how much money was to be paid out, all things David did not care about. That was Phil and John's side of the business. All David wanted was the basics. The notes from his team had more meaning to him than the documents from the people that requested the job. The FBI, like MI6 paid his family well for their work and their silence. The family's relationship with most US agencies had grown since the hit on a famous singer in 1980. James had done that job, even though he was a fan.

David finished his review of the notes while he downed the last of his coffee. He took one last look at the photos then rolled up the notes, photos, and garbage. He placed it all in a plastic grocery bag. David got out of the car and walked to the garbage by the door to the coffee shop. He dropped the bag and its contents into the garbage can.

Rush blasted 'time standing still' on the radio while David drove through Niagara Falls, down Clifton Hill and along the waterfront. This little tourist hot spot had a soft spot in David's heart. He always enjoyed a visit to the Falls, for a weekend or just a day. He enjoyed a bike ride on the bike trails that ran the length of the river at least once a year with Phil. When family would come out to visit from back home, this was always a place they wanted to see, the marvel of the falls. Most trips across the border would happen over this bridge. His good luck bridge, he called it. David crossed the bridge and had two cars in front of him before his interview with a customs agent from the States.

He got out his ID, ready to hand it over to the authorities when asked. There wasn't much difference between this and the checkpoints he encountered in Northern Ireland. Except for the fact there weren't four snipers with guns pointed at the occupant's heads as they were being questioned.

"Good afternoon, citizenship, please," asked the tall muscular guard.

"Canadian," David said and passed over a driver's license.

"How long are you planning on visiting?"

"Three days," David said.

"Where are you going?"

"Buffalo."

"What's the reason for your visit?"

"Get away for a couple days, do some biking along the river and catch a Bills game Sunday."

"Have a good trip, and go Bills," the guard said as he handed back the ID.

David smiled, "Thanks" and pulled into Niagara Falls, New York.

David had no intention of seeing a Bills game or staying three days. If all went well, he would be back in his own house by supper tomorrow. He drove through the city of Niagara Falls, and headed for Grand Island and his hotel.

•   •   •

Tom's house was a short distance from the hotel where Phil booked a reservation. A quick bike ride to the house would not be an issue for David. When he arrived on the island, David resisted the temptation to drive by Tom's house. Instead, he took the main road to the hotel to check in, *'always keep to the original plan until you can't,'* his granda would say. He arrived at the hotel and parked the car at the edge of the lot outside the view of the security camera's range.

His room on the main floor was ready for him early as requested. David carefully unpacked both bags, he confirmed he had all the tools he needed to complete the job. He spent some time with his bike, he checked tire pressures and the mechanical devices, he made sure they were not damaged while in the trunk of the car. Even though he biked almost every day at home or away, this was his back up bike he only used for jobs. Unlike some of his other bikes, this one, a Bianchi he bought three years ago had no real sentimental value. If someone stole it or saw it on a job, he would ditch it. The bike sat mostly in the basement only used for special occasions. It did not stand out like the other paint choices some of his bikes had. This week the bike was a dark blue. It had bar tape that was changed more often than he oiled the chain, for obvious reasons. This bike was not super light or fast, but it was quick to clean, easy to paint and sturdy for dirt roads if needed.

David unpacked the bike knapsack. Then carefully packed it again in the order items should come out of the bag. At the bottom of the bag was the gloves and balaclava. Above those items were the coveralls folded and placed in a way, when he took them out, they would unfold properly so he did not struggle to find the top of them. The side pocket had a small towel and bottle of soapy water, if he got blood on his skin. There were two pockets that held the two knives, sharpened, cleaned and ready to do their job.

David headed back to the front reception area of the hotel and made a couple calls on the pay phones. One was to Phil to let him know the job would happen today, and the second was to the last man of the team, who still followed Tom. They discussed where Tom was and if he had kept to his regular schedule. He was, and with that confirmation, David released Sean from the reconnaissance work and had him head home. David would take care of the rest of the business agreement alone.

David changed out of his clothes and put on his bike shorts and a tee-shirt, being mindful of Tom's schedule. He had fifteen minutes before he needed to leave on his bike. He sat on the bed cross legged with his head bowed and prayed. It brought him into a quiet peaceful state quickly. After a few minutes of meditation, he reviewed all the steps he was going to take to finish this job. There would be no conversation, no mercy, and no opportunity for Tom to beg for his life.

David left the hotel room with his bike and backpack. He used a side door to enter the parking lot. Once off the curb he mounted his bike and pedaled. *'Time to make some money,'* he thought.

David always found a bike ride relaxed him, before a job. It took him out of the situation he was about to enter and put him into a relaxed frame of mind. This being his first job alone, he needed the quiet prayer and the bike ride to calm his nerves and his mind. David watched the numbers on the mailboxes, as he biked. He looked for the house, he knew he was close. The house had blue cedar siding and a backyard that overlooked the river. The property had lots of old trees that surrounded it in the front yard and blocked a lot of the house and property. He saw a spot to the side of the property where he could easily hide his bike. David checked the time, he calculated he had about half an hour before Tom would arrive home, hopefully alone. He continued to bike on the road. He enjoyed the beautiful fall afternoon and the colors of the leaves as they began to change and fall. After a few more miles he slowed, and when he did not see any cars, turned around to head back in the hotel's direction. At a location he noted on the ride past Tom's house, where he had a view of the driveway, David stopped the bike and got off. He took the front wheel off the bike and set it to the side. He took off his backpack and opened the front pouch. He took out a spare tube and some small tools. David pretended to change a flat front tire on his bike. A few cars passed him, no one took any notice of the biker as he made the repairs to his bike.

As he worked on his tire, he heard the rumble of a Harley Davidson motorcycle in the distance. *'This should be Tom, right on time,'* he thought, as he checked his watch.

Tom rode past David, looked at him and nodding. David continued to work on his front tire, now with a mini pump in his hand. Tom pulled into his driveway, parked the motorcycle, and headed straight for the front door. David lost sight of him as he continued to work on his wheel.

After a few minutes, he cleaned up his tools and put his wheel back on the bike. David biked slowly towards Tom's house. He looked around for any witnesses as he turned onto the front lawn and rode to the trees where he had noted a spot to hide. He quickly got off the bike and crouched down. He surveyed his surroundings, he was in a blind spot behind some bushes and trees, no one could see him in this location, from the house or the road. He had a view of the backyard from his location. There were noises from the backyard. He opened the knapsack and dressed for the job. Two special pockets were sewn into the coveralls for his knives, one pocket was for his favorite knife, it was located horizontally over his left chest. The other pocket was on the outside of his right thigh, just above his knee. David placed the knives in their spots and reached into the bag for the Balaclava and gloves. Ever since his first kill David wore a balaclava, not to hide his face but to prevent blood from getting into his mouth or nose. It was a bit of a phobia he now had.

He surveyed the property and neighbor's sight lines again, with no one in sight he walked to the backyard. He approached the back of the house and smelt meat being cooked. Near the back corner of the house, still protected by trees and bushes, he crouched down and crawled to the edge of the house. His black coveralls blended with the shadows. He poked his head around the corner of the house to survey the backyard and see what issues could arise for him. There was an outdoor table and chairs for guests to eat meals on the upper deck. A lower area where outdoor loungers faced the lake and chairs circled around a fire pit, shadowed by large trees. The landscaping looked professionally done and the dock looked like it recently had a facelift. The BBQ was part of a built-in outdoor kitchen on the upper level, closer to the house.

David thought, *'I would love a backyard like this one day.'*

There were a few boats on the river, but none close enough to identify David.

David located Tom by the BBQ. He had just opened a cold beer from the fridge. Tom opened the BBQ and flipped the chicken breast. He adjusted the temperature and sat at a chair that faced the river.

David would not have to enter the house and locate Tom. Anytime an assassin could do a job outside it was an advantage. No sneaking through a house, no surprises hidden behind a door.

David saw the opportunity to pounce and made his way quietly to Tom's location. He crouched behind the chair Tom relaxed in.

David took in a deep breath and released it, he reached for his knife. The loud music that played from the speakers by the fire pit, Guns and Roses-Welcome to the Jungle, dulled any noise David made as he pulled out his knife. One last deep breath, in and out, then he stood up behind Tom.

David grabbed a handful of Tom's salt and pepper hair with his left hand. He thrust Tom's head forward, then snapped it back quickly. Tom's neck popped and cracked as David exposed this throat. Tom wide eyed, with his mouth wide open, had a look of shock and horror on his face. He stared at the sky then his eyes moved to David. His beer fell to the ground, it spilt over David's shoe. Before the can of beer bounced a second time, David's right hand stretched across Tom's chest and in one seamless, smooth motion he pulled his hand back across Tom's neck. The knife did what it was built for, it became an extension of David's body. It punctured Tom's skin just to the outside of the left artery. David's hand recoiled as the knife sliced through the left carotid artery, then the windpipe and finally the right carotid artery. The action was effortless, like a spoon entering pudding. David could already feel the heat from Tom's blood on his glove as it escaped from the arteries and bubbled up through the windpipe. David's hands did their job as David locked eyes with Tom and smiled. Tom's eyes showed the surprise and confusion of the moment, the pain of what had just happened to him and finally, emptiness. To be sure the job was complete, David forced the knife into Tom's head just below his right ear. The wheeze from Tom's severed windpipe was the only noise he made during the entire assault. David removed the knife from Tom's head and wiped the blood off the blade on Tom's shoulder. In a matter of seconds, a man who had plans to enjoy a fall evening by the lake was dead. David's left hand released Tom's thick hair and the body twitched before it slumped over onto itself, like an old man who had taken a nap in his favorite chair. David reached down and grabbed some of Tom's loose t-shirt. One last wipe of the blade before David put the blade back in the sheath, another notch on the handle.

David was relieved and satisfied by his first hit alone. His first job alone could not have gone any better.

The only thing left to do was bike back to the hotel and call John. He removed the blood-soaked gloves and put them in a small plastic bag he carried in the coveralls.

He replaced those gloves with a clean pair, and he headed back up the patio to the house. The BBQ smoked heavily. David opened the BBQ; the chicken was a little burnt but cooked. He turned the BBQ off and took the chicken off with the tongs Tom had used earlier. David stood and admired his work, the backyard, and the river with the boats on it. *'What a beautiful view this guy had,'* he thought.

Once the chicken cooled enough to handle, David took it and headed around to the front of the house to pack up and go. He carefully removed his gloves, balaclava, and coveralls. Then pulled out a plastic bag from his knapsack and placed all the articles of clothing in it.

He took a couple bites of the chicken, *'damn, I wished I asked Tom what the sauce was, it is very good and flavorful,'* he thought.

After he ate the chicken, too good to throw away, he got back on his bike. From behind some trees, he leaned out, he saw no cars on the road and no neighbors outside. After he ate the chicken, too good to throw away, he got back on his bike. From behind some trees, he leaned out, he saw no cars on the road and no neighbors outside. He rode back to the hotel with the knowledge the bastard they hired him to kill was dead. After a shower, change of clothes and a quick call to John from a pay phone, David's assignment was done. He knew his grandfather was proud of the work he was doing in North America and how his skills and confidence had improved. He couldn't wait to tell his granda about his first job alone and how well it went.

The next day David went for an early morning bike ride. He started on the route the same way he did the day before. As he passed by the late Tom Elliott's location, there were no extra vehicles, no sign anything had changed from when he left the job. With all the wildlife on the island he wondered if any animals had picked at Tom's body yet, maybe stole a finger or chunk of cheek. For some reason, that made him feel better. His experience in these matters squashed any urge to see for himself. David had a nice long ride around the island before he headed back to Canada.

Tom was to check in with the agency at three that afternoon. When he did not, and certain people already knew he would not, a contact at the agency called the police. He was found where David left him. An investigation began on Tom's death, but the one who did it was already across the border.

• • •

David headed to the shop to debrief with John, James, and Phil. They were happy the job went well and that their money had been wired to them.

The group who contracted the kill were, like all the family's customers, happy with the team's work. The documents Tom had in his office were shredded as were all notes from the meeting. His team was reassigned around the world away from any areas close to the safe houses. Tom's house in DC was ransacked. All computers and papers were retrieved and destroyed.

The compound in Texas and the safe houses worldwide, remained open for their clients and victims.

CHAPTER FIFTEEN

Northern Ireland, 1989

Kenton summoned James and David back to Northern Ireland to catch up on a few jobs. They used the usual routes and fake IDs to get out of one country and into another. British Intelligence requested one job a month ago, but because Kenton was ill, it was delayed.

Kenton and David wrapped up the first job outside of Newry, where they ambushed a truck full of explosives headed straight to Newry police barracks. The plan was the suicide driver would drive through the security gate and detonate the truck once he got to the building's front doors. This would kill many police officers and destroy the building and most of the paper documents inside it. David and Kenton were able to slow the truck on a back road, take the driver and with their own explosives blow up the truck with only one casualty, a cow who was a bit too nosy about the crew's work. The driver was taken back to the shop, James and Scott worked him over for information before they disposed of the body in a garbage bin outside Wade's pottery.

With that job complete, Kenton and David headed to Belfast to meet another contact of Kenton's, they picked up a shipment of guns.

Two nights later the crew gathered outside of Portadown, on Dungannon Road. They owned an old stone farmhouse and some land. Just like the properties in Canada this house was used to hide and move people or things.

The crew sat around the dinner table for the first time since James and David arrived. They discussed the jobs they just wrapped up and some future work and shipments that would require David to manage. They joked about the steaks they could be eating for supper, if the cow was only a few feet further away from the blast.

The room was very small with a large solid maple dining table and hutch, it made the room impossible to walk through. Kenton purchased the house back in 1984 to use as a safe house and a place to store items given to him by the government. It sat atop a hill overlooking open farmland. Ancient stone walls built over hundreds of years of Ireland's history were the only thing that broke up the different colors of green grass owned by various property owners in the area. Most walls were only three feet tall, enough to keep grazing animals contained. The house, built in 1745, held the dampness. David had lit a fire in the living room fireplace. He could see his granda's arthritis bothered him, and the dampness in the house did not help. The fire brought dancing lights and dry heat into the dining room. The walls were bare, and the house was very light on furnishings. No one lived there, except the ghosts of previous homeowners. Most people were moved in and out within a week, on to another safe house or a new life and identity somewhere else in the world. Indoor plumbing was installed in 1963, a fact David found to be so strange growing up in a new country like Canada. He enjoyed trips out to the house, he constantly looked at the construction of the house and sat on the back porch. The view looked over the farmland, David was always amazed by the beauty of the view. 'You didn't see that many colors of green in Canada,' he would tell anyone who would listen.

After Kenton made some tea, the group reviewed the plans from the British government. There were a few jobs left to do before James was to head home. David still had a couple jobs to complete with Kenton and Scott but first he had a trip to Boston. He would escort a shipment of guns to Boston and meet a new client. The guns, tactical vests, and ammunition was packed and ready to head to the airport the next day.

Tonight, they were to bring a smaller shipment of guns across the border. They would trade the weapons for a person who needed protection. This person had information on two rogue IRA fellas who had successfully bombed parts of downtown London. David was excited to meet the man they were picking up. He had lots of questions for him. He knew where Nigel was, and David hoped his information was accurate. David made a private request of his grandfather, if the information was true on the location of the bombers, he would like to handle the job personally. This guy was responsible for tearing the family apart and David wanted to do the same to him, if it was authorized by their bosses. He knew he was not to make any of his work personal, but this one person, the one who identified his father years ago, seemed to have a connection with David. This enemy of David's would haunt him until he could look him in the eyes, touch his skin and slowly rip out his heart. David sat at the table with the others, he thought of the wars this guy had prolonged, the fear and mourning he had caused around the world.

David had learned years ago; wars don't have winners and losers; they have profiteers and agendas. In Northern Ireland his family was one of the profiteers, so was the man that identified James. Yes, his family had a strong Protestant background and a loyalty to the Union Jack, but if someone needed to have someone disappear, or if items needed to be sent to either side for money or information, his family would do it, for the right price. His grandfather would remind him, when David asked too many questions, the truth of war and what the news images of war were two different things. All wars are designed for certain people or businesses to make money. David understood this the older he got, but still all he wanted was this one guy's location.

Something about this job did not sit right with David, he wasn't sure if it was excitement about the information they could get about Nigel, or if the job was a set-up to take down the family.

Around lunch he was in the shed and thought he saw movement under a vehicle. Already nervous about the job, he ran to the front of the house to see a rabbit hop from under the Range Rover. That little voice in his head repeatedly said, *'Be alert David, watch out for the crew.'*

Kenton reviewed the drop point location with the crew. "On Clay Road a mile over the border there will be a farmer's gate on the left of the road, that is where we will drop off our package. It is a high point, so we should have good visuals on any vehicles as they approach. Scott will be in the car with me while you two control the traffic on the road. It is roughly fifty miles from here so we will need to leave the house around half past ten to be set up in our locations for the drop at quarter past one. My contact has assured me if we stay on this route, there will be no police or military checkpoints to slow us down. There will be military in the area on routine patrol so we will have back up if needed. David, you will carry the flares and the radio. Tonight, we will use channel twenty-eight if we need backup. Scott and I will drive the Land Rover and we will do the drop. James, you take the Ford and be the lead car. David, you get the Austin and the back for this one. Once we transfer the weapons, and take our man, we will take these three routes back to the shop where we can store our new tenant until we can approve proper transportation. Until then, he is ours to question. Again, question only, hands off. I want to re-state this. We could be targets tonight. We need to be ready for anything. Guns should be kept loaded and live at all times.

"Granda if I am in the rear, do you want me to pull off here and take this position? It is high ground, and I would have visuals of the road from both directions and the fields."

"Aye, David your skills are improving. I like that idea. David will cover us from this location," said Kenton.

"One more question. Why do I always get the junky car," said David with a grin.

"You are the young one here. We old guys can't handle driving in a wreck like that. If it breaks down, you're Mr. Fitness, and can run five miles to a house. We can't," said Scott. He reached over to rub David's hair like he was six again. David was the only one left in the room with a full head of hair.

"So, questions on tonight's job?" asked Kenton.

"Where are we dropping the cars," asked David.

"Back at the shop," said Kenton. "We can hide the cars in there until we return them to Gary's for recycling."

"Okay" said James. "The military in the area, are they aware of the drop? How do they know, if shit goes bad, not to shoot us?"

"We will wear bands on our arms that are dark to the naked eye but very reflective to their night vision equipment. That is our only means to differentiate ourselves. The platoon on patrol have been informed there are some covert troop operations happening in the area so they will look for the bands if we call them for backup. Okay, if there is nothing else, let's get prepared."

The men broke apart, and James put on the kettle for his traditional cup of tea before he began work. David went out to the back porch with Scott.

"This is what I miss about not living here, the view everywhere is so beautiful. You don't get this in Canada," said David.

"No, that is why it is so hard for me to leave here," said Scott.

The two men stood in silence for a while as they ran their parts of the plan through their head.

James' kettle had boiled, and he made a cup of tea, "Dad, you want a spot of tea as well?"

"No, I am fine. How is Elizabeth and Amy doing?" said Kenton.

James sat back down at the table as Kenton cleaned up the papers and maps.

"Fine, Elizabeth is doing her usual bitching 'when will all this end' but she also likes to spend the money we make quicker than I can launder it," James said with a smile. "Amy is good, she is in High School. Her plans are to go to University and major in Psychology. I think she thinks she can crack this old skull and see what is truly inside one day."

Kenton laughed, "Well, there would be a career of analyzing if she got in there. I can only imagine if she got into wee David's head."

The two men sat together at the table. "What is the other job for David? Anything I can help with?" James asked.

"No, I just need someone reminded who their allegiance is with, seems they have forgotten and need a refresher. Small things like that. Then a trip to Boston. You can sit that out and spend a couple days at the house in Portrush, before you head home. David is my new guy for these jobs," Kenton said.

"Yea, good, bad, messed up or fine, David outshines us in our careers. It is turning into a full-time job just laundering his money. These jobs, here, don't even touch some of the CIA money. He was in South America a month ago for two weeks. You should see the money they paid him for those jobs. I guess the Americans used him, working with CIA agents to help topple a small country's government."

"Aye, good for him, we talked about it last time he was over. Let's face it, the troubles here are dying down. There won't be much left on the bones for him to have in a few years. All this talk about peace and one united Ireland. It is a wave that is growing in the distance," said Kenton.

"Aye, it is good we diversified years ago, or we would be in trouble now," said James as he drank his tea.

"Well, we should get the cars ready and move out," said Kenton.

James took one last drink of his tea and headed to the back porch to get the other two.

"Time to roll," he announced.

"Aye, I guess it is," said Scott.

The three of them re-entered the house. They grabbed the keys for each vehicle and headed out the front door.

Scott said, "I need to grab something out of the Ford, start her up Dad and I will be right over."

Kenton's Land Rover was backed up to the shed door. The other two cars were parked in front of it with the brown Austin closest to the road and the red Ford sandwiched between the two vehicles. Kenton walked to the back of the Rover and opened the back door. He looked at the inventory to ensure it was all secured for the drive.

Scott and James were at the trunk of the Ford. Scott removed the bag he carried with him on all of these jobs. It was a canvas shoulder bag; it had some medical items to sterilize and bandage up any body parts that might take a hit from a knife or a bullet. It had his pistol; the one Kenton gave him when he came of age. He had only fired it once to kill a person, but had spent thousands of bullets while he worked on his aim and speed. Of course, there was his fake wallet with all his fake ID's and cards. And the one thing people made fun of since he was a kid, his Daffy Duck. Some people had statues of Mary or Saint Christopher or a wooden or gold cross as a protector of life, but not Scott. Scott had a small key chain sized Daffy Duck. Daffy was about three inches in height with one hand in the air, it held a white top hat, the other hand held a wooden cane, and his body covered in a white tux. That was what Scott used as his religious charm, heavenly protection, or good luck, it depended on how he felt about religion that day. Daffy had been on every job with him. He had traveled the world with Scott. If Daffy could speak Scott would have a lot to answer for to any authority that would listen. But every person had their good luck charm, even if it was a cartoon duck with a lisp. Scott reached into his bag and pulled out Daffy, looked at it and placed him back into the bag.

David passed by Kenton and gave him a wave. Kenton smiled and waved back to David, the grandson he loved. The only grandchild he would allow into the inner circle of the business. The other grandkids might dabble a little on the outside with reconnaissance work or delivering parcels at drop points, but they never knew why they were doing it. David knew as much, if not more, than James. David had met with all of Kenton's contacts and had planned and completed many jobs for Kenton.

Kenton climbed into the Land Rover and fumbled around for the ignition key. He checked his pockets then remembered he left the keys above the sun visor, an old habit he had a hard time breaking. He took the key and inserted it into the ignition. He turned the key to the right to start the car.

The explosion under the Land Rover came from the rear axle area of the car. The detonation caused the rear of the vehicle to lift into the air a foot, then slam back to the ground.

The light from the fire ball blinded David, who was the closest to the Rover. The blast wave of the explosion threw him back onto the grass. He lay on the ground as the car became engulfed in flames. His ears rung like the Notre Dame Cathedral bells on Christmas morning. His skin was burnt, and his nose bled. The blood from his nose ran down his cheek and around his ear.

James, the furthest away, and protected by his car was the first to react to the fire ball. He heard Kenton's screams echo in the Rover as he burned alive.

The explosive placed by the back axle was only enough to explode the back of the car and engulf it in flames. Only an expert could measure out the right weight of explosives to have that happen to a vehicle.

In Kenton's last moment of consciousness, he attempted to open his door, but the explosion had twisted the frame and doors. Kenton, not killed immediately, fell unconscious. His clothes melted to his skin and brought him back to consciousness. The heat melted his hands into the steering wheel and the plastic that surrounded him dripped on his burnt skin. Trapped in the vehicle, Kenton drew panicked, short breaths. Each breath brought more hot, toxic air into his lungs.

He turned his head to see David sit up, his last action before he suffocated.

Scott spun around in time to see his father turn his head to see David sit on the ground dazed. James ran to David, he slid on his knees as he dropped to David's side. David, still in shock from the explosion looked up to his dad.

"What happened," he asked. He could not hear anything but the muffled mumble of his voice and the even louder church bells that still rang in his ears.

His skin was hot and tender, worse than any sun burn he had ever felt. He struggled to focus his eyes on his dad. Even though James responded to him, he could not hear his dad's response. David lay back down on the grass and cried. He did not need to focus on the car or his dad to know Kenton was dead. *'His mentor, his grandfather, the man he looked up to and had involved him in a way of life he only believed happened in movies, killed by a car bomb, in our own driveway of our safe house. How could this have happened? Someone did this while we were inside the house,'* David thought.

He came out of his shock and sat up. The ringing in his ears quieted down, and looked at his dad. Tears ran down James' cheeks.

James embraced David when they heard Scott yell, "The shed is on fire too, help!"

David and James jumped up and ran to the side of the house. They had put in a hose connection years ago to water the plants; not too often did they need them watered by hand in Northern Ireland. James ran to the side of the house and turned on the hose. David pulled himself fully out of the daze and confusion his mind was in and ran to the Austin. He took a quick look under the car for anything that looked out of place on the frame before he pulled it away from the fully engulfed Land Rover.

Scott had already done his check under the car and was in the Ford, he moved it away from the fire to a safe area on the road. He ran to David to see if he was okay. David gave him a thumbs up as he moved the car further from the house. They both ran to James, who had the small fire under control in the wooden shed. He watered the Land Rover, he tried to control the fire that was already dying down. The smell of burnt flesh wafted from the car, it was only dulled by the stench of burning plastic, paint, oils, and fuel. There were two more explosions, as the front tires finally gave up the air within them. James jumped back and tripped on the hose, he soaked himself. Scott and David watched as James struggled with the hose while he lay on his back. With the tragedy that had just occurred, the two men were able to muster up a laugh at James and his comedic action entangled with a simple garden hose. The three men gathered and investigated the burnt vehicle. Kenton's burnt body had fallen forward, and his head now leaned on the steering wheel. His hands were still melted into the steering wheel, like someone stressed in a traffic jam.

Scott went to the back of the shed and started the tractor. He pulled it around front and moved the burnt car away from the house and around to the back, out of sight from anyone that might pass. James and David followed the tractor, arms around each other.

David looked out over the moonlit fields. He noticed a reflection two fields over. He looked again, he could see a person with binoculars held to his face. David sprinted the half mile to where the person was located. Despite all the pain he felt from being thrown to the ground and his burnt skin tighten, adrenaline had taken over.

The person jumped to his feet and headed to his car, hidden behind some bushes. David sprinted with all the power and speed his legs would muster. He made it to the location just in time to see a white Vauxhall Cavalier speed away. He stopped at the place where the man had hidden, David investigated the area for any evidence. There was a handful of cigarette butts and the binoculars the man used to watch the house and explosion. David assumed this guy was an amateur, paid to confirm the bomb went off and there was at least one death. No professional would leave this stuff. David gathered the items as he tried to catch his breath from the sprint.

Scott had grabbed the garden hose from the front and worked on a couple spots where the vehicle was still smoldering. James looked closer at the Land Rover then the shed. The Rover was completely engulfed in flames earlier, but now only smoked. Kenton's silhouette against the moonlight was now mostly muscle and skeleton.

"Where did you go? You took off like a dog chasing a fox. We didn't know if you had cracked and were running away," said James, to David when he returned.

"Never, Dad. I would never do that," he answered between gasps for air. "I saw a light reflect off something. The second time I could see binoculars and a man. I sprinted as fast as I could, but I couldn't catch him. I saw the car he left in and he left a few things on his perch. We can discuss that later. We lost Granda, I can't believe he is gone!" he reached out to Scott and James the two men pulled David close to themselves. The three men held each other and cried. They had lost their father, grandfather, and boss.

"Dad, I know it is too late to say, but I had a feeling earlier in my gut about something going bad and didn't speak up," said David.

That gut feeling or little voice in his head that he ignored this time would be his guiding star in the future. Never again would he ignore that voice or feeling, especially during a job.

James broke the embrace of the other two, "We will need to get this cleaned up, it doesn't sound like the fire brigade is coming so I guess no one called in the fire."

"Thankfully, it is bonfire season," said Scott.

"I will go inside and make some calls; we will have to let the client know we will not be making the drop. Hopefully, they can reach out to their people and inform them. I will call Gary and tell him we need a tow truck out here tonight," said James.

"Aye, we will keep watering down the vehicle to cool it off and see if anything is salvageable in the Rover," said Scott.

David had a rush of emotions run through him, "I could take the Ford and drive around the area to see if I can find that car. Find the bastards that did this to us. Many people will die for this, maybe not tonight but blood will spill for this. When I get my hands on them, they will die. Very, very slowly and painfully. I bet that fucker Nigel had something to do with this."

The three men broke apart and took to their tasks. David drove the ancient roads around the area, he looked for the car or anything out of what he thought was the ordinary. James made the phone calls. Scott continued to wash down the Rover with a hose and was able to hide his tears by the spray of the nozzle. As the three men went about the chores, they all had the same mantra run through their heads. There will be a time to mourn and a time for payback. They all knew that.

David returned after an hour. He drove the roads around the area. While alone in the car he had many emotions run through him, the one that settled into his heart was one of revenge.

James finished with the immediate phone calls. He sat outside on the back porch alone with his thoughts while he waited for the police to arrive and write their report. Scott emptied the vehicle of all the weapons and removed as many embedded bullets as possible. The police contact James called would not search the car too carefully, he had worked with the family and knew what they were involved in. The vehicle would be brought to Gary's Garage where an investigation team would remove what remained of the explosive.

The police did their investigation and Kenton's body was removed from the vehicle. His remains were transported to the morgue to wait for Keith, a family friend and undertaker, to claim the body. He would prepare what was left of it for burial. They called an ambulance for David; he had more injuries than first realized. David sat in the ambulance and answered questions from the police while he received stitches on his arm and his thigh. They gave him some pain pills and told him to take it easy for a couple of days.

James finished up with his interrogation, went into the house and looked for some whiskey for himself and Scott. He found a bottle and brought it out with two glasses and sat on the back porch. The excitement of the evening had quieted down. There were only the three of them left with a couple of police officers. The Land Rover was towed away. David asked Gary to bring back a clean car and remove the other two vehicles. The police were satisfied by their quick investigation. They made sure that James, Scott, and David felt safe and did not need any protection. James reassured them that they could take care of themselves.

Gathered on the back porch, James poured drinks for himself and Scott, David grabbed some water from the house to wash down some pills.

"To Dad, and all he has done for us," toasted James, and then drank the whole shot.

"Aye" said Scott and David in unison.

"I cannot believe the night we just had, what the hell happened here," said David to no one.

"Well, we need to figure this out. I guess in the morning we will need to call people to let them know our dad has passed," said Scott.

"Aye, I should call Elizabeth now, she will need to get flights for herself and Amy. I will call John after that," said James, two conversations he did not want to have.

James spent the next half hour on the phone, he repeatedly explained to Elizabeth that they, especially David, were all safe. Scott and David cleaned up the front of the shed and took out the travel bags and all the other personal items that were in the other two cars. Gary had the cars towed away and a new Ford Escort dropped off. None of them slept that night, or for a couple days after that, except for the quick nap. The next few days were a whirlwind of funeral plans, visitations, and questions. The person the team were to pick up in the trade was also found dead at the side of a road. His tongue was cut out of his mouth and placed in his left back pant pocket. The crew had a good idea who was behind the two deaths.

David's wounds continued to heal, at least the physical ones. When he had a quiet moment, he sat, and thought, *I am in all the way now, any doubt about my loyalty is in the past. All I want is Nigel. Nigel, Nigel will pay for this and any acquaintance's he might have. He doesn't know who he just started a war with.'*

Elizabeth and Amy arrived, she interrupted the quiet and reflective atmosphere. She scolded David and screamed at James about the risks they take in this line of work. Elizabeth continued to scold, preach, and scream, every chance she got at James, David, and Scott. She might have caused permanent damage to James' hearing. Edward and his family came back from Australia to pay their respects but made it clear he was not home to get involved in anything to do with the business. John and Phil flew over for the funeral and to help if anything needed to be cleaned up afterwards. David was happy to have Phil there. He was able to show him around the area and lean on him during this time of confusion, anger, and sadness. Amy, confused by the whole situation, as she thought her dad and brother were camping in Algonquin Park, had to be filled in on some of the lies they told her over the years. David and Phil took her out for a long drive to answer her questions and help her understand some of the truths about her family. Elizabeth was furious that Amy was told any of the truth and threatened to go back to Canada before the funeral. She was reminded of her role in public and to play along nicely, to ensure her own safety. Doris and Sarah took Elizabeth out for a good talk and reminded her of what they all had signed up for.

• • •

The ceremonies ended, the flowers at the grave had begun to die and people were back to their normal routines. The casserole dishes were emptied, washed, and returned to the mourners who brought the family food. Elizabeth, Amy, and John flew back to Canada. Amy asked John lots of questions on the flight while Elizabeth slept.

James, David, Scott, Phil and Eric, Scott's son, sat down in Kenton's old shop, Scott's new shop, to talk about the future.

James began the meeting with a prayer, he asked for forgiveness for Kenton and all the men who sat around the table.

"Amen. Okay, we have all had slightly more than a week to think since Dad's funeral. Who has thoughts on where we go from here? I will be honest; I would like to step way back from all this. We never got to say goodbye to Dad, and I don't want that for David and you, Phil," James began. "Scott, Dad has been grooming you for this side of the Atlantic, but with the troubles dying down there isn't much left for us here. We are a great depot for weapons, making and selling them around the world and a few other items you have on the go. You know I will always be here to support you, but I would like to spend more time in Canada and travel a lot less."

"I completely understand James, I have Eric coming along with me on business meetings and other jobs. You could take your break, you know, you always have a place to lay your head if you choose to visit or come back for a job," said Scott. "David, you will still be available when we need your skills?"

"Of course, I will. More than ever, Uncle Scott. I am a pager beep away, anytime you need me. Phil and I have enough to keep us busy in North America and other areas, but you will always be a priority to me," said David.

The crew sat for three hours, they talked of jobs they did with Kenton, the rules he had, how he trained them and the jokes he always had when they needed to hear one. For James, David, and Phil their flight time approached. The crew hugged each other as a group. Tears flowed like champagne on New Year's Eve, and no one wanted to be the first to release from the group hug. Finally, James stepped back to break the hold of the others.

• • •

Eric drove David and Phil in one car while Scott drove James, there were a few other items to discuss amongst themselves without the others present. Scott reminded James there was no getting out of his duties for the family business. Death was the only true escape. Edward had moved away, but he wasn't fully in the inner circle. James agreed with Scott, but he wanted to step back for a while. David would assume his duties as the lead of the business and would continue to travel for John. Phil now ran seventy percent of John's side of the business. Scott could keep the money he brought in here for himself and Eric to build a safe place to live. Phil secured another large contract for a shipment of weapons from the Chinese military to a new group in Afghanistan. They wanted a large amount delivered monthly and paid sixty percent up front. That would be Scott and Eric's big customer for the next few years. They agreed to still have weekly meetings to ensure both businesses continued to grow together.

At the airport, there were more hugs and tears as the families said goodbye.

They waited to board the plane, James, David, and Phil talked about Amy. The things they hid from Amy upset her, and she wanted a lot more information. They were all sure Elizabeth would fill her in with the wrong information. They devised a plan to give Amy the full truth and maybe even a small piece of the action if she was interested.

PART THREE
A New Era

CHAPTER SIXTEEN

The 1990s were a different time for the family. The loss of Kenton, their leader, in 1989 was hard on everyone.

In Northern Ireland, Scott continued to make and ship weapons, but stepped back from the hands-on work. Sarah, and Eric, managed the orders and shipments of weapons from the many ports on the island. 'The Troubles,' that made a few people very rich, had begun to die down. The talks of peace was constantly in the news. The British military and government continued to contact John and David for jobs in Ireland and the Commonwealth countries.

In Canada, John, James, and the boy's, worked hard throughout the 1990s to triple the business they did in the 1980s. With the fall of the Soviet Union, peace in Ireland, and the political changes throughout the Middle East and Africa, they continued to diversify themselves and the business.

Inside North America, the U.S.A. took a stand against the Italian Mob, bike gangs and strengthened their stand on drugs. John hid more people, under the family's 'witness protection program,' than the U.S. government did with theirs. John and James worked closely with Scott to move weapons, of all sizes, around the world. With the 'can do' attitude they continued to build relationships with governments and agencies around the world.

David, everyone's 'go to guy', had perfected his skills and was known by many around the world, some he worked for, some he helped to destroy. His kill numbers grew every year and his skills changed with the new technology. Phil and David had new directions they wanted to take the business. John and James supported the boys' expansion of the family business. The only downside of the expansion was John and James had to become even more creative in how they hide the money that flowed through the office.

David had a network of people to look for Kenton's killer. Most were expected to check in with Phil weekly. One of his contacts, found a Nigel, but before David could get to South Africa, Nigel had left for a new location.

The family's presence in the world during the 1990s was never fully known, except by a few.

So much happened to The Family over that decade, too many tales for one book.

●　●　●

Guelph, 2002
David had been away for a week. This time, in Daytona Beach, Florida. He was hired to do some work for John and after the job he attended an auto race. On his way home, airport security pulled him out of the line to board the plane and questioned him. He resembled a person wanted for the murder of three Cubans in Fort Myers. They brought him into a small, windowless room and questioned him about his location during his stay in the great state of Florida. They showed him a pixilated image of the person—David—they were looking for. He always had a secondary story and showed them a ticket for a tour he was on in Daytona at the date and time of the incident, thankfully, Phil always covered the details. On this job Phil did not mention or know of the camera.

David stood at his parents' front door with coffees. He balanced the tray of coffees while he rang the doorbell. James came to the door to let him in.

"Hey Dad, I thought I would stop by since I am back from Florida. I went to the Firecracker 400 while I was there," said David.

"David, where have you been," his mother said from the kitchen. "I haven't heard from you in over two weeks. I didn't know if you were alive or dead," said Elizabeth.

"Hello Mom, sorry to disappoint you, but I am still alive," David said.

"Everything good, son?" said James.

"Yes, all good, Dad. Mom, I brought coffee."

"Why would you do that? Is mine not good enough for you? So where were you this time? I don't suppose you were actually on a vacation with someone, were you? Or were you off doing the work of the devil?"

"Away with Satan himself, Mom," David said, as he smiled at his dad.

"Ok, well, you and your Dad disappear into his office and chat, like you always do. I will just continue to worry about my son and his safety. Why don't you just take over the plumbing business from John and settle down?" she said. She already knew the answer.

"Mom, I didn't come here to be preached at, here is your coffee. I am going to talk to Dad."

"Of course, you are," she said.

James was already in his office, tired of the banter between the two. Over the next hour David told James about his trip to Daytona and the success there. He explained how he contacted a new customer in Miami, who needed a lot of weapons, explosives, and vehicles. He discussed his conversation at the airport and his concern that since 9/11 the US has stepped up its camera surveillance of its citizens.

He slipped a stuffed business envelope across the desk to James, full of money that needed to be laundered.

James opened the envelope and counted the money. "I never made money like this in my day."

"Yea, being third generation in the business and the training you and granda gave me makes me irresistible."

They talked about some business that happened when David was away.

David felt the vibration of his pager and pulled it from his belt buckle and hit the read button. *'Need some credit cards cut,'* said the message.

"I guess it is back to work for me. This is becoming a full-time gig. The guys in the shop are noticing how much time I am missing at work," David said.

"I guess you should go see your mother before you leave," James reminded David.

"I guess so. I thought it would be different once I moved out, but nothing has changed."

Elizabeth was downstairs in the laundry room when David found her. "Hey Mom, so what is new with you?"

"You need to stop this. When I can't get hold of you, I panic. I went through this with your father and now I can't handle going through it with you. And stop talking to Amy about your extra work, she was never to find out. Until your granda died she thought you were a plumber."

"Mom, you know one call to John, and you can put your..."

"I am not calling that heathen; I curse the day we came to Canada to work with him. We were to be here to avoid all the troubles, not to create them worldwide. No, I will not call him."

"Suit yourself, Mom. How is Amy anyway?"

"She is good too. Doing an honest day's work at her new job."

"That's good, I will give her a call later. I have to go to work."

"Okay that's good, you need some honest work to save your soul from what you have been doing."

"Yes, Mom. I didn't—never mind. See you later."

David reached to give her a hug, but she turned and continued to load the dryer.

"Dad, I am heading out." David yelled to James, who was still upstairs.

James met David at the front door "Take care. All the best with this one, stay smart and safe."

•　　•　　•

Michigan, 2002

"May the Lord bless you and keep you, may his face shine upon you and be gracious unto you and give you peace," Pastor Paul said to his large congregation and the TV audience around the world.

David sat in the audience. He couldn't believe the spectacle that was this church service. It certainly was nothing like the church services he attended when he was young. The building itself, just outside of Detroit, Michigan, would put any music hall or European cathedral to shame. The gold leaf, the artwork, and the sound quality in the sanctuary were eye and ear popping delights. David sat at the back of the packed four-thousand seat, two-tiered auditorium.

The service ended and the crowd filed out. The camera crew shut down their equipment as the director removed the microphone from Paster Paul. David sat and watched as Paul went to the crowd to shake hands. He only approached those in the front three rows. David's notes mentioned those were the big money people. If you gave the church more than $300 thousand annually you had reserved seats in those rows. *'I guess those are the guaranteed seats for heaven,'* David thought. The rest of the seats were general admission.

This was one of his strangest assignments ever. Take out a pastor who on the surface, looked to be a normal, God fearing, television evangelist. He was very rich, but a person with a normal family who worked hard to 'save the world from Satan's grip' or so the church's pamphlet on him claimed. He had a personality that drew people to him, and with his sermons on prosperity and giving back to the Lord, how could you not love him? Typical of all churches, this one did not pay any taxes even though its net worth was over $250 million. It gave back enough, to the community and the world by the works the church did, or so their booklet would tell you. Pastor Paul was one of the best-known pastors, not only in the Detroit area, but also around the world. Millions of television viewers saw his church service every Sunday and it ran all week around the world in syndication.

The package for this job was one of the thickest he had ever received. David usually only wanted the details he needed to do the job; Phil would filter the rest for him. This job, David had to know a bit more. When the job was presented to him a couple of weeks ago, David remembered the lesson from Kenton. *'You never do anything to a man or his family while he is in a church or attending a church service.'* That unwritten rule stuck with David even now. Easy as it would be today to finish the job, he would not do it in a church.

David, sat in his seat, he watched how the Pastor interacted with his high rollers, just like a manager at a casino.

"Sir, the service is over. We will be locking up shortly, is there anything I can help you with?" asked an usher.

"Oh, I was hoping to see Pastor Paul, I traveled from Canada to see him today. I have a sister that needs healing, I was hoping he would pray for her."

"Sorry Pastor Paul only sees people through appointments, he has a very full schedule."

"Oh, I understand. He is just down there. Could I not speak with him? My family is hoping to donate to one of his foundations, we understand we need to give back to God to see his miracles happen on earth. Who would I talk to about that?" David said.

"You could come to the main building tomorrow and set up an appointment with his staff. One of them would gladly help you. They will help you find the right ministry for your donation and they would pray for healing for your sister. If the Lord wants her healed, she will be healed."

"Okay, thank you for your help, this was a blessing to my heart today," said David humbly.

David slowly made his way to the front entrance of the building.

"Sir, sir, please don't use that door there are protesters outside. We recommend you leave by the back door to get to your car," an usher said as he helped an elderly man back into his wheelchair.

"Thank you. I would hate to walk out into a mob of angry sinners," said David.

"God bless, sir," was the usher's farewell.

David headed down a long hallway. Photos of Pastor Paul with members of governments from around the world, music stars, actors and military personnel hung on the walls. Not one photo of a homeless person or an average Joe. The security in the building was very tight, like no church David had ever attended before. He headed out the back door and sat in his borrowed car.

A helicopter lifted off from the roof of the building.

David shook his head, "I can see why they are protesting him," he said to only himself.

•　　•　　•

"Okay Sean, I need to make a stop on the way home," Paul said as he approached his helicopter. "Can you have the pilot stop at the hospital I have a couple people to visit?"

"Yes sir," said Sean.

Paul had just returned from a tour of Afghanistan where he visited with soldiers, led church services, and spent time one on one with higher-level officers. This was all to help them get right or stay right with God during a time of war. These men needed to be saved to get to heaven for all their good work they did, for God and country, he would say when anyone asked why he went to visit soldiers. Of course, many of these soldiers would give money during the church services 'for the Lord's work.' Paul sat in meetings, high-level meetings, where they discussed information, and drew up plans. As the Spiritual

Advisor to the President of the United States, no one considered him a national security threat.

Paul's helicopter landed on the roof of the hospital. Paul and Sean headed to the elevator to take the ride down to the wing Paul donated and built five years ago.

As Paul walked the hallways of his wing, he stopped into rooms and spoke with people. Sean would keep the visits short, but each person received a 'blessing of healing' from the pastor. Paul's team had talked to the nurses and knew what rooms to have him avoid due to someone with a contagious disease, or a possible complaint for the pastor. The people recovering from physical ailments, Paul touched and blessed them, he even had a person stand or walk. Of course, these quick miracles only happened if the cameras were on. Once Paul moved to the next room, the hospital staff would carefully return the person to their bed for a rest before more physio and procedures the next day.

On the second floor of his wing, they built a room for him to have meetings. It had a second back entrance, there were no security cameras, in the parking lot or in the hallways. This allowed his special guests to remain anonymous. Paul made his way through the hallways while his guests, a couple of umpires from Major League Baseball and a few officials from the ATP, Association of Tennis Professionals, waited in the room. They were all members of his church and would help any way they could, for the right price.

Paul sat at the head of the conference table. He discussed upcoming games in the MLB, who to bet on or who to bet against, of course his friends would umpire those games. Everyone's big money maker this summer was to pick an underdog at the US Open tennis tournament. Like they had done in the past the winnings would be shared with those around the table. The group reviewed the games and tournament picking who he would bet on. Paul slid four envelopes across the table. Everyone's big money maker was to pick an underdog at the US Open tennis tournament and guide that player to the championship.

Paul was indebted to the mob and a few other organizations. Even with his friends manipulating sporting events he was losing money. He owed almost eight million dollars in gambling loses. He had been reminded a few times that his debt needed to be paid before something bad happened to him or a family member.

Paul and Sean left the meeting room and walked through his wing. He stopped at different rooms to bless people before he returned to his helicopter and headed home to his fifteen-thousand square foot mansion that backed onto Orchard Lake.

• • •

Early the next morning, Paul took the helicopter back to the church where he prepared for his weekly staff meeting.

"Hello, ladies and gentlemen," said Paul, as he entered the full boardroom.

He missed two of these meetings due to his visit to Afghanistan, so the room had more staff than usual. The meeting lasted over three hours. It finally ended with a Bible study and prayer. The Bible study Paul prepared reviewed the ethics of the church and how each member must stand above his or her friends to show others how a great Christian should look and act. Once the meeting ended, Paul went to his office to meet with his managers. The three men had been with Paul since he first started his ministry in the gym of a public school. As Paul grew his ministry, they became his top leaders. They took care of most of his business matters, his personal appearances and the oversight of the many churches started under the Paul Richards Church franchise name.

"Welcome back, Paul. You had a good trip?" asked Bruce.

Bruce was the only man dressed in a three-piece navy suit, and Paul's business manager.

"The church service yesterday morning was especially powerful. The part about fighting the war on poverty not only in your neighborhood, but around the world, well timed with the news this week. From what the overnight numbers show, our viewership was up thirty-five percent from last week's sermon at the air force base. Not too bad at all, considering last week you had a plea for help with the war," said Bruce.

"Thanks, Bruce. Whatever I can do to line our pockets, I mean do the Lord's work," he said as he touched his chest with his right hand. "What have I really missed while I was traveling?"

"Here is a rundown of personal appearance requests for the next three months, a lot of requests for visits to South America," Bruce said, as he slid a folder across the table to Paul.

"Okay, I will review them. More soup kitchens and homeless shelters, I suppose? Why can't strip joints request my service?"

"Congress would like a prayer service for the troops. It would be you, with them on the steps of the Capitol Building this Wednesday. It's a good photo op for us. It is last minute, but you need to attend. The President would also like a few minutes of your time when you are in Washington."

"Okay, what else have you got? I could use a bit of fun. Being stuck on military bases in a war zone is boring and lonely."

"Yea, we can make Washington an extended trip, I will make the travel arrangements. We can jump on the plane and hit Washington tonight, enjoy the city for a day, then attend the prayer meeting, hopefully sober. I have been looking forward to some of our shipments you brought back from Afghanistan as well," said Sean.

"Okay, extend the trip. I forgot to mention, our Christian camps, in the Middle East, are working well and the locals are being converted to Christians and more importantly, drug mules or sex slaves. That country is messed up. Our government has destroyed many local economies to the point there is nothing left for the people but, to move arms, drugs, or fuck, for money. Our charities have moved many people out of

Afghanistan, to do the company's work in other nations. We now have an agreement with a few more organizations to transfer the right people from our camps, however they see fit, to South America and Africa. I don't care if it helps to bring down some of my gambling debts. The number of missing children is astonishing in some parts of Afghanistan. I can only imagine where they are ending up, someone has a large organization taking these kids. Anything else, at this point, fellas? If not, I have a couple meetings then we can be wheels up at four o'clock," said Paul.

"Paul, I am getting a little stressed over some of the extra projects we are taking on overseas. Yea, 9/11 has made us all richer, but is this why we all got into the ministry? The money from the television rights and donations should be enough, why are we jeopardizing it for the illegal stuff? Our donations are up thousands of percent since 9/11. Are we not going to bring some unwelcome attention to ourselves eventually? I mean, we must be stepping on someone's toes as we expand, even with the blessing from certain sections of the government. We can only hide this behind the church walls for so long. Think about it, we are building camps to help those affected by the wars and then using those people as mules or prostitutes, with the promise of a better life somewhere else in the world. I know the other organizations are too, but do we need to? I wonder if even you, can convince God to have our sins forgiven for all this."

"I don't see you complaining when you head home to your trophy wife and car collection. Get off your high horse and fall in line, Bruce. No one would suspect our ministry to be doing any of these things. We just need to continue with our good work, the side the public sees. Our pastors are doing great work across the country, hell the world, spreading God's word, they don't need to know about our secondary business structure. That was why we became non-denominational, remember? When we broke away from the Baptist community to stop giving them ten percent of our earnings and the constant auditing.

"Yes, I know, but I feel we are pushing some limits here, that's all. Look, we can talk on the plane, you have a news briefing in half an hour at a soup kitchen. Don't forget to mention your trip to Afghanistan and the good work the church is doing there."

Paul left the room with Sean.

"Sean, I want Bruce followed to ensure there are no issues with him or the doubts he has," said Paul. "If we feel he is going to talk, we have people that can deal with him and his family.

"Yes, I agree. His questions concerned me."

David left his hotel room, dressed as a homeless person, and headed to the location of Paul's press conference. Paul was at a soup kitchen in Ann Arbor. He was scheduled to feed the multitudes of needy people and donate $250 thousand dollars to upgrade the building.

David shuffled along the line of people to finally meet Paul. David had no plan to kill him today, but if the opportunity arose, he would be ready.

David approached the Pastor, he was told by a helper, "Smile, say thank you, and move on. Do not stop to talk to him or reach out and touch him."

David nodded in agreement. "Who is this guy? Is he really trying to help us," he said to the lady behind him.

"Why would you say that? He is here to save us, to help us. If we believe, God will raise us up to greatness," she said with a trance like cadence to her voice.

David shook his head and turned away from her. Three more people and then he would reach his target and stand in front of him. The man in front of him reached out and shook Paul's hand. The security team jumped the man, his tray of food was spilt, and he was led to the back door, without supper. David received his 'gift of love' from Paul and continued. He now knew how he could get to Paul. He left the building and went to the back where security had escorted the man. He sat on the ground beside the door.

"Here, take this, sir," David offered as he placed the container of food on the man's lap.

"No, No. I don't deserve it. But I touched him, I actually touched him. My life will be better now that I touched him," he said.

"Okay sure, but please take the food too, it will also help you."

The man took the food from David, and with a large smile on his face, he ate. David walked past the front of the homeless shelter. He could see Pastor Paul, he stood on a table and preached to the homeless as they ate their free meal.

• • •

'This might just work,' he thought as he packed his bag to head back home. He needed to discuss his plan with John and the team.

David sat on the bed and quickly made notes on his plan to assassinate Paul. The timeline would need to be stretched out a few extra days. Paul's next scheduled public appearance was at another soup kitchen in Denver the next week. That would give David some time to rig up a device that could kill the pastor.

The next morning David was back in Guelph meeting with Phil, James, and John on how he thought the job could run. John had already contacted his customers to let them know they would need to delay the job by seven days.

David, as had become routine, asked Phil for an update from all his contacts. He wanted to know if there were any leads on his granda's killer. Once David was satisfied with Phil's update, he turned his attention to the job he was currently being paid to complete. Both Phil and David knew if something went wrong while David stood and talked to Paul, the congregation would tear him to shreds.

David and Phil sat at the boardroom table. They reviewed and broke down the steps required to successfully complete the job. David had CNN on and noticed, Al-Qaeda ambushed and killed two CIA agents and a small, specialized crew of American soldiers out on patrol. They were killed on a reconnaissance mission while they searched through caves in Afghanistan. The team was one of the Army teams Paul had just visited.

Phil, as usual, would take the trip with David for support and help. With all the press at any public event Paul did, David's identity would need to be protected.

They spent a couple days in Denver before the job. They rode their bikes through the hills and trails and relaxed at the hotel. It seemed over the last year, each job David did, it weighed on him more. He looked for a way out of this messy life that had entangled him. He used to be happy with the challenge of the jobs and bored with the plumbing job. Over the last few months, especially since 9/11, David wanted a life where he did not constantly look over his shoulder, worried someone was after him. Lately he had a couple jobs that were close calls with the authorities or had bullets just miss his head. His grandfather died while he fought the good fight. David couldn't see the line between good and bad anymore.

This job he did lately definitely had blurred lines. The few days in Denver again played with his emotions, *'Here I am chasing down a pastor, once again those lines are blurred,'* he thought, *'a man of God and I am here to kill him.'*

"Phil, this is it; I am out once we are home. The money we will make on this job will take care of us for a long time. I am done with this shit," David said.

"David, this is why I come with you. Lately every time you do a job you go through this. Focus on the job at hand. We can discuss this on the plane ride home. What is eating at you lately? You used to get up for these jobs, no questions, no emotion, just in and out. We spent four days here planning. We never did that before; we would come in, do our thing and be home within thirty-six hours."

"I know, I know. Maybe a person can only kill so many people? My number is up there, maybe I need a break. This has been a busy year. It seems the world is getting more fucked up, and for some reason, I am the answer. Or maybe it is the way we are killing him, this is a new way that we have no control over, usually it's all in my hands how they die. I cannot believe Dad and John got this method approved, but that is why they hire us, I guess," David said.

The lack of emotion in the joke he just cracked concerned Phil as he pulled a bag out of the closet in the room. "Is your head in this dude? I am worried, this one is a lot more complicated than the other jobs we do, you need to be focused. Want some music on?"

"Yea, that might help, throw on some Matthew Good, for me."

Phil did, and David found his groove as they prepared to leave for work.

They prepared for the job, while the album played. Phil got out their equipment while David laid on the bed, he mentally reviewed the procedure, visualized the food shelter and how he would approach the Pastor and ask for a blessing, the way he would hold the cross then receive it back.

"Let's get going," Phil said. "Are you feeling better now?"

"Yea, I am good. I guess this is why I bring you on these jobs. You are my voice of sanity that helps keep the rest of the voices in my head quiet."

"What? I thought you brought me because I pay for everything and act like your bloody butler."

The two headed out to the van that was left for them at the airport when they arrived in Denver. An unmarked white Ford cargo van. You could see the road through the floorboards and each time they took the van for a drive they joked that another couple of parts were left behind somewhere on the road. They knew like most vehicles they drove on their excursions once they returned this van to the airport it would not be around for much longer. The two climbed in and headed downtown.

• • •

"Park over there, it's not our first choice, but we considered it and the space is available," David said.

Phil pulled the van into the parking spot. David climbed into the van's cargo area and changed into the worn-out clothes he had in the bag. Phil helped him put on the wig and baseball cap.

"Do we want to use the nose, or do you think this is enough?" Phil said.

David looked in the rear-view mirror, "I think we should be good. The hair covers my ears and since I haven't shaved in a couple weeks, the beard covers the features on my face. Let's go with this look. Plus, we had issues with the nose staying on yesterday, I don't think they would buy that I had leprosy if my fake nose fell off."

"Okay, here is the cross. You know how to hold it, correct? I have the antibody here, but there is no guarantee it will help you if you get any poison on your skin," said Phil.

"I know, the chemist we got this from scared the shit out of me on this chemical. Yes, I have practiced this all week. It is amazing what they can make in a couple days. I can't believe I was able to come up with this plan and they had it built and ready to execute within a week. Granda would never have believed it. I really hope he is looking over my shoulder on this one."

"Okay, here is the vile. Load it in the cross and good luck, brother. I will be around the corner ready to go, just like we planned."

David placed the cross in one pocket and the vile of Batrachotoxin in the left side pocket of his oversized, worn out and torn raincoat. They shook hands and David exited the van by the back door. He headed to the soup kitchen so the world's favorite Pastor, Paul, would feed and bless him.

• • •

David stepped into an alley beside the food kitchen and loaded the deadly chemical into the cross. The safety was still engaged on the cross, but still, David feared even a drop of the liquid on his skin. His hand shook a little as he placed the hidden cap on the cross. He tossed the vile into the dumpster, couple rats scurried out of it. He proceeded to the long line at the soup kitchen.

David couldn't believe what he heard in the line around all these homeless and poverty-stricken people. They all talked like this man was the second coming of Christ. The excitement of the crowd was like bunch of teenage girls at a Britney Spears concert. *'If they only knew the secrets he kept, and they would soon, if I do my job right,'* David thought.

The man behind David asked, "Are you going to have him touch your cross?"

"Yes," David said with excitement, "If he touches my cross my life will be complete. He is such a wonderful man who walks in the footprints of Christ. We will break bread with him today. Being in his presence is enough to make my life change for the better, yours too!"

David noticed security at this appearance was incredible. There were people all throughout the building. Like the last soup kitchen David attended, security monitored the lines for anyone who looked like they had any agenda. Pastor Paul's promotion team did not want anyone to jump out of line or misbehave in front of the cameras and press. The closer he got, the staff instructed and constantly reminded David, and all the others in line how to handle themselves when they met the great man himself. David asked the final controller before he got to Paul if he could have his cross blessed. He took out $1,000 and explained how it took him a month to save this for the betterment of Paul's congregation. They gave him permission.

David continued to shuffle closer to his target. He hit the button carefully that released the safety on the cross, it was now armed. As he held the safety button his hand cramped, if he let go now or relaxed his grip, his life would end quickly and painfully.

David held the trigger tight. He reviewed how he would hand the cross to Paul, he needed to be precise. Paul needed to take the cross a certain way or they both would be flailing on the ground like fish out of water.

One more person.

●   ●   ●

"Bless you, may God use you for the betterment of his world. God bless you," said Paul to the man in front of David.

David stepped up to be blessed by Paul. The man he showed the $1,000 to whispered in Paul's ear.

"Sir could you bless me and my cross, I saved $1,000 for you to use for God's work," David said, in his rehearsed nervous voice.

"Yes, for your generous donation to the church I will take your cross and bless it," said Paul.

"Thank you."

David handed the cross to Paul. He guided him to take the top of the cross. As David's hand released the trigger, the cavity inside the cross pressurized slightly. The pressure released the Batrachotoxin out through the small needles placed throughout the cross. To Pastor Paul, it would just feel like the sweat from David's hand all over the cross, but it would be the Batrachotoxin being absorbed into his skin.

Paul took the cross, he gripped it firmly with both hands.

He raised it over his head and said, "May God bless this man and may he hold this cross as a symbol of God's love and protection for him. May Jesus' love and compassion enrich his life."

Paul lowered the cross to his mouth and kissed it, the small needles pushed the last of the poison into his bloodstream. David couldn't believe the time Paul took with his cross, obviously, the longer he held the better. The chemical transferred from the cross to Paul's skin and like a bullet leaving a gun headed for his nervous system.

"Here you are my son, God has smiled on you today, go and spread the good news."

"Thank you, Pastor Paul, yes I feel He has smiled on me today. Thank you for your love and comfort," said David.

David carefully took back the cross from Paul. There were two spots on the arm of the cross David could safely touch, the rest potentially still had poison on it. David received the cross and carefully put it in his satchel. He then took the tray of food and moved down the line. David knew he had about five minutes to get to the van before the effects of the poison would take over Paul's body and kill him.

He sat at a table while Paul continued to bless people and hand out food. Then, suddenly the line stopped and there was a commotion, Paul's people gathered around him and helped him to the back of the kitchen. David saw this and took his opportunity to leave. He left his food untouched and headed to the van. The sound of sirens drew closer to the building as he made his way to the parked van.

"How did it go?" Phil asked once David buckled himself in.

"Good, he actually kissed the cross once, he rubbed it and blessed it. It didn't take long after that for the poison to kick in."

"Nice, let's pull away from here and drop off the van, you can change while I am driving. Did you get any on you?"

"No, it was perfect. I was worried he would rub it all over the cross, but he held it in one hand and placed the other on top as he held it, he raised it up, said some bullshit, then he lowered it to his lips and kissed it right on the intersection of the cross where most of the chemical would be. That bit of showmanship sealed his future."

David and Phil left downtown Denver and headed to the airport. A car waited for them closer to the airport where they planned to drop off the van and its contents. When the pair made the exchange of vehicles, they hid all their items in the back of the van. David knew with this operation the van would disappear before they even reached the airport.

They stopped at a bar for some food and to celebrate quietly, with six hours to wait before their flight. The restaurant usually showed sporting events, when they arrived Fox News and CNN were on every screen.

Their food arrived and a *'breaking news, update'* came on the screen. *'TV evangelist and spiritual leader to many of our Presidents and great man of God has been rushed to a Denver hospital. We currently have no information on why he was brought to the hospital. We have a reporter at the hospital now with a full update coming at the top of the hour. What we do know is, Pastor Paul was at a food bank in Denver helping the needy when he was rushed to St Luke's Hospital. A press conference is scheduled for seven o'clock tonight.'*

David smiled at Phil. He raised his glass of water and Phil raised his Coors.

"Wow," David said. "That was a crazy one, but we did it."

The two sat quietly and ate their meals, David still did not feel right about this job.

"Phil, I know I don't do this, but do you have the full document on this guy? I would love to know what he did that was so bad. Not many people have more than one organization that wants them gone."

"Yea, I can get the package out of the car, it is in my bag. I meant to leave it with the van." said Phil.

"Can you grab it please. Then, we can find somewhere to destroy it before we leave for the airport."

While David waited for Phil to return, he received a text message over his pager. 'TY' was all it said, another successful job confirmed by his contacts. Phil came back in and slid the folder across the table to David. "Here read up, then go throw up."

David opened the booklet and read the report.

David whispered, "Is this a misprint? He owned that much in gambling debts, and he paid officials and players to throw games? How the fuck do you pay officials and still lose money on sports? Well, that explains the Mobs donation to this job. Military locations, to the Afghani's or whoever asked and paid? No way. Prostitution and sex trafficking too? After all the work his church does to help prevent sex trafficking? Wow, now I wish I had done him in with my own hands. His whole inner circle was in on it? Why am I not helping more of these guys see the real heaven? How the hell could he be so squeaky clean on tv and be running all this in the background, unreal."

"Yea, I think over the next week they will round up the rest of his associates and that is how they will release all this to the news."

"The money people sent him, life savings, I don't know what to say. Well, I guess the catholic church will enjoy having the spotlight taken off them for a bit."

"How do you feel now?" Phil said.

"About this, or what we talked about earlier?" asked David.

"About the earlier conversation," said Phil.

"I think I still want out, maybe not right now and maybe not fully. I have a bad feeling in the back of my mind something big is coming and we want to avoid it. My grandfather always said, 'Listen to the voice in your head, it won't lead you down a bad path, it knows things you can't.' Granda would walk away from jobs if his little voice spoke up. I am at that point; the voice is saying I only have so much time."

"Come on, you don't believe that, do you? I don't expect to see you do this when you are sixty, but we are still young, now is the time to make money, we can enjoy it later!"

"If there is a later for us?"

"Dude, you need to get laid or something. This is why I drink to get away from it for a bit. You need to find a way to get away from it. I have been telling you that for a while now. We need to get our bikes back out. Hit the roads like we did when we were young. Stop taking every job."

"Yea, you are right. We should be on our bikes more. Let's head to France this summer and watch the Tour. Maybe even see if one of our contacts can get us to meet Lance Armstrong. If we donate enough, we could probably even ride with him after the race. Alright, when we get home, we can get some new bikes and get back into it."

They headed to the car where David put his head back, and just like his grandfather taught him, was asleep within a minute. Because you never know when you will have time to sleep.

CHAPTER SEVENTEEN

Northern Ireland, 2004

Nigel and Liam were happy to be back on Irish soil, even if it was, Northern Ireland. They were contracted to blow up a Member of Ulster's Parliament. After many years of service, this MP decided to retire. Throughout those years of service people had attempted to end his life. While he served the people as a Member of Parliament he supported, wrote, and voted for many laws that strengthen the punishment of those who terrorized the citizens of Ulster. These laws and this man were partly the reason that many people, including Nigel, had to hide in other countries, away from family and friends.

The job was scheduled for the night before Parliament planned a celebration of the career for the Honorable Member from County North Atrium.

Nigel and Liam were experts in their field of explosives, generational men like David. Like David, they had become world renowned for their professional skills and the ability to keep secrets. Many of the same organizations that contracted David also used Nigel and his crew. They were able to get in, get the job done right, and get out of the country without a trace, just like David or James.

There was professional respect between Kenton and Nigel's father until the contract James took to kill Nigel, and was identified by him. After that, the families were at war. Nigel's crew took and completed the job, the night they killed Kenton. Then there was the funeral for a fallen police officer who worked closely with Kenton. Three police officers were killed, and fifteen mourners died after a series of explosives detonated in the graveyard.

David was in Oklahoma in 1995, the CIA had contracted him to do a hit on a high-level Iraqi, foreign dignitary. The same day Nigel was hired to blow up the Alfred P. Murrah federal building with a couple fellows from the Michigan Militia. The explosion at the federal building was a distraction for the news. David's high-profile kill was the important job that day but received only a quick mention during the evening news, just like his customer planned. David did his assigned job and then attempted to catch Nigel. He knew the CIA had designated a patsy named Timothy to take the fall for the explosion. David met up with Timothy after the blast, he hoped Nigel and Timothy would be together. Unfortunately, Nigel was already on a flight home. David had Timothy drop him at a gas station where Phil waited for him. Moments later, McVeigh was in custody.

• • •

Nigel and Liam scaled the fence of the car lot with their equipment in the backpacks. Their contact at the depot informed them which car would pick up the Member of Parliament for his trip to work. They also paid their contact to forget to let the dogs into the yard that night.

"I have a bad feeling tonight," said Liam as he took his backpack off.

He carried the explosives and tools while Nigel had the electronics.

"Nah, it is just the fact that we are back home. When was the last job we did on the island? I have it a bit too. I think it is more the excitement of finally getting this bastard. We never get paid and get revenge on the same job. He has had this coming since the seventies," said Nigel.

"I guess. I am going under. Hand me my tools," said Liam.

Liam climbed under the car while Nigel kneeled by the front of the car and passed tools and equipment. Neither man spoke. They each knew what needed to be done and in what order. The two men were so focused they did not see the commotion that surrounded them. Men in black clothing moved in on them. Military men surrounded Liam, Nigel, and the car.

"Excuse me, can I see your hands please," asked the polite team captain as he put the muzzle of his gun against Nigel's head. "You under the car, one move and we will shoot you. Stretch your hands above your head."

A soldier reached down and grabbed Liam's ankles. He dragged him out from the underside of the car, pieces of skin and hair were left on the gravel.

A tip came into the British Army at five o'clock in the afternoon and turned out to be accurate. They gagged and cuffed the two men while the bomb squad moved in and removed the equipment under the car. They led the pair away to an armored vehicle. No one spoke as they loaded them into the truck and transported them to a military base where they met with officials of the Army, MI6, and police. The SAS did their job and got their men, Kenton would have been proud.

Liam and Nigel refused to speak or answer questions without a lawyer. Even with the lawyers, they were told not to speak. A couple of high priced internationally funded solicitors from Dublin worked hard to have the men released. The lawyers, no matter what angle they tried could not get their clients released. The military moved the men to solitary confinement and questioned them separately. MI6 knew who they caught, and the ripple effect this arrest would have across the planet. They also knew two more people needed to be picked up before they left the country.

• • •

Dermot and Conner waited in a safe house for their team to return to Dungiven. They expected the pair to return before sunrise, with a full report on another successful mission. Conner became worried when the sun cracked over the horizon and Nigel and Liam had not returned. Conner knew these guys were not good with schedules, but they were now hours past their worst-case scenario, time frame. Conner made some phone calls, and a worried look came over his face. Dermot stood up and packed their equipment. He knew Conner well enough, that look of concern meant it was time to run.

Conner hung up; he explained the situation to Dermot. The pair jumped in their car and headed for the Irish border. Not sure if Liam and Nigel had talked, they knew they had limited time to get out of Northern Ireland before their names were leaked. This was a high-risk job, that was why they brought in the best but even the best mess up and talk.

Dermot knew he couldn't have them rot in prison. They knew too much and couldn't be trusted not to talk. He decided an anonymous call to Scott would help his situation. Scott would pass the information on to David, and he would find a way to get to them in prison. Everyone knew David wanted revenge for his grandfather's death. Dermot decided once the boys were settled in a prison, he would make a call to Scott.

What Conner did not realize was the police already had eyes on them. At the final checkpoint, the police instructed them to pull into a holding area. Conner knew they had been compromised, and that either Nigel or Liam talked. He panicked and he tried to drive through the checkpoint. The tire spikes did their job and punctured three of the four tires. As the car slid out of control, eight military men jumped out of the tall grass and surrounded the car.

Three months after Nigel's and the crews arrests and interrogations, David received a call from a British intelligence friend.

"Hello," David answered.

"Hi mate, can we talk, is now a good time," said the voice from far away.

"Yes, I am clear," said David.

"Okay, listen up. A few months ago, we had a good night over here. We captured four men, two who were high-level leaders from the old IRA, and two were world renowned bomb builders. We have interrogated them since then and have received a lot of information. Some of it will confirm your doubts about your dad and your grandfather."

"You captured Nigel?" Got have him?" David said.

"Aye David, But not just him. They are moving these lads into a prison next week. I know you have been looking to meet Nigel for a while. And you will but you need to work with me. I could lose my job because of this phone call. The BBC is all over this transfer, so we need it to go right. Once in prison, they are yours to play with. Nigel is there, his partner Liam assisted him on the night your granda died. Then there is these two, Dermot and Conner. They were the ones who authorized the hit on your granda. If you don't have a contact for the prison, I can get you one. They are going to Maghaberry."

"What? How did you catch them?"

"Too much to say over the phone. I have a package for you,"

"Okay, thanks for the information. I will make a trip home within the next couple days. Can you drop your package to Scott at the shop? Give him everything you have, please."

"Aye, I will."

David arrived at Scott's shop the next week. He completed a job in Kenya, flew to Belfast and headed straight to the shop. No one was around, but there was a note on his bed with a large yellow envelope. *'David, headed out on vacation. This came for you. Will see you if you are still here when we return. Love, Scott.'*

David read through the report, he discovered some additional information about the crew but most of the notes he had already discovered through his team and their investigations. The four men were sentenced to life in the Maghaberry Prison. David had a couple contacts who worked there as guards. He met them years ago when Kenton and he did a special job inside the prison.

He made some phone calls to his contacts. David arranged to meet Dermot, he ranked the highest out of them all and could release any information David gave him to the rest of the crew.

They booked the meeting. He would enter the building through the staff doors where they would escort him to a meeting room. The only request he had to honor was he could not touch Dermot.

David visited his grandparent's graves, ate a lot of British candy, and visited some relatives to fill the time as he waited for his meeting.

He prepared for the face-to-face meeting with Dermot. He researched, acquired names and addresses of the wives and kids of each man. He studied and knew details about each family. Usually, he would do a job with as little detail as possible. This was different. He wanted to know everything he could about the families and extended families, ages, hair color, the schools they attended and their schedules.

* * * *

David entered the prison and checked in under an alias. The guards escorted him to 'A Wing'. This wing was the home to the four men he wanted to meet and kill. Today would only be a meeting, he would have to wait for the opportunity to kill them.

Handcuffed and shackled at the ankles, Dermot did not move quickly. Once David saw Dermot, he could feel the hatred and anger emanate from himself. He wanted to kill Dermot in the lunchroom with his bare hands. He needed to get his emotions under control, or he could ruin not only this meeting, but any chance to get back in for more visits. David took a few deep breaths and focused on his long-term goals with Dermot.

The superintendent who let David in would easily and happily cover up a mysterious murder for David, if needed. The little voice in David's head spoke up, *'Always prepare for a kill and never kill for revenge.'*

There was no plan today to kill anyone, easy as it would be, but it would make it more difficult to get the other three.

Dermot did not recognize who David was and made that very clear to the two guards who walked him into the room. Even as he struggled and yelled, they forced him to stay with David. The guards stepped out of the room and closed the door as Dermot protested the meeting and the lack of security.

"Who the fuck are you," said Dermot.

"Aye, I am your guardian angel. As long as I am around no one will hurt you or the other three lads in here with you. You have my protective hand, and I will always be a phone call away, friend," said David, in a thick southern Ireland accent.

"What? Who sent you? Why are you here to look out for us, no one mentioned you in other conversations?" said Dermot.

"No, I wouldn't think they would. See, I am your protection because one day I will be the one who will put you in a grave. Not today, but one day. You put a hit on a family member of mine, Kenton Grant, a few years ago, do you remember? You and your partner had the other two place a bomb under his car, just outside of Portadown."

"Nope, don't know what you..."

"Shut your fucking mouth, or I will," David said, the fake accent now gone. "Only speak when I give you permission. Here's the way I see it. There is enough evidence to prove the four of you were involved. Now you are all locked away for a long time. But the good news is your families are all out and about, free, and maybe even missing you. Your mom, Francis, she lives at 101 Greenstone in a small-town north of Dublin. Three houses down from her, your brother with his wife and three kids..."

Dermot jumped up from his seat. David did not flinch as Dermot tripped over the shackles. He fell and hit his head. David walked around the table and kicked him in the gut, all missed by the guards, unfortunately for Dermot.

"So, would you like me to list off more family members as you take your seat? I can also list off all your other friend's families and their addresses. Liam just had his first grandson six months ago. He might not see seven months, the mood I am in. Conner's grandfather just had his ninetieth birthday—how exciting. Oh, and not to exclude Nigel, whose daughter is eight months pregnant with the twins. Huh, wonder what could happen there?"

"You are all talk," said Dermot. "Anyone could get that information. You government agents think you can come in and intimidate me? Not a chance. We know we are innocent, and it will only be time before a judge sees it too. Your threats will not get me to confess shit."

David heard the nervousness and fear in his voice. David knew this would hit a nerve, and it hit hard.

"You are just some punk. That is all talk, you don't scare me at all. I don't even know a Kenton. I can make a call from here and have you disappear in about twelve hours. I don't think you know who I am."

"Right, if you did any research on Kenton, and I know you did, you know all about his family of killers and how James was good, but David, aye David, was better than them all."

"Okay, maybe I did. What, are you going to tell me you are David?" he said, with a sarcastic tone to his voice.

David raised his eyebrows and smiled.

Dermot blinked twice, all his confidence and color in his face disappeared, like a ghost had just walked into the room and shook his hand.

"Friend, how do you think I got in here? You know I don't work here. I don't even live in this fucking country anymore, thanks to Nigel. But I made a special trip and called in some favors just so we could spend some time together. See, I am going to visit you and your shithead friends every chance I can. Sometimes I might even come with a gift, maybe a photo of a shallow grave, a finger, or a teddy bear. Who knows what I will bring, but you will be in here with your fucking boyfriends while

I fuck with all your families and friends. They will know who I am and why I am in their lives."

David laughed at the fear and shock on Dermot's face.

"Get me out of here," Dermot screamed at the guards.

"Not until I am done, do you get to leave. So, you go back and tell the other three how you met a new friend today, everyone's guardian angel. Explain to them what I told you. My friends over there will keep me updated on the four of you. I will know when you eat, shit and sneeze. They will also happily tell you before anyone else knows which family member went missing or, who knows, as I take my time working through each one of your families. It is a shame, I had so much fun chasing Nigel and Liam around the world. We were so close, so many times working for the same people. But now instead of killing him quickly, I can enjoy my time getting to hang out with you guys. Now, I think we are done here. Enjoy your time in hotel hell. Just think, you know every day that while you are here no one will hurt you. You guys are safe in jail, no other inmate will even cross your path. You will have many, many years of wondering what is happening on the outside, missing funerals, births, and special occasions. The good news is, I will come tell and show you how I was involved in those good and bad times."

David walked out the door and told the guards he was done with Dermot. He planted the seed in Dermot's head. Dermot would never forget David's face.

Once the guard's shift was over, David took them out for supper and arranged for them to receive a monthly care package for all the information he required on his friends.

●　　●　　●

David did not want to be known as, 'all talk no action,' so headed down to Dublin before he went home. He wanted to make sure his new friends understood he did not make idle threats.

Dermot's sister had to lose a child. It was unfortunate for her family. Like they say, 'you can pick your friends, but you can't pick your family.'

David spent a couple days and followed the family. He decided the middle daughter would be his target. He broke into the house at night, the family were exhausted from a day at the park where they played and picnicked. At least they had pleasant memories of their final day together. He took the seven-year-old girl from her bed, just to make a point, he left a note for the family to find.

'Dermot will have answers for you.' He wrote on a blank piece of white stationary and left it on her pillow.

The next morning when the family reported the missing child, there was no mention of the note left on her bed to the authorities. Dermot's sister, Carol, headed to visit Dermot the next day and asked him to explain the note. He was very apologetic to his sister and explained that her daughter, his niece, was likely dead. He couldn't give her many more details of what he knew.

Three days after the child had went missing and after another more informative and detailed visit between David and Dermot, the little girl was returned to her family by taxi. Dermot was told the next time the person would not be returned alive.

CHAPTER EIGHTEEN

Washington D.C. 2005

Corey Green looked forward to his flight home to spend a day with his wife and child. Then he would have to return to the road with Senator Woolwick and his campaign for his sixth term in office.

Corey was in his office, held up by his secretary who wanted one last moment alone before he left her for a couple weeks. Beth was a tall ginger with an athletic body, Corey became infatuated with her the first day they met. Corey tried to remain faithful to his wife. But the long hours at work with Beth and the weeks away from home were too much for him. The first night he hooked up with Beth was after an office party the Senator threw for his staff.

Beth wanted to make her way up the office ladder and helped suppress Corey's loneliness and lust. After the first night together, Corey, out of guilt, asked his wife to move to Washington to be with him. They had a young child together, and her family lived in Phoenix. She refused to move; she chose her family over Corey. That decision devastated Corey. He worked longer hours, drank bigger bottles, and saw more women.

Corey looked to make a change, but this trip would not be the time. The re-election campaign for the Senator, began last month. The senator enjoyed his alcohol, drugs, and women, he was not the mentor Corey needed in his life. Corey's plan was to finish the campaign with Senator Woolwick, hopefully help him win his re-election, then quit, not just his job, but Washington, and find a job closer to home. The guilt of Washington's lifestyle destroyed Corey self-worth and he knew the only escape was to move back to Arizona.

Corey did not know his wife knew about the women, the booze, and the drugs. When he would go home, he would act the part of a good, clean, and sober husband. He would tell her stories of lonely nights and long hours at work. She filled in the rest of his story, from the phone calls from Washington when he drunk called her with the moans of his whores in the background. The worst night was when he used a new technology, a camera on his computer. Poor Paula had to watch her husband fuck two ladies, he did things and had things done to him she never would or could imagine.

●　　●　　●

David was on a bike. He followed Corey as he traveled around Washington. The day was warm and sunny, and Corey was scheduled to be on a plane in two hours to head home. David also had to make that flight. David was concerned by the pace Corey took as he walked up the reflective pool towards the Lincoln Memorial. He knew he couldn't pull out a special pass or ID and get on the commercial flight if he was late, this wasn't pre-9/11, and he did not believe Corey could either. They gave David a package which confirmed the flight home, and so far, the schedule Corey kept had been right.

He continued to bike different paths beside the main reflective pool. He watched Corey fumble with a cigarette, check out women in short skirts and drink from a bottle of water, or another clear alcoholic liquid that replaced the water. Corey continued to the stairs of the Lincoln Memorial. He turned to the south and walked around the perimeter of the memorial where he met a man. They acknowledged each other and walked side by side.

David got off the bike and watched as the two men stopped behind a short hedge. David positioned himself where neither man would notice him, but he could clearly see any interaction between them. He watched as the men exchanged envelopes. They shook hands and parted ways. Corey headed to Independence Avenue and hailed a taxi.

David saw the direction the taxi headed. He biked to where Phil had parked the truck and put the bike in the back.

"All good?" asked Phil.

"Yea, strange. There was a meeting beside Lincoln. He exchanged envelopes with another guy. I would like to follow him, but that is not our objective right now." he motioned towards the taxi, "He better be heading to the airport, we are cutting it close. Maybe I should be reading why people hire me for jobs. This one is confusing. It seems this guy knows he has a number on his back."

David wrote down the description of the second man. He would discuss it with the customer when he gave his debrief. When David accepted this job there was a quick turnaround, he had less than a week to complete the task. Usually, the US governments reports were filled with details, this one had two pages and some airline tickets. To David, this whole job felt like it was thrown together quickly and with little care how it was completed. Phil did not receive the report until they arrived in Washington. All David received while they were in Italy was, 'need credit cards cut, Washington, details upon arrival, short deadline.' When they called John, he only knew the customer had a strict deadline and details would be ready when they arrived in Washington. David wasn't too concerned, he had his targets name, some details of his schedule, and a dead by date. John's contact in Phoenix had scouted Corey's house and street and passed the information to Phil. Simple as that, just like he had been taught by his grandfather and father.

Phil parked the truck in their usual airport parking area. This truck would have more time to put miles on its wheels, unlike most vehicles they dropped off at airports. They waited in the departure area and watched Corey read a magazine. The only time he looked up was when a shapely woman walked by his chair.

"We know he is heading home to his family but in the last twelve hours he drank enough alcohol to kill an elephant, did lines of coke off a lady's chest in his car and took her to a hotel. Then he leaves the hotel this morning without her, heads into work and walked the historic area of town. This guy is a player for sure. He must have a constant supply of coke going up that nose, to keep up his energy," said David. "I am going to make some calls, grab me when we are about to board."

With the job wrapped up in Italy and the immediate demand for his presence in Washington, David missed his weekly check in on Nigel, Dermot, and the gang.

"Any update?" Phil asked when David returned.

"Nothing new, Nigel tried a hunger strike, it lasted thirty-six hours. Pussy. Dermot has had a few visitors, I have their names, I will get Scott to follow up and see who they are. Peter said they were not his usual lawyers or brother-in-law. Liam and Nigel had the usual visitors, one snuck in some drugs for them and another updated Nigel on a new start to the IRA. Again, Scott can dig further. Hopefully, they will release them soon so I can invite them back to the shop for a skinning and burial." David said.

The flight loaded and David paid extra to sit at the back of the plane while Phil sat closer to the target.

David was perched atop a hill, it overlooked a large house in a subdivision just outside of Phoenix, Arizona. He looked through a pair of high-powered binoculars at Corey, Paula and their six-year-old daughter, Karen. Corey was relaxed in his blue lazy boy as Fear Factor played on the TV. Paula played with their daughter on the couch.

'This guy is amazing,' David thought, *'comes home to his family, then plants himself in-front of the TV with a Pepsi. Good quality family time.'*

David enjoyed the outdoors. James took him camping and hunting, it wasn't just always a cover story in Canada. In Southern Ontario, there was not much in the wild that could kill or scare a person. David lay on the sand and dirt and wondered what creatures; snakes, scorpions, or spiders could strike at him. Back home he had seen bears, at a distance, and the odd rattlesnake further up north. Nothing small and deadly that could crawl up his pant leg or into a shoe. The assassin that many people feared, was scared of a small spider.

He had twenty-four hours left to eliminate the target. Once Corey headed out on his next trip, the contract ended, and David would be out of pocket for his expenses. He followed this man in Washington for a day and now home to Phoenix. He had opportunities in Washington to complete the job, but the request was to do it at his house away from Washington.

Now at home with his family, Corey had a life and a family that counted on him. Corey now became a person to David, not a target. When David first started out, this did not bother him. A job was a job and money ruled. But now he had empathy for those with families. David remembered his lessons from his grandfather. He had a job to do, and he would do it well.

Paula got up from the couch and picked up Karen, who had fallen asleep. David watched as Paula turned lights on when she entered rooms. She ended up in Karen's bedroom.

Joe Rogan had sent the show to commercials, Corey had two minutes to step outside for a smoke. Perched on the hilltop, David would have a perfect shot with a sniper rifle at his target. But that was not how the job was requested. They hired David because he was the best with a knife. He would do the kill the way he was trained, with his hands and in close contact. He could not do that now. No, tonight he would observe the target. Tomorrow when Corey came out for his morning smoke alone, that would be the last thing Corey did.

The sun had set, the temperature dropped, and the wild animals made noises in the distance. Once it was fully dark, he would move into the backyard of Corey's house and wait for him. David took one more glance through the binoculars. He noticed a figure emerge from the side of Corey's house.

"What the fuck," David said out loud.

The person came around the side of the house, he had a rifle over his shoulder and a pistol hung off his hip.

'What's going on here,' David thought. *'It can't be another hitman, could it? If it is, who called him. The package specifically said no guns to be used, that is why I am here.'*

David positioned himself to crawl down the hill if needed. He watched the person crouch behind the BBQ on the patio of Corey's backyard. The rifle, the stranger carried, was a Stoner SR-25 and the pistol was a Glock. The Stoner was a sniper rifle issued by Mossad's marksmen.

'If it is a sniper, why would he take a close position,' David thought to himself. *'What is this guy doing? He should be up here for the shot. It is the dominant position. He is way too close for that size of rifle.'*

David decided to wait and see what the guy's next move would be. David lay down in his nest. Corey headed up to Karen's bedroom and tucked her in. He came back down to the couch, all timed between commercial breaks.

David had a perfect shot at the back of his head if that was what the job would have allowed.

'Why isn't the other guy up here, using this position?' David thought again. He walked back through the trail towards the road. He looked for another set of footprints, there were no footprints in the dirt, but he noticed a snake had left a trail as it crossed the path.

David lay in his nest, he looked for the stranger and Corey. Both the stranger and Corey were gone. Paula was on the couch, but Corey had left.

'Maybe he went to the garage for his final smoke of the day,' David thought. *'But where is the other guy?'*

David located the stranger. He came back around the side of the house without the rifle and only a pistol. Not crouching, not trying to hide.

'What the hell,' he thought, *'this can't be Mossad.'*

David watched the guy for another half hour. He couldn't figure out what this guy was up to. The way he held the pistol, the way he exposed himself to the hill side. There were too many mistakes for a pro. David decided he would approach the stranger.

'Moving downhill, something strange to investigate,' David texted Phil.

Phil was on a side road hidden from any traffic that might use the subdivisions alternate entrance.

'Problem?' Phil replied.

'Going to find out, stand-by,' David typed.

Slowly David rose and put on latex gloves and his balaclava. He carefully made his way down the dusty hill in the dark. Once down and on the grassy area of the yard, he hid behind the fence. The stranger did not hear him come down the hill, or all the stones that raced him to the bottom. He was now twenty feet from the stranger, exposed behind the BBQ. David slowly walked the perimeter of the fence to get within five feet of the BBQ. The stranger still did not see or hear David approach, this confused David. He now took three steps and stood behind the stranger.

David grabbed the intruder's right arm; he broke his wrist and had his mouth and nose covered all in one quick swift move. The gun dropped to the ground as the stranger's hand lost all its strength. The strangers only reaction to this change of position was he fell backwards. David fell with him, he placed him in a headlock and wrapped his legs around the stranger's waist. There was no struggle from the stranger as David tightened his grip. David moved his hand to uncover the stranger's nose, it allowed him to breathe again. There was no fight from the man, only his left hand moving to support his broken right wrist. David loosened his grip and rotated onto the stranger's stomach and chest. David leaned down, covered the mouth with his right hand as his left forearm pressed into the stranger's throat. The stranger's eyes were wide open, the look of shock was comical to David. There was no fight from him, David expected to be in a full fight with a Mossad assassin, instead he was on a man that now, very likely wet himself, from the warmth David felt on his belly.

"You will not scream, understand?" David said.

The stranger nodded with eyes as wide as a tunnel entrance.

"Okay, I am going to sit back and take my hand off your mouth, one noise from you and it will be your last. Plus, did you just piss yourself?" David said. He moved away from the stranger's face.

"You broke my wrist, you fucking asshole," the stranger said when he took a deep breath through his mouth.

"What did I say, not a fucking noise," David said.

The stranger pulled back into the ground as if he expected a fast punch to the face or throat.

"Right," he whispered.

"I am going to get off you and pick up your gun, do not move, understand. I promise you, if you behave, I will not use the gun, if not—well—it sucks dying by your own weapon," David said.

The man's eyes widen, David thought they would pop out of his head. David slowly looked around the BBQ for the gun, he found it and checked the safety, it was on this whole time. He looked again at the stranger confused. He placed the gun in the back of his waist band and moved back to the stranger.

"Okay, we are going to leave the backyard and head up the hill, slowly. Understand?"

"Uh huh," was the quiet whisper from the stranger. "But who are you? Did Paula hire you too?"

David ignored his questions and helped him to his feet. He pointed him in the direction he wanted his prisoner to go. They walked along the side fence, then slowly up the hill. The stranger lost his footing a couple times and fell on his shoulder once.

"Fuck, that could have hurt if I landed on my broken wrist," he whispered to nobody.

The men got to the top of the hill and David grabbed the man's shoulder. "Okay stop walking and sit down."

"What? Why? Who the fuck are you anyway," the stranger asked.

"How about I ask the questions? You answer them right, you walk away from here with a beating heart. You fuck around, and well, the cops will be looking for you. Got it?" David said.

"Well, who.."

David reached for his broken wrist. "Maybe you are confused by what I said. If I do this, will you understand?"

David twisted the stranger's hand; he heard the broken bones grind. The man went to scream as David covered his mouth again.

"Listen, I am not here to fuck around. Either way works for me, you either answer my questions or I kill you. There is more than one place to hide a body around here," said David.

"Who are you?" David said, with authority.

"Umm—well my name is..."

David reached for the broken wrist, "Okay, the hard way it is then."

"No, no. Daniel Fraser, okay? People call me Dan. What's your name," Dan said.

"Nope, I ask, remember? Why are you here?"

"Well, that is not so easy. Are you a cop?"

"No, I am not. Answer the question because a cop isn't allowed to give you the option of losing your life for not answering, I do."

"Okay—okay, so the lady in there, Paula, hired me." Dan paused, while he waited for a response. "She knows her husband is cheating on her and she wants him dealt with. She hired me to break into the house and scare him. Rough him up a little, act like a jealous boyfriend from one of the ladies he is cheating on Paula with. You know, scare him straight. She would leave him, but she believes they can fix things."

David had the largest smile on his face. "Continue,"

"So, tonight was the night—uhh—she wanted it—umm—done, before he headed out for a weeks trip with his boss. Umm, he is only home until tomorrow—umm—afternoon and she wanted to give him something to think about while on the trip. We had it all worked out—umm—what we would both say, how she would respond, everything," Dan lifted his left hand to look at his watch. "I should be going into the house, right now to play my part."

David looked back at the house and could see the kid's bedroom light was turned off and it looked like the couple were on the couch together.

"What about the gun?"

"It was just for show. Let him know how mad I really was. I wasn't going to use it. The safety is still on and there are blanks in the clip."

"I saw that. How much did she agree to pay you for this job?"

"$1000. $400 up front, $600 tomorrow when he gets on the plane beat up, but alive."

"How did she find you to do the job?"

"Well, that is just it, I am a friend of a friend."

"What? Did you have a mask, anything to hide your identity? You are carrying your wallet, what is wrong with you? How did you think this was going to work? And what about the rifle, what was the idea of that if this is all fake?"

"Oh, right, I meant to—umm—leave my wallet in the car, idiot. Yea, I thought the rifle would look good. Then I realized he could grab it and swing it at my head, so I put it back in my car."

"Where did you park your car?" Dan nodded to the street in front of the house.

"Oh, come on. Out front of the house? Dude, you are lucky I was here to stop you. You would be going to jail for a long time. He is a government official. So, this idea is not happening. In fact, this is your lucky day, not only do you not have to do this and probably get yourself hurt, but I am going to give you two grand and you are going to walk away from this. You will never talk about it. You never met me; you never came here."

"So, are you his personal security, because of his job in Washington?"

"Yes, that is what I am. You are lucky I didn't shoot you when I saw you walking into the backyard. I have to protect my boss."

The lack of critical thinking dumbfounded David.

Right, I wear gloves and a mask to protect my boss, while perched a hill. Wow!' he thought.

"Shit, she never mentioned personal security. I am glad you caught me before I went into the house. I guess if I had gone in, you would be having a different talk with me. Or a doctor would be."

"Or an undertaker."

David texted Phil, *'issue dealt with bringing you company for the night, suit up.'*

Phil read the text and pulled his balaclava over his face.

David walked his prisoner down the road to where Phil was hidden and opened the truck door. David pulled out an old gym bag and dug to the bottom. He pulled out a roll of cash and counted out $2000.

"Okay, you are going to get in the truck with my partner and sit there until daybreak when our shift is over."

Phil looked at him quizzically but knew when they were on a job, he should never speak up and always go along with the story line David presented.

"So, the new security detail will be here to start their shift around 0800. Also give my partner your wallet and car keys for safe keeping."

Dan pulled out his wallet from his back pocket. Phil took out the driver's license and went to the back of the truck. He pulled out a small instant camera and took a couple of photos of the license. "Call it insurance in case you talk about tonight to someone," Phil said when he got back in the truck.

"Okay, I won't be talking to anyone about this, promise."

Dan held his wrist and asked, "So no medical attention until morning?"

* * *

David went back up to the nest and packed his equipment. He returned to the truck, dropped off the surveillance equipment and checked on Phil and Dan.

David surveyed the house and noticed all the lights were out. His plan was to stay in his nest until 0400 then head to the yard and wait for Corey to come out for his morning smoke.

David, cold and hungry, waited for 0400. The sounds of the night beautiful, like an orchestra of animal calls. He used this time to quiet his mind, he reflected on his granda and how they hunted around the world. Kenton taught David the different calls of animals, how far a pack of coyotes were. David missed his granda. A day did not pass David did not think of him and the fun they had. David thought back to the night Kenton surprised him with a visit to Canada and baptized him into the inner circle. A night that changed him forever.

* * *

Guelph, 1988
David felt like his entire life had been a series of unanswered questions about what James, John and his grandfather really did. Kenton answered many of his questions when he worked back home, and James would answer a few questions or tell him to ask Granda next time he was home. David knew until he

was finally brought into the inner circle, he would always have more questions than answers.

James and David pulled into the unpaved parking lot of John's Plumbing Wholesale and Service. They had the iconic colored toilets and tubs from the fifties and sixties lined up on the old wooden loading dock. A classic sixties Mustang, on blocks and under a tarp, was in the corner of the parking lot. Skids of pipe lined the back fence. James pulled the car into his spot. They walked up the old, worn cement stairs to the service door. Frank opened it for them as they approached.

"Hey guys, how you doing? Another gold star job, I hear David," said Frank. "You are putting the old guys to shame."

"Thanks Frank. I think I have a long way to go to be on equal ground with Dad," said David.

"Kid, we already know you are a superstar," Frank said, as he winked at David. "John and Phil are down in the office; I am just locking up and will be down."

"Thanks, Frank," James said.

"I know I don't have to say this but listen and don't talk. There will be plenty of time for questions after," James said to David as they approached the office.

James knocked on the door and entered with David behind him. The office was bright, clean, and modern, unlike the upstairs warehouse. John sat behind his large cherry wood desk where he reviewed some papers. To the right was a large twelve seat conference table, where Phil sat.

"David!" Phil exclaimed. "You're here."

Phil ran over to David; he edged his way past James. The two embraced.

"How was your trip?" Phil asked.

James walked over to John's desk and hugged his father, Kenton. David hadn't seen him in one of the chairs by John's desk.

Kenton turned around and called across the room, "Hey David, you not going to give your old grandfather a hug too?"

David, in shock, spun on his heels, he ran from Phil to Kenton. "Granda, I just left you a couple days ago. How—why—what are you doing here?"

Phil walked over to the group. He had spent some time with Kenton while they waited for David and James. Phil sat in bewilderment at the stories Kenton told him.

"David, what is going to happen tonight is much too important for me to miss. We were going to do it back home, but we decided Phil should be with you."

"Dad, what is going on, what is all this about," David said.

"I have supper coming and we will sit and talk, then we will really talk. Phil can tell you about what he has been up to while you were back home. I know Phil would want to know what you did, as do I," said John.

Frank opened the office door with his hands full of brown paper bags, some stained with grease on the bottom.

"Supper is here and smells great," said Frank.

David and Phil grabbed a couple bags from Frank. There was enough food to feed twenty people. They walked over to the conference table and spread out the food. John grabbed a bottle of wine and some plates. James grabbed the utensils and cups from the large armoire in the corner.

David and Phil opened the bags and took out salads, whole chickens, veggies, and bread. They served the food and poured the wine. Everyone took a glass except David. He decided he would never indulge in drinking or smoking, partly because of religious beliefs, the need to be ready to work, and also because of his uncontrollable temper. From what he had seen in his short life, a bad temper and alcohol did not mix.

"Before we eat, Kenton will you say grace please," asked John.

"Dear Lord God, thank You for the food in front of us, thank You for the friendships around the table and the families they come from. Be with us all gathered here and let us have long healthy lives. Amen."

"Amen," the rest repeated.

The men dug into the food. David and Phil sat beside each other, John and Kenton sat at either end of the table.

"David, do you want to tell of your trip home?" asked John.

"Sure" said David after he swallowed a mouth full of potatoes. David repeated the events that led up to his trip home and all the details of the trip. Kenton only had to interrupt him a couple times to correct his story. Phil sat and listened with incredible interest to the story.

"Phil, why don't you tell David what you did while he was gone. By then we should be done eating and we can get down to business," said John.

"Okay, where do I start? The day you left for Ireland, sorry Northern Ireland, Dad called me into the office, and we talked about the business and the trip he had planned," Phil described his trip to New York. They collected money, had meetings with heads of mob families and a couple bike gangs. They made agreements for a few shipments of weapons, and three dirty cops would need to be moved to the safe house, before Internal Affairs completed an investigation on them. They traveled to Chicago and repeated the exercise, with Russian, Asian, and more Italian families. They met with a few foreign statesmen, there was more requests for large shipments of weapons and David's services. They returned home and met with business owners in Toronto, Mississauga, and Hamilton. They collected money to clean through their businesses. Phil finished his story, and the crew sat in silence.

"It looks like you two have a bright future together," said Kenton.

"Gentlemen, I am sorry I don't have anyone to clean up after us. So, before we begin the second half of the meeting, can I ask that we all do our part to clean off the table. The wine can stay, and I will get us another bottle for the occasion," said John.

The crew worked together and cleaned up. David ran the food scraps up to the garbage bin while Phil gathered up the dirty plates and brought them to the other room, for the cleaner in the morning. Kenton and John went back to the desk to gather up some items for the next part of the meeting. Frank wiped down the table as James stacked the leftovers in the hidden fridge.

David met Phil in the hallway and asked, "What is happening? What is this, second part of the meeting stuff they are talking about? Are we in shit for something?"

"I don't know, David. I was sworn to secrecy this morning about picking up your granda. I don't think we did anything wrong; I thought my trip with Dad went well. Kenton had nothing but praise for you and your skills. Let's just get through whatever they want to talk about together. Whatever it is we are a team."

"Agreed, we will stick together."

"I have spent the whole day listening to your Granda's stories. No wonder you love going back there, he has some crazy tales. And they somehow end with a lesson, it is insane!"

"Okay, we should get back in there, as a team."

• • •

"Now that we are all back at the table, we are ready to begin," said Kenton. "First, David, your uncles, aunt and grandmother wish they could be here for this meeting but we all couldn't leave the country without raising some suspicion. But they are here in spirit and all send their thoughts and prayers to you."

"John, do you want to start?" asked Kenton.

"Our families have worked together for," John paused and looked at Kenton, "almost forty years?"

Kenton nodded in agreement.

"David, you are the third generation in this business and Phil, you are second generation. We all could not be prouder of you both. David, since you came to Canada, I have watched you grow up with Phil. The two of you are like brothers, no, closer than even brothers I would say. We have all watched you grow and have helped you both learn skills to help you become fine citizens in both the worlds we all live in. We have also taught you other things, most people would never learn or want to learn. For years we have planned and worked on our businesses combining them where we needed to for strength and separating them when we needed secrecy. Kenton and I have always trusted each other. You two can continue with that business plan as you grow your parts of the business. You both have the skills and talent. Phil, you have proven you can manipulate and work in the community to sell our products as well as hide our money. David, you have a skill set we have needed here in Canada and with some more training will become a world famous highly demanded killer. You both have the skills to plan and execute any program needed to keep the businesses secure. Kenton, would you like to speak?"

"When we moved your dad, and you to Canada the plan was to have you stay a couple years and then come home. That changed because of your mom."

"What?" David said as he looked at James.

"Shh" James said.

"You guys settled in here and you and Amy had friends and a life here that was safe. As you grew, we taught you martial arts, and other skills. I would plan training for you two, and your fathers have taught you well. To be honest, as you sit here now, you might not know it, but you have more training and skills than a Navy Seal or any SAS soldier."

"Phil," John began, "ever since you were a child, I have shown you the business side of the plumbing companies and the other businesses even though you didn't exactly know what I was showing you. You have now seen the 'hands on side' of the business. We have shown you, and will continue to show you the rest of the business as you grow up. The one thing I would add is, you both need to take care of each other as you grow up."

"David, Phil, you have a choice to make tonight and it won't be an easy one," said Frank.

James said, "You two have your whole lives ahead of you, working together and apart as Dad and John have. But always looking out for each other and protecting each other at any cost. That being said, none of us are going anywhere soon, we will continue to support each of you. We all just want to begin backing out of some of this work and enjoy the spoils of our pasts. So, let me start by saying, even though you are our sons, if you decide to go against us or speak of this evening to anyone but us here present now, we will have to dispose of your bodies. Understand?" said James.

David and Phil looked at each other. David said, "I think we have proven we are in for the long haul."

"What do we need to do to help and grow the businesses?" David said.

"Well, the way we have discussed this is you, David, would deal with the operations side of the business and the overseas customers. Phil, you would deal with the financial items, trafficking money, guns, and people. You would be David's support, his negotiator, travel agent and psychologist," said Kenton.

"What we do now, you two would naturally move into as you grow older. Phil, you would be best to take some business courses. David, you need to keep your physical skills up. As a cover, you two would work for the plumbing company. You would do plumbing apprenticeships and become plumbers," said John.

"This is where your life becomes tricky. We all make a lot of money with the jobs we do," Kenton began. "The thing is, we can't live a life where others would ask, how we can afford those things. So, on one hand you can afford to live a very high-class life, but on the other, you can't show that because your money isn't trackable with the government. That is where the plumbing companies and the other companies come in. We run them like true honest businesses with employees, overhead, losses and profits, as you know. If the books get audited, no one would see any issues. You two will complete a full plumbing apprenticeship and become plumbers with master licenses. You will learn how the business runs and, on most days, will be out working in a truck doing service work. That is how people will see you and expect you to live within those parameters of your wages. Where you can enjoy your money is with items people who see you daily don't know about, like the safe house on the farm. All the off-road vehicles and the boat we have up there, the property down south and in Europe. No one knows we have them. Plus, vacations, you can take the craziest trips you wish, unfortunately you just can't tell people too much about them. Like we keep stressing, keep your two lives separate, David the plumber guy and then the one no one knows about, he is the one that gets to enjoy all the fruits of the business."

"The next thing especially, for you David, is you need to blend in. No tattoos, no piercings nothing to make you stand out in a crowd. You wear regular clothes from whatever style is in at the time. When you travel, you need to know what the clothing style is where you are going. Usually, Europe differs from North America for clothing, as you know. You must act like anyone else your age, but with the wisdom of someone much older. Shave your head so you don't leave hair samples behind on jobs. Limit any scars. No drinking or drugs, you need to always be alert, constantly watching your surroundings," said James.

"You will have to be very careful with the girls, I assume girls, you date for more than a week or two," Kenton said. He laughed at his, assumption of girl's, comment.

"The biggest issue you two will have to deal with, and it will be easier once you are out of school, is living two lives. You will have to go and finish high school. Act like regular well-behaved students. Then you will get a call and must turn your mind over to the business at hand. A client might need weapons moved, a snitch tortured or someone to incite a riot and kill a target. Then two days later, you will be back in school reading Shakespeare. It is not an easy transition, and you will have no one to talk to about this except us. It can be very lonely." said John.

There was a quiet pause in the room. David could feel the weight of the world upon his shoulders. He enjoyed the risk when he worked with his father and grandfather. He liked the respect they gave him when he made a pickup or delivery for John. What would his mother think of him if he told her, he now locked himself into Granda's crew? Would she see him even more differently, or would she treat him as the paid killer he would be instead of the son she gave birth to?

"Can I take a minute and run to the washroom, please?" asked David.

"Aye, of course," said Kenton.

David left the room and headed to the bathroom down the hallway. He entered the room and went to the toilet; he bent over and threw up his supper. His nerves were on high alert. He couldn't tell if this life scared or excited him. He sat on the floor, his back against the white toilet bowl. He knew the right thing to do was to be what his father wanted. But a little voice asked if he wanted that or a normal life. But with what he has already done and seen in his life, what was normal? He washed his mouth out at the sink and headed back into the office.

"David, you okay?" said Phil, in the hallway, he was pale. "Do you want to do this; you have a lot more to risk than I do in this. If you do, I will be with you on every job, if you want as eyes or whatever you need. We have done everything together, if you want out, so do I. I won't do this without you. But if you are in, we are in together. I will be there to run the jobs and protect you."

"Phil, really, do we want to do this? I really think when we walk back in there, we will need to make a decision. This is forever. Plus, would they really kill us, that comment hurt."

"I know, we are talking rest of our lives. But I do enjoy it, I know you do too."

"Dude, all for one in this case, if you are in, I am too. I am fine, it just all came crashing down on me. We are getting into the inner circle tonight. I wasn't expecting this, we are in Phil. My emotions just took control. Let's do this brother," said David.

They hugged and headed back into the office together, united, and ready to die for each other.

"Alright?" said John.

"Aye John, all good just had to make some room for dessert. Or isn't there any?" David said with a smile.

"Later we can go out and celebrate. There is one last item to discuss. You need to show your dedication and commitment to the business and family. It is an ancient ritual that was started back before Moses wandered the desert. Kings and hidden societies passed this tradition down through the centuries. Once you complete this then you are in for life, and life will be all you have."

"When Moses was wandering the desert, God asked a sacrifice of the Jews, circumcision." James began.

"What? Hold on, no way I...." David started.

"Let me finish, David. Way back in time, just after Moses' death, when the Jews were a new religion, people noticed, as their cities were destroyed that certain member or the Jewish leadership had their third finger, on their left hand scarred, or as we call it the ring finger. Other civilizations realized that all the Israeli special fighters, spies, and certain leaders worked for both sides of the wars and had scarred or marked their fingers as an identifier. When the people the Israeli's enslaved, asked about the scars on the fingers, they were told this was a separate mark of commitment to each other, to God and to the promotion of chaos. The Egyptians, Greeks, Romans, Templar's, medieval militaries, Celtics, and many secret societies adapted this tradition through the ages. And it continues to our time," James said.

Each man showed David and Phil their fingers. James had a scar in the shape of the cross, John had an arrow scar the length of his finger, and Kenton had the tip of his finger removed, including the nail. Frank did not have any marks as he was not part of the inner circle. If Scott was in the room, he would have shown a triangle on the pad of his finger.

"I never noticed these before," said Phil.

"I noticed Granda's before, but I figured it was an injury from work. So, we need to commit to the business and have our finger scarred to be full members in the group?" asked David.

"Phil will have a scar of his choosing, you David will need to have the tip removed and replaced showing the circumcision of the finger and the true commitment to your God, family and the honor of all those mentioned earlier. Only a professional assassin has this honor of the removal and replacement of the tip, like mine." Kenton once again showed his finger, David noticed it was all there, it looked strange because there was no nail, and the tip was crudely sewn on.

"When did you do this," David asked.

"Another time son, tonight is about you two," said Kenton.

"Okay, do we need to do this?" asked Phil.

"Wait, he gets a scar, but I lose part of my finger?" said David.

"Yes, we will give you the ancient treatment thousands of men have received in the past. Some well-known historical figures and some no one ever knew were part of this society of assassins. You will become one of the chosen few alive today. I only know of one other member alive, and he has a double circumcision, his finger and," Kenton nodded his head towards his crotch, "being part of Mossad and an Israeli."

John had grabbed some medical equipment and a knife. They wiped down the conference table and set out some towels to catch the blood. Everyone, except Frank sat around the table again, only this time a lot closer to each other.

"Phil, do you take the responsibility of protecting our secrets, putting the family before yourself with no concern for your personal well-being. Will you give your blood and your life for your family that sit around this table?"

"Yes, I will," said Phil.

"How would you like to be marked, a permanent mark you cannot explain to anyone but others around the world will recognize?" asked his dad.

Phil hesitated to answer. He did not expect to have a question like that asked of him tonight, or ever. Phil sat silently as the others waited for his response.

"I would like a Celtic triangle cut out around the base of my finger. Or as close as you can get to one, please." He placed his hand out, palm up. "Right here."

He pointed at his fleshy part at the base of the finger.

John wiped down the finger with alcohol and looked at his son in the eyes, "I am very proud of you for doing this. We all are. I love you."

John looked down and grabbed Phil's hand, James stood behind Phil and held his shoulders so he would not move. John took the medical scalpel and dug into the flesh of Phil's finger. Phil yelled out in pain and struggled to free his hand. John clamped down tighter and Kenton reached over to hold down his forearm. John worked the scalpel in deep enough to ensure the skin would not heal over without scarring. The blood made it harder to see as he worked into the flesh. He worked the scalpel in and out and side to side, John saw a Celtic triangle form with the lines he cut. Phil almost passed out with the pain but was now through the worst of it. Frank grabbed a clean towel and wrapped Phil's hand.

"Welcome, Son, to the life I, we, wanted for you," said John.

Phil stood, pale in the face, and wobbled on his feet. John stood up and hugged him. Each man hugged him. James sat in the seat where John was seated.

"David sit down please, your turn for the ritual," said James.

Kenton pulled out his knife and handed it to James. "He is your son, you do the cut," said Kenton.

"Wait, I have my knife, can it be used?" asked David.

James smiled at Kenton and then at David. "I don't see why not?"

David ran out to the car and retrieved his knife. In a moment of weakness, he almost kept running, away from the chaos and uncertainty of life.

"Are you ready, Son?" said James.

David nodded, pale from Phil's ceremony with the knowledge his would be worse. John washed David's hand with alcohol.

"We don't use pain killers for this because each man must face his pain head on, and know the pain, he will cause others. David, your ceremony is different from others. Yours is for the elite of the elite. You are entering the brotherhood of assassins. There are few of you alive ever on the planet. Throughout history your brotherhood has toppled governments, started, and ended wars, destroyed monarchies, and served them, all at the same time. The brotherhood is restricted to only a few on earth at one time, you will meet others but never speak. A nod of acknowledgement will be all you ever see. Before I begin, you must understand there are rules and responsibilities to this. You must never kill in anger. You must never kill while intoxicated from alcohol or drugs. You can only kill for others' needs and money. The only time you can kill in anger or for revenge is if someone kills one of us, or a blood relative. With this responsibility you must never speak of the work you do to others besides those involved with our family business. Your life will always be in chaos, from the conflict of a normal life and the elite life you will bounce between. God has called you to do his work on earth, to cleanse it for the good of his name. Do you agree to these terms Son?"

David nodded, "I do."

With David's confirmation, James dropped the knife onto David's finger, the tip was severed halfway up the nail. It was quick, and at that moment painless. Then the nerves in David's finger realized there was a problem and pain took over.

David saw the chunk of flesh as it rested on the now red towel. He squirmed as large black dots formed in his vision.

"David, Frank is going to sew it back on now, okay?" said his dad.

David floated between consciousness and unconsciousness as Frank sewed the tip of David's finger on crudely.

After what felt like a year to David, Frank finished. The h stitches would never heal his finger right, the nail would never grow normal, but the ceremony was over. Both David and Phil had their hands wrapped in white towels. Both towels showed marks of red through them.

"Okay boys, you are officially part of the inner circle. We are all so proud of you both. You did it and did it without too much screaming. Once you guys come through the shock, we can head out. Frank will wrap your fingers for you, so they don't get infected. Obviously, it will take a couple weeks to heal, then it will be time to work," said Kenton.

"One last thing boys, here are a couple pagers for you guys. When any of us have work for you, we will page you. David your code will be, *'need some credit cards cut.'* Phil yours will be, *'pick up some oranges at the store'*. When you receive those pages, find a pay phone, and call the office. Understood?" said John.

"Yes," said Phil.

"Yep," said David.

"Okay, I can tell you both right now, the worst part of the pain will happen in the morning when you get up," said Kenton.

"How do you know that will be the worst time?" asked Phil.

"Because that's when both mothers will see what we have done here tonight." Everyone in the room laughed at the comment. "Believe me, we will all be feeling pain tomorrow."

"If you guys want, we can head over to Cagney's for a few drinks to celebrate," said John. I reserved a portion of the restaurant just for us.

"Okay, you guys feel up to it?" said James.

With the care Frank gave them, he slipped some pain killers in their care package to take the edge off once they were home.

Frank cleaned up the bloody towels and knives, while John and Kenton, sorted through some items on his desk.

"Dad, John, can I ask something? Maybe it should wait," said David.

"I am leaving if you need your privacy. Thank you for letting me sit in Kenton, it was an experience. I will see you two lads tomorrow. I will stop by your houses and change your bandages," said Frank.

"Thank you for your help, Frank. See you tomorrow," said John.

Frank left the office and David sat at the table.

David nervously asked, "Can I ask one question, dad?"

James and John sat at the table, while Kenton answered the phone.

"Okay, so the part about killing Phil and me, if we mess up, did you mean it? You wouldn't kill us, would you?"

"Would you ever give me reason to? You have seen what happens with some of the mob family's when things go wrong. Look how they handle it. They bring us in to clean up the mess. So, maybe I wouldn't actually do the act."

"You guys would kill us, or have us killed, if needed?" said Phil.

"Why the questions? Are you two planning to get rid of us? James, we better have a chat alone. Sounds like there is dissension and treason in our ranks," said John.

"Dad," said David. "I have already lost one parent, mom, at least emotionally. I don't want to lose you too. I love you; I love what we are doing. But Dad, would you really kill me? I already look over my shoulder, I don't trust anyone, except who is in this room. I worry when I bike, a white van is going to pull up beside me and take me prisoner or shoot me. It's not like we are making many allies these days. Now, I have to worry about you guys?" David said, tears ran down his face.

Kenton stood up from the desk and walked over to the group.

"James and John, these boys have been through enough this evening. Will you two stop playing with their heads. Fuck me, I feel like throwing you over my knee and thumping you on the backside James. Stop it," Kenton said. "Look, the boy is in tears; he just had his bloody finger cut off. Stop it."

James burst out into full belly laugh. John bent over the table as he laughed.

"David, Phil, you are our sons. No, we would not kill you, if you betrayed us. This ceremony tonight, if we had any doubt about your faithfulness to us or the business, would never have happened. Son, stop. David, come here," said James.

He grabbed David and squeezed him tight.

"Now you two are, no, always were, part of this team. We are family, we are one," said James. "Yes, dad had to straighten a few family members out. But not us, inner circle son, inner circle, that is where you two are now. I am sure dad has told you stories about me. You can't be as big a fuck up as I was at your age! So yes, we are hard on you guys, but for your own good. No, we will not kill you no matter—no matter, what happens. Now your mother's, they might. I think we all might be sleeping with one eye open for the next week."

"Boys, this life has hardened us, all of us, and probably even you two, by now. But not to the point we would kill our own blood," said Kenton. "David, I have told you stories about your father, but still, he is above the ground, barely, some days. Never think any of us would betray another person in this room. We are bound by blood. We just wanted you to know the magnitude of the decision you both made tonight. That comment was made to make you think about what you agreed to. We wanted to see how you would react, that is all. We know you would never betray our trust and we would never betray yours. Hell, you two are our pension plan."

"Okay, so we are all in this to death, but just not at each other's hands," said Phil.

"It seems the only family members we need to worry about is our mother's," said David.

"Again, I am so proud of you both," said John. "David, we know you will surpass all of us with your skills. Phil, I don't envy you having to keep up with him. You are going to be busy running his jobs and the business. Listen, don't ever think that again, we are one team, together, to cause chaos while making a shit load of money. We are all on level ground here, the inner circle. You two will be involved in all the business decisions and plans going forward. You thought you were busy before? Well buckle up because this ride just got real."

David woke to the sound of his mother in the kitchen. His finger throbbed, and the dressing needed to be changed, Frank said he would do the first couple to be sure there were no issues. Taped to David's bedroom door was a note from Amy, 'Frank was here. He needs to see you around 4. Don't be late!'

David was hungry but he was scared to go to the kitchen. He knew he couldn't hide his finger from his mom. The courage it took to have his finger cut off was a drop in the ocean to what he needed to muster up to walk into the kitchen.

He entered the kitchen and greeted his mom with his hand hidden as best as he could. Elizabeth, the distant mother, took no notice of him until he reached for a cup out of the drying board.

"What happened to—no—NO. You didn't David, did you? Let me see your left hand, don't you dare hide it from me. LET ME SEE YOUR HAND," she yelled.

"JAMES GET OUT OF YOUR BED AND GET IN HERE NOW!" she screamed. Loud enough for the entire street to hear her.

David heard his father fall out of bed and run down the hallway to the kitchen, his eyes half open, a loaded pistol from his night table in hand. The pillow had etched wrinkles onto the right side of his face.

"What—what is wrong? Is everyone okay?" The panic left him when he saw David wave his left hand at him behind Elizabeth.

"You two and your secret boys' club. Now you have disfigured David? What the fuck is wrong with you, James? We came here for a new life. Now our son is deformed like you and your father? Why would you make him do that?" she said.

"Mom, I chose to do it, no one made me. They even gave me a couple opportunities to pass on the ceremony. So, you can't blame anyone but me."

"David you are my son, but I can't have this. You two will be ⸺ death of me. I just can't do this anymore. Just leave me alone. I want to be alone, get out of my kitchen now. Go, you are both dead to me. It is the only way I can handle this. What will you tell Amy if she asks?"

"I had an accident at the shop. It's not that hard Mom, or Elizabeth, if that is how you want things to go now. You have been a horrible unloving mother these last few years, so why wouldn't I go to where I am accepted."

"How dare you say that about me, you ungrateful little runt."

"Let's go David, we can get food downtown," his dad said. He gave up on Elizabeth and her stubborn nature. "You know this was coming for a long time. You chose how you wanted to handle it. I, no, we don't care anymore."

James changed and they left the house with Elizabeth still baking. The rage she felt was be enough to cook a pan of brownies.

•   •   •

David checked his watch. He put on his coveralls, gloves and balaclava and carefully made his way to the backyard. Corey should come out around six for his smoke. David positioned himself behind some outdoor toys close to the door Corey would come through.

He checked his watch; it was 0615 and still no lights were on in the house. And more importantly, no Corey in the backyard. David did not want to break in and do the kill in the house.

'Half hour then the sun will be up I will have to go into the house and do the job in front of his family,' he thought. 'Where are you, Corey?'

A light came on in the kitchen, as if Corey heard David call for him. Corey quietly opened the door and stepped outside into the cool dewy morning. He walked to the edge of the patio and looked out into the darkness as he lit his cigarette.

David moved like a lioness in the wild, pouncing on her prey. Before Corey knew there was an assassin behind him, David cut his throat and twisted a warm metal object into his brain from under the back of his skull. David cut wide and deep to ensure he disengaged the voice box. David guided Corey to the ground where he fell on his right side and rolled onto his stomach. The body twitched and a dark puddle of blood grew around Corey's head, like butter melting in a frying pan. David, like he was taught, confirmed the body was dead. The body had fallen behind the BBQ and out of site from anyone in the house. David wiped the blood off his knife with Corey's track pants.

He stuck his head into the house to listen for any commotion. All was quiet, just like he had hoped. He slowly closed the door and followed his steps back up the hill. There he packed up his clothes and knife and headed to the truck. Now to deal with Dan, the man!

. . .

Phil was still wide awake, but Dan was sound asleep, his drool ran down the passenger window where his head rested.

"All done, let's go," said David.

"What about this jackass? You owe me for listening to his shit all night. He finally fell asleep around three. Do you want to do him in and hide the body? We could leave him in the back of the truck. This one is scheduled for full disposal once we drop it off."

"No, we can wake him, he can't identify us. Plus, I slipped him some money. I think he is happy just to be alive."

"Yea, can I wake him," said Phil. "Get your balaclava on."

"Right," David said.

Phil had not waited for a reply, he headed to the passenger side door. Quietly he lifted the handle then quickly opened the door. He watched Dan, still asleep, spill out of the truck and onto the ground, with an enormous thump of his head. It was either the bang on the head, or the sharp pain as his broken wrist slammed on the ground, but Dan was awake and med in pain.

Phil kicked him in the ribs, "Shut up, be quiet before I kick you in the head."

"Dan, remember we were never here. We have a photo of your license with your address. Working for the government, we can track you down. So, I would suggest you take my money and the little you got from your friend and disappear. Do not contact her or anyone else. You never came here. You got cold feet and fled. Understand?" said David.

"Yes, totally. What do I tell the doctor about my wrist?"

"Whatever you want, just not the truth. Now get up and get out of my sight before I have you arrested," said David.

Dan picked himself up out of the dirt.

"Get out of here before we change our minds," said Phil.

"Oh, your shift is over? Okay, can I get a ride to my car," Dan asked as he tried to get back in the truck.

"I will count to ten and if I can still see you, we will bury your body. One–two–three..."

Dan held his wrist and ran down to the main road.

• • •

Dan waited in emergency at the local hospital as people coughed and babies cried. A nurse who had seemingly lost all enthusiasm for her job called patients names. The two TVs that hung from the wall had the local news channels on. Dan noticed the breaking news crawl across the screen. *Local resident and Washington DC staff member, Corey Green was found dead, by his family this morning, in his backyard. Police are investigating. Corey worked for Republican Senator Woolwick.*

Dan quietly sat and watched the news. He now knew he just spent his last few hours with the killers and they had his license. He would not speak to anyone, once the doctor tended to his wrist, he would go home and pack. He always thought Florida would be a nice place to live.

What the news did not report was, Corey had recorded audio and video of elected officials, and their after-hours activities. He attended many parties with his Senator, Beth, and other elected officials. The Senator of Georgia saw a recording device with Corey at a party and began an investigation. He called his investigator and told him what he saw. When Senator Woolwich was informed of the situation, he had Corey travel for a few days. He believed it was a mistake. He stated that Corey was an outstanding employee and would never betray his trust. A team entered Corey's apartment found tapes, photos, and documents hidden in his apartment. The tapes showed, multiple offences that no elected official should ever be involved in. Once the report was returned to the Senators, David received his page. David boarded the plane to Phoenix while tapes were being deleted and documents were destroyed. While David waited for Corey to step outside for his smoke, James took care of Beth.

CHAPTER NINETEEN

Northern Ireland 2011

David kept a close watch on his four targets in jail. Rumors were the British government had started to release "POWs" in good faith. Those arrested for minor crimes were being released quietly at first, then it became a newsworthy story as more prisoners from the troubles were freed.

David and Phil increased their contact with the guards and military. Government officials interviewed Nigel and Conner, but neither talked, this just extended their time in prison.

Forensics and technology continuously improved, Nigel and Liam were tied to more jobs around the world.

David received an update on a rainy day while in Turkey, he was on a job for a Russian millionaire. Liam, wanted out of jail, his dad was dying, and he wanted to be with him before he passed. In exchange for his freedom, he admitted to many bombings, this included Kenton's. David confirmed a flight to Dublin. He spent thirty-six hours in the Dublin area before he headed back to Canada. By the time he was on a plane to Canada, each man in prison had lost a family member and the guards left photos in each man's cell while they ate their suppers.

David turned from a world-renowned assassin into a revenge, starved, serial killer. He broke his vow to the family and to Kenton.

Exhausted and guilty for the murders, not paid killings, David called Phil and told him to meet him at Pearson airport. He needed a vacation somewhere warm.

•   •   •

Guelph, 2011
David knocked on John's office door.

"Come in," a voice said.

David opened the door. John and James were at the board table with a third person. He wore a hat and had his back to David. James walked towards David as the third person turned to look at him. David stopped; he couldn't believe it.

"Uncle Scott," he said.

"Hey, Son," James said as he hugged David, "Welcome back."

"Hey Dad, why is Scott here, I wasn't expecting to see him?" David said.

He walked over to Scott and gave him a big hug.

"How are you? It has been a while. Is everything okay," David asked.

"David, stop with the questions. We will get to Scott in a minute, first how did the job go."

"Well... Where do I begin?" said David.

David recalled the whole mission in Venezuela as he constantly looked at Scott. He knew there would be no answers about why Scott was at the table until he gave out every detail of his last job. David recited the details, as his mind raced through reasons why Scott was five feet away from him.

"I dropped the car in long-term parking and here I am." David concluded. "Now why is Scott here. By the look on your faces, it is not for a vacation."

"No, not at all. We have a real problem back home and I need your dad and you to come home and do a job for British Intelligence," said Scott.

"Okay, what is going on? We usually have this conversation over the phone, so this must be serious if you are here in person. How quickly do you need us? Dad, are you coming out of retirement for this one?" said David.

"Yes, I guess I have to. It is going to take more than just you for this job."

"Okay, so big job back home, am I going to get more details? Is it about Nigel and the other three?"

"Let me pour some drinks. This will take a while to review. Scott gave an overview of the issues, but we knew you were on your way here, so we waited until we were all together to get all the details," said John.

Phil helped John with the drinks. David looked at Phil and knew, whatever was coming was bad. David could read Phil like a book, and Phil looked like a horror novel. David went to the fridge and grabbed a couple bottles of waters and some left-over pizza; he couldn't remember the last time he ate, and after this briefing he wasn't sure when he would eat again.

The men settled in and Scott began.

"Couple days ago, I got a phone call from an unknown number. The voice on the other end of the phone asked to meet me at the shop."

• • •

"Hello," answered Scott.

"Hi, could I book an appointment for tonight at ten, please," the voice responded on the other end of the phone.

"We don't book that late we close at five," said Scott.

"Is this Scott?" asked the customer.

"Yes, who am I speaking to?"

"An old friend of Kenton's, let me just say, the TRAFFIC around here these days is so bad you need to GUN-IT to get through a green light."

"Aye, I see now. Yes, I can book you for ten. Please use the back service door when you arrive."

"See you then, mate."

Scott hung the phone up and closed the shop early.

Something was wrong with this; he had no contact in a couple years and did not want any contact. He immediately called James to inform him of the meeting that night. James, halfway around the world, couldn't get there in time, and David was in South America on a job.

"Aye, I can take the meeting," said Scott on the phone with James. "It is strange, I thought this all was going directly through John. I was only to ship and receive weapons. I don't like this, James. We had an agreement. Maybe they need some help with a few guys who shouldn't be let out? But that should go through you and John. The fact he used an old code to identify himself, again strange."

"Just be ready for anything and only let in one person so they do not outnumber you. Call me before they arrive and leave the phone off the hook so I can listen in," said James.

"No, I can handle it, there isn't much you can do anyway. If it goes bad, do you want to hear me being killed over the phone?" said Scott.

"Aye, be ready for anything and call right after he leaves," said James.

They chatted for a bit about their family's and some other business, then said their goodbyes.

Scott heard a knock on the back service door. The cameras around the building only showed one man, an older gentleman possibly in his seventies. Scott cautiously opened the door. The man looked familiar, but Scott couldn't put a name to the face, a much younger face.

"Scott?" said the voice outside.

"Aye, come in. Are you carrying?" said Scott.

"Aye," the man said, he touched his chest, "chest holster."

He slowly took the pistol out of his jacket and handed it to Scott. You can pat me down if you like, I am not here for trouble, I am here for your help. Your Queen and government need you and your family again. Plus, David would be very interested in this information. I reached out to David first. When I couldn't get hold of him, they asked me to try you. This is time sensitive so if David is off in some foreign land, I can't wait for him to get home to return my call. Wheels are already in motion."

"Aye, I am not sure what help I can be," Scott said. He patted the man down. "How about we start with names. You know mine, what is yours?"

"Son, you don't remember? We met a few times back with your dad, I guess time hasn't been kind to me, I am Brigadier Williams, I was one of Kenton's direct contacts from the government."

"Aye, now I remember, you looked familiar, but with time we all change. Please come in."

The two men went into Scott's office.

"What brings you here after all these years? I thought you would be retired by now."

"Retired? Soon, I hope. I know you still have contact with your brother, James, and his son David. I came to you to help bring them all back for this."

Scott got up and went to the fridge and grabbed a couple bottles of beer.

"Continue," Scott said.

"As you know from the news, the government is releasing old IRA and UDA members from jail, for arrests that were questionable, at best. What they are offering is immunity for any crimes they committed, if they talk before they leave. The four guys David has been in contact with, and getting updates on, are to be released shortly. Over the last year they have begun to talk more. They confessed to many, many jobs, including how they knew you guys would be together the night your dad died. They had prepared bombs for all of you, not just your dad. They had bombs for all the cars but ran out of time."

"So, you are going to give me the release date and times?"

"We will get there, but first there is more to this story."

"The gentlemen are also responsible for many other killings. There were so many bombings in the eighties and nineties.

Bombings in England, North America, Asia, and the Middle East. I know I am not telling you anything you did not know. I will skip the details. The military, not just ours, do not want them released, but they are part of the agreement the British government has signed. There are also many other countries that had dealings with those four. No one wants them to talk. We know they will disappear once we release them in Dublin, that cannot happen. These men need to be dealt with swiftly when they are released before they go into hiding. We, by that I mean a few of us, were around when this was all happening and have lost friends during the troubles. We want these four killed and we all know David wants them. They don't deserve to spend their remaining years with their families free on some tropical island."

"Okay, you are asking me to pass this on to James. You know he retired from the work when they killed Dad. David will be very interested, but this seems like something more than a straightforward hit. David is the contact for all that."

"Yes, it will be. I will work on things from my side to ensure there is a window of opportunity. We feel we might have some people with alternative agendas on the current team, so I decided to come directly to you. There are only three other people that know I was asked to come here, and one is Her Royal Highness, The Queen. This has to be completed with no one talking to David's new contacts."

"Okay, you said there was another item you need us for? What is that?"

"We have evidence there is a new IRA being built up. We want to cut the head off that snake before it grows too big to handle. Britain does not have the appetite to start the troubles up again. We have names and addresses; it could be handled in one night, a quick sweep of four houses and hopefully that puts an end to it."

"Again, this needs to be kept between us? What has happened to our government and task forces?" said Scott.

"It has changed. It used to be so simple." Williams shrugged his shoulders. "Technology and other wars halfway around the world have a higher importance than fighting for Northern Ireland. I guess if we dug a hole and found oil that would change things. Plus, we all agree, the four guys who killed Kenton, you guys deserve that one."

"Right, so when is this all going to happen?"

"You tell me. I can have my people hold them for a few more weeks, but that is about it. Their lawyers are looking for a confirmed release date. If you can gather up your team, I will have my team organized so we have drivers and guards ready to go. You will have to do the rest. I am still gathering information on the other four."

"Okay, I will head over to Canada tomorrow, to talk with James. You will have a date by the end of this week. This deserves a face-to-face talk. Can you get me a packet by morning? I will need as many details as you currently have. We can fill in the rest later."

"I have one in my car. I didn't want to assume we would get this far."

"If David found out we had this opportunity and I said no, I believe I would be hunted."

"Do we need any of them kept for questioning or torture?"

"No, just a quick bullet in the head, I would love to see them suffer, but it will need to be quick and simple. No discussions or looking for confessions."

Brigadier Williams finished the bottle of beer.

"I appreciate this, and like before, your government will appreciate it too, they just don't know it. This is my number, it is secure. Call it any time to confirm the times and dates. I know David will be ready for this, he had his eyes and ears in that jail for years. I am not only giving you the two guys that did the job on Kenton and the one who identified James, way back in the day, but the two who masterminded the whole job."

"Yes, David will be on a plane the minute he hears this."

The men shook hands, Scott opened the door to the back of the shop. The cool fall wind blew on their faces as they confirmed cell numbers and contact by the end of the week. The Brigadier returned with the notes on the job.

Scott walked through his shop to the office, *'Well, I guess I better check flights to Toronto and call James,'* he thought.

"So, I got on the next flight and here I am," finished Scott. "Sarah is not too happy about any of this, but she understands."

The group sat there shocked of what they just heard. James broke the silence, "Well, I am in. I would like to take the time to make them suffer, but I understand the reasons we can't."

"Oh, I am in with both feet. But I need a break. I need to make this my last job for a while," said David.

"Just remember David, you can step back, but you can never leave," said John.

"Aye, don't I know it," said Scott.

I did not say out just need to wind it down for a while," said David.

"I can understand," said John. "You have been very busy."

"I want to come for this too," said Phil. "I only met him a couple times, but David has told me so much about him, I feel I owe it to him. I am not sure what part I can help with, but whatever you need I am there."

"Yes, I am in too. Not sure what I can do. It has been so long since I got my hands dirty, but fuck this, I want to see the assholes that killed my 'brother' dead," said John, as he slammed his fist on the table.

"Okay, I will let him know we are in. How soon do we want to do this? I am thinking we hit both jobs in one day and get out," said Scott.

"I was thinking the same thing. Get it all done before news gets back to the new crew," said James.

"Okay. I will get IDs made and book flights for Thursday. No, screw it. We are flying private for this one. Thursday gives us two days to prepare here before we head to Northern Ireland," said John.

"Okay I will call the Brigadier and tell him we will be home Friday. We want him to release the four lads on, Sunday? My flight leaves at eleven tonight so I will have a couple days to prepare some stuff before you guys arrive."

"Sunday will work," said John.

James called David over to the corner of the office. "You okay with all this?"

"Dad, I have spent all these years dreaming about getting these guys. You know I had guards keeping me updated on these pieces of shit, now we get to end it. They finally think they are being released and guess what? We will appear to end their joy. I just wish we could bring them back to the shop and take our time sending them to meet their maker. I know Granda always said not to prolong a killing, but this should be an exception to that rule."

•   •   •

James and David entered Scott's shop from the front door, with John and Phil close behind.

James called out, "Hello can I get some help, please?"

Sarah came out of the office from behind the counter.

"How can... James, David?" she said with surprise. "How are you guys?"

"Hi Sarah, how are you doing?" asked James.

"We can talk about me later. How was your trip? Hello, John. Phil, welcome. Scott is out back," she said as she hugged James, then David.

The four men followed Sarah into the shop area. The size was the same as James remembered it, but Scott had replaced all the older equipment with newer machines. There was an old Austin Healey sports car in the corner. Three men worked on metal parts at a large workbench. They looked up, and then went back to their work. James did not recognize any of them. The floor had an epoxy grey coating, and the walls were a brighter beige color. James looked around in amazement at how bright and clean it all looked.

"I can see in your face the changes surprise you. It's like when you don't see a child for a while, your mind holds onto the last image you had of them. Right James?" said Sarah.

"I suppose," he said in amazement.

Scott came out of his office. "Hello, welcome. Come on into the office."

"Wow, Scott you really have modernized this place," said James.

The office, used to have, dull lights, an old wooden desk, and a rickety old drafting table, but now it had bright lights, a large drafting table, and a modern wooden desk with a lot more space. The big old conference table was moved further back into the office, out of the sight line of the shop. That made room for a second desk that faced Scott's desk, where Eric sat.

"Yea, it has been a work in progress. As the money allows, I update the tools and machines. We are one of the biggest machine shops in Portadown. We have contracts from here to Dubai."

"This is crazy, Scott," said James. "I need to come home more, I guess it has been a few years. Well, since time is tight, do we want to talk about this now or wait until we are alone?"

"We can talk, the office is soundproof. I can't have them hear any of the weapons deals we do in here," said Scott as they all laughed.

"Do you want tea, booze, water? Before we start."

"I would take a water," said David.

"Tea for me," said James.

"Something hard, please," said John.

"Whiskey?"

"Perfect, double shot would be good," said John.

"I always hear about the beer here. So, if you have any, I would love one," said Phil.

Scott gathered the drinks, and the men settled into chairs around the large wooden table made in the 1800s.

"This is a beautiful table," Phil said, as he ran his hand over it. "The craftsmanship is outstanding."

"Aye, I purchased it at an estate sale in Londonderry. It was made in 1830, for the Earl of Ranfurly. So please, use a coaster on it, guys."

"Yes, Mom," David said.

"So, the flight was good, and the car was waiting for you at the airport?" asked Scott.

"Everything was fine, how are you doing?" said James.

"I assume, just like you with Elizabeth, things are a little tense. Sarah is not too happy with what we are about to do," said Scott.

"Yea, I am surprised you didn't hear Elizabeth yelling from here," James said as the others laughed. "She was so mad she told me to stay here and not come home. If she only knew how easy it would be for me."

"Okay talking to Williams, we have until Sunday to be ready. Sunday at noon they will release the four assholes and transport them to Dublin. There they will hand them over, to family and friends. I expect there to be a large celebration. The assumption is they will be in Dublin for about twenty-four hours to celebrate and visit with family before they are transported to an undisclosed location in Europe. Looks like our Russian friends are paying the bill. We must hit them before they leave for their trip. That is one assignment. The second one could be a little harder. The members of the new IRA are located across Dublin and its outskirts. This will be more of the challenge to hit them all at once, preventing communications or warnings sent out. I have three trusted members of the Black Knights watching them now. Ideally if we could get at them while they met together over the next couple days then we could clean up before the release. I should hear from them around 10:30 tonight regarding the weekend schedule for these guys.

They will be at the celebration for the others, but that is not the place we want to do the job," said Scott.

"What about these four they want disposed of. Who are they?"

"They are," Scott replied, as he looked for a piece of paper. "William Begley, Dessie Farrell, Sean Hughes and Tommy McKee."

"Okay, so how are we breaking this work down? Who is taking what?" asked John.

"I would love to have the prisoners; I have enjoyed my one-on-one time with them. I would love to have one last conversation," David said.

"Yes, me too," said James. "But they will be the easy target. I would think we might need our skills in Dublin, not on the road."

"Depending on timing, you two might be a go for both jobs. If we let the released prisoners get to the outskirts of Dublin, you could hit them there. There are two targets that are in northern outskirts of Dublin less than an hour away from where the prisoners hit could happen. We know they will take some of the smaller roads, not the M1," said Scott.

"What kind of vehicle will they be in?" asked David.

"Just an unmarked SUV with tinted windows."

"That will stand out here, it is not like it is Washington DC," said Phil.

"Just a wee bit," said Scott.

"Okay, so what is the situation with the driver and the guard? Are they aware of this? Are they in on it," said David.

"No, they have not been told anything, but Williams is making sure once they are across the border and in Ireland, they are not to fight anyone. If there are any issues, they are to step aside and let nature take its course. They will instruct them to only protect themselves," said Scott.

"Are they expecting any other issues while they move these guys?"

"There are rumblings the new IRA doesn't need, or want any old farts coming back from the dead and trying to run things like they used to. So, there is a concern they could be out to do a hit. Intelligence feels it won't happen while they are being transported since the route is not being released."

"Okay, so we need to be alert."

"We will need to hit them all at one time. We can get more information shortly, from your contacts Scott. How about dinner while we wait?" said James.

"I am starving," David said.

"Aye, let's get some food, then come back, to hear from the others," said Scott. "We really can't fully plan this until we have both schedules to review."

The crew climbed into a couple of cars and headed out to the Irish Road Restaurant.

• • •

The group gathered back at the shop and waited for the phone call from Matthew and his report on the leaders of the new IRA.

"Hello Matthew. What did you find out?"

"Hello, Scott, we might have a bit of luck with this matter. There appears to be a meeting at 1 p.m. on Sunday. It will be in a public place; they will all be there. I will give you the details when I get back in the morning, this looks like our best attempt as a group. Plan the job for then. I think they might have something planned for the lads traveling down the road and want to be in a public place as it happens."

"Are there any other windows?" asked James.

"No, not before the other matter happens. The only other way would be to hit their houses overnight Saturday."

"Okay, leave the others to continue with surveillance, you come back with what you have."

"Night."

Scott hung up.

"Okay so we have roughly thirty-six hours to put a plan in place and be in two locations to make it happen. This window of them meeting in public might be our only chance to have them all in one location. If we go that way, it will have to be a shootout. No quiet and polite with this one," said Scott.

"Aye, is that what we want? The news could hit the prisoner transport before we get to it, then what?" questioned John.

"How capable are the three guys you sent down there to do the job? It looks like our only option will be to do the hits simultaneously. We can't risk the news getting to either party," said James.

"I agree," Scott said.

"Let's get some sleep and meet in the morning. Matthew should arrive around 9 a.m.," said James.

• • •

David went to bed.

James walked to his room. His joints hurt and a nervousness was in his gut. He felt like he could throw up. He thought, *I am too old for this shit. Now I know why I retired from it.*

James climbed into bed and was asleep before his head hit the pillow. John took the extra room. Phil took the couch; he lay awake excited about the next couple days. He had a feeling something might go wrong. His gut did not feel like this job would end well. He knew they would assign him to David, and that meant seeing the other David he hated to see, the killer, inside David. This time could be worse because this job was very personal. He knew David had obsessed over this very moment for over twenty years.

• • •

The next morning James was up early and cooked breakfast. David woke to the smell of bacon which put him in a time warp of memories back to his youth.

"Morning Dad, how did you sleep?" asked David.

"Like a baby," said James. "You?"

"Yes incredible. I guess that might be it for a couple days," said David.

"We will see. Maybe a nap in the car tonight, see how our plans go today."

"How do you feel this will go down, do you have a good feeling?" David asked.

"Yes, this will clean up some loose ends that have bothered 'The Family' for years," James said. Something did not feel right about this one. Something bothered him about how the two jobs came together at one point in time.

"Dad, if we are doing the jobs at the same time, I want to do the guys who blew up granda."

"Yes, you and me both, Son."

"Okay just to be clear I am on that assignment; I want to do them in real bad. I just wish we would have time to make them suffer a wee bit. I would love to bring them back here for a couple days."

"This is my only concern about you being on that assignment, what were you always taught?"

"That I should never be connected to the person I kill. No emotion towards that person because it will always fog my judgement of the situation."

"Exactly. So, I don't know if I can trust you on this job. You are too emotionally close to the person you are assigned to kill. You had them monitored in jail for years with weekly reports. You know them better then you know me, I think."

"I know Dad. I have killed many people for a lot of money over the years. This is the first job I am doing for free. This is the first one where there is an emotional attachment. The first one where I really want to kill the person. All the others were just jobs, this one is very personal. Dad you know some of this. I used to come home and visit Dermot in jail. I used to play with his mind and the other three in prison. Dad, I am sorry, but I have already killed a few of each of their family members while they were locked up. I am sorry Dad; I should have told you when I did it. I was embarrassed. It could have been you or me in the car that night, not Granda. Those fuckers actually targeted us and Granda. I want this job as bad as a fat guy wants his next meal."

"I know, but to do the job all emotion will have to be put aside. I can't have you screw up and shoot one of the guards, you need to run this operation professionally. Like you were taught."

"Yes, I am aware of that Dad, I have been involved in enough of this to know that."

"Alright get the others up, breakfast is ready, and I am starving," said James.

. . . .

The crew had breakfast together. They told stories of the past. Matthew arrived and met with the team; he disclosed the information his team had gathered. Brigadier Williams showed up with some extra information Scott had requested for the job. Once the details were reviewed, there was no option but to do the jobs at the same time or as close as possible to the same time.

The Brigadier's information noted, once the meeting of the New IRA members concluded, they would split up for a couple weeks and travel, to help build support. William was headed to Boston to raise funds for the cause, Dessie would stop in Syria to purchase weapons, Sean was to stay in the Dublin area to keep the home base stable, and Tommy was to leave for Russia to meet with some government members. The New IRA had already begun to stretch it's legs like the old IRA had, to gain world support. The crew now knew this would be a tough job. The Brigadier confirmed the time of the transport, the route, and the stop points. He explained that two vehicles would be used on the trip and not one. Brigadier's informant also found evidence there would be kill teams on the roads around into Dublin. More evidence that the new leaders of the new IRA did not need historians telling them how things were done in the old days.

The final details were put together; David would run the crew to hit Dermot, Nigel, and the rest, as he requested and desperately wanted, with every living cell in his body. He would take Trevor and Phil. They would meet Greg, on the road coming back from Dublin.

James would run the other crew; he would have John and Scott. Peter would meet them in Dublin at the meeting location, St. Stephens Greens by the bandshell. James' crew would hit the four men at quarter past one. At the same time, David's crew would meet the vehicles where they were scheduled for a lunch break. They would take the prisoners, and send the drivers and guards back onto the road. The teams broke apart. Each member reviewed their roles and the finer details of their jobs. James who had been out of this work for almost a decade, stepped back into his role, just like riding a bike.

• • •

David met Scott in the office.

"Scott, do you still have Granda's knife he used on his jobs?" said David.

"Yes, it's in a storage box above the office. Why?"

"I want to use it tomorrow. I want to kill those bastards with his knife."

"David, the plan was to shoot them, not to get that close to them. You need to stick to the plan. We can't have this go sideways."

"I know, I know. I at least want it with me as part of my crew. Like having Granda beside me while I work, I wanted to do so many other things with him."

"Okay, it is above the office. The box is marked with a large K, you will probably need to clean and sharpen the knife before you go."

"Yes, no problem there," said David.

David found the knife; it was dusty, and the blade had some surface rust on it. As he held it in his hand, his mind bounced from memory to memory of his grandfather. He remembered the first time he held the knife, the first job they did together without James or Scott, and how well Kenton could move with his knife. This knife was not as nice as the one Kenton had given to David. The blade was an inch shorter, made of carbon steel, and the shaft was worn. The words Kenton had inscribed on the shaft when he was in the SAS, had all but worn away. The leather on the end of the handle was brittle, the dried blood of many a victim soaked into it. David looked through the box. He found other keepsakes of Kenton's, his necklace, all his military metals and an envelope addressed to David. David stared at the envelope with his name on it. *'Now is not the time to read this letter. I need a clear mind for tomorrow,'* he thought.

Scott came up the stairs.

"Did you find it?" Scott said.

"Yes, also there is an envelope addressed to me. Why haven't you given this to me?" asked David.

"I forgot all about it. I am sorry David. Honestly, I forgot this stuff was up here. You can have the box. I think it is time to pass it all on."

"Do you know what it says," he asked.

"Not a bit, open it and see."

"No, I will leave that for later. We have other business to attend to first."

David stood up and headed back down the stairs with Scott in silence. He took the knife to the grinder and worked on the blade. He thought, *'if I get the chance, this is going across at least one of their necks.'*

The busy afternoon turned to evening without anyone from the crew noticing. The cars were loaded with guns, maps, and clothing. Plans were reviewed by each team. At 9:30 p.m. they had tea and their final meeting. Everyone would discuss, and recall, their role for the next day. James noted he would feel better if there was at least one more person on the crew in Dublin but did not want David to be short on his team.

"This will be challenging to get all four at once without at least one running away," said John.

"We can only do as we are able to do. If we need to, we should be prepared to run them down if we miss a shot," said Scott.

"If there are no further questions or details then wheels up at 0500, so get some sleep," said James who broke his silence.

They sat together, a bit longer to chat and share some tea. Then those who had beds went to them and the rest found couches or cots to sleep on.

• • •

Both crews were at the cars and ready to go before 0430.

"Okay, Son, take care of yourself and your crew. Don't take any chances. You know to keep yourself and your team safe by not taking any foolish chances. I will see you back here for dinner. Love you," said James.

"Love you too Dad. This is it for us. We can finally put the ghosts of the past to rest. We can go back to Canada and lead somewhat, normal lives. Be safe Dad, love you."

The father and son hugged. They went to each member of the team. Each man shook hands and wished each other 'all the best.' The cars pulled out of the shop, headed in two different directions.

• • •

Trevor drove the car with David and Phil. It would take them a few hours to reach the meeting point on the old back roads. The three men sat quietly, lost in their own thoughts, as they drove to the destination. They met Greg and drove the road they planned the roadblock on. It was busier than they expected, but it would be manageable. The quartet parked the cars a mile away from where the targets would stop for a lunch break. They walked to where the operation would happen. They hid behind a berm, hidden until they needed to move on the SUVs. With several hours to wait David reviewed the plans with Phil, Greg, and Trevor. He reminded everyone he was the only one to kill the targets. Their jobs were to secure the vehicles and the military personnel. He noted that he would be changing the plans. Phil protested the change, but David overruled Phil.

James and his crew searched for a parking spot close to the park to ensure an easy getaway once they completed the job. There was no parking in the area, a detail Matthew missed in the report. The team found a space and walked to the site. They met Peter who had surveyed the area all morning. It was the quieter part of the park, and there were no activities scheduled at the bandshell. Just like David's crew there wasn't much talk amongst the men, just enough to make it look like a normal group out on a social walk. Peter noted, if the targets did meet in the location the report showed, the team would have an elevation advantage to shoot from. If they did run, they could contain them, the only way out was the walking trail or run towards the team. Each man on the team found a position around the bandshell where they were visible to each other.

•   •   •

David pointed to his watch and signaled his crew, to be ready for the vehicles. Phil identified the vehicles first, as the SUVs came over a hill. David's fear was the prisoners would drive right by them. If they did not stop, for lunch, David's team would have no chance to get back to their cars and chase the vehicles. They watched the vehicles pass and continue their trip. At the last moment, the SUVs slowed down and pulled over to the side of the road, 400 yards from the team. David motioned to his team to follow him as he hopped over an old stone wall and continued through a field to the vehicles.

The driver of the lead SUV exited his vehicle and stood at the side of the vehicle while his partner helped the two prisoners out. The driver and guard in the second vehicle did the same. All four prisoners were hand cuffed and shackled.

"Look, they are shackled too, that will help us," David whispered to Phil.

David pulled down his balaclava and put on his latex gloves. All the butterflies in his gut disappeared. David had his game face on, and his body took the cue. Time to go to work. He checked with Trevor, Greg, and Phil, once each person confirmed they were ready, David stepped over the wall and onto the road in front of the first vehicle. Phil flanked the first SUV, Trevor flanked the follow up vehicle, Greg took the back. Each team member had a balaclava pulled over their face and had an AK-12 Kalashnikov in hand and a GLOCK pistol, strapped to their hip. The lead driver was the first to see the crew.

"Nope, hands up where we can see them. We are not here to hurt you or your partners," David said to the driver.

Greg tapped on the back window of the second SUV. He used the muzzle of his gun to direct the driver and guard to step away from their vehicle.

David instructed the guards and drivers to take their side arms out of the holsters, slowly and gently place them on the ground. Then walk to where he stood. Trevor and Phil gathered the four prisoners and brought them to the front of the lead vehicle.

"Okay, everyone on the ground spreading your arms and legs far apart," David instructed. The guards and drivers slowly got to the ground. Greg patted them all down, he took away a couple of knives, cell phones, and a smaller gun hidden in a guard's sock. Phil went through the SUV's. He found a couple automatic weapons in the back locked up, spare magazines, and two-way radios. He placed the weapons and accessories in the back of the second vehicle.

"How long is your break here?" David asked the driver of the second vehicle.

"Quarter of an hour, sir," he said.

"Okay, so seven minutes before you leave. All we want are these four gentlemen."

David pointed to the front of the SUV where Nigel and his partners stood.

"Fuck you, we are not going anywhere. Why are you fuckers not protecting us? We are your responsibility. You are to get us to Dublin where we receive our freedom," said Nigel.

"Shut, the fuck up," David aggressively yelled to Nigel. "Or I will save you for the last. Oh wait, I was anyway."

"Why are you lying there? Get up and fight for our rights. We have an agreement," yelled Nigel. A bit of fear snuck into his voice as he yelled.

David walked over to Nigel, "Nigel, right? Hello old friend. We have been playing tag together for a long time. Looks like I got you. I was so close so many times but—well—here we are. It looks like I won."

"Fuck you, asshole," Nigel said. He spat at David. "I don't know who you are."

David took off his balaclava. With no need to hide his face anymore, he wanted these guys to see who he was. Dermot recognized him immediately.

"Oh, fuck," was all Dermot could squeeze out.

"So, you four assholes took part in killing my granda, and now it looks like it is my turn to play with your lives," said David. "Nigel my friend, it is over."

"Maybe it is, maybe it's not. A car could pass by and just like the night I identified your dad, someone could interrupt your fun, mate. Oh, how I wish I had got to the house an hour earlier. You, your dad, and uncle would have baked like your grandfather—no, what did you call him? Granda. Baked like your granda. One of my best jobs."

"Shut the fuck up," David said.

Nigel laughed at David's shocked reaction to his comments. "I said shut up."

David raised the butt of his gun and connected it directly to Nigel's mouth. It hit so hard blood exploded from his lip and three teeth fell to the ground. Nigel dropped on top of his teeth.

"Stand up now," David said. "I SAID STAND UP NOW."

David grabbed him by the top of his head and lifted him back to his feet. David looked deep into his eyes, "Now, not another word from you. Do you understand?"

Nigel tried to respond, but his broken jaw just hung there.

David again swung the butt of his gun. It connected with Nigel's ribs. David heard the snap of a bone. Again, David pulled Nigel to his feet by his hair.

"How you feeling friend," said David.

He cocked his arm, swung, and connected with Nigel's shattered jaw. Nigel fell to the ground, he bounced his head off the SUVs bumper on the way down.

"Help him up," David instructed Liam.

Phil was nervous. David had diverted from the plan. Phil could see David's emotions begin to take over. Phil needed to refocus his partner, before mistakes were made.

"You guys," David said to the drivers and guards. "You need to be leaving so the GPS doesn't alert anyone."

"What about these four, or three and a half now," said the guard of the second vehicle.

"You don't need to worry about these four, they are now under our loving care. We will get them home."

"But we were to..."

"Look I know what you were to do but your plans have changed," David interrupted. "I have changed them. So, continue down the road as planned, then you can get home tonight and kiss your wives or girlfriends. Just be happy to be alive. I have nothing else to say. You are scheduled to leave, so I need you guys in your vehicles and rolling out. One at a time stand up and get in your vehicles, starting with the guards, now."

Each man took their turn, stood and entered their vehicle. David felt bad for them, they were all young and probably never had any real combat experience. This was likely the first time they had a loaded gun pointed at them. He could see their fear, he could smell it.

"You, come with me," David said to the driver of the front SUV.

The driver came over to him as the four targets looked at each other in confusion.

"Yes, sir," asked the driver.

David put his arm on his shoulder and walked him to the berm they hid behind. David opened his bag, "Here, take this. Share it amongst yourselves for the good work you have done here." David handed the driver eight thousand pounds. More money than they would make in a couple weeks' worth of military life. "One piece of information. Once you get close to Dublin there will be people looking for you, for them. I want you to continue driving for an hour. Stop and report you were carjacked. Don't worry, they know about us and them. Do not get too close to Dublin. I want you lads home safe, understand."

"They know about you? They were sending us to a potential shootout for those pieces of shit?"

"Son, it is the military, it is what they do. Be safe. You have done well today. Go enjoy the rest of your life. Remind your team they need to forget this face. If I meet you guys again, I won't be so pleasant. If you know what I mean. Thank you for your help today. Remember I need an hour. Do you want me to talk to your team as well?"

"No, I will pull over, up the road, and tell them about our new plan. Thank—thank you, sir,"

The driver, shocked, walked back to his vehicle.

⬤   ⬤   ⬤

James noticed the first member arrive. He sat on a bench in front of the bandstand. It would be a simple kill right now; he was thirty feet from the target. He could quietly walk behind him and cut his throat before the target knew James was even there.

After a few minutes, the second and third men arrived. John had those two lined up. Again, it could be quick and simple, but the plan was not to engage until all men arrived. The fourth man was late, and James could see the other three were agitated. Finally, the fourth man showed up, laughed, and pointed to the back of the bandstand. He had a backpack and a shoulder bag. The men shook hands and walked to a second bench. The fourth man, Sean, opened his bag and took out file folders and handed them to each of his partners.

'He must be the guy that is staying in town.' James thought. 'He is the base manager for them, his job is just like John's.'

The men sat quietly with their heads down and reviewed the documents. There was some talk between them, but they mostly studied the documents.

'This might be too easy,' James thought.

They could all go behind each man and do the job quietly. James looked around; he did not see anyone in the area. It was too late to change the plan. James knew he would not have missed this detail years ago. James motioned to the crew to get a closer position on the targets. Scott stood up and walked to close the distance between himself and his target. James drew his gun and took aim.

The team pulled out their guns and were ready to shoot their assigned targets. James locked in on his target, before he pulled the trigger, he surveyed the area for witnesses. This part of the park was empty; he couldn't ask for a better scenario.

•   •   •

David stood at the side of the road and watched the vehicles pull away. Trevor, Greg, and Phil came over to David, who stood by the four men shackled in front of him. Phil felt bad for them and what they would experience in the next few minutes. Ever since Kenton died, he knew this was the moment, in time, David had waited for. David would tell him how badly he wanted to slip into their jail cells. Then, one at a time, slowly torture each one of them.

Now the four men were in front of their executioner. The police could be here in less than fifteen minutes, so David got down to business.

Phil knew David turned into a monster when on jobs. He tapped Trevor and Greg on their shoulders, "We should leave him to his business. He doesn't need us here. I don't need to see the person that takes over when he is all business, it's not pleasant. Let's get the cars."

"Okay, mate, if you are sure he can handle this on his own."

"Oh yea, nothing to worry about there. We don't want to see this, believe me."

Phil, Greg, and Trevor walked towards the cars. Phil looked over his shoulder and winked at David.

David was confused, this wasn't part of the plan, but he understood why they were leaving. Phil had told him before how he did not like to see the Mr. Hyde side of him, and this time it would be a lot more than just Mr. Hyde.

The four men were in the middle of the road. They knew David, and his skills. They had spent seven years in jail and did not even survive seven hours on the outside.

Liam spoke up first. "You, you–you can't kill us, we made– we made a deal with the government. You can't kill us."

"Shut the fuck up, I will do the talking, Liam. You and your wee friends will only speak when prompted to. Plus, you might want to save your voice for the screaming, begging, and crying you will be doing shortly. Now, walk over to the side of the laneway and get yourselves over the stone wall.

Conner said, "Why should we? You are just going to kill us anyway. We have a better chance if we stay here. Maybe a car will pass by and help us."

"Maybe, or maybe that car will be my friends running you over, so get moving."

Conner fell to his knees and lay in the road while the others slowly shuffled to the side of the road and rolled themselves over the wall. David bent down and grabbed the shackles around

Conners feet and dragged him to the side of the road. His face bounced off the road as he pleaded, "Stop, stop, I will walk!"

"Sorry that option has been revoked, for you," David said.

Conner's clothes tore on the pavement. Pieces of skin were left on pebbles across the road. The other men made their way to the stone wall, a wall that had probably stood for 300 years. It had stood tall through all kinds of weather, and the progression of mankind. The wall was sturdy, made of old field stone and held together with a small amount of ancient cement. David dragged Conner over to the wall. He let go of his ankle shackles and stepped over Conner's head. He grabbed a hand full of bloody hair to help Conner to his feet. Conner was shoved hard enough to fall forward. He smashed his face on top of the wall. Blood poured from his nose, now broken, and his eye, pierced by an old, jagged stone that stuck up out of the wall. David grabbed Conner's legs and lifted them to the top of the wall and rolled him over. Conner landed on Dermot, he cut Dermot's cheek with the handcuffs.

"I am going to have fun killing you Conner, making me work so hard today. I am in no fucking mood."

"Go ahead then kill me. Get it over with, or are you all talk," Conner said. Each word Conner said spewed blood out of his mouth. He turned to see out his left eye. David jumped over the wall and landed on Liam's mid-section.

A large cry came from him as a couple ribs broke. One punctured his left lung.

Dermot stood up and walked away. David grabbed him by the hair and dragged him back to the wall.

"All of you, up on your knees and face me," said David.

"No, I won't make this easy for you," said Dermot.

"Oh, you haven't, but not to worry, at least I am going home to my family tonight. You guys are not so lucky, but hell has a no refusal policy to all who show up. And the good news is, I have already sent some of your family there. They are waiting at the gates of hell to welcome you with open arms. Well—except your Uncle Freddy, Liam, I cut his body up so he doesn't actually have arms anymore."

Liam who had been quiet most of the time finally spoke up. "Look, I just want to go home to my kids and family, see my mom, pay respect to my dad and live a quiet life. I paid the price for what I did, I told them everything they asked, and I helped as much as I could. I, we know you took your anger out on our families, so I think we are even. I just want to go home."

"Oh, I understand. Let me think, hold on let me ask my granda. Oh, shit, I can't, he is dead. And who did it? You two put the bomb under his car while you two planned it. How many others did you kill before you were caught?"

"Fuck you David, don't give us this holier than holy shit. You are no better than us. How many have you killed?" said Dermot.

"I am better. I haven't been caught."

"How do you know this? How did you know we were being released?" asked Dermot.

"Boys, boys, boys, we are not here to play twenty questions, so enough chit chat. Pray to your God for forgiveness for your sins," David said as he pulled out his grandfather's knife.

David grabbed Liam's hair and pushed it away from himself and exposed Liam's neck. In one motion David sliced his arteries and windpipe. His so-called signature move. The blood exploded from Liam's neck. The blood came to rest on Nigel's legs and midsection. Nigel screamed to the best of his ability with a broken jaw.

"Now your turn, you need to suffer I think, don't you? You were a bad boy today and need to be punished, you know I stabbed a guy fifteen times in strategic places so he would suffer but not die until I was ready to let him. Do you think we can do twenty-five on you?"

"No, please, I am sorry, no, please," Nigel pleaded. The sound was more of a mumble, like a man with no teeth.

"No need to plead. You need to get right with God, not me. We are done here. Satan is the next thing you need to plead in front of, I am just the means to get you there. If only your clients could see you now. One of the world's top bomb builders crying and pleading for his pathetic fucking life."

"Fuck you, tell yourself you are no different than us. Go ahead get it done. Kill me, let's go—can't do it?" said Dermot.

"Uh—uh—no stop," Nigel was able to get out through his broken jaw. David stuck the blood-soaked knife into Nigel's kidneys, then thigh. He then rolled him onto his belly and dragged him in front of the last two.

David swung the knife. He pushed the blade into the side of Nigel's neck, he twisted the blade and pushed forward.

That was the end of the two men who placed the bomb under the vehicle that blew up his grandfather, and the one man who identified James in 1977.

Conner pleaded again, "No, no, stop I am sorry. I ordered many people to be killed but have never been up close like this, always at a distance. I am so sorry. Please," he said, the tears rolled down his cheek. "I have, I have asked for forgiveness for my sins. Please let me go, we don't deserve this, please."

David enjoyed how he pleaded for his life. He stood Conner up, "You are right, I should let you go. Please, go find a car to take you to safety."

Conner confused, smiled, and turned to climb over the wall. David in one flash stuck the knife under the back of Conner's skull, it pierced his brain. Conner fell to the ground, his body shook. David lifted his head and slit his throat. Always make sure your target is dead. Conner's blood puddled on the now red grass and dirt. Dermot cried while his friends were killed, he curled up on the ground. He kicked at David, but the shackles prevented any real action from his legs.

David stood over him. "So, my friend. After all our visits in jail, all my promises to you, and here we are. Not exactly how we would talk about it, but close. The ending of all my stories will be the same. You were the mastermind to many attacks in Northern Ireland, big man on campus, they say. What should I do with you? I have so many ideas but not enough time to do them." David said. He pulled out his pistol and shot Dermot in each knee. Dermot screamed out in pain.

"How many people did you order, the ol' shot in the kneecap, punishment on. Sucks, there is no one around to hear you scream," mocked David.

David sat on the wall and waited for Phil to arrive with the car. He sat with his three dead victims, and one who wished to die. David had stabbed Dermot a few times, as he waited. Finally, Phil pulled into the laneway.

"Well mate, that is my ride. I have to be off," said David.

Dermot, on his belly turned to look at David. David pointed the gun at Dermot and pulled the trigger. Dermot's head exploded onto the grass. David headed to the car.

"It is done," he said. He still held the gun in his right hand and the knife in his left.

"You need to get cleaned up before we go too far," said Phil.

"Yea, let's move away from here first, I have clothes in the back."

•   •   •

James steadied his hand, took in a breath, and as he breathed out, took his shot. The bullet pierced through the air and headed to its target. The sound from the gun, not muffled fully by the silencer, echoed through the trees. The bullet connected, it made a tiny hole in the back of the targets head and pushed out both the eyes and right cheek bone, in the front. James heard three more shots pierce the air, then a fourth, and a fifth. The targets, three of the four were either slumped on the bench or on the ground in front of the bench, with blood pooling around them. The fourth man, Dessie, had moved just enough to avoid the first shot, but the trail of blood showed he was shot. James' crew moved in on the shot men by the bench. Dessie, spotted James and ran towards him. James ran from his spot under a tree to cut off Dessie. As the two men approached each other, James had missed another detail, Dessie had a pistol in his hand. Dessie shot at James as he continued to run. The first bullet just missed James' head, the second found its way into James' shoulder, it wedged itself into the muscle.

The momentum of the bullet pushed James backward onto the ground. Dessie stopped and took aim at James. Another shot rang out. James' body tensed for the pain to follow. But no pain arrived. Scott's shot hit Dessie between the shoulders, the bullets momentum knocked him to the ground. Scott stood over Dessie and put a bullet in his head, the shot that killed him, and hopefully, the rebirth of the IRA.

The sound of police sirens filled the air around the team. Peter headed to the car, he instructed John where he would pick them up in five minutes.

People entered the area, curious of the gunshot sounds. John was the first one to get to James. James tried to get to his feet as John took him by the right shoulder and helped.

"James, we need to get to the car, this is not the job we are getting caught on," said John.

"I am fine. The bullet feels lodged in my shoulder and it broke some bones, I think. I can move where are we heading now that the plans are changing."

"We need to move now. Peter went to get the car and will be at the meeting point in five minutes, max. We need to hide your injury from the people gathering, and avoid making contact with the police," said John.

The three men made their way through the trees, away from the path and crowd. The Police were behind them, where the shots were fired. They combed the area for witnesses. More police arrived and cordoned off the park. James knew, they needed to be in the car and out of Dublin. If he wasn't hit, the need to be out of the park would not be as great. But the police would have a lot of questions for the men, and their friend with a bullet in his shoulder. As they came to the road a police car passed at a high rate of speed, luckily they did not take any notice of James' blood-soaked shirt. Peter pulled up to the traffic light a few yards away from them. He took the green light and proceeded. The crew were on the other side of the road as an ambulance ran through the red light. It almost hit the front of the car. They placed James in the back seat of the car and John jumped in beside him. Scott slid into the passenger seat and the car pulled away before all the doors were closed.

John immediately pulled off James' shirt to look at the damage. The bullet was still inside of James and it looked like it broke his collar bone.

Scott phoned Dr. Whitten, a second cousin who had helped them out many times in the past. Scott arranged to have the Doctor meet them at the shop, eight hours away. As in the past, the shop would be used as an operating room.

Peter drove the car cautiously as police cars sped to the scene of the crime. The car worked through the streets of Dublin and headed north on the M1. Out of Dublin they stopped and got some first aid supplies, from the trunk.

"Do we pull the bullet out now, or wait," asked John.

"Can you see it?" Scott said.

"No, but it feels like it is right under the skin back here," John said. "I could go in there and see."

"Let me call the Doctor. We had a successful operation. The last thing we need is to play Doctor and lose James now."

Scott called the Doctor, who reassured him he would be ready to work the minute they arrived at the shop. They were to do nothing heroic on the way back, just control the bleeding and keep him as still as possible.

"Did you do what you needed to do, David," Phil said.

"Yes, they are all dead. Funny, I have been planning this for years, what I would do to them, but when it came down to it, I did my usual thing. The only difference is I used granda's knife, my new knife," said David.

"Do you feel a sense of relief knowing they are dead?"

"No, let's not talk about it right now. You know I appreciate silence when I do a job," said David. "Has anyone heard from the other crew? They should be on the road north by now. Turn on the radio, see if there is any news."

The music station had stopped playing music a while ago. Like every other radio station from Dublin, they reported on the murder of four men.

"Hey, I might know some guys that were involved," said Phil.

"Shh," David said, annoyed. "Listen to the report."

'Four men were shot in St. Stephens Green earlier in the day. Police have not released their names. There will be a press conference once the police finish their initial investigation. The police confirmed, four men were shot dead. Police found three men around a park bench. A fourth was located 100 meters away from the others. Police cannot confirm if the man found away from the bench, was an acquaintance of other three. Police have no other information at this time.'

David clapped his hands, "Yes, it sounds like their job went well too."

• • •

James and his crew listened to the same news report.

"Has anyone heard from David's crew? Anything?" James asked.

"No," John said, as he applied pressure to the wound to control the bleeding.

"Not so hard, John. Maybe I am getting old and soft, but less pressure, please."

"Sorry James, how do you feel, you have lost a bunch of blood?"

"I feel okay, the pain-killers have kicked in. I would feel better if we heard from the other team."

"I just tried David's phone, no answer," said Scott.

"They should be back in the car, heading home by now," said James.

"James let's not worry about it right now, you focus on yourself and getting back to the shop," said Scott.

"I will call Phil's phone," said John.

The phone rang a couple times before Phil answered, "Hey Dad, we are just listening to the news reports. Sounds like things went well for you guys."

"Yes, the job went well," John said.

James tapped him on the leg, he motioned not to mention the wound.

"How did your job go?"

"Everything is good here we are heading back to the shop. Should be there before you guys."

"Yes, we are still about six hours away."

"Okay, we will celebrate tonight."

"Yes, we are all glad your job went well. See you soon."

The men drove back to the shop in silence. The only conversation was when John took another piece of gauze from Scott to control the bleeding which had slowed down as the wound congealed.

"We need to speed up and get him to the Doctor. The wound has begun to close with the bullet still inside," said John.

Peter sped up to the threshold of the other traffic. The last thing they needed was a police officer to pull them over. There would be too many questions to answer.

•   •   •

David and his crew arrived at the shop first. They pulled in, and David saw the Doctor. He had prepared a work bench with linen and towels.

"Hey, why are you here? What are you preparing for?"

Phil jumped out of the car, "David, who is he?"

"He is Doctor Whitten, he is my cousin who does some side work for us," said David with confusion in his voice.

"David, how are you. Is that your blood on your pants?"

"No—I—am—we are all fine. Why are you here?"

"Did you not hear? Have you not talked to the other crew?"

"Yes, they said everything was fine."

"Oh, okay, well that is not true. Scott called me and told me your dad was shot."

"What?"

"I am sorry, I thought you knew."

Phil had already dialed John's number.

"Dad what the fuck is going on? There is a Doctor here saying James got shot. What is happening?" asked Phil.

Phil turned on his phone's speaker.

"Phil, it is fine, James got clipped in the shoulder. The bullet is still inside him so the Doctor will need to pull it out and stitch him up."

"John, put my dad on the phone," David demanded.

"David, it is okay, I am fine, just grazed, we are forty-five minutes away. I will see you shortly, don't worry and do not call home, understand?" James said.

"Dad, that is the last thing I would do right now."

• • •

David paced the shop as the others helped the Doctor set up. The bay door opened. To David the time he waited to see James felt like three lifetimes. The car doors opened, and all the men got out.

David ran straight to James, "Dad, dad, are you okay? How can I help you?"

"Yes, I am fine. I can walk over there on my own. Phil, can you watch David please, the Doctor will need some space." John said.

James got to the makeshift medical bed and pulled himself up on the bench.

"Okay let me see what we have here," the Doctor said while he examined James' shoulder and arm. "You have a broken collar bone, and yes the bullet is still in there, I can feel it, it almost came right out the back of your shoulder. Probably would have if it didn't bounce off a few bones."

The Doctor asked John and Scott to stay with him and assist. All three men went to the sink and washed up. James was given some local freezing and pain killers; he would be awake for this operation. Over the next half hour, Phil and David paced around the shop, while the Doctor removed the bullet and a few fragments. There did not seem to be any other damage to the shoulder structure. Once he was satisfied all the bullet fragments were out, he stitched James up, set the broken bone and explained how lucky he was.

Trevor went out and brought back supper. David and James thanked the Doctor for his help and asked if he wanted to stay to eat. He declined the offer. He knew the crew would want to debrief each other and discuss other matters, nothing he wanted to hear or have any knowledge of.

The crew sat down and gave thanks for the food and that they all got back safe and alive. David reviewed his teams' job. He left out the one-on-one time with his targets.

They all raised a glass in memory of Kenton and that fateful night. James wished he had a chance for some time with the prisoners but knew David had done a fine job.

James, and his crew, reviewed their assignment and explained how he was shot. There were a couple things they could have done differently, but it did not matter. Everyone was here, alive.

The men sat around until almost midnight. They talked and celebrated when James realized no one had called home to tell the family in Canada they were all okay. James went into the office to talk to, or be yelled at, by Elizabeth. John went into the apartment and made his call home.

"See Phil, this is what I mean. Who do we have to call? No one, unless we call our mommies but that's who they're calling."

"I know I hear you; I feel the same way. Things need to change. Was that a knock at the door?"

"Yes, I heard it too," said Scott.

The men ran to the cars and grabbed their guns and took positions around the shop. Scott went to the door. James saw the commotion through the office window and cut the conversation short with Elizabeth. He hung up and came out to the shop floor. His freezing had worn off; he was in no shape to help.

"What's going..." Another knock cut him off.

David waved James back to the office. Scott looked through the eye hole to see who was standing on the other side of the door.

"Stand down, it is Brigadier Williams," Scott informed everyone.

The crew relaxed and Scott opened the door. The Brigadier had two other men with him.

"Come in," said Scott.

"I brought a couple others with me."

"Come sit at the table and we can do the introductions there."

The crew came over to the table. James came out of the office and Phil went to get John. Once together, Williams introduced the men as top management from MI6.

"Now gentlemen, congratulations on your operation today, they were both successful. David, it seems you personalized your work and did some damage to your targets, but I am not here to ask what happened or to judge."

"Couldn't stick to the plan," said James

"Well—well the outcome was the agreed upon result," said David. "I just took a small detour to get there. So, what happened to my old contacts from MI6 and the military."

"Well, we did a little house cleaning and sanitizing. That was why I approached Scott alone and didn't have the proper contacts for you, John. These two are your new contacts for all matters to do with Great Britain."

"It is nice to meet you both and I look forward to a future with you. But tonight, we are celebrating the past," said David.

"Yes, that is why I brought these," said Williams as he pulled out two bottles of whisky from the bag he brought. "Let me pour you all a glass, we are all very thankful for your work today."

"Yes, I just spoke to my wife. Your money transfer was very generous. I was thinking this was a free one, for the information on Kenton's killers," said John.

"It was going to be, but you guys did excellent work and deserve something for your troubles," said Williams. "Whatever happened in Dublin, right now the police are suspecting the gentleman who moved away from the others was the killer. Plus, this is my last job with you fellows. I might as well spend some of the budget. Can I get some glasses please to pour a drink before we all leave you men to your celebration."

Scott grabbed a tray of glasses and Williams poured the whiskey. David's new contact, Jack, handed out the drinks.

He placed one in front of David, "None for me thanks, I have a water. Always need to be ready for action." David said with a wink.

Williams held up his glass, "A toast to the end of the IRA and the troubles in Ireland, for now. The Queen and government will forever be indebted to this family for all the work they have done over the years."

Everyone tapped glasses and drank. Williams and the crew stayed and celebrated with 'The Family' and shared some stories from the past.

•   •   •

The next couple of days the crew laid low and stayed around the closed shop. David and his dad visited with family and the graves of David's grandparents where they left flowers. They spent a day in Bangor with John and Phil. It wasn't the Bahamas, but it was home to David. On the last day before they headed back to Canada, James and David went to the house where their lives changed forever, where it all started, for David.

A few families had bought and sold the house since they lived there.

James knocked on the door and an elderly lady opened it.

"Hello," said Mable, the current owner.

"Hello, I have a very strange favor to ask of you. My son here was born and raised till he was seven in this house, back in the seventies. If it is not a bother, could we come in and just walk through the house? It is probably our last visit to Northern Ireland together and it would mean a lot to us," said James.

The lady paused and stepped back, "Are you the family who were rushed to Canada? I heard rumors and stories about you and your family. If you don't break anything yes, come in. I will put on a pot of tea."

"Thank you," said James.

James and David walked through the house. A wall had been removed on the main floor, many coats of paint had covered up their original paint, from the seventies. They walked up the stairs and along the hallway and stopped at David's old bedroom.

"Dad this was my room," said David.

"Yes, it was."

They stepped inside the room. The memories of that night, when he was stolen away from that life, came back to him and slammed into his head like a Mike Tyson knockout punch. David cried into his father's chest.

"Dad, I can still see you leaning over me telling me to get up. A lot of water under the bridge since then."

The room was now Mable's sewing room. The walls were covered in wallpaper with flowers and pots, the old hard wood floor was now covered with a light blue carpet. In the middle was a desk with wool, thread, and books with patterns for clothes. Beside it was her black Singer sewing machine, well used. A small radio sat on a shelf in the corner.

"I am sorry Son. This was not the life I had planned for you."

They stood there for one last moment, memories raced through their heads. James took money from his pocket and left it on the sewing machine. Father and son stood in the room and cried.

"Tea is ready," Mable called up the stairs.

James and David wiped their eyes and headed down to the kitchen.

Mable looked at them, "Everything okay, my luvs."

"Yes, never better, thank you," replied James.

They spent an hour with her. They listened to her stories of when she grew up in the troubles and made connections with people from their pasts. James and David thanked her for her time, and treats, and headed back to the shop.

● ● ●

The next day, after a long flight, David brought his dad home to recover under the love and care of Elizabeth. He visited with his mother and explained what had happened. She yelled and vented at the two of them about their trip home, and how jobs like this were killing her emotionally. Not once, did she seem concerned about them, or what they were through. She was more concerned about how the gunshot wound would change her life more than it did James.'

David, finally on his own bed, was exhausted. He reached into his pockets to empty them. He set his keys, phone, and wallet on his night table. From his back pocket he pulled a note to himself, *'don't forget to bring home granda's box.'*

"Ah, crap," he said to himself. He put the note on top of his wallet. "Don't forget to call Scott tomorrow and have it sent over."

He dozed off and wondered what was in the envelope. Within minutes he was in a deep sleep. His cell phone woke him, he rolled over and read the text, *'We need some credit cards cut...'*

About the Author

Stephen is an Associate Director of Utilities at the University of Waterloo. A plumber by trade, he enjoys making sourdough bread and walking with his wife and dogs.

His one addiction is cycling, something he does regularly. He has been told that he owns too many bikes... that is a matter of opinion, mainly his family's. The longer the ride, the better for Stephen. He uses the time to create new story lines, develop characters or just listen to podcasts.

Born in Northern Ireland, and raised in Canada, Stephen is married and the father of two, twenty something boys.

Note from the Author

Word-of-mouth is crucial for any author to succeed. If you enjoyed *Family of Killers*, please leave a review online—anywhere you are able. Even if it's just a sentence or two. It would make all the difference and would be very much appreciated.

Thanks!
Stephen W. Briggs

We hope you enjoyed reading this title from:

BLACK ROSE
writing™

Subscribe to our mailing list – *The Rosevine* – and receive **FREE** books, daily deals, and stay current with news about upcoming releases and our hottest authors.
Scan the QR code below to sign up.

Already a subscriber? Please accept a sincere thank you for being a fan of Black Rose Writing authors.

View other Black Rose Writing titles at
www.blackrosewriting.com/books and use promo code
PRINT to receive a **20% discount** when purchasing.

9 781684 338573